The Season Of The Cerulyn

being the second book of the *Travalaith Saga*

by LUKE R. J. MAYNARD

• CYNEHELM PRESS •
TORONTO

Sale of this book without a front cover may be unauthorized. If this book is coverless, it may have been reported to the publisher as "unsold or destroyed," and neither the author nor the publisher may have received payment for it.

Copyright © 2020 by Luke R. J. Maynard.
All rights reserved. Luke R. J. Maynard asserts the moral right to be identified as the author of this work.

A Cynehelm Original
Published by Cynehelm Press
www.cynehelm.com

Trademark notice: all characters, places, fictitious creatures, languages, neologisms, and the names and distinctive likenesses thereof, are trademarks owned by the author, except where they previously existed in the public domain.

This book is entirely a work of fiction. The names, characters, and events portrayed in it are the work of the author's imagination. Any resemblance to actual events, places, or persons, living or dead is entirely coincidental.

No part of this book may be reproduced in any form or by any electronic or mechanical means, including information storage and retrieval systems, without written permission from the author, except for the use of brief quotations for review purposes.

Please respect the copyright of this book. It enables writers & artists to keep on producing the creative works that enrich our lives and our culture.

Our books may be purchased in bulk for promotional, educational, or business use. Please contact us directly.

To receive advance information, news, and exclusive offers online, please sign up for the Cynehelm newsletter on our website: www.cynehelm.com

Manufactured in the United States of America

Cover art & design by Luke R. J. Maynard

First Edition: March 2020
ISBN: 978-1-989542-04-0 (paperback)
978-1-989542-03-3 (hardcover)
978-1-989542-05-7 (e-book)

10 9 8 7 6 5 4 3 2 1

The Season Of The Cerulyn

from *Minstrelsy of the Selikhan Border Towns*
Volume II: Songs of the Annexation & Uprising

— Att kuyn zuo gitek imn oula, ai Daž?
Att kuo Anat se zue krjek aet sacaž
Pem kirahaf sajra inkern pallje saf,
Im sajra injomë kižil ter œt kraf?

— Gito wic laf ik kapriz başka neryc,
E henyen enur dažaren delilic,
Zyelë şik konwort, ik şikel gonulpaž,
Im humbati in wizye yomë arye daž.

"O when will you go the the lowlands, my lover,
And which of the Ladies shall hallow your going
Through frost-dappled pastures of kine softly lowing
To meadows made dank with the red sweat of war?"

"I go by the word and the whim of another:
The light of the Moons is a lover's distraction;
It brings little comfort, and less satisfaction,
To men lost in lands whither love comes no more."

— "O When Will Ye Go," c. A.M.3413

ONE

ONCE THERE WAS A SOLDIER who lost his right arm to a rebel's blade. His coat of mail was not well-forged; it might have stopped the clumsy swing of a longsword, but few rebels could afford the nobleman's weapon. In truth, although the sword is beloved by poets, and casts a noble shadow when brandished overhead, the ugly bearded axe that took his arm was a far better tool for such a grim job—a job it undertook on a wet spring day on a battlefield east of the Danhorn.

The axe had been a fine one, unshouldered at sunrise with a keen and hungry edge, but by highsun it was as weary and battle-scarred as its owner, damp with the red sweat of war after a morning of desperate fighting. And so the soldier's arm did not come away cleanly, but fell to a fast alliance of hatred and persistence, ad a rain of ever harder, ever clumsier blows that left a queer sinewy mass where an arm should have been.

In the end, he lost the arm not just to an axe, but to the saw-backed dagger of his commander, who finished the deed and meticulously pried a dozen broken links of iron out of the stump. The severed links of iron were cleaned, oiled, and sent back to the rearward smith, to be forged into a new coat of chainmail. The severed arm was left to the crows.

The Battle of the Danhorn, fought and lost on the blasted red heath of the Surreach, left many Travalaithi soldiers with the same story to tell. Some lost an arm, some a leg. Some, by great skill or luck, lost only a small part of either. Many took to rot and died of their wounds, for it was well-known that the sorcerers and witches trained under Jordac could lay a curse on the wounds they caused. But many of the wounded survived; and this one who watched awestruck from the command tent as the crows fought over the flesh of his arm was named Rendon.

Called Rendon the Reckless by his company, he was a young and vigorous man at the time of the battle. Tall, wild-haired, and proud, he was one of the first to cross steel with the rebels, and his great size and reach served him well. He was strong enough to survive the wounding, but in the weeks that followed he was never again quite the same man. Once known to the men of his quire as a fast friend with a generous heart, he grew sour and unpleasant, like a bad wine left too long uncorked. A shadow fell upon his mood, and he grew easy to enrage. So pronounced was the change that the few surviving men of his company toasted his riddance when word came from the Capital that he was excused from regular service, never again to return.

For a time he lived in a city barracks on a modest pension, which he squandered on wine from the outlying vasilies. He ate with the soldiers, but drank alone in a room no larger than his bed, with thin wooden walls and a mattress of beaten straw. In time, once he had relearned to crack a single-tailed slaver's whip in his remaining hand, Rendon was reassigned to the iron mines at Fingrun, where he earned his keep overseeing the prisoners of the Uprising, driving them to harder toil than was ever endured among the free miners of the Outlands. In each of the imprisoned rebels, he saw the shade of the man who took his arm; as a result, he was not kind to them, and in a few short weeks his whip had taken back, by small degrees here and there, more flesh than he had ever lost.

It would not have been unfair, then, to call Rendon a cruel man, but his life of cruelty did not please him. When he left the iron mines, it was to drink in the city; when he left the city it was to toil in the mines. With the coming and going of the seasons, the memory of the scent of flowers was lost to him. He had not walked on grass, nor felt the wind of the open plains upon his face, nor tasted the clean water of a country spring, nor known the touch of a woman, as he had done often on campaign. And those women, too, had been willing: in many of the lands well back from the fighting, the soldiers of the Grand Army were talked of as heroes, and Rendon before his maiming had been handsome of face and noble of bearing.

On his travels to the Iron City, Rendon's usual boarding-room was in Greymantlehouse, a low thatched building in the lee of the Shadewall. It was a murky place, sheltered even from the light of midday, and though he drank till dawn and slept into the afternoon, he did it all under cover of a profound gloom that never seemed to lift.

In the years since the Siege of Shadow, the city of Travalaith had outgrown the terrible black wall that now wreathed the citadel. On the outskirts of the city, a descending spiral of storehouses, inns, cottages, and even small farms stood thriving on land once blighted. Within the Shadewall, no tree had borne fruit, nor had so much as a weed taken root, since before the Occupation. But the ravaged city lay upon a rich countryside whose fertile soil was not so thoroughly despoilt; rich carpets of flowers adorned the rolling hills to the east and west beneath its wind-blasted plateau, and the forest of Vosthome to its south was skirted by bands of rich farmland.

It was here in the surrounding hills that perfumed woods were burned to mark the passing of those brave men who fought and died under the Imperial banner. Rendon could smell the sweet smoke of the fires when they were kindled atop the Imperial shrine at Vairhurst, a monthly occurrence when new reports of casualties came in from the provinces. It was in its way a pure smell, a living smell; and after too many weeks in the city, Rendon found himself climbing the steps to the memorial without quite knowing why.

The cemetery at Vairhurst was ancient, but not crowded since the Occupation: few suffered themselves to be buried within the Shadewall in dead graves uncovered by grass. What endured here were the memory stones, a garden of gleaming monuments erected to the honoured dead of every Travalaithi legion, from the Imperator's personal bodyguard to the lowliest of the "hostile conscripts" in the field. Rendon's company, the Fifteenth Legion of the Blade, was represented by a tall limestone pillar adorned with clay panels bearing the names of each season's casualties.

When Rendon came close enough, he found not only the scent of aromatic woodsmoke, but of flowers: the city's flower-girls had wreathed the stones with garlands of flowers brought in from the hill. The Three Maidens—the red poppy, the heart-petaled violet, the dazzling blue cerulyn—were traditional flowers of state, and their use in the city was tightly regulated. Rendon was pleased, somewhat, by the honour, and wondered if they would lay flowers for him when he died, or if that was a commendation reserved for those who died in battle. He almost thought to ask the caretaker, but lost his nerve in the end.

The second visit, then the third, were much the same. Rendon was a man of habits, and his habits in the mines were broken by this season of reporting and politicking, all work for which he had no stomach. As his sojourns seemed to grow longer with every passing season, he began to make himself new habits in Travalaith—the first, we have said, was a habit of heavy drinking; the second, though not the last, was his regular climb to Vairhurst, his daily walk through the barren gardens of the honoured dead.

In time his duties began to fall aside as his habits grew worse. He had taken to buying his wine from the merchant who supplied the Black Bridge Inn—innkeepers' prices, he thought, were for men who took their drink in good company—and he would climb the hill to lie among the withering cut flowers—and, perhaps, to wither there himself. It was on these trips that he collected his modest wage as overseer of the

Fingrun Mine, and by the second year of his intolerable work, he would starve through the season in Fingrun, come to the city every equinox, every solstice, and drink his pay away by the time he returned. The mines were a place of austerity and hard sobriety—the city, a place of sickness and excess. Through it all, the pain of his missing arm never left him, and when strong drink settled his nerves there was still pain to be had in other, deeper places. His friends might have marked the change in him with some concern, if he'd had any. But penniless, friendless, long wounded, and sick at heart, Rendon lived out his days as a solitary slaver, driving the convicts in his power with cruelty as he waited for death.

As the seasons rolled on, the Battle of the Danhorn was followed by others, and it became clear that the Mages' Uprising had not been fully quenched. Rumours of fierce fighting in Selik, in the Surreach, even as far north as the river Ban, reached the Capital—as did the ongoing tally of the dead. The monthly ceremonies began to happen more frequently. Names of Rendon's acquaintance—old friends, estranged companions, with whom a two-handed Rendon had once broken bread and shared filthy jokes—began to appear on the memory pillar of the Fighting Fifteenth. And with increasing regularity, Rendon would pass his days beneath those names, leaning against his company's memory stone with a clay pot of cheap wine, taking in the sweet but fickle scent of the violets and marvelling at the weightless feeling in his own head as he rocked it to and fro. He felt aimless, relaxed, and free, like a dead soul on the wind, and the time soon came that it seemed a better fate than returning to the mines.

Neither Rendon nor the Grand Army ever replaced his sundered armour—there was neither need nor money for it—but his sword and dagger he kept in Travalaith, and meticulously maintained them from old military habit. It was late in the summer of the year 3413 that he took his dagger from its resting place and climbed the steps at Vairhurst for what he was sure would be the last time. There was no night at the tavern this time—only a real glass bottle of the Black Bridge's best and strongest wine, and the majestic purple tabard and lined cloak of his uniform, which had at first seemed torn and stained, but with the passage of time had come through the war better than he had. At the foot of the Black Bridge, outside of the inn that bore its name, there was a stagnant fountain in whose reflection he had seen himself for the first time in many years. His wild hair, always unruly for a soldier's, now fell about his shoulders in a tangle of curls, like a woman's or an Esman's. His neat beard had grown to a snarled mess, and his sunken eyes were shielded by heavy lids and cavernous lines that had stolen all his youth. However tall and lean he remained—and there was no natural defect in his body, even now—the tiredness and coldness of his steel-grey eyes, once such islands of power in his face, spoke strong words of the ruin they concealed. It was a sight that disgusted him, and one he was glad to leave behind as he made his way to the winding cemetery stair.

The climate was never quite hot, not even in summer, but the blazing sun on the desolate, ruddy soil and the wide grey flagstones of the path made the warmth of the day uncomfortable. It was poor weather for death, perhaps—but the days of Rendon's short life had been poor weather for many things. With a less careless hand than he expected, he parted the withering violets from the earth in front of the monument and sat down with the memory stone at his back. He glanced one last time at the inscriptions as he lowered himself down: nine men, now, that he had known. More would soon come. He wondered, again, if the name Rendon Cowler, or even Rendon the Reckless, would find a home there. Perhaps when they found him, beneath this stone in particular, they would find an officer to identify him.

Or perhaps not.

When some good wine was in him, he tried to carve his own name with the point of his dagger. It was far harder than he expected. Barely lettered at the best of times, Rendon could write simple things and tally figures well enough, and sign his own name with ease. But carving with a metal edge on clay was nothing like writing with a quill on parchment or a stylus on soft wax. And it seemed to him, now, that there would never be an end to discovering what skills he had lost forever along with his dominant hand. After a few defacing scratches beneath the ninth name, he fell back to the earth in despair, clutching his dagger and waiting for the strength to open his veins.

He knew just how to do it, too; any soldier would have. But the coward's answer, as he had heard it called, took no small resolve to come by at the end of a heavy blade. He had thought to open his wrists, but of course, could not open both of them—nor, he found in frustration, could he open even one with the long dagger held in that hand. He would have to do it at the armpits and thighs, and that meant cutting very deep. He finished the wine—which went down easy and seemed not half as strong as his errand demanded—and settled in to gather his courage.

In the late afternoon, as Rendon's hand closed tightly around his dagger, a woman in black ascended the steps. She was hunched as if very old, but moved with a grace that belied her bent frame. Cradled in her arms, held protectively over the swell of her breasts, was a fresh bouquet of flowers from the summer fields. The intoxicating scent of them hung as thick in the air as the echo of her weeping among the standing stones.

Whether she ignored him, or whether his outline was impossible to discern in the falling light, Rendon watched as she crossed the path, searching the inscriptions in vain. Beneath the bouquet, she clutched a tiny pendant of blue glass whose shape was all too familiar.

With a degree of wonder, forgetting himself, Rendon watched as the woman knelt by a tall stone surrounded by wilted blue cerulyns and laid down her own bouquet. She uncovered her head at the foot of the shrine, drawing back her hood to reveal a shower of cinnamon curls that shone almost gold beneath the lowering sun. With her pale forehead pressed to the stone, she whispered something too low to make out. Her eyes fluttered shut, then, and she knelt very still for a long time, as if gathering courage of her own.

He would shake his head, in later years, and ask himself why he slipped his dagger back into its sheath and poured himself upright onto shaky legs. There was no ready answer, then, nor would an answer ever come. He loathed to think it was because she was beautiful. He hoped, for the rest of his days, that he had come to her side because some grain of kindness, some redeeming sympathy for fellow creatures broken by sorrow, refused to die in him to the very end. On feet that felt very distant to him, with only the familiar rocking of his drunken head to keep his thoughts company, Rendon went to her and knelt beside her at the stone.

"He was a tower guard," said Rendon. It was all he could think to say.

"Yes," she said. "How did you know?"

"Cerulyns for a Cerulean."

She smiled sadly. "It's the tradition."

"Was he kin to you?"

She turned her eyes to him. They were the sparking green of forgotten fields, of places he had not seen in many summers and might never see again.

"He was my husband," she said.

A man who had not known such a burden might have offered his condolences. Rendon nodded and sighed, and that was enough.

"Whom did you lose?" she asked. The question caught him off guard.

"Myself, I suppose."

She looked a little betrayed by that. Her seeming scorn wounded him and stopped his tongue.

"I go to be with one I loved," she said. This time, it was his turn to shake his head.

"Widows I've known," he said. "So many widows. So many young women. They return to their families. They grieve with their sisters. They seldom come to this place—leastwise, never to die."

Her eyes widened. "How did you know?"

He gestured with his gaze at the pendant in her hand. "I was considered for the Cerulean Guard, once. I know a Mother's Drop when I see one. Every one of them gets one, I hear—more symbolic than practical, they used to say. I've never heard of a Cerulean being taken alive, so it's a moot point. They say it's actually quite sweet. They say you just go to sleep. I wish to the Ten I'd been selected, if only for a Drop of my own."

She nodded slowly. "You a soldier?"

"Was," said Rendon. He pulled his cloak back from the maimed shoulder. It was the longest anyone had talked to him without…noticing.

"You're a big man," she said. "Lucky they didn't get the rest of you."

He might have laughed, then. Even in the moment, he wasn't sure if he did. But she did.

"Rendon the Reckless, they called me," he said. "Can't imagine why." This time he did laugh, broadly, from the belly. The laugh filled him like light streaming into an opened tomb. She laughed with him.

"I was named Lysandra," said the beautiful woman. "They never called me reckless. I married a guard of the tower. I thought he'd live longer than the men on campaign. A fat lot of good it did me—no, you're no worse off for recklessness in this life than you are for caution."

They sat in silence together for only a moment before Rendon said, out of nowhere, "I never sold my sword."

"Oh?"

"I never thought to. I was sure I had nothing left. It'd be worth ten times, now, what it was before the Uprising. That much fine steel, now, would be a handsome prize."

"I've no such loose ends," she said. "No wealth to speak of. None to give it to."

"Have dinner with me," he said, impulsively. She laughed, but seemed to find the idea charming.

"What?"

"I'll sell my sword and buy you dinner."

"I can't," she said.

He looked toward the memory stone. "What are you doing tonight?"

"I'm dying."

With strength in his grip, he answered by brandishing his own dagger, showing her its wicked edge, and tossing the weapon carelessly away into the blood-red soil of the hill.

"Have dinner with me tonight," he said again. "We can both die tomorrow."

Through the last days of summer and deep into the fall, they would chase the day on which they swore they would end their lives. But after that first night together, neither was eager to catch it. They had little to talk about, but bore the burden of their suffering together, and Rendon in particular found that the company and touch of another lightened his load.

Like the Travalaithi sun in the autumn, Lysandra's smile shone brightly and often, but with little real warmth. Rendon understood. He had already stepped beyond his own life, in his mind, and made his peace with that. Everything he could say of himself—his childhood far inland, his love of heroic stories and his fear of the sea, his father's trade and his short tour with the Grand Army—seemed distant now. These things were part of another man's life, and in the drifting days with her, he had no life of his own.

Lysandra was much the same. She spoke little of her husband, except that he had dwelt in the city and had died there, too. She had spent her whole life in Travalaith, though her family had long since gone to their graves. She had no children, nor hope of any, now; and what friends she kept had been parted from forever.

"I am already dead," she said, and the bleak resignation in her eyes convinced Rendon it was true, in spite of her laughter.

"It is liberating, I think, to be dead," said Rendon. "I have gone on to a good judgment, I think. I dine now in a bright hall with a beautiful woman—just as they say the best warriors will, on the night of their death. I am late returning, now, to my post in the mines of Fingrun. But I need never return, now. If ever there was a place in all the world more like the Pit Beyond, I have never seen it."

She seemed surprised and interested in that. "The Fingrun mines?" she asked. "In these hard times you are doing vast, important things with that iron, though you may not see it."

"Those hard times are behind me, now," said Rendon. "As I say, there is great freedom in being dead."

She touched his hand. "This is the most alive I have felt in a long time," she said. "And you, dead man, cannot imagine the freedom of a dead woman."

"I imagine it is much the same as the freedom of a dead man."

"I am beholden to no man," said Lysandra. "I have passed out of my father's house. My husband is gone on ahead of me. I have no children to raise, no house to keep ordered. I answer to none but Tûr, who seems content to let me conduct my life as I will, and find my fate where I may." She fixed him with a glance tinged with desperation. "I thought it was my destiny to end my life tonight. But now…I cannot even say whether I'll die in the morning."

"We will see," said Rendon. "We will see."

Their lovemaking was somehow both desperate and dull, passionate and lifeless, in the same long instant. They staggered home to Rendon's simple room in Greymantlehouse, unaccountable to any but themselves, and in a tangle of arms and legs they fell to his bed in the darkness. Rendon was glad for that darkness, ever mindful of his infirmity, but she touched with her fingers the site of his shame, felt it fearlessly and with an almost solemn acceptance. After baring the wreck of his arm to her, no other part of him was so intimate, nor so vulnerable, and there was no great fear to overcome as she brushed her hands across his body and traced his ribs with kisses left too long untendered.

Her green eyes were pained and distant in the lamplight as she received him, but her flesh was warm and his was willing. He wondered, then, how he looked—whether he, too, was so wounded by war that it showed even in eyes determined to love. His hurt felt fresh, and hers seemed very old, but it did not stay him, nor was the dullness of their time together a disappointment to him. He did not feel he could demand much passion from a woman in mourning, much less a woman as sick at heart as he knew now he had become himself. There was, for the first time in years, a tenderness in his thoughts, though he wondered whether it would fade like summer dew in the first heat of the sun.

But the sun never shone too directly on Rendon's little cell in the boarding house. When morning came, he counted a few coins out from the price of his sword—there were considerably more than he expected—and set out in search of breakfast.

They dined together on his straw cot, on a breakfast of game eggs and battered bread cooked over his fireplace, and they lay together all through the morning. She wept for a time with great wailing sobs, and he sat with his strong arm around her and wanted for another to brush her hair. But he found that in caring for her, he was capable of many things he thought he had surrendered forever on the field at the Danhorn. By the time the sun had begun its descent, he found himself wondering what else he might learn to do again, if only to stifle a woman's tears.

"It is nearly dusk," Lysandra said later as she watched the colour of the sky turn. "Shall we go again to the hill?"

"You took the best strength out of my legs, lady," said Rendon, not disapprovingly. "I reckon it's too hard a climb. We can die tomorrow, if it please you."

One day turned to several, and the summer spun into the autmn. Like dogs slowly losing scent of a fox, they chased the evening of their shared suicide from one day to the next until it had slipped away from them, perhaps forever. The price of a sword—still a nobleman's weapon, in spite of its widespread use in the Grand Army—was enough to live a long time in poverty. The room was wet and unfriendly when the summer rains came, and Rendon found himself wandering with the widow Lysandra to parts of the city he had never been, all the while watching the notice board for word that the other overseers had come in from their own mines. He was long overdue—weeks overdue, in fact—to return to his post at Fingrun. But the seasonal assembly of overseers could not be called until the absentees from all across the Empire had come. Rendon enjoyed the wait as well as he could, grateful for the gift of time he had been given.

Lysandra, for her part, seemed worse off than he was: she was often sick, and seemed to wear the wounds of her mind more keenly upon her daily routine. The touch of a woman, let alone the attentive pride she bore him, brought to Rendon some of the vigour he thought he had lost. Each night, he would hold her to his side and kiss her lips, and promise her they could die on the morrow—and each night, the thought of death crept farther and farther from his mind.

In time the Master of Iron, to whom the overseers answered, sent a rider to Selik to ask after the missing man, and within the week the grand assembly was called without him. Unbound as she was by the legal bonds of fathers and husbands, Lysandra was free with her tongue and outspoken in a manner that pleased and flattered Rendon. When he confessed that she had rekindled in him the will to see to his work and attend the meeting, a joy crossed her exquisite face that seemed more genuine, somehow, than all the times she had lifted him with a sweet smile of polite affection.

"May I be proud of you?" she asked him.

"Someone ought to be," he replied. "It's not in me, not yet, to be proud of myself. The Imperial Harper will be in attendance—the Mouth of Travalaith, the voice of the Imperator himself—and I feel like a common vagrant before him. I can barely remember my figures. I can barely read my own writing. I have been remiss, I have been lost, and now I shall be found out."

"I will help you," she reassured him—and, much to his surprise, she did.

At that time in Travalaith, there were many good reasons to be lettered. Most citizens, even the labourers, knew an alphabet and could string it together. Even if they could not read in silence, as the priests and clerks often did, they could draw from letters the sounds hidden there, and hear in their voices the words committed to the page. Lysandra, however, was marvellously literate: she looked over Rendon's report from the mines with interest, asking him questions, and producing in her own hand for him a fair copy of all that he had scratched out half-drunkenly with his weak hand upon arriving in the Capital. Her skill with letters far exceeded his own, and he was moved by her interest in the work that he had come to loathe in large part because he felt it was given to him out of pity.

"Meet with the Lord Harper," she urged him. "You are a man of the Grand Army, charged with a great responsibility. Give them the best that's left of you this week, and we will see what comes. We can always die next week."

She rose at dawn, and made him breakfast, and washed his uniform, and woke him with a kiss. As he ate, she rubbed down his sleeves and leggings with a soft rag, working an inky black dye into the faded wool. He looked up from his eggs with some surprise at the sour, woodsy scent of it. To him, it was a scent he associated with officers and rich men.

"Is—is that trueblack?" he asked her.

"It is," she said.

"Lysandra—we can't afford—"

"Maybe you're not the only one with an old sword to sell," she said.

"It won't last the day in this heat," he protested.

"It doesn't have to," she said. "Just the morning. Just long enough to make you stand out. You're a handsome man, Rendon the Reckless. Rendon the Handsome, more like. Or have you forgot?"

He had exhausted, long ago, the tears he would shed in his lifetime. He was a hardened soldier and would not weep again until the day of his death. But for a long moment, he could not speak.

"Why are you so kind to me?" he said at last. He thought the words would make her smile; instead, she looked away from him with a great sadness.

"Hurry up," she said, "or you'll miss your audience."

TWO

THROUGH THE LAST DAYS OF SUMMER and deep into the fall, they would chase the day on which they swore they would end their lives. But after that first night together, neither was eager to catch it. They had little to talk about, but bore the burden of their suffering together, and Rendon in particular found that the company and touch of another lightened his load.

Like the Travalaithi sun in the autumn, Lysandra's smile shone brightly and often, but with little real warmth. Rendon understood. He had already stepped beyond his own life, in his mind, and made his peace with that. Everything he could say of himself—his childhood far inland, his love of heroic stories and his fear of the sea, his father's trade and his short tour with the Grand Army—seemed distant now. These things were part of another man's life, and in the drifting days with her, he had no life of his own.

Lysandra was much the same. She spoke little of her husband, except that he had dwelt in the city and had died there, too. She had spent her whole life in Travalaith, though her family had long since gone to their graves. She had no children, nor hope of any, now; and what friends she kept had been parted from forever.

"I am already dead," she said, and the bleak resignation in her eyes convinced Rendon it was true, in spite of her laughter.

"It is liberating, I think, to be dead," said Rendon. "I have gone on to a good judgment, I think. I dine now in a bright hall with a beautiful woman—just as they say the best warriors will, on the night of their death. I am late returning, now, to my post in the mines of Fingrun. But I need never return, now. If ever there was a place in all the world more like the Pit Beyond, I have never seen it."

She seemed surprised and interested in that. "The Fingrun mines?" she asked. "In these hard times you are doing vast, important things with that iron, though you may not see it."

"Those hard times are behind me, now," said Rendon. "As I say, there is great freedom in being dead."

She touched his hand. "This is the most alive I have felt in a long time," she said. "And you, dead man, cannot imagine the freedom of a dead woman."

"I imagine it is much the same as the freedom of a dead man."

"I am beholden to no man," said Lysandra. "I have passed out of my father's house. My husband is gone on ahead of me. I have no children to raise, no house to keep ordered. I answer to none but Tûr, who seems content to let me conduct my life as I will, and find my fate where I may." She fixed him with a glance tinged with desperation. "I thought it was my destiny to end my life tonight. But now…I cannot even say whether I'll die in the morning."

"We will see," said Rendon. "We will see."

Their lovemaking was somehow both desperate and dull, passionate and lifeless, in the same long instant. They staggered home to Rendon's simple room in Greymantlehouse, unaccountable to any but themselves, and in a tangle of arms and legs they fell to his bed in the darkness. Rendon was glad for that darkness, ever mindful of his infirmity, but she touched with her fingers the site of his shame, felt it fearlessly and with an almost solemn acceptance. After baring the wreck of his arm to her, no other part of him was so intimate, nor so vulnerable, and there was no great fear to overcome as she brushed her hands across his body and traced his ribs with kisses left too long untendered.

Her green eyes were pained and distant in the lamplight as she received him, but her flesh was warm and his was willing. He wondered, then, how he looked—whether he, too, was so wounded by war that it showed even in eyes determined to love. His hurt felt fresh, and hers seemed very old, but it did not stay him, nor was the dullness of their time together a disappointment to him. He did not feel he could demand much passion from a woman in mourning, much less a woman as sick at heart as he knew now he had become himself. There was, for the first time in years, a tenderness in his thoughts, though he wondered whether it would fade like summer dew in the first heat of the sun.

But the sun never shone too directly on Rendon's little cell in the boarding house. When morning came, he counted a few coins out from the price of his sword—there were considerably more than he expected—and set out in search of breakfast.

They dined together on his straw cot, on a breakfast of game eggs and battered bread cooked over his fireplace, and they lay together all through the morning. She wept for a time with great wailing sobs, and he sat with his strong arm around her and wanted for another to brush her hair. But he found that in caring for her, he was capable of many things he thought he had surrendered forever on the field at the Danhorn. By the time the sun had begun its descent, he found himself wondering what else he might learn to do again, if only to stifle a woman's tears.

"It is nearly dusk," Lysandra said later as she watched the colour of the sky turn. "Shall we go again to the hill?"

"You took the best strength out of my legs, lady," said Rendon, not disapprovingly. "I reckon it's too hard a climb. We can die tomorrow, if it please you."

One day turned to several, and the summer spun into the autmn. Like dogs slowly losing scent of a fox, they chased the evening of their shared suicide from one day to the next until it had slipped away from them, perhaps forever. The price of a sword—still a nobleman's weapon, in spite of its widespread use in the Grand Army—was enough to live a long time in poverty. The room was wet and unfriendly when the summer rains came, and Rendon found himself wandering with the widow Lysandra to parts of the city he had never been, all the while watching the notice board for word that the other overseers had come in from their own mines. He was long overdue—weeks overdue, in fact—to return to his post at Fingrun. But the seasonal assembly of overseers could not be called until the absentees from all across the Empire had come. Rendon enjoyed the wait as well as he could, grateful for the gift of time he had been given.

Lysandra, for her part, seemed worse off than he was: she was often sick, and seemed to wear the wounds of her mind more keenly upon her daily routine. The touch of a woman, let alone the attentive pride she bore him, brought to Rendon some of the vigour he thought he had lost. Each night, he would hold her to his side and kiss her lips, and promise her they could die on the morrow—and each night, the thought of death crept farther and farther from his mind.

In time the Master of Iron, to whom the overseers answered, sent a rider to Selik to ask after the missing man, and within the week the grand assembly was called without him. Unbound as she was by the legal bonds of fathers and husbands, Lysandra was free with her tongue and outspoken in a manner that pleased and flattered Rendon. When he confessed that she had rekindled in him the will to see to his work and attend the meeting, a joy crossed her exquisite face that seemed more genuine, somehow, than all the times she had lifted him with a sweet smile of polite affection.

"May I be proud of you?" she asked him.

"Someone ought to be," he replied. "It's not in me, not yet, to be proud of myself. The Imperial Harper will be in attendance—the Mouth of Travalaith, the voice of the Imperator himself—and I feel like a common vagrant before him. I can barely remember my figures. I can barely read my own writing. I have been remiss, I have been lost, and now I shall be found out."

"I will help you," she reassured him—and, much to his surprise, she did.

At that time in Travalaith, there were many good reasons to be lettered. Most citizens, even the labourers, knew an alphabet and could string it together. Even if they could not read in silence, as the priests and clerks often did, they could draw from letters the sounds hidden there, and hear in their voices the words committed to the page. Lysandra, however, was marvellously literate: she looked over Rendon's report from the mines with interest, asking him questions, and producing in her own hand for him a fair copy of all that he had scratched out half-drunkenly with his weak hand upon arriving in the Capital. Her skill with letters far exceeded his own, and he was moved by her interest in the work that he had come to loathe in large part because he felt it was given to him out of pity.

"Meet with the Lord Harper," she urged him. "You are a man of the Grand Army, charged with a great responsibility. Give them the best that's left of you this week, and we will see what comes. We can always die next week."

She rose at dawn, and made him breakfast, and washed his uniform, and woke him with a kiss. As he ate, she rubbed down his sleeves and leggings with a soft rag, working an inky black dye into the faded wool. He looked up from his eggs with some surprise at the sour, woodsy scent of it. To him, it was a scent he associated with officers and rich men.

"Is—is that trueblack?" he asked her.

"It is," she said.

"Lysandra—we can't afford—"

"Maybe you're not the only one with an old sword to sell," she said.

"It won't last the day in this heat," he protested.

"It doesn't have to," she said. "Just the morning. Just long enough to make you stand out. You're a handsome man, Rendon the Reckless. Rendon the Handsome, more like. Or have you forgot?"

He had exhausted, long ago, the tears he would shed in his lifetime. But for a long moment, he could not speak.

"Why are you so kind to me?" he said at last. He thought the words would make her smile; instead, she looked away from him with a great sadness.

"Hurry up," she said, "or you'll miss your audience."

Among all of the flower-girls who laboured on the Lornock Stair that day, Iria's hands were the smallest and cleverest, with thin delicate fingers like petals themselves. Although she was small and sometimes had to be lifted by the older girls, she could reach places among the Iron Hedge that they could not. Where her older sister Maddie's hands were callused and scarred from a few years of the work, hers were soft-skinned and unmarred. She bragged among the other flower-girls that the Lornock Hedge had never stung her even once—though it had, earlier that spring, and she ran home crying and would not come again to the stair until the festering scratch in her thumb had healed to a pretty white scar she took care to hide.

Broader than a house and eleven flights long, the city's tremendous central stair was the only approach to the profane citadel of Lornock and the looming black spire of Cîr-Valithar. The stair itself dated from the old city, before the Siege of Shadow. Before Iria's time, before her parents or grandparents, it had been the main causeway to the old palace, whose ruins were now dust beneath Lornock's foundations. Where once it had been lined with gently sloping gardens, it was now bounded on both sides with winding coils of glossy black iron, tipped with razors and spikes in the manner and mockery of natural thorns. The weird iron was immovable, nor did it rust in the weather, nor dull or wear with the passage of time. It was the same stuff of the Shadewall and of the citadel itself—metal that could not be marred or melted down, though the best smiths had tried.

It was from these unwanted relics of the Siege that the Iron City took its byname, and the uneasy dreams they inspired were not lost on children of Iria's age—nor even on grown men like Rendon. His ascent to the citadel was an unsettling experience and one he made only once on each reporting visit—usually when the cerulyns were in bloom, if he could help it.

Here, in the harvest season just before first frost, they were still in abundance. Fast and hardy even in the autumn, the cerulyns were from ancient times the flower of the city, and of the Imperator's own arms, a symbol of Travalaith's victory over the powers of darkness and its indomitable will to survive the horrors of its past. On the day of the Iron City's liberation, local legend said the whole Stair was strewn ankle-deep to welcome the arriving generals. Now, the flowers remained a gesture of resistance, a refusal to live with the ugliness brought to them by Tamnor's occupation. Girls and sometimes boys from the poorest families would harvest the cerulyns where they grew beyond the Shadewall, and weave them through the razor-sharp wires for a state pittance and the alms of passersby, concealing the wicked vines behind a curtain of sweet-smelling flowers that were nevertheless quick to wither within the confines of the city.

Against the backdrop of that horrid iron, whose unsettling presence the cerulyns could never quite conceal, the sight of the young girls with their hampers of brilliant blue cerulyn blossoms excited a profound pity in Rendon's breast. Iria, most of all, whom he deemed too small for this sort of work, pierced even his coldness, and he stopped on the third landing to press a silver harp into her palm.

"I thank m'lord," she said softly, as she had been taught, slipping the coin into her little apron. In her tiny hands the little coin looked ten times its real size.

Others had stopped, here and there, to leave coppers for the children, but traffic on the foreboding stair was sparse for such a pleasant day. The ministers and magistrates were closed up in their chambers; the messengers and chattel runners from the city below made up most of the stair's traffic, and they were not inclined to dally. Their pace up the steps gave Rendon a feeling of urgency after his moment of charity. Against the pleas of the other children, who could smell a man made generous by pity, he doubled his speed up the long stair.

The reports from the state mines were the business of a magistrate called the Master of Iron, a title Rendon found both laughable and ill-suited. The first year he had reported, he expected a stern, powerfully built man, late of the Grand Army himself—not a fat, pasty, white-bearded egg of a man like Mardon Black. There was nothing very ironlike about him, nor particularly masterly: his family was no more notable than Rendon's own, and how he came into a position among the Magistrates' Council was a mystery to more and wiser men than Rendon. It was an indignity, of sorts, reporting to this man; but today, with a polished report in a trueblacked uniform, Rendon was looking forward to making a show of his dignity as he never had before.

Under the watchful eyes of blue-cloaked tower sentries, Rendon passed through the looming barbican of the Lornock Gate into the citadel courtyard. The citadel itself was mostly new construction, a connected series of palatial sandstone buildings raised around Cîr-Valithar where most of the Empire's day-to-day administration was carried out. This was as close as he had had to come to the Spire itself, for which he was glad at heart. The Victory Tower erected by the Company of the Owl just adjoining the central building was an impressive structure by the standards of any city engineer, but seemed nearly laughable before the eerie, unblemished black needle that stood as an immovable, eternal symbol of the Iron City's dreaded former occupant. There could be no winding about of that eyesore with a garland of flowers, he thought. An unfriendly wind beat against his clothes until he made his way indoors.

As it happened, Rendon was not the last to arrive. The Master of Iron himself, rubbing his pasty hands together thoughtfully as he entered with his page, was perhaps ten minutes behind him. Gathered in a small chamber awaiting his arrival were the overseers of a dozen other iron mines throughout the Empire. Fingrun, a modest prison mine on the westernmost edge of the vasily of Haukmere, was neither the smallest nor the largest of these.

The overseers were mostly former officers, survivors of the battlefield whose duty there had come to a sudden and unpleasant end. They were rugged and physical men of great stature, and stern prisoners, for one reason or another, of their own bodies. When Mardon burst into the room, Rendon felt the climate turn cold. He was a man clearly unaccustomed to hard labour—a man who had been given the gift of good health and a whole body who had carelessly let both fall to ruin by his own dissolution. The distaste for him, among the maimed veterans in particular, was immediately palpable.

"Providence and a good day to you, gentlemen," he began, as usual. "I hope the road has been kind, and the city giving."

"Good day," a few of the men mumbled in response.

"I would begin," said Mardon, "with a summary of conditions in the Empire, and with your figure reports from the Outlands inward. Afterward, we will be joined by His Excellency, Lord Olferth Tarbeck, Vasil of Creslyn and Patriarch of House Harford, declared Imperial Harper and Mouth of Travalaith by His Illustrious Majesty the glorious Imperator Valithar, who will be presenting the Empire's strategic vision for the mines in about an hour's time."

"Fifty minutes' time, after a title like that," muttered one of the other overseers, who knew Mardon was hard of hearing.

"We shall hear first from the Outlands," said Mardon. "First from the River Ban Encampment, then from the Cliffs of Orrath, then the Danwyn family mines of the Surreach."

"Not Ban River, then the mine at Selik, my lord?" asked one of the men.

Mardon fixed him with beady, unreadable eyes. "Our rider has confirmed," he said, "that the Selikhan mine is no longer under Travalaithi control."

A low murmur went through the room.

"Make no mistake, gentlemen," said Mardon, "these are perilous times. If pitch is the blood of the Empire, as Lord Olferth says, iron is the bone. Since very old times indeed, iron has been the bane of old magics—and it will serve well enough for men, too. Our output has been insufficient, and our stores are not so great as we had thought them. The wax-iron tribute we have been taking from some of the outlying vasilies has gone to rust in places. Dampness in the waxing process and other impurities are to blame, I am told; but we have not the reserves we anticipated. I am desperately awaiting some good figures from you, gentlemen, and better figures still next season."

Rendon smiled at that. His mine had done well, and although Haukmere was among the most secure of the vasilies, scattered fighting in Orrath had brought in so many live traitors that they had to be shipped by the wagonload into Fingrun. Fresh manpower was driving production; the more rebels came out of the Outlands ready for a fight, the more iron there would be to skewer the rest.

The other overseers, however, had less to be proud of. Production was down in most of them, and working the prisoners harder through the hot summer had proven to be disastrous. Even the coastal mine of Orrath, which was much like Fingrun and had many of the same good fortunes, had too much of a good thing. Its influx of traitors was so pronounced that they had the numbers to revolt, and the survivors did not flee the mines, but fortified them and settled in for what surely would have been a protracted siege, if Ashimar himself had not come down with his private bloodguard and laid waste to the resistance.

As it was, the overseer at Orrath—a poor beleaguered man named Vanneck—wound up without any labour force for weeks. During the disturbance, his strongest incoming prisoners were rerouted to Rendon. When Ashimar finally came, he was thorough with his sword: there were no survivors among the rebels that night, and no one left to dig graves for them until a new shipment of prisoners came. When word reached the camps at Fingrun that the Orrath uprising had been slaughtered to a man, the morale of Rendon's workforce was broken while their health remained unspoilt. It became clear from the two reports that Vanneck's loss was Rendon's gain—the first time in years he felt had got the better of someone—and though it was mostly the fault of happenstance, he took a long-dormant pride in it.

Without fanfare and without formalities, the Imperial Harper joined the meeting through an all-but-hidden side door toward the end of Rendon's report. Where Mardon was a dominant presence in the room, Olferth was almost eerily subdued; his plain robes were trueblacked, like Rendon's, but otherwise without adornment, save for a tiny gold brooch in the shape of a harp—his only badge of office. The immovable helm of his hair was the colour of ashweed, a hoarier shade of the straw colour common to many of pedestrian Asdi descent. Throughout Rendon's speech he was utterly impassive, resembling nothing more than a wax figure. When he smiled at last, at the end of the report, his waxy lips pulled back to reveal a bucktoothed smile as cold as it was effusive.

Mardon waited to acknowledge the lord's arrival until after Rendon had said his piece. "Your Excellency," he said simply. Olferth waved for him to continue, and listened pensively throughout the final reports before speaking. When the last overseer had spoken, he rose to make the most of his average height and coughed once to clear his throat.

"Let me be clear," he began, "about the needs and the expectations of the Imperator. The citizens of Travalaith who have suffered so much under this insurrection expect a degree of justice. Above all, they want to see decisive actions and strong deterrents for insurrectionist behaviour. To an extent, laying aside the peacetime importance of the mines, your work serves to satisfy this demand. Our response to our enemies must be as visible as it is harsh. But make no mistake, the mines are not places of idle torment. They are a practical resource of the Travalaithi Empire; we cannot afford for them to be anything less. What matters to our friends on the battlefield is not how much suffering comes *to* their captured enemies; but how much aid comes *from* them."

"My lord—" Mardon began, his smile unsteady.

"This one," said Olferth, with a gesture toward Rendon, "understands the importance of results. I suppose it should be expected from the mine nearest Haukmere. And yet every man at this table, I think, can clearly see the quality of your ambition. Look at these ledgers." Here he lifted Rendon's parchment in his clammy hands, turned it around in the light, leafed from one page to the next.

"Positively elegant, my lord," said Mardon, eagerly.

"Every detail," said the Imperial Harper. Rendon didn't dare tell him Lysandra had helped him with his penmanship every step of the way.

"My advice to the rest of you," said Olferth, "is to maintain order with the same sort of precision, from the pen to the whip. Losses are inevitable, and we will face them bravely. But the losses at Orrath might have been handled with greater precision."

Vanneck, who was used to being the absolute power of his settlement at some distance from the capital, could not hold back his sigh. The room went silent as stone.

"I trusted in Lord Ashimar's gift for precision," he volunteered, feeling the judgment of the room upon him only as the words emerged.

Olferth was unimpressed. "Ashimar is precise in nothing but his cruelty," he said—words to which the room might have agreed even if they had come from the mouth of a flower-girl rather than the Mouth of Travalaith. "Besides which, he acts with the confidence of a man who is not easily replaced. You would do well, Overseer, not to share in that confidence."

"Your Excellency," Vanneck said, and was silent.

The rest of their audience with Olferth was a dull affair dominated by figures and logistics. He left them soon after, having pressing business with the Imperator himself, and bestowed on Rendon the final favour that his name would be mentioned in that exalted company. There was no shortage of bad blood and jealousy when the meeting broke; but a few of the overseers looked on Rendon with something like admiration. He had not long been a figure of much reckoning, and they marvelled at the change that had come over him in so short a time. Even Mardon, the Master of Iron, was drawn to his company: he had a keen nose for Imperial favour, and had come by his position, perhaps, by standing beside favourites whenever he could.

"Well done, my boy," he said afterwards, bobbing his broad head with enthusiasm. "The Lord Harper is a hard man to please, and those who do please him are never stuck in the Outlands for long. I hope you have a taste for city life."

"Fortune smiled on me; that's all," said Rendon. "Vanneck's loss was my gain. My leadership's had precious little to do with it these last months."

Mardon threw a stubby arm over Rendon's shoulder—or at least, across the middle of his long back.

"You come here from a world of genuine and honest men," he said, "so I'll counsel you on one thing: the Lord Harper is a man who cares about results. You are his champion today because you brought him good ones. But results, not facts, are what matter in his house. And make no mistake; until the Imperial Family come down again from the Tower, and rule the common folk with their own damned hands, this is very much his house, from the lowest brick to the highest turret."

"My thanks, your worship," said Rendon a bit hastily.

"Results," said Mardon again, walking with him some distance as he moved to disentangle himself. "Even putting down a revolt too harshly is bad for results. Dead men do not work, and badly beaten men work poorly."

"I understand," said Rendon.

"Do you?" asked Mardon. "Twice the beatings for half the men will give you exactly the same effect with fewer casualties. You've been given an extraordinary gift in Vanneck's castaways, though. You have a surplus of manpower. Kill one, from time to time, when the other poor bastards least expect it. That's my advice to you. It'll save the lost work from beating the others. Keep them hale of body, and broken of heart. We'll see what the winter holds for you."

"Yes, your worship."

The Master of Iron pressed something heavy and cold into his hand with fat fingers. "What's this?" Rendon asked.

"You run a mine," said Mardon. "You know damn well what that is."

The thin gold coin was almost half as wide as his hand. On its polished face, a golden harp gleamed opposite a wide, prominently drilled hole, as if a man could somehow earn a second such coin to tie to it.

"What's it for?"

"Results," Mardon said again. "Change it with the Treasury before you go, if you must. You're missing an arm, my boy; that's a liability in the business of sowing fear."

"I don't take alms."

"Nor do I give them," said Mardon. "Go down to the stabler—any of Harrod's men will show you the way—and hire yourself one of the Master General's pet karach for the season ahead."

"Karach?"

"Dog-men," said Mardon. "The beasts we conquered in the West. Put the whip in its paw, and watch the sweat run and the iron pour in. A strong back and a broken will. That, my boy, is the heart of any mine."

Lysandra shrank from him when he kissed her on his return. He settled for an embrace she did not reciprocate. Her hair smelled softly of the sea.

"You've been out," said Rendon.

"I've been down to the wharf," she said, distantly. "I bought us a hakefish for supper. It's fresh."

Rendon smile belied his uneasiness. "I love fresh hakefish," he said. "You can't get it in Fingrun. Boggles the mind, the keep being so close by the Pale Sea."

"You'll have to come home for it, often," she said.

Rendon's heart sank. Gently slipping out of his uniform tabard, he let it drop carelessly to the rushes that covered the floor.

"You mean not to come with me," he said.

"I—I can't."

Rendon sat on the edge of the bed and beat the mattress once with his fist. "Fortune gives me nothing it cannot take back," he said.

"I don't know what to say."

"Say nothing, if you please," Rendon spat. "Though a shred of disappointment in your eyes would flatter me."

She didn't even flinch at the comment. "It's not you," she told him evenly.

He shrugged. "Who is it, then?"

"That's not fair."

"Fair?" he barked, shooting up from the bed. "What do you know of fairness? This one day—this one and only day—my luck had begun to turn. This one day, I saw a future without suffering. I saw my labour come to something, something more than this; I saw a house beyond the Wall, where a green thing or two might grow, where the smell of evil doesn't get in your hair. I saw a feather bed, and a woman to fill it. I saw a life that was worth something! *I* was worth something, this one day. And now… now…"

He had been fighting hard with the knots and laces of his uniform, brushing away her hands as he spoke. Pacing and jerking, his lithe body eventually slithered out of the splotchy black tunic, its surface now flaked with a shower of peeling grey flecks.

"This is my luck," he said, throwing it down. "As false as trueblack, they say. Give it a day, and it all turns to shit."

"I've given you no cause to be cruel to me," said Lysandra coldly.

Red-faced, Rendon sat, then stood up again. His every movement betrayed his fury, though he dared not come near her.

"If I were half a man," he muttered, "I'd give you cause to be so cruel to *me*." But he met her eyes and she knew there was no real danger in him—only hurt. However many seasons he had spent driving the slaves, he was a man who understood when violence would not give him his desires. That left him without a second tool to try, and he knew it. She sat beside him, as if a sudden weight had pulled her down. He dared not push her away.

"You had good tidings to bring from the meeting," she said.

"They are my tidings now," said Rendon. "Not yours."

"Rendon—"

"They will keep me company when you are gone."

"You can't mean—"

"I can mean it as well as you can. Take what's yours. Don't forget your Mother's Drop."

She looked suddenly afraid; the tears that had been hidden burst onto her face. "Don't send me away," she sobbed.

"You have sent yourself away," he said.

"I...cannot travel," she said. "I cannot make the journey. That's all."

Rendon nodded his head across their only room. "The door is not far," he said. "Take whatever journey suits you after that."

In tears, she stood, and took small steps toward it, turned back, wiped her face with her hands. It was his turn, now, for a moment, to fix his gaze upon nothing, to feel nothing.

"I'm pregnant," she said.

He later wondered how far out the door she might have made it, if he had let her. But she did not move from that spot until the words met him and sank into him, until he looked upon her with wonder, until he rose in full control of his movements and crossed the floor and swept her gently into the embrace of his good arm.

"Impossible," he whispered in disbelief. "It's impossible."

"Oh, it's very possible," she told him. "I'm sure I needn't explain how."

"It's—already? I can't believe it."

"I've been to see a—a midwife," Lysandra blurted out. "She said I can't travel. Too dangerous...for me. For the baby. Our baby."

"Our baby," said Rendon, carelessly; then, with a little more thought, "our baby." He felt the weight of the heavy gold coin in his pocket. "You can't come with me."

"I can't," she sighed, clutching him to her.

"And I can't stay."

"But I'll write you," she said. "As often as I can."

"Gods, how I love you," he said.

She smiled contentedly in response and nestled into his chest.

He sniffed at her hair. "You went down the docks to find your midwife."

"Oh," she said. "Yes. But don't worry; I wasn't lying about the fish. I brought it, too."

"I have coin," said Rendon. "There's more of it to come, if I work hard. I don't want you dealing with those cut-rate beet-pullers who hang out in the harbour. Midwives for whores and strumpets, all of them. You deserve better."

"My midwife is very good," said Lysandra, very hastily. "An aeril. A true, pureblooded aeril. She's been birthing children a hundred years."

Rendon didn't look convinced. "I don't trust their kind," he said. "Natural witches, I hear."

"She saved our baby's life once already," said Lysandra. "It won't be an easy pregnancy. It's why I can't—"

He kissed her once. "Stay with her, if it please you. But care for yourself, above all. I'll speak with the Warden about keeping the room. Do you need something better than—this?"

"No," she said. "It's fine."

"I have gold, Sana. Gold. Not much, but I could—"

"It's fine. I'll stay here. This is my home. Your home."

"I've never kept a room through the season," he said. "Never had a home to return to."

She held his hand to her flat stomach. "You have a home in me," she said. "How long—when do you go?"

"A detachment heads west on the Iron Road in six days," he said. "I'd meant us both to ride with them."

"Write to me," she said. "Every day. Tell me everything. Paint me into the mural of your days, as if I were there with you."

"I swear it," said Rendon. "Every day. They'll have to butcher a herd for the parchment."

She smiled gently. "You say the sweetest things."

The next five days were an uneasy mix of contentment and sorrow. Mindful of the work to come, Rendon lay whole afternoons abed with Lysandra, who welcomed his embrace but pushed aside, as usual, his most ardent advances for reasons he only now understood. They climbed to the Imperial shrine at Vairhurst and walked among the memory stones, though there was no more talk of killing. Four names had been added to the stone that would have been Rendon's, and he found himself glad not to be counted among them. On the last evening before the detachment set out from the Legions of the Shield, they went walking out beyond the Shadewall, among the clustered houses, inns, and farms along the Iron Road.

In the rolling hills to the west, between Vosthome Wood and the high cliffs of the northern coast, great fields of violet had come and gone in the spring, ceding the fields to the late-blooming cerulyn. But in a few shady places, hardy violets cultivated for civic reasons still cast their own hue into the mix, their blossoms dark and rich, their green leaves ringed with gold in the light of a late summer sun. When the drabness of the city proved too much, they often came out with bread and sweets and wine to the heart of a field and lay down among the flowers. They did so again on their last evening together; Lysandra wove a brilliant purple crown for his head, in flagrant defiance of the law concerning the Three Maidens, and Rendon found it, to his frustration, one more favour he could not return with a single hand. "I've heard violets in autumn are bad luck," he said, but suffered his crown anyway.

"Of all the Maidens," said Lysandra, "violet is the most fickle. Smell this—the delicate fragrance is like nothing else. But smell it again, and she is far away. She is the humblest flower, the most modest. She hides her face beneath the leaves, and she hides her scent away in the wind."

"It's the oldest flower of Travalaith," said Rendon. "An emblem of the city, from long before Valithar, before the Occupation. The Baron-Kings revered them. Even the True Kings, a thousand years before them. I think there is no shame in a man wearing such a crown as this, flowers or no."

"Those days are long past away," said Lysandra sadly. "I am no minstrel, no court skald. I wish I could better sing of them."

"I have no head for songs," said Rendon. "I know 'The Watch at Vostarban,' of course, like any good soldier. It has a verse or two about the violets."

"I know it much too well," said Lysandra. She shut her eyes tightly and lay back in the grass as Rendon, with a deep voice much unused to music, began to sing to her:

There ran a river red as blood,
There ran a river blue as sky,
There too a river violet ran,
At Ban! At Ban! At Vostarban,
The ground of those who will not die!

The Watch that rode upon the flood,
The heroes who, at Outlands' end,
Bore Vostar's blood and Vostar's clan
Within their breasts at Vostarban,
With valour still that land defend.

The Maidens Three upon its banks
Attend the war-spent where they lie,
Ensure the men who lie unmanned
Reclaim unto their bloody hand
The fallen sword—

He stopped. Rivers of tears were streaming silently down Lysandra's face where she lay, wracked with sadness on the hillside.

"Hush," he breathed. "Hush, Sana, darling. I've no talent for melody, but I'm not all that bad."

She shook her head. "My…my husband," she said. "He was my husband."

Rendon nodded silently, and cradled her in his arm as best he could. "I'm sorry I've upset you," he said.

"I was a bad wife," she sobbed, "and I've been a worse widow. The things I've done…"

"Hush, love," said Rendon. "None of it matters now. You are my lady, for good or ill, and you are good to me. We've all lost something to those vile outlanders. Me, I've only lost an arm. I can't imagine your pain. But I understand. I understand."

"You understand nothing," she said, but buried into him and

clutched at his shirt just the same. They lay on the hill a long time in heavy silence, until the night had come down and there was no more time for regret.

When the morning came, she rose at dawn, and made him breakfast, and washed his uniform, and woke him with a kiss. She had done all this before, and it had such familiarity now that she could do it, as she did this morning, nearly in her sleep. There were more things to be packed, and provisions to be arranged; the provisioner came in advance of the troops, and then the Warden of Greymantlehouse came to inspect the room, and to pass the keys for the little dwelling directly into her care. He asked no questions and took little notice of who she was to him; the soldiers took to women, and frequently to young men, of all kinds, and a formal marriage before Tûr, the Ten, or any other gods was not so common as the magistrates pretended. She would serve as tenant in his stead, and he passed to her the cured leather badge that identified her as an inhabitant of the House.

The soldiers massed in the adjoining square, many of them on horseback, with little ceremony but an abundance of noise. Their parting was faster than either of them expected, with more words and touches of the same sort hastily exchanged. No one was with them when they parted, and no one was with Lysandra after he had gone. She sat on the edge of the bed for what seemed a long time; then, with almost precise efficiency, she rose, went out into the barren courtyard, and retched, emptying her stomach into the rain-gutter until she was shaking, cold, and thoroughly purged of her breakfast. But the sudden disgust that filled her stomach, a disgust at many things, was not a load so easily unburdened.

She cleaned her face with water from the rain-barrel and set her hair as well as she dared. With only a moment's pause to pry up Rendon's original, barely-legible copy of the Fingrun report from beneath a courtyard flagstone, Lysandra came down from Greymantlehouse by way of the beggars' alley and made for the harbour.

THREE

ODI WAS PLAYING the other fishermen at four-tower—and losing handsomely—when he saw the woman he knew as Madge Dunny come down onto the wharf. He ought not to have drawn attention to her at all, but the morning had been unkind to him, and he could ill afford a cruel afternoon.

"Look at that one," he said. "A work of art, that."

The other sailors craned their necks backward. "The laundress?" one asked.

"No, the one behind her, on the steps," said Odi. "Hair like a cloudy sunset."

The other men grunted their approval. "I could break that in two," said one.

"Careful," added another. "That's an army cloak keeping her warm. That's no harbour whore, that. She's some watchman's wife."

"Watchman's wife," scoffed Odi. "I know a whore when I see one. Maybe the cloak's part of her trade. You know well as I, some of the men too long at sea come home with tastes and fancies for pages and junior officers."

"She'd have her hair bobbed short, then," said one of the others, "if that's her trick."

Odi flashed a small silver coin in his hand. "I've got one rider," he offered, "that says she's bound for one of the merchant-boats—and belowdecks, if she's got a lick of decency."

The men shook their head.

"Any number of reasons she could be headed onto a boat," said one.

"Give me two for one, Loric," said Odi, "and I bet I can tell you *which* boat."

The men leaned out incredulously, casting their eyes over the sea of masts collected in the inner harbour. A few seemed determined to count the odds; a few threw a couple of coins onto the four-tower table.

Loric eyed the silver coin in Odi's hand. "Is that a Celithrand rider?" he asked. "The Foundry's recalled them. They're up in value since he turned traitor to the Empire."

"I hear he escaped again," said Odi. "Gave us the slip out west of Wescairn, right under the local censor's nose. It could be worth twice its weight, now, to the right collector."

"One boat," said Loric. "One guess."

Odi stroked his chin deeply in thought, then pointed straight at a single-masted trade cog moored far down the pier.

"That one," he said.

Loric shrugged, considering the choice. "A very clever guess, but a wrong guess. I've seen beautiful young girls go on and off that ship all morning. Exotic ones, from all over. That merchant keeps a floating whorehouse; that much I'll believe. I've seen them. But I've seen my share of whores, son, and that's not what your lady is."

"You sure?"

"She doesn't…"

He hushed himself for a moment as she passed him close by.

"She doesn't have the eyes for it," he finished.

The third man scoffed. "What's eyes got to do with it?"

"Too much sadness," said Loric. "A man can smell that kind of grief. Ruins the whole business, sad eyes like that under you."

"So turn her 'round," said the third man.

"I'm telling you—" Loric began. He fell silent as the woman stepped up onto the gangplank.

With hasty steps, she ascended to the deck of the merchant cog. A tall, green-eyed man met her at the railing and took her below decks at once. Odi cheered.

"That's two silver riders," he said, beaming. "Or I'll take a harp and a half, if Imperial coin is all you've got."

Loric thumped two coins onto the table with a snort. "S'what I get, I s'pose, for looking 'em in the eyes."

On the deck of the *Wyrmsbolt*, a tall, green-eyed man in opulent merchants' robes extended a hand to the woman.

"You must be the lovely Lysandra," he said. She took his hand and hoisted herself over the rail, but did not look him in the eye.

"It's Madge, if you please," she said. "Call me Madge."

"Well enough," he said. "My name's Hendec. Your cargo awaits you below deck."

She eyed him with tired skepticism. "You're not her usual man. You're new. Why should I trust you?"

He jerked his head toward a distant set of masts—tall, whitewashed masts that towered over the nearer ships like the upturned fingers of some skeletal hand.

"You know whose ship that is?" he asked.

"The *Providence*," she said. The slight blush in her cheeks drained to sudden paleness. "Lord Ashimar's warship."

"Aye. If I was come here to double-cross you, dear widow, I'd pop you over the head now and we'd be having this talk with him."

"Take me down," she said, her voice breaking. "Get me out from under all this sky."

The hold was accessed by way of a small hatch in the low sterncastle. Hendec went ahead in the dark like a man accustomed to the way, and she followed him eagerly into a shallow space stacked with colourful bolts of linen and silk.

"It's a little tight," said Madge, turning sideways and inching through the narrow aisles.

"We like it that way," he replied. "The city guards are iron-crazed. Longswords, the lot of them. Longswords, longswords, all they carry. Nowhere down here to swing one, if it came to that."

"Will it?" she asked him. "Will it come to that?"

"Not if you weren't followed," he said, and pushed open another hatch.

The makeshift meeting-room in the hold of the *Wyrmsbolt* could have fit in any one corner of the room at Greymantlehouse. There was barely enough room in it for a small table, a pair of coarse wooden stools, and the two people—both women—already seated. They, like Madge, were of slight build, youthful in appearance, the very picture of what men like Hendec understood to be delicate feminine beauty. But the woman seated in the rearmost corner of the little room was hidden beneath a cloak of grey silk. Her thin lips and narrow chin were all that could be seen of her in the flickering glow of three fat candles, and even that was too much. The softly iridescent glow of her skin, pale and shimmering in the candlelight, was a telltale sign of her pureblooded heritage: here, surely, was one of the aerils, and surely the one whom Madge had been told to expect.

"You are late, Lysandra," said the aeril.

"It's Madge, if you please," said Madge.

"It's Lysandra," the woman countered. "Until you leave the city, your name is Lysandra, you were born in Travalaith, and your husband was a tower guardsman."

Madge frowned. "It's good to see you, Baran."

"I am your new contact with the Mage," said the aeril-woman. "Your *only* contact with him. This is Hendec—he is your escort in the city, and your urgent contact if things go poorly. This young lady is Catrine, a Vairhurst Widow like yourself. There are a few others still active, but you will not meet them."

Catrine extended a willowy arm in greeting. "Most simply call me Cat," she said.

"You used your truename," said Madge, with some disdain.

"Pleased to meet you," said Cat, ignoring the slight with a practiced smile.

"We've been waiting to debrief her since you arrived," said Baran. "Some solidarity among the Vairhurst widows will be necessary to maintaining your sanity. But you will meet here and only here, and only when the *Wyrmsbolt* is in harbour."

"There is much to tell you," said Madge. "Most of it will please you—at least, more than it pleases me."

Catrine shifted uncomfortably in the narrow hold. "What I have to say will please you less," she said softly.

Baran eyed the younger girl with curiosity. "Let us have the bad news first, then. Catrine, tell us of your work."

Catrine cleared her throat, shaking the candle-flames on the small table. "Rasten is his name. He's a tower guard—a Cerulean, appointed by order of merit," she began. "He grew up in Carmac, youngest of seven children, and came to the city. He worked as an enforcer, a heavy at the Black Bridge Inn, and made his way into the Grand Army. No particular loyalty, at first. The coin was good, and his sisters were spinsters for want of a dowry. He fought under Thurmod the Dark in Selik with his brother, and was sent home highly decorated for valour, but he suffered no maiming on the field. They posted him to the Tower last year, but not in a pensioner's post. He was hand-selected for special duty."

"What kind of special duty?" asked Baran suspiciously.

"Inner guard to the Imperial chambers," said Catrine. The others let out an audible breath.

"I thought you said this would displease me," said Baran. "None but the bloodguard themselves come closer to the Imperial family. Catrine, I am delighted. You could not have chosen a better man."

Catrine cleared her throat and nodded timidly. "I feel the same way…but for different reasons."

"Explain."

The three women started as Hendec stirred behind them, shifting uneasily on the crate where he had settled.

"I can smell where this is going," he said. "She's gone moony for the poor bastard."

Baran shook her head. "No, it's not possible. It's only been a few months."

"The lives of ordinary men—women, too—are shorter than you think," said Hendec. "I'm going up to keep an eye on that white ship. I've no stomach for lovers' gossip." He roused himself with a grunt and twisted his tall frame out of the makeshift meeting-room.

"Is this true?" asked Baran. Catrine's eyes shone wet in the candlelight.

"He speaks often of marriage," she whispered. "He is utterly disarmed. He tells me so, and I know it. There is a kindness in him I did not expect from…from the men who fought us in the East. He writes me poetry. And though I came to him and seduced him in the lowest of circumstances…he means to court me, as a man should court a woman."

"He serves the Imperial Grand Army," said Baran sharply. "You would do well to remember your husband."

"Aden was a kind man, too," said Catrine. "He would not want me to be unhappy. We spoke of it, the year of the yellow plague. He said if he died, I should remarry. I'm sure he meant someone from the village, but…"

"You have no village," Baran reminded her. "The Empire burned it. The esteemed Imperial Harper bought out the Danu, just as he bought out the thanes and bondsmen of the Fanes fifteen winters ago. The Battle of the Danhorn made short work of the fighters, and those blood-crazed men made short work of your husband soon after."

"Not Ras," said Catrine. "He was in the East."

"Ah, the East," said Baran. "We know how Selik has fared. Tell me, do you love this brute?"

Catrine hesitated. "Yes," she said. "It feels strange to admit it."

"And do you trust him?"

"In a manner of speaking...I do."

"And what have you told him?"

She swallowed hard. "N-nothing, yet. He knows nothing."

Baran's expression was unreadable in the stillness of the hold. Madge dared not interject, though an anger—and perhaps the seed of jealousy—roiled in her gut at the idea that a Vairhurst Widow could ever dare fall in love with her mark.

"Do you want out?" Baran asked at last.

"I...don't think so," said Catrine. "He's a Cerulean—as you say, only the bloodguard themselves are closer to the Imperator. What I can learn, we can't get from anywhere else. Only... I love him, is all. It complicates things. I thought you should know."

"I must consider this," said Baran. "The Mage must consider it. You are in a very delicate position, Catrine. But the Mage will know what to do." She paused thoughtfully. "If the Mage demands it...will you kill him for us?"

"Yes," said Catrine.

"You're lying," said Baran. "That came out far too quickly to be true. Don't look so frightened for him, Catrine. A bodyguard to the Imperator is far too valuable an asset to put a knife in just yet."

"Not so a Vairhurst Widow, though," said Madge with casual coldness. "We widows are the one thing, the only thing, of which Jordac has no shortage. Travalaith makes him a few more widows every day."

Baran fixed her with sparkling eyes. "Do not utter the Mage's name in this city again," she said.

"My pardon," said Madge, though she didn't sound sorry.

"What of you, then?" said Baran, her attention suddenly deflected. "I don't suppose your man has likewise slicked you with poetry and sweet words."

"Hardly," said Madge. "He can barely read or write. He's a bitter cripple and a cruel slaver...and a fool, if you ask me. He lost an arm at the Danhorn, and some days he's so blind I find it hard to believe we didn't take his eyes, too."

"He's a soldier?" asked Baran.

"As you say," said Madge. "Rendon Cowler's his name. They call him Rendon the Reckless, and I've seen it bear out. All tinder and no fuel, that man."

"Where does he come from?" asked Baran.

Madge shrugged. "He doesn't speak much of his old life. Much less important than where he is now. He's the Overseer of the iron mines at Fingrun."

Baran nodded with respect. "He's a rare find."

Smiling with some pleasure, Madge hoisted a sheaf of parchment. "His seasonal report from the mine," she said. "Delivered to the Imperial Harper himself. I had him write out a fairer copy, since the penmanship of this one is so poor."

All three women leaned in to look over the document, still smudged with soil from the courtyard.

"It's not bad," said Baran. "I can read every word."

"It was bad enough to warrant a second copy for us," said Madge. "Fingrun is clearly overproducing and undermanned, and not far from the coast. They've taken on far more prisoners than they should have—all revolutionary men, and none of them broken down by the mining yet, if we act quickly. A dozen of us, under the right moons, could take the fort, put to death the lot of them, take what we can carry from the bloomeries, free the prisoners, and roll a season's worth of iron ore into the sea."

"A bold plan," said Baran. "You've dwelt on this thought a long time. And you would count your new lover among the dead?"

"I wish his usefulness would end soon," said Madge. "I feel...it feels disrespectful. A betrayal of my husband's memory. Not because I love Rendon, you understand...but rather, because I do not."

Surprisingly, Catrine reached a delicate hand across the small table and took Madge's hand in her own.

"I envy you for that," she said with sad eyes.

Madge paused uneasily. "And I envy you," she said.

Catrine blushed in spite of herself, but looked away. "Stories like mine always come to bad ends," she said.

"My love story ended long ago," said Madge coldly. "It ended when the Imperial soldiers took my husband's life, and I swore I would settle his debt to them—with the very iron, it seems, with which he was paid. You are young, Catrine. Whatever years you had with Aden I will not discount. But you may yet have another love-story in you…and if tales of love end badly, believe me, tales of revenge end worse."

"Enough," said Baran. "Too many are the tales of woe under this vile Imperator. I will not have you compete like boastful men, to the detriment of the cause. We work to bring these days to an end, to overthrow the wickedness of this Black City once and for all. You have given much to the Mage—your bodies, your hearts. Your souls, if you like. Your lot is one of sacrifice. But if you wallow in that sacrifice it will be for nothing. We are each of us wounded. But the day you settled your widows' inheritance, and took up the fortunes of your men, you took up their fates, as well. You are soldiers, both of you. A coat of mail would ill become you, but do not forget that you are warriors."

"I—do not feel like a warrior," said Catrine.

"The Mage must decide what you are to us, now," Baran replied. There was coldness in her tone, but not hostility. "Until then, you will both go back to your business. Catrine, you will lie with your love, and find what peace you may, and learn all you can about the workings of the Spire. Everything about the Imperial Family. We have heard so little of them for many years. You are the closest source we have to them, which tells me things will not go badly for you with the Mage."

"I will do my best," said Catrine.

"If you truly love him," Baran added, "if you love him with your whole heart and he returns it in kind—perhaps he can be turned to the cause, for your sake. I can give you no more hope than that. But do nothing until you hear from me."

"I have been away too long," said Catrine. "He dotes on me. I will be missed."

"Go," said Baran. "We meet again the morning after the first white-wax. Look for Hendec or Odi in the harbour."

Catrine bowed as well as she could in the narrow space, and passed from the hold. But Madge lingered after she was gone with a heavy tongue that at last unburdened itself.

"There's more," she said.

"I would hear of it," said Baran.

"He wanted to take me to those awful mines," said Madge. "I would have been no good to anyone. When I would not go…it was nearly the end. He nearly had done with me there. I…I told him I was pregnant. There was no choice."

Baran stood from the table. She was smaller than Madge, her leanness almost harsh, but her eyes burned.

"That's a hard lie to make true," she said. "Or an inconvenient one, at least. How long is he gone?"

"Long enough to miscarry it," said Madge. "I…I told him I had a midwife in the harbour. An aeril."

Baran scowled. "Few of us linger in your lands," she said. "My presence will be noted."

"He told no one. He is gone to Fingrun, just this morning."

"We will see what comes of it," said Baran. "Some coin will make its way to you. Send a letter on to Odi as soon as you have one from Rendon."

"He said he'd write me every day when he arrives."

"Don't worry. It never lasts."

The sun had come up over the grim crest of the Shadewall, bathing the harbour in a blazing light that shone without warmth. Catrine's pale golden ringlets gleamed as she tucked them away under her hood. A few lewd whistles came up from the fishermen hauling in their first catch, but she lowered her eyes and kept walking.

"A different woman," she heard a too-close voice say, with the loudness of a man drunk at dawn. "A fine one."

Her rising fear was cut short by a sneering voice she knew to be Odi's. "Nah, same one," she heard him mutter. "That filthy young merchant just knocked all the colour off her." The fishermen roared with laughter, and Catrine had to raise a gloved hand to hide her own smile. Odi was an artisan of crudeness, when the occasion called for it. But she knew with him stationed in the harbour, she had nothing to fear. She looked back, smiled at him for just a moment, and heard the fishermen whoop and cheer him accordingly. He fixed his beady eyes on her with concern that melted into gratitude. Things would go easy with them, now. She understood how it all worked.

She stopped for a fresh hakefish, just as Madge—Lysandra, she corrected herself—had done. The water in the walled bay was choppy and there would be no denying the scent of it on her. Fresh thyme she would have bought, too, but the merchant was unused to the city, and a day or two within the Shadewall had withered his bunches to rotting brown sprigs.

But where Lysandra would have followed the Saltway straight on from the harbour, skirted the Lornock Hedge, and crossed the bulk of the city to her wicked lover's hovel in Greymantlehouse, Catrine turned her course eastward up a narrow, hilly road into tightly packed laneways of grey and white limestone. The Storm Quarter was not much cleaner than the streets below, but the gutters flowed downhill, and the cool autumn winds were baffled by rows of high terraced buildings. Compared to the sights and smells of the lower quarters, the Storm Quarter was almost palatial; and Catrine counted her blessings that the man she had chosen to shadow, to seduce, and finally to court with an honest heart, had won such renown under Thurmod the Dark and lived to boast of it. When the Grand Army were driven out of Selik, many of the front-line soldiers were simply wiped out—a defiant decimation that pleased Catrine immensely. That Rasten was not himself numbered among those dead, though, pleased her even more.

The iron-banded door to the shared great-hall was well-made and moved on its hinges with an easy silence. A tall fire blazed in the common hearth, and the thick, briny scent of fish stew had no trouble filling the place to its high ceiling. Her quarters—Rasten's quarters—were up some stairs, which she ascended almost noiselessly.

He was hard asleep on the bed when she found him, splayed across it though it was not yet noon. The feather mattress was wider than she was used to, but his broad shoulders filled the space. As a man often in motion, the size of him often escaped her notice—he was not long in the body, not really, but thick and muscled like a bull, the sort of man for whom the women of old Selik would have envied her. Some time in the city had rounded his muscular frame at the edges, but she could trace with her hands the hard muscles, a warrior's muscles, that lay in wait beneath this new layer of softness, a layer she found not unappealing.

"Ras," she whispered. He barely stirred.

In spite of herself, she found her cloak unclasped and her shoes slipping off her small feet as she slipped beneath the blanket of thick, coarse wool and curled up against him. She struggled to lift his thick arm over her; even his hands were heavy. She curled her fingers around his big hand and felt small and safe against him.

"Ras," she whispered again.

"Mm?" She was surprised to get even that much.

"It's past noon."

"Mm."

"You asked me to wake you."

Ras groaned as he shifted against her lazily. "You are making it no easier to get out of bed."

"I could make it easy," she teased, poking him where she knew it would make him jump. He only groaned and recoiled from the touch.

"Oww," he said. "That's fresh."

She drew back the blanket with curiosity, then alarm. "*Ai džeb!*" she spat, forgetting herself. "What happened?"

Ras rubbed at one of the long, purple welts striping his torso. "Training," he said. "I've been out today already. Harder than I'm used to, that's all."

"Training?" she said. She ran her fingers across a bruise and he winced.

"It's the Imperial Harper's orders," he said. "I've been assigned to the Imperator's daughter. Olferth wants us nothing less than master swordsmen on every floor of the Cîr-Valithar. And I…I am no master swordsman."

"No need to be so rough about it," she frowned, reaching out with concern. He brushed her hand away gently.

"Master General Thurmod put those there himself," said Ras. "They're like badges. I'm amazed a man of his importance had time to train me."

"I'm not sure he *did* train you," said Catrine, eyeing the long welts with her head cocked sideways. "At least, not very well."

"Oh, stop," said Ras, though he was smiling.

"Either he's the greatest swordsman in the Empire, or the very worst teacher."

Ras pulled gently at his arm—he was growing restless, as was his way.

"I like to think he's both," he said. "It saves the ego some."

They lay in bed a while longer, but when it was time to rise, he was decisive and wasted no time.

"You're awfully spry for a man beaten senseless," she said.

"Not much choice in the matter," said Ras. "It's Keddensday, and a sunny one at that. Illyria meets with her tutor in the state building's upper block—he refuses to enter the Cîr-Valithar, for which I can't say I blame him."

"Illyria?" asked Catrine. "I thought she died in the birthing bed, not long after her mother."

"Apparently not," said Ras. "Her lessons are the only time she leaves the safety of the Tower. You can imagine, in wartime, how much it displeases the Imperator."

Catrine rolled away, feigning disinterest. "I can imagine," she said, as calmly as she could. The very existence of the Imperator's daughter was a matter of rumour that even Jordac's agents had struggled to confirm it.

That she had a name, and a routine, and that she left the impenetrable Tower for a building whose walls could be breached, was more information than she could have hoped for—but the discovery left her hollow inside and sick at heart.

"You should not speak of such things," she warned. Ras only shrugged.

"If a man can't tell his…his…" he began. He stopped, thought for a long moment, looked for the right words, then held her face in his hands and kissed her forehead instead.

"I trust you," he said at last, his grey eyes shining. "With all that I am." It took all she had to return his smile with practiced pleasure until he turned away. Draping his linen tunic over a muscled arm, he fastened the little blue pendant of the Cerulean Guard about his neck, then reached up high for the double-bladed axe he kept mounted on the wall.

"Besides," he added, hoisting the axe with effortless familiarity, "I've sworn an oath to protect the Imperial family to the death. You come after her, my love, and I may just have to put you down."

"Is that so?" The humour was gone out of it, now, for her.

He smiled. "Yeah, that's so."

She gestured at his ribs as he pulled on his tunic. "Well, you're dropping your guard on the right side."

"Better than the wrong side, I suppose," he said, and laughed a little too heartily at his own cleverness. "I'll be home not long after dark." He kissed her, again, the way most men only kissed in love-ballads, and moved to the door with the grace of an agile man unburdened by cares.

"Rasten," she called after him, and he turned.

"Hm?"

"I love you," she said. "You know that."

Ras smiled, a little off-guard. "Of course I do," he said. "And I love you. Don't you forget it, either."

"Not for a moment," she beamed, though her smile was already fading as he pulled heavy door open and slipped into the hall. Her tears were not long in coming, and she stifled her sobs against a fine feather pillow whose airy softness only worsened the burden of her guilt.

"I'm sorry," she whispered in her grief—to herself, to her lover, to her lost husband, to all the world, to no one in particular.

Even several months in, Ras was still unused to the pleasure and privilege of making the long walk from the Storm Quarter to the Tower without being hassled by every street urchin and beggar who lined the lower streets. His broad shoulders and muscled frame made him seem taller and more imposing than he was, but his face was round and friendly, and made him all too approachable. Before he was posted to the Cerulean Guard, it had made him a sympathetic target for every beggar and swindler in the Empire. So long as he was careful to let his cloak billow proudly, flashing its blue lining as he strode with purpose, the people kept their distance, for the most part. Even the flower-girls on the steps backed away, knowing too well the urgency of the city's most prestigious regular military order.

Behind the great-chambers and central receiving hall of Lornock, behind its domed library and magistrates' offices, within the central courtyard of the newer Imperial fortress, lay the great and ugly Inner Wall. A work of foul immovable iron like the Shadewall itself, the Inner Wall surrounded the imposing black finger of the Cîr-Valithar; during the Siege, it was the only protection the Spire needed. Faces of unspeakable agony were wrought into the iron of that wall, horrendous sculptures of writhing men and women, tormented by nameless Horrors that still lingered on the edge of living memory. Ras would never quite get used to seeing the Inner Wall across the courtyard; and while foolishly optimistic artisans had draped immense tapestries over the Wall in the city's three colours to hide the handiwork of the Second Craftsman, the winds on a day like this were enough to tug at the edges of the hanging banners. Screaming faces in spotless black metal peered out at him when the wind picked up and shook his usually strong stomach until he felt sick.

A small squad of men, perhaps a dozen, in their own Cerulean cloaks were performing combat drills in the tower square. Some had heavy wooden practice swords and some had weapons of live steel. In their midst was a familiar face, noticeable in the squadron even at a distance. Standing to the side of the most heated contest of wooden blades was a soldier whose head was banded in the style of the far South. His face was the colour of stained mahogany, and he was cloaked not as a Cerulean, but in the same Imperial purple as the regular troops. His rank and decorations—for he had many—were marked only on a sash he had laid aside.

"See the new arrival at your backs," he called out to the men, nodding to Ras. "The whole battlefield has just changed. If your stance has not, you are not making swordplay. You are just swinging steel."

A few of the men noted Rasten's arrival and went on with their routines. A few greeted him from afar and got stung for it by their focused partners. The dark-skinned officer approached him with a glowing smile as he crossed the yard.

"Rasten," he said, interrupting the bigger man's courteous bow with a handshake at the forearm. "It feels as if you just left us."

"Master General Thurmod," said Rasten. "I'm afraid my ribs would have to agree with you."

Thurmod's smile flashed smug for only a moment. "And yet I see you are still carrying that meat chopper."

"It was my brother's axe," said Ras, as if that would explain it. "Beside which, two weapons are always better than one."

"Impractical," said Thurmod. "Knives for skirmishers, maybe. A mother-and-pup, if both are light, I have carried. But these? You must be very sure of them both. And stronger than most men, besides."

Rasten shrugged. "I'd be glad for more practice," he said. "You honour me—you honour all of the Ceruleans—to come and play among us."

"You are the best warriors in the city," said Thurmod. "The Tower Guard are better fighting men than any in my whole army. You were chosen because you were deemed too deadly for the front lines of an Empire at war, and that is saying something. I like the company of my officers, but when it comes to training I would take your comrades over my own karls ten times out of ten."

Something in his measured voice, more than a mere trick of the accent, chilled Rasten to the bone. He looked back to the men, to the intensity of their training, and felt the ache in his side as he twisted round.

"You're deadly serious," he said. "About the training, I mean. You're not just shepherding some border town this time. You're headed somewhere dangerous."

"Jordac has men south of Selik," Thurmod conceded. "How many, and exactly where, we do not know. A rider for Magistrate Mardon brought us the news, and was lucky to escape with it. The Mage comes and goes like dew on the grass. But the mines there were laid waste, and Master General Harrod was driven back from the edge of Estelonne Forest."

"Master General Harrod had ten thousand men with him," said Ras. "And whips them, no doubt, to fight like twenty thousand."

"I have been sent to bring aid, and troops, and fresh supplies," said Thurmod. "And figure out what under sun or moon he ran into out there. Magic or no, Harrod could not have been turned back by a small force. There is a real army in those trees, I wager. Large enough, perhaps, that we can catch them on the move for once. Give them fair answer for what they did to us at the Danhorn."

"I wish I could be there with you," said Ras, and not long ago he might have meant it. But strictly speaking, it was now more idle pleasantry than truth. He had come away from the madness of war to an easy life, steady pay, and the love of a good woman. The mud and cold of the campaign had lost their allure to him, even before the prospect of being burned to death by strange sorceries was factored in.

"Do not wish too hard," said Thurmod. "You may be needed here. With both Master Generals in the east, I have no doubt trouble will come from the west ere long. A rider came, just this morning, from Wescairn with troubling news from the frontier."

"Oh?"

Thurmod frowned. "It seems the fugitive Celithrand was caught making his way to the coast. Not by my men, nor Harrod's. Some glorified clerk from Haukmere with a few vasily men. The moment they had him, they let him slip away."

"Celithrand," Rasten said, shaking his head. "That one hurts. He was one of my heroes growing up."

"I hear that is so for many in your country," said Thurmod. "But the Mage's powers are growing in the East. If Celithrand's magic is returning too, if he comes at us from the West with the druids at his back…"

"That will never happen," said Rasten. "The druids never fight. They never choose sides, not in political squabbles."

"Even so," said Thurmod, "he cannot be allowed to reach the coast."

"You mean to go after him?"

Thurmod shook his head. "Not I. Lord Ashimar is handling the matter personally."

Rasten shuddered. "Poor old man. That's not how I wanted things to end for him."

Thurmod put a firm hand on his shoulder. "We are at war," he said. "If we could all have what we wanted, *tsat'e hālzi*, I think we should not be at war."

At his back, the drills and clashes of the fighting men were growing steadily sloppier without the attention of their senior commander. It was a rare occasion indeed for a fighting man, even a Cerulean guardsman, to bend the ear of one of the two Master Generals. Rasten could have spent the afternoon in talk, but he knew when the time had come to let Thurmod go.

"I'm for the tower," he said simply. "I ought not to keep you from your duty. Safe journey to you, Master General."

"Safe journey," said Thurmod. "You go on to your preferred misery, soldier, and I shall go to mine."

"Farewell," said Rasten.

The Inner Wall had a single point of entry, a broad gate and barbican of the same black iron that had once been wide enough to admit… something altogether unnatural. The builders had fashioned a gatehouse of wood and stone that surrounded the inner gate and narrowed the passage considerably, concealing, at least from the eye, the terrible façade. The yard within, much smaller than the surrounding Lornock courtyard, was wreathed about with curtains of black metal that were solid in some places, and in others wrought of woven bands of iron. They were twined after the fashion of layered, thorny cobwebs, and had proven impassable to men during the Siege, but not to the oil and fire spat down upon them.

Here the builders had done a fine job, too, of concealing the atrocity of the place. False veneers of exquisite marble stonework were piled against the eerie iron web-walls and the stark foundation of the Spire itself, and a grand mosaic depicting the Company of the Owl and their tremendous victory adorned the stonework here. Superstitiously, as if their very names protected him against the evil of the Tower, Ras named them and ducked his head reverently to them as he crossed the last threshold:

"Valithar. Garim. Janus. Celithrand."

Even now, he would not unname one of the four heroes.

Within the impenetrable Spire there was no need at all for defenses, and the wickedly aggressive architecture of the outer walls gave way to a spartan space that was more easily decorated by the builders, who concealed the original vileness with far more art and thoroughness. The rushing water of the great baths echoed distantly in the hallways, where the Craftsman's waterworks and the Black Forge itself had been repurposed into a bathhouse of unmatched opulence for the Imperial family and its most honoured servants.

Passing a dozen other Cerulean guardsmen on his way, Ras mounted the first stair and began the ascent to his post, marvelling at the stillness and silence of the tower while Thurmod's men went on with their practice outside. He was stopped at the fourth landing by two immense karach, who crossed the ceremonial spears of their forgotten clan in front of him and bared their wolfish teeth menacingly.

"I am the bodyguard for today's outing," he said, his voice not quite faltering.

"Speak the words," one of the karach growled.

"Today's flower is the poppy," he said. "Today's number is five. Today's charge is a rampant boar."

The karach parted their spears and let him pass. No matter how routine his passage became, their presence always unsettled him. They took their job seriously; that much was for sure.

A raspy chuckle greeted Ras as he entered the tower's lower keep. He recognized its owner by scent before sight.

"If you ask me, milord," said the wretch, "memorizing the whole chart is a rampant bore." The tower's stoolman shuffled in from the Lady's hallway, his hunched back further bent under the load of an ornate wooden commode, lidded and fastened, that looked far more beautiful than it smelled.

Ras smiled at the servant. "As you say, fellow," he said. "It changes every day, and I've not much gift for memory."

"I comes and I goes three times a day," grumbled the stoolman. "You'd think I'd have it by now." He limped to the stairs with his burden to take it down to the baths and dispose of it, but Ras stopped him with a look of concern.

"How is she feeling?" he asked. "Really."

The stoolman sloshed the little cabinet in his arms appraisingly. "Better, sounds like. But they don't let a pot-porter like me see her, mind you. Might ask her yourself."

"They don't let me see her either," said Ras. "Nobody sees her."

"Nobody but the Imperator's bloodguard," said the servant, "and they's picked from birth." He shook the cabinet again. "They sounds healthy, too."

It felt strange to leave the hunchbacked servant without some sort of farewell, but that was how it worked for officers, after all. They'd crossed paths often in the past few weeks; tower security was unreasonably tight, he found, and the changes of staff happened for servant and Cerulean alike at the safest and surest of times.

It all seemed a little much to him: as far as he knew, common knowledge was that when the Imperator's wife had died in childbirth, the baby had died with her. He had told none save Catrine that the girl even survived, and knew that every other Cerulean was bound by the same secrecy. The precaution of an armed escort for the shuttered sedan was altogether too much, he thought, and might even be counterproductive. On his long walks he'd had time to imagine what he might do if he were Master General, or stood in charge of tower security. If he had to move her, he'd often thought, he would do it with stealth rather than strength of arms. There were quite a few women who worked in the citadel—wash maids and ladies-in-waiting, ubiquitous mistresses, even a few lady Magistrates. The whole production of moving Illyria to her lessons would be much more secure, he thought, if they abandoned her armoured litter for a drab linen dress and gave her a pot of water to carry like a common servant.

The hallway led down some distance, almost the width of the tower, before reaching the latticed gates beyond which he had never set foot. He held the keys for the first gates himself, and no sooner had he drawn them from his pocket than the thunderous barking and growling began.

"Easy, Heward," he called. "Easy. It's me."

Beyond the first set of gates, the shuttered sedan waited. Without its poles, it was little more than a metal box, a gilded cabinet whose door was not readily apparent and whose windows, it seemed, were little more than a few holes to let the air through. Beyond that stood the heavier second gate, and on the far side of that, a red velvet curtain that blocked everything beyond from view. The curtain swayed and trembled now as Heward stirred behind it. Ras took a knee as the dog's bark of warning subsided and waited for the bloodguards to come.

It was not they who quieted the dog. As Heward's massive paws kicked and clipped at the floor beyond the curtain, a pair of small and dainty bare feet—a girl's feet—joined them from somewhere behind the arras. Heward's barks turned to gruff snorts and finally to silence as a rhythmic scratching quelled his alarm.

"Hail, Your Imperial Highness," said Ras, bowing even though he knew he could not be seen.

"Rasten?" came her voice, small and high and precise. "Is that you?"

"It is, Your Imperial Highness. I'm here to escort you to your lessons."

"There's no need for such formality," her voice said. "Just plain 'Your Highness' will do nicely." He let slip a chuckle and so did she.

"I presume your men are busy."

"For the moment," she said. "They're unhappy with the poles on the sedan. The wood rots too quickly here, and they don't want me tumbling down the tower stair or some such thing. They're adjusting new ones. We'll be out in a moment. Sit."

Ras hunched down on the wall by the second gate, as usual. Her bare feet padded across the stone to stand near him. Her ankles were delicate, her toes nearly the white of cream.

"I dare not refuse Your Highness," he said.

"Then tell me," she said. "I would hear it all."

Rasten sighed. "Illyria…"

"Out with it," she snapped. "Every word! What did she say? Wait…how, where did you ask her? First, are you to be married or no?"

Rasten searched for words and found none.

"You didn't ask her." The girl's disappointment was audible. "Why not?"

"I meant to," said Ras. "But the time has not come."

Illyria coughed, cleared her throat. "Do you not share a bed with her?"

"Well, yes…but we have not had the time together for such things. You know how it is."

"No. I don't know."

"I…I wrote her a court poem…I made it in the old lord's verse, as you taught me."

"Let me hear it," she said.

He hesitated. "My lady…"

"Do you think I see many suitors here?" she asked him. She was not angry, but her impatience was clear.

"I could not presume—"

"Of course not," she interrupted. "None at all. I am young, so says my grandmother. And it is dreadful and dull here, and the great breathless heartstorm of the old romances is denied to me. You have not won my confidence by shyness, Rasten. I've waited all day to hear how you fared. You must give me something!"

"Illyria…"

"Please," she urged him, in a voice that was at once whinging and commanding.

"Yes, yes, yes my lady," he said at last. "Let me get it out. I wrote it down. I've not much gift for memory."

"Hurry," she said. "They'll be coming."

"Right," he said, and from a scrap of parchment in a rushed voice, he read:

> *Cat, your kindly kisses*
> *Can command this man's heart;*
> *All the length of my life,*
> *Long it dwelt in shelter.*
> *Wildcat, witching woman*
> *With your fire inspiring,*
> *How you shape and shine it,*
> *Shake it with love-making.*

"That's dreadful," she said. "Really, really terrible."

Rasten frowned. "Be honest, now," he said. "You shouldn't pretend to like it if you don't."

Her laugh was high and delicate, like windchimes of blown glass. "You weren't listening at all."

"Did I get it wrong?"

"No, it's not *wrong*," she said. "Metrically, it's exactly right. It's just—just—*awful*. 'Shake it with love-making,' really?"

"I—it had to fit."

"You're sure you haven't read it to her?"

"Oh yes."

"You're a lucky man, Rasten the guard," she said. "She'd be out to sea on the first ship. Even Heward thinks it needs work, don't you,

Heward?"

Rasten was at a loss. "It's stupid," he said. "I ought to forget the whole thing."

"You can't!" said Illyria, a little too loudly. She coughed and took a deep breath. "Your little love-story is all I have to sustain me here."

"Perhaps you ought to marry her yourself," said Ras. "You certainly have a better head than I do for poetry."

"I have the taste, but not the talent," she said.

"Ah, so you critique the poetry of others but dare write none of your own. There's a word for people like that."

"And what is that word?"

He caught himself. "It's not for the ears of a princess."

"I am no princess," said Illyria. "My father was bethroned by popular choice. His rulership is not hereditary. I have no proper title and no rank, and I assure you I am not afraid of your rude words."

"Just the same, I'm afraid of speaking them to you. We are told not to speak at all."

"Yet here we are," she said, "the best of friends."

"Here we are," he repeated.

"They're coming," she said, in a hushed whisper. "Will you be on guard tonight?"

"Tomorrow night," he said. "We'll speak then."

"I expect you to be engaged by then," said Illyria as the great hound barked once more at the arrival of someone new. Rasten did not dare reply.

In a moment, the outer layer of curtains parted. Through the latticed second gate, a bloodguard appeared, tall and fearsome in his Haukmere war helm and red-enameled armour. This one's helm had the roaring face of a striking tiger. With deft hands, he wordlessly unlocked the gate and swung it open with a creak. Illyria's feet had disappeared back behind the curtain as three more bloodguards emerged---bear, boar, ram. They hoisted with them two long, iron-banded wooden poles, and threaded these into the mounts of the sedan. With the ease of practice they lifted it and marched it backward through the curtain and into a space unseen;

and with a moment's care and the shuttering of many bolts, they emerged again, a little more slowly under the load of their Imperial passenger.

"Good afternoon, fellows," said Rasten. "If you'll follow me—but I believe you know the way."

Ras felt the bloodguards' eyes on him unceasingly as he led them through the first gate and down toward the stairs. For rankless men, they radiated an authority that unsettled him—and worse, confused him. He had no head for protocol at the best of times, and was never quite sure what they expected of him. Dutifully, he passed the two karach at the door, drew his weapons on the stairs, and manoeuvred his way down as if expecting Jordac himself to come leaping out of the shadows at any moment. Moving tactically down the heavy stairs, he recalled those few times he had been called upon to fight on such ground, on the steps of an old watchtower in Selik, and kept his wits about him.

It was a challenge to stay alert amidst the drudgery: once again, there were no mages, no monsters in the dark, no assassins lurking in the shadows. There were only a few onlookers—fellow Ceruleans, servants, and tower clerks—who peered in at the lower landings as the sedan passed. At the bottom of the stairs, with his burden emptied and cleaned, the hunchbacked stoolman waited in deference to the procession; though he had dared to look Ras in the eye, he lowered his face in abject submission as the bloodguards passed—nor could Ras blame him. Even on the winding stair, whose incline and direction ought to have frustrated men with such an unwieldy load, the bloodguards barely slowed at all, canting the litter's support-poles sharply forward and bringing the girl down with comparative ease. It was a route to which they were clearly accustomed, and Ras suspected each of them to be far stronger in the back and arms than any servant had right to be.

As they came out to the Inner Wall, the Ceruleans who had been training with Thurmod broke their drill formation to attend the procession immediately. It felt good to have their company, and to be out from under the oppressive weight of the Cîr-Valithar, but under a naked sky Ras felt much more vulnerable.

"Hail and well met, Rasten," said one of the other soldiers, an older, white-bearded veteran, clapping him on the shoulder.

"Elmore," he said, smiling. "It's been too long."

"That it has," said Elmore. "Tower duty again?"

"Tower duty."

"All that sitting, you'll have the strongest backside in the Empire before long."

"All that sitting," he agreed. He dared not admit to his conversations with Illyria, not with the bloodguards in close rank behind them. "How's Gwen?"

"Doing better, most days. How's your—the new lady friend?"

"It's a long story," said Ras. "Longer than your beard, old man."

"I'll have hours to hear it out," said Elmore. "We're being sent—"

"Eyes open," one of the bloodguards hissed, and they fell silent. Elmore's face betrayed how little and lightly he thought of the red-armoured bloodguards; that put Ras at ease, too.

Elmore's clever blue eyes were lit by some hidden thought as they led the procession across the courtyard and into the citadel. Ras never relished the feeling of leaving Illyria in her private study with the bloodguards, but the weight of that thought was so heavy on him that he could not wait to be free of them and ask the old man about it.

Illyria's study, tucked just beneath the yawning rotunda of the Imperial library, was a well-appointed but modest room, with no more than a dozen large books adorning its otherwise empty shelves. Among the furnishings there was open space for the sedan, but not much else, and as the bloodguard brought their silent load into the chamber, it was easier for the Ceruleans to slip out into the lobby and give them room. Today, Ras took his leave gladly, and pulled Elmore aside as the others returned to the courtyard.

"Our young charge is safely delivered to her lessons," he said. "Now cough it up, El. Whatever news you've got, cough it up before you choke on it."

"Nothing exciting, I'm afraid—at least not for us," said Elmore. "We're being put on cargo duty, soon as we're given leave. Likely for the rest of the day. I'll have ears aplenty for all your woman problems then."

"Cargo duty?" Rasten groaned. "Pots and tossers! That's your big news?"

"You must be new to the blue," said Elmore, tugging playfully at Rasten's cloak. "Cargo duty's no news at all to a common soldier. But to assign Cerulean Guardsmen to cargo duty—that's another matter."

Rasten stopped in his tracks. "Go on."

"The way I hear it, this came down from the Mouth himself. We're going down to Whiteport, to load up the *Providence* for a sunset departure. Short-haul provisions and rowers brought up from the Rattle. Lord Ashimar sails home to Wescairn tonight, then marches wet-kneed for some unknown destination."

"I've already heard," said Rasten, suddenly proud to be in the loop for a change. "Trouble in the west, wasn't it? Thurmod told me just this morning to expect it."

"Rumour holds that Celithrand was seen in Haveïl. He took on a full squad of the Grand Army. Blinded their marshal, so I hear." With an imaginary sword, the old man demonstrated the druid's deadly strikes for emphasis.

"Eleven shits," breathed Ras. "Just one old man did this?"

"Celithrand fought in the Siege," said Elmore. "Survived the Battle of Lornock. Those men were of another age, and aerils like him most of all. If I'm surprised by anything, it's that he left enough survivors to get a message back to Travalaith."

Ras shook his head. "I'm just glad I'll be safe behind the Shadewall when Ashimar catches up to him. It'll be a day for the Hanes, no question."

"I hear Ashimar flayed the poor messenger half to death," said Elmore. "I can't begin to imagine what he'll do to the traitor."

The two men fell silent as one of the bloodguards passed them. Rasten leaned in close and lowered his voice to a whisper.

"I'll take cargo duty anytime over the company of the lady's attendants," he said. "The common labour of loading a ship would settle my uneasy mind, I think."

"Aye, and good for your mind," said Elmore. "But not for my uneasy back. I was a curator, Ras. Meant for the library. Not for the high honour of loading crates of salt pork in a fine uniform."

"You could always refuse the office," said Rasten.

Elmore sighed. "Does your lady-love care much for silks and jewels?" he asked.

"If she does," said Rasten, shrugging, "I've never heard about it."

Elmore clapped him on the shoulder. "Then you marry her soon, lad. Be quick about it. You hang onto her, or you'll end up with a lovely, queenly wife like mine, and like it or not, you'll be wearing blue till they bury you in it."

"I mean to," Rasten said. "I've meant to ask her for some days, only…there is some shadow on my heart. Some fear I cannot place."

Elmore's eyes twinkled. "That's called being a young fool in love. I assure you, it'll pass."

"Something more," said Rasten. "Just some nagging doubt, some ghost of a worry that haunts me. She's a young woman, El. It's a long road ahead if I wed her. And I can't shake the feeling I'll hurt her, somehow. Or that she'll hurt me, in the end."

"Oh, *life* will do that," said Elmore with a chuckle. "Have no fear. Life is already sharpening a knife for you, son. For all of us. All we can choose now is who stands close enough to wield the blade. You fought at the Danhorn, yes?"

"No," said Rasten. "I was in Selik, thank the gods."

"Just the same, you've locked swords with some right ugly foes, haven't you?"

"I have," said Rasten.

"And likely will again. Look, you can't live a whole life behind your whirling swords. You have to let someone slip in under your guard. We all do. And if it's a beautiful woman who puts a knife in your heart—better that, I say, than an ugly man."

Rasten laughed. "Not the most inspiring of lectures," he said.

"Just the same," said Elmore. "You avoid the suffering that comes of love as if you'll somehow be spared from suffering if you do. Don't be fooled. We all suffer. But to suffer *for* someone you love—that's a higher calling, and a sweeter pain."

"I once heard," said Rasten, "that even the sweetest pain is worse than the bitterest pleasure."

"Sounds like nonsense to me," Elmore warned. "Who told you that?"

"You did," said Rasten. "In this room, at this time, last week during Illyria's lesssons."

"I did?"

"You did."

Elmore nodded sagely. "Hmm. Wise words, yes. Very wise words."

FOUR

ON A BLOOD-SOAKED DRESSING-TABLE in the bowels of the Rattle, laid out with his grisly stripes to the ceiling, Kellan Fyldron moaned high and loud like a cow at calving as he cursed the day he had ever met a man named Castor Stannon. At his back, just out of the light, a cellwife hummed softly to herself as she churned up some sweet-smelling mixture of honey and liquor in a wooden bowl.

"Oh, have done with it," he bellowed. "Leave me in peace, woman."

"Hush up," she said. "I know my trade, sir." She came into the light to daub her pungent concoction across his shoulders. It stung like fire and he winced.

"Where are my clothes?" said Kellan. "I asked for none of this."

"Turn on your side," she commanded, and he complied, content to be facing away from her. She was not an ugly woman, but she repulsed him just the same: ashen-faced, well past the thick of middle age, she smelled like torture, and there was no smell Kellan hated worse. It was rather like the scent of the ocean in port, he thought, itself a strange pungent concoction of salt and brine, trash and excrement and cool fresh air, decaying driftwood and sun-rotting fish. The scent of the harbour was not so offensive on the whole—some even called it picturesque—but it turned a man's stomach, if he thought too hard on each of its components. The smell of medicine, the smell of torture, was something like that, and Kellan knew a great deal about the things that made it up.

"Poor lout," said the cellwife. "I ween you didn't hardly ask for a lashing from Lord Ashimar either. They never do."

"Who?" he asked.

"The messengers," she said casually.

"This happens often?"

"More often of late," she said. "More ill news of late, you see."

"He flogs the messengers," Kellan muttered. "He actually flogs the messengers. I thought that was just a damned proverb."

"Proverbs are nothing but the legacy of unfortunate truths," said the cellwife. "Other side now, prithee."

Kellan hoisted his weight up onto his elbows and gingerly turned over.

"Figures I'd get stuck with a philosopher," he groaned. "How long have I got to endure all this?"

"I've cleaned out the venom from Ashimar's scourge," said the cellwife. "Nice to know who dealt the blow, so I knew what to expect. Gatekeeper to the Empire, they used to call him, on account of those wicked keys hung on it. The welts will go down on their own in a few hours or days. These parts where you're bit deep, they'll scab over, but they'll scar for life unless I tend them a while."

"I haven't that kind of time," said Kellan.

"You've got more time than most he sends down here," she says. "They don't often come to me. Straight to Van they go, mostwise."

"Who's Van?" he asked.

"The embalmer," she said dryly.

She ministered to the wounds on his back for some time—and to her credit, the sharp sting of every deep stripe seemed to fade. They pained him again when she turned him onto his front, to tend the blows landed there; but Kellan had been flogged hard before, and his ill cheer softened as it became clear just how skilled she was.

"I've been unkind, old woman," he said. "You know your trade well." Distantly, a wooden door creaked open, echoing down a hallway of stone.

"As you know yours, young man," she said. "You've seen more battles than most men survive."

"Aye," said Kellan. "These aren't my first marks, nor my last."

She touched a small scar at the top of his chest with gnarled fingers, just above his heart. "They used to call this a yeoman's nipple," she said. "All my days, I've seen only one other man survive being shot through here. Supposed to be a mark of good luck, to them that survive."

"Count the fresh scars as you tend them," said Kellan, "and tell me then, old woman, what you think of my luck."

"I think your luck is about to change," said a man's voice.

Kellan looked up to the doorway as two men entered, one of whom he recognized as a figure of some importance from his unpleasant debriefing in Ashimar's receiving-hall.

"For the better, I hope, milord," he said deferentially, not quite sure what to make of the man. The other behind him—an attendant of some kind—unbundled a fresh change of clothes from a dark cloak.

The man in charge made a plaintive gesture to Kellan's immense body, stretched across the table with his big feet hanging off the end.

"Well, it can't get much worse, can it?" he said with a waxy smile.

Kellan was nonplussed. "Always could be worse, milord," he said.

The cellwife, until now focused entirely on her patient, drew back from the table and bowed her head as the smile triggered her memory. "Lord Olferth," she breathed—a name that raised Kellan's eyebrows as well as the throbbing pulse beneath his wounds.

"Tell me, soldier," Olferth said. "You're clearly a strong fighter, as the hag says. But that is not what I saw this morning. I saw a man twice my size fold at the waist and cower like a Lornock flower-girl."

"Aye."

"Why? The Imperial Scourge is mostly an empty title. He's not your commander, he has no formal rank in the Grand Army, and he's given up his vasily. You could have fought back. Why didn't you?"

Kellan would have laughed in the face of a less powerful man, but kept his composure.

"When I draw steel," he said carefully, "It's a vow to my own self. It's a promise that I'll eat another meal and see another sunset. I draw my sword when I'm fixing to be the man who walks away with his guts intact."

"And you don't think fighting back would have kept you alive."

"We both know better than that, Your Excellency," said Kellan. "I'd no sooner draw steel on Lord Ashimar to stay alive than light a fire to keep cool."

The Imperial Harper nodded approvingly. "You fear him."

Kellan looked down at the lashes adorning his body, slick with medicine but still gleaming red. "I pray you tell me, Excellency," he said, "if I shouldn't."

Olferth clapped his hands together. "Splendid," he said. "Then you'll get along very well indeed with him on the *Providence*."

Kellan let the silence hang a long moment rather than let slip something unsavoury in the Imperial Harper's presence. "There must be some mistake," he said at last.

"Oh, there's no mistake," said Olferth. "Get him dressed."

"He needs more care—" protested the cellwife, but a glare from the Imperial Harper silenced her. The aide with the clothes began unfolding them; they looked large enough to fit.

"The Censor of Haukmere is not unknown to me," said Olferth. "Castor Stannon would not have sent you with this news of Celithrand personally if he had not meant you to be rewarded."

"That was his plan," said Kellan, "and it was charitable enough. He thought I might be rewarded with silver for finding you the traitor Celithrand. Not paid in my own blood for losing him again soon after."

"Just so," said Olferth. "You know the way to this village, and you were one of the last men to see the traitor alive. That is why you will be joining Ashimar's personal guard. You will lead Lord Ashimar to the place where Ashimar disappeared, and he will pick up the trail from there. When Celithrand is dead, I assure you, the reward will be so fat, you'll have to hire Castor Stannon and half his treasurers just to count it."

"I'm flattered, Excellency," said Kellan. "But Ashimar's men are bloodguards, same as the Imperator's own bodyguards. I'm not fit for their ranks. Those men are brought up from birth for it."

"Nonsense," Olferth said with aggressive cordiality, slapping the big man on his shoulder where the lash-marks were fewest. "You'll do for a season, no doubt. And now you have the blood to prove it. Do you know how many red cloaks there are in the Empire?"

"No, sir."

"Fewer than forty, my boy. Fewer than forty. Even this old woman could count them. And most will serve the Red Captain for life. Very few of such a rank ever have the luxury of trading on it."

Kellan frowned. "You mean to say they nearly all die in his service."

"Those born into the red have no option to resign," said Olferth. "You will be different. When this is over, you can trade in a seasoned bloodguard's cloak for…anything you want, I suppose. Be a Cerulean captain, if you like. Sit at the war-table of either Master General. If you please Ashimar well enough, you may wind up a landed lord in Haukmere. The Kelmors may be his own beloved family, you see—but even they dare not oppose his will for long, once he has made it clear to them. No one, my boy, would be so foolish as to refuse him, you understand."

Kellan took in the Imperial Harper's words with patience, and chose his own with great care.

"Milord," he said at last, forcing the words out, "it sounds to me as if you speak of easy money."

In all regions below his icy eyes, Olferth's smile was warm. "I think we understand each other," he said.

Kellan shifted uncomfortably. "I believe we do."

The cellwife's sad, sunken gaze was her only form of protest as Kellan was dressed by the aide in warm soldier's clothes. They were light and cool on his fresh wounds, and in their quality far surpassed the tunic and coarse shirt that had been torn off him in strips only a few hours before. He wrapped his belt around his waist, wincing as the movement pulled at his wounds, and tested the weight of the small purse that was strung to it. The cellwife had not taken his silver—of that he made sure.

"You have an uncommon prudence in a man-at-arms," said Olferth. "The Mages' Uprising gives us no shortage of seasoned veterans, and skill on the battlefield is cheap and in easy supply. But a man of your quality will flourish under Ashimar; of that I have no doubt."

"We did not meet on the best of terms," Kellan warned.

"You had bad news for him," said Olferth. "That day is past. Those hurts will be remedied when you lead him to Celithrand."

As Kellan's cloak was at last unfurled, it shone dark like blood under the guttering torchlight of the little room. It looked like the sort of thing an ambitious man would wear—and ambitious men, he found, had notoriously short lives ahead of them.

The Imperial Harper smiled as he fixed it about his shoulders. "I trust that soothes the hurt of an unfair flogging."

Kellan set his mouth hard and spoke with forced deference. "Aye," he said, "I didn't particularly earn a flogging. But this, Excellency—this, truly, this is more than I deserve."

"I'm glad you're pleased," said Olferth. "The Imperator offers you his personal congratulations on your promotion, I'm sure. I have official business to attend to, and so I shall leave you to finish your dealings with the hag. Report to the *Providence* by sunset. You'll be helmed and armoured as befits a bloodguard before you depart. Don't be late—not then, not ever."

Kellan nodded curtly, and ought to have stopped there. Olferth was already turning to go, and would have gone away quite happily with his silent aide in tow, if Kellan had not suffered a rare lapse in judgment and wagged his tongue a moment longer than necessary.

"Your Excellency," he asked, "may I know one thing?"

Olferth stopped and the icy smile returned. "Ask."

In his hands, as he thought out his words, Kellan fidgeted with a coin from his purse. It was a late Imperial issue, minted on one side with the displayed owl of the Travalaithi Empire, and on the other with the small silver harp that represented the Harpers' Guild—and that rare and ancient position of court advisor to which Olferth himself was the heir. In his youth, Kellan remembered the old silver riders—so called because they had borne a spearman atop a thundering horse on one side, and Celithrand's laurelled head on the other.

"The traitor Celithrand," he said slowly, "was of the Company of the Owl. He fought at the right hand of the Imperator himself, gods protect him, in the Siege of Shadow. His mosaic still stands a dozen feet tall against the very Cîr-Valithar."

"A structural oversight that will soon be corrected," said Olferth.

"How did it come to this?" asked Kellan. "They were heroes of the people. They were brothers in arms. It's true what they say of me—I saw the old man with my own eyes. How did the Lord of Druids come to betray the Imperator, in the end?"

"You are gifted, as I said, with an uncommon prudence," said Olferth, his smile never faltering. "That is the sort of question I have every confidence you are too wise to ask."

A century or two past, the parchment bound up in the old codex had been skinned from calves whose short lives had not been pleasant. One after another, the page edges were sharply curved at the outside, suggesting that calves with full-size skins had been hard to come by. To Illyria's keen eyes, under the well-lit windows that circled the rotunda, the marks of a thousand biting and stinging insects were visible, and even the pale scarring where some ancient and pustulent illness had come and gone in the herd. She sometimes heard the lowing of cattle in the street, and imagined what the pungent smells and shuffling sounds of the herd must be like to a girl standing among them. There was as much story in the pages, to her, as in the ink that stained them.

Her own pages, the loose ones to which she copied the text, were exquisitely fine by comparison, cut from a delicate paper of rice and silk that was made by some secret art in the distant south, far beyond even the homeland of Thurmod the Dark. It felt as thin as dragonfly wings under the coarseness of her quill; and while it took the weight of the point without complaint, more than the thinnest touch of the runny ink would smudge across its surface, leaving a single wounded letter bleeding grotesquely alongside its companions.

The process was meticulous and tiresome, but she was disciplined and well-schooled in the craft. With exceeding care and slowness, and many return trips to the inkwell, Illyria had already copied out the first of four stanzas, transcribing from the ancient script of the aerils to more pedestrian common script as she did so:

> *Aruili gructi throldomi ştilacti*
> *Kirilai mi nuili vuş nisil,*
> *Ic* íla *thirit valda ve duralai—*
> *Mi nuali mor foriammillas.*
> *Ai! Lor umal fenamailu*
> *Mi curind ionai vindaceni*
> *Throldon malada ei fondact,*
> *Allisil* şae *luonai licairract.*

Today, under the watchful eye of old Osgrim, whose sternness belied some inner warmth, she had begun the process over, copying the same stanza letter for letter from the opposite leaf, where it lay simply rendered in the Merchant's Tongue:

> *The fighting moons whip frenzied foam*
> *Within the waves along the coast*
> *And turn a woman's heart from home*
> *To seas where she would soon be lost.*
> *Alas! O when shall come again*
> *Into the reach of mortal men*
> *The valour of my vanished kin,*
> *The beauty of their banished host!*

When she had finished, she read the verse aloud. Her voice, unused to speaking, cracked under the effort, but it felt like a verse that needed to be proclaimed. Osgrim, reading his own book at the far end of the long table, raised his bald head from the pages and listened with interest. He had a marvellous voice for reading, sonorous and sibilant, deep and resonant in the vowels that sounded just a bit off, a bit exotic—an accent that was not quite Northern, but from somewhere she imagined to be very far and ancient. She had never set foot outside the Capital, at least not that she could remember. He could have been from somewhere as near as Carmac or Vosthome to the south, but sounded to her untraveled ears as if he had come down from one of the moons.

"Good," he said, with more power in his voice, it seemed, than in her entire verse. "Do you know the poem?"

"I think so," said Illyria. "It's 'The Fosterling,' I think."

Osgrim smiled enthusiastically. "That's right. Its original title? In Viluri?"

She hesitated. "The—raised by four—"

"*Vaimactal*," he said. "Four-parented. In Varphann it was called *Burunimactal*, the wind-parented girl. You shan't need to know that. Let's see how you've done."

He rose from his creaking chair and moved down the table. His lean, tall frame in its simple black schoolmaster's robes seemed to glide along the table's edge, as if he were a piece in a game of four-tower, pushed down the board by an unseen hand. He craned his bald head in so closely that she could feel his short black beard brush the crown of her hair.

"Hm, very fine," he said. "We'll start with this, and move on after."

She watched him perch on the edge of the table rather like a bird of prey. He had learned all the postures of a stern schoolmaster—for she had known many such masters—but they did not suit him.

"You've read both, now," he said. "Tell me, what is lost when you put it into Tradespeak? What has fallen away in translation that you cannot get back?"

She compared the verses, turning them over in her mind. "*Throldon*," she answered at last. "*Throldoni*. Antics or acts of boldness—or here, valour."

"It's just a different idiom," said Osgrim, leading her. "I quite like 'frenzied foam,' myself."

"The fighting moons beat angry valours into the waves," she said. "Literally. Can I say 'valours' like that?"

"Not really," said Osgrim. "Angry valour, perhaps, in the singular. So it's the same word twice. Why does it matter? The word 'water' appears in three flavours: *nuil, nual, nisil*. Why does the conceit of valorous waves matter so?"

"Because the valour of her people—pardon me, of the aerils—is vanished. Yet it survives in the waves."

"In the sea whither her kin have gone," suggested Osgrim. "The sea of the Merging."

"But they're not her kin," said Illyria.

"The verse calls them her kin," Osgrim said.

"It's ironic," Illyria answered. "She has no kin, not among men, and not among the Fei. She is all alone."

"How do you know?"

"I—I don't know," said Illyria. "Because I am alone, and I see myself in her. Because they are gone, and she is not."

Osgrim shook his head sternly. "What have you lost?"

"*Throldon*," she said again, shaking her own head. It was just a word to her now, just a sound. "Boldness. Courage."

"She means to drown herself," suggested Osgrim.

"Yes."

"A woman who commits suicide by drowning. And suicide, to the Vosi of old—remember your teachings in the summer—"

"It's the coward's answer," she said. "As the proverb says."

"For her? Yes."

"But not for the aerils," said Illyria. "At the end of their life, the aerils Merge with the sea. It is an act of bravery. But drowning herself in the sea—for the Vosi, it's just a way out of her own suffering. She knows in that moment, even in death, she could never be kin to them."

"Good," said Osgrim with a beaming smile. "Very good. You'll see it bears out as we go on." She meant to protest, meant to interrupt and admit her laziness, but he had started in on reading the next verses in Tradespeak—and once that voice began, there was no stopping it:

> *On feet of ice she takes her ease*
> *Where teasing waters tongue the sand*
> *And hears the roar of sweet release*
> *That lulls her from her native land:*
> *Alas that she who shares the call,*
> *The fosterling in aerils' thrall,*
> *Who Merges as her people shall*
> *In death alone discovers peace.*
>
> *The Eldest shall emerge again:*
> *The silver drawn upon the deep*
> *Is but a veil betwixt the men*
> *Who find in death a fitless sleep*
> *And they—O Father! Mother! They*
> *Who in their time are torn away*
> *To life, beneath another sky,*
> *Not slumber, like a slaughtered sheep.*

> *But here upon the Tunderstrand,*
> *Where aerils came ere final hour*
> *To meet their Change, and meekly stand,*
> *who weakly spanned, by secret power,*
> *The bridge of worlds: here in the gloam*
> *The fosterling upon the foam*
> *In hopeless search for hearth and home*
> *Has wilted like a fleeting flower.*

"Now," Osgrim proclaimed happily, breaking the spell of his words, "what has been lost? What have we given up, in bringing the words across to the Merchant's Tongue?"

Illyria hesitated; there was no way out of it, now. "That's all I have," she said. "That's all I've done."

Osgrim clucked his tongue in surprise. "Illyria," he said. "That's all? In three days? One stanza?"

"I've been busy," she protested. "It's not my fault."

"Busy playing fetch with Heward, for three days?" he chided her. "You never leave the Cîr-Valithar. What have you been doing, wagging your studies like that?"

"I—"

"Are you painting the whole Spire in there? Have you been hosting lavish parties when Olferth's back is turned?"

Above in the gallery, at Osgrim's mention of his name, Olferth nearly gave himself away. Controlling his breath and suppressing a snort, he shifted his weight off the front rail and slithered farther back into the gallery, where even less of the light streaming down from the rotunda reached him. He retreated from sight until he felt the fat arm of his companion against his shoulder.

"Hush," she whispered. "Listen."

The silence was unbearable as a very cross Osgrim bore down on the girl with piercing hawkish eyes. He never raised his voice in anger, not ever—but he took her lessons very seriously, and demanded that she do the same. Of the few men and women in her life, only he called her by her given name and nothing else. She felt like an ordinary girl in his presence—a boon, usually, until she was an errant student found out by an offended master.

"I was busy," she said. "Working on—other poetry."

"What other poetry? Do you write?"

"No, I—I am helping someone. I—am teaching him, as you have taught me. An unlettered soldier."

"Illyria."

"Well, he's nearly unlettered—or he used to be. He's fallen in love with a girl, really in love, and I think in love with reading as well. He has a gift for it, but it's very late in coming. He never read as a child. He has written the most awful lord's verse—"

In the gallery, Olferth was fuming.

"Who's been speaking to her?" he asked in a barely-controlled whisper.

"Hush," entreated the old woman at his side. "Let her speak."

"Enough," said Osgrim, frustrating both of the eavesdroppers. "I'm pleased you've absorbed enough that you feel ready to teach. But Illyria, you know what trouble you could bring upon yourself if it comes out you've been speaking to outsiders."

Illyria closed the old book loudly. It was the only thing within reach on which she could exert force.

"I suppose they'll confine me to the Tower," she said dryly. "Lock me up like a princess from the old stories—ah, but wait. That piece has already been played, hasn't it? They have no more pieces to threaten me with."

"Not while you enjoy the Garden," said Osgrim. "That's a rare privilege indeed."

The thought of the flowers that impossibly bloomed below the tower, in fragrant defiance of the city's withering curse, was enough to cow her into contrition.

"I'm sorry," she said. "You won't tell them, will you? I meant nothing by it. You must understand, Osgrim, it can be unbearable sometimes, this life in the Tower. I don't suppose you can understand, you who come and go as you please."

"We are all of us chained," said Osgrim. "And the chains lie thickest, sometimes, on the very powerful. Even the heavy circle of a crown, as the proverb goes, is but one link in the long chain of history."

"I do not feel powerful," said Illyria, "for one so chained."

"That is one function of the chain," said Osgrim. "I do not feel powerful either, anymore—but the difference is, that pleases me. Power is a burden, as I am sure you will learn in time. But that is not the sort of lesson I am here to teach."

Illyria was unsure what to make of his words. "Do not mistake me," she said. "I am grateful for the lessons you give me. I am sure that Rasten is too."

"Rasten," Olferth repeated in the shadows.

"There you go," said the old woman beside him. "I told you to be patient."

Illyria had begun leafing idly through the old book, turning its pages with gentle fingers—a sign of distraction that heralded the end of her lessons for the day.

"The languages are a drudgery," she said, "but the Hanes and the sagas take me far beyond the citadel, to places I shall never see while my father lives—places I know well it would endanger his rule for me to visit."

"As you say," said Osgrim, turning away. He clapped his own book shut. "But I think you've had enough of your lessons for one day."

"He is going to be married, you know," Illyria blurted out. "Rasten, the guard. Now that he has found some real fortune as a Cerulean, he means to take his lady's hand. I just know she will accept."

"Do you?" said Osgrim, distracted by something.

"I think it's romantic," said Illyria. "Is there something I can do to help him? Would my father honour him, if I said that he was the noblest guard who ever lived? If I said he showed me real kindness when the others offer only silence? He is my friend, Osgrim—my only friend. I would play some part in his fortunes, if I can."

"I am not sure that's possible," said Osgrim. Reaching for the shelf in the study, Osgrim rang a heavy bell, signalling the end of the lesson.

"It must be possible," she said. "I had a dream about it."

He paused in his steps. "A dream?"

Her golden tresses bounced as she nodded emphatically. "I was decked in jewellery and fine gold, and spoke from a throne of white, and my word was law."

"It is fitting that you dream of power," said Osgrim. "Your chains are certainly as heavy as the chains of the mighty."

"If I had power," she said, "I should choose to make Rasten a Master General, or head of the Grand Army, that he might be a worthy prize for the lady Catrine."

Osgrim cracked a smile in spite of himself. "That is unlikely, Lady," he said, "given that he has broken the oath of his service in speaking to you."

"But if I had power," she said again, "I would speak to whomever I choose."

Osgrim had a clever reply on his tongue, no doubt, and she a petulant retort for that. They could have gone on that way most of the afternoon. But as the doors swung open and the bloodguards entered with the heavy Imperial sedan, both of them were fazed into silence. Their demeanour together, familiar both in its affection and its frustration, evaporated into formality as the servants unlocked the covered litter and helped the girl onto the luxurious cushions within.

"Farewell, Your Imperial Highness," Osgrim said with an appropriate bow.

"Farewell, Lord Magistrate," she said.

When she was properly secured, the doors opened again to admit a senior member of the Cerulean Guard to the study, to guide Illyria and her servants back to the tower. It might have been Rasten himself, who had not been long away from her. It might have been his friend Elmore, or some other Cerulean altogether. By that time, Olferth was out of sight, having slipped away into the oldest and narrowest hallways of the Lornock citadel with his companion close at his heels. Head bowed and lips pursed, he strode on with a grim resolve, and the old woman hustled to keep pace with him.

"You see what I have to work with, Moriath," he said. "Enemies on all sides, in every season."

The lady Moriath sighed. "They are not created equal," she reminded him. "One ham-fisted thug of a soldier is nothing compared to Jordac and his growing army of outlanders."

"We'll know soon enough," Olferth fumed. "A few hours in crocodile irons will tell us what ties he has to the Mage."

"He is a Cerulean Guard," she said. "If an old woman's memory serves, they are vetted very carefully indeed."

"Even so," he said. "We will learn what we can of him."

"Torture a Cerulean?" asked Moriath. "Many of the city guards will hear about it, in time. And why was he tortured, they will ask? Because he dared speak to the Imperator's daughter—the daughter few even know he has? She will become the talk of the city over it. And if you are afraid of spies in the citadel proper, you can be damned sure there are spies in the Iron City at large. I think not. Find another way."

"Remember your place, dowager," Olferth growled in his frustration; but some moments later, he seemed to soften. "What would you suggest?" he asked, forcing his resentment into civility with absolute transparency.

"Do as the girl asks," said the old woman. "Promote him—but promote him to the Red. You are dispatching the Scourge to hunt down Celithrand, yes? Send the man west with the Red Captain when he goes."

"Promote a traitor?" Olferth asked. "To Ashimar's own bloodguard?"

"Not everyone is a traitor," said Moriath. "If he *is* a traitor, you've taken him away from the girl, and cast him out into the thick of the wretched provinces. And you've done so without ever showing a sign that you suspect him. If you promote a mole, Jordac will figure you for a fool, and will be more careless when he sends on this Rasten's replacement—which he must do immediately, if this Rasten was truly his spy. You could watch for the emergence of such a replacement, and trace him back to the Mage. And do not forget what becomes of the men forced into the bloodguard."

"Killed, aren't they?"

"Every one of them," said Moriath. "If he dies a bloodguard, no one will ask questions. But if you execute him as a traitor, the others will want to know why. News of the Imperator's daughter will spread. Name him to the bloodguard, and the others will hear only that a man once promoted for distinguished service was promoted again."

Olferth smiled. "That's not bad," he said. "I knew I kept you around for something," he said.

"You keep me around because I'm a venomous old snake, and that pleases you," she told him. "And because a cup of my venom is just the thing to keep the wrong people from having the wrong dreams." She turned her back on the Imperial Harper as the passage came up into the citadel proper and split off in two directions.

"I would prefer if you passed on the secrets of your venom to the healers and cellwives," he said.

"Of course you would," she snapped, without turning round. "But I'm a frail old woman, you trumped-up pitch farmer, and I'll be dead soon enough. I've no desire to divest myself of my last valuable secrets and speed up the process." She hastened to leave him alone in the passage, her cane clacking and rattling along the stone as she hauled herself upward toward other duties. Olferth watched after her a long time, though there was no shortage of things to be done. Perhaps he was simply putting off the clerical duties of his office: it would upset things among the Magistrates, he knew, and he despised stirring that particular pot.

With fewer than forty true bloodguard left, and all surviving members raised from birth, it would not go unnoticed that Olferth aimed to appoint two men in the space of a week. There would be opposition, no doubt; but a side effect of the growing power of his office was that he would hear no one's dissent directly. He had no doubt that Moriath would pick up some of the chatter and relay it to him—she was Janus Veritenh's widow, after all, and had been politically adept in her day. But he depended on the old woman completely for one thing already, and despised the idea of counting on her for a second.

He was hungry, too. He hadn't eaten all afternoon, and that only made matters worse.

Burdened by the weighty chain of his thoughts, the Imperial Harper came at last to the Chapel of Slaves, a grim sepulchral space left over from the Occupation, an unseelie iron structure like the Cîr-Valithar that could not be unmade by the Lornock's new tenants. It was a highly defensible place, devoted as it had been for the worship of the god-king Tamnor, but it was one that few tenants would have suffered in the aftermath of the Siege. In spite of his pragmatism, Olferth dreaded coming here, but it would wait no longer. He reminded himself of the particulars of his position, steeling himself with the knowledge that in an official capacity, his word was every bit as absolute as Valithar's, and his command as unquestionable. At last, straightening his robe and clearing a few flakes of crumbling trueblack from the collar, he pulled open the outer doors and nodded with what looked like pompous authority to the three red-armoured sentries within.

"I have come to relay orders to Ashimar," he said icily. "In the name of his Illustrious Majesty Valithar, show me in."

FIVE

"TELL ME ALL ABOUT THEM," whispered Illyria. "I want to hear it all."

Rasten leaned hard against the iron wall, his legs finally beginning to tire. "It's late," he protested. "Haven't your ears got tired yet?"

"I haven't had my tea yet," she said through the curtain. "I'm wide awake. I'm bored to tears—and I fear there may be little time for such stories."

Ras smiled in spite of himself. "You going somewhere? They planning to marry you off to some border vasil?"

"It might be worth it," she said, "to be gone from here."

"It might not," Ras countered. "I've seen the border vasilies. Ruins, many of them. Half figurative ruins, half literal. Vosthome has been swallowed up by the sprawl of the Capital beyond the Shadewall.

Carmac's run by a glorified innkeeper. Haukmere, well, I'll not say a bad word about it while the White Ship is moored here, but I can't imagine you'd be happy there. Draden's abandoned, and Fane Castle's razed to the ground, home now to none but ghosts. Any farther out than that, and you're into contested territory. I'm sure the Mages' Uprising would sell their own grandmothers to the Rattle to get their hands on you."

"Perhaps I'd be kidnapped by bandits," she said wistfully. "Like in the romances."

"Oh, I'd not wish it," said Ras. "Daring rogues in the ballads, to be sure, but there's plenty they do that doesn't make it to the page. It'd break my heart to think of you suffering that way."

Illyria was silent a long time.

"Tell me about the other Ceruleans," she said at last. "None of the others dare speak to me."

"If there's any who would dare," said Ras, "his right name's Elmore. He's been with the Cerulean Guard a long time. A former curator in the Lornock Library, which always agreed with him more than the sword, I think. He's a good man and a good friend."

"Do you think he would talk to me as well?"

"He'd talk your ear off," said Ras, "if you don't mind a little flirting from a man old enough to be your father—*my* father, if it came to that."

"It might be nice," she said. "Who else?"

Ras mulled it over. "You might try your luck with—" he began—then held his tongue as Heward's thunderous barking filled the hall. The great hound was not easily silenced as the two karach in the doorway came into view, leading two smaller figures—one wide and stocky, ambling on a cane, the other small and hunched.

The karach warily handed their keys to the pale old woman, who snatched them with some disdain and ushered the hunchbacked stoolman ahead of her as she eyed Rasten with absolute suspicion. In her far hand, she carried a mug of steaming tea that smelled inviting even to Ras, who had confirmed his faithfulness to ale on more than one occasion. With a practiced twist, she swung open the inner gate and passed into the welcome of the bloodguards, who brought a commode out to the stoolman, exchanged it for the clean one he had brought up from below, and waved him away.

"Evening," said Ras. No one—not the bloodguard, nor the karach, nor the old woman, nor even the stoolman—paid him any mind.

Sick as he was of repeating the same boring stories of his fellow Ceruleans, Ras longed for a chance to break the uncomfortable silence and stillness that followed. Illyria, who moments before had been so eager for more people to talk to, was silent as death while the woman was with her. They had moved away from the curtains and far back into the chambers on the far side, where only an occasional rustle or murmur of the old woman's voice betrayed their presence. The bloodguards, as usual, were as silent as the beginning, or the end, of a plague. Only Heward was restless and noisy, padding back and forth behind the curtain on his immense clawed paws. He breathed and snorted and occasionally growled, still dissatisfied that someone lurked beyond his curtain.

"I don't suppose you want to hear about Elmore and the others, pup," he whispered.

That set the dog off barking again—great, rolling barks—and there was no one to quiet him.

The whole Age could have passed, he thought, before the old woman returned through the curtains. The sky was red in the west—he could see it dimly, through the sole distant arrowslit of a window on this level of the Tower. It would be after dark again when he made it home to Catrine, who might be asleep, or away on one of the long walks she took outside the city walls for her health.

To his surprise, she had not returned alone. The irregular tapping of her cane was the only sound as she approached, but the soft-booted bloodguards—first two, then all four of them—came at her back.

"Let us out, damned beasts!" she called down the hallway, though from the look of her she was not wrathful. She noticed Ras looking at her, thought to say something, then shook her head.

"No matter," she said cryptically. "You'll be sent for, soon as they're ready."

"Sent for?"

Both karach returned, pushed him aside with nothing but the fierceness of their yellow-eyed gaze, and unlocked the door. All four bloodguards followed her out and down the hallway with their usual, measured gait. It was she who set the pace, cane tapping furiously as she led them to the stairs.

"Come along," he heard her say. "It's after sunset already. All this waiting will not please him."

Then he was alone again, alone with the constant simmering growl of the pacing dog.

"I don't suppose you know what this is all about," he said to the dog.

Another string of furious barks followed. The karach looked back down the passageway with curiosity as Heward sounded his usual alarm, and eventually grew tired of staring suspiciously at the lone guard. In time, Rasten heard the familiar sound of Illyria's whisper as she quelled the dog's fit in some soothing language he did not understand.

"Rasten?" she said, when she had calmed him. "Are you still there?"

There was something wrong with her voice. She had been crying.

"I'm here," he said.

"Can you come in?" she asked.

His breath stopped in his throat. "I—I can't," he said.

"Please."

"No, really," he said. "I can't. I haven't the inner key."

In near-complete silence, the curtains parted. There, floating on her toes like a specter, was a willowy young girl, pale as parchment under a disheveled mass of silver-blonde hair whose exquisite braids had fallen loose. The eyes that met his, though they were bloodshot from crying, were the most dazzling shade of turquoise he had ever seen, a colour he had only heard described to him by tower guards who had once sailed the far northern seas. There, in those eyes, was the girl to whom he had long spoken; and although her nightdress was scandalously sparse, he could look nowhere but into their depths. Truth be told, she was not the icon of perfect beauty he expected: while he had imagined her from her voice and her station to be thin, delicate, and fair, she was waifish and gaunt with hollow cheeks, fragile and white like the wings of a moth.

Even her big, bright eyes were sunken and raw. She had spoken of herself so often as a princess in a tower that his thoughts of her were wound up in all the old stories, and he had never imagined her as anything but the fairest girl who could exist. In that speechless moment, a small part of him took secret pride in knowing that his Catrine was fairer still, from the tips of her fluttering eyelashes to her unforgettable—

"Take it," Illyria urged. "Hurry, take it. They don't know I have it."

He shook himself from his thoughts to find her fingers stretched against the elaborate mesh of the inner gate. She had worked the fat end of a gleaming, double-sided golden key through the largest opening in the gate. He took it almost without thinking, tried it in the lock. It was unusually heavy in his hand—surely it was solid gold throughout, though it was terribly rough in its craftsmanship. He turned it very gingerly, slowly in the lock, wincing at its softness.

"Will this break if I twist it too hard?"

"It may bend a little," she whispered. "I'm sorry. Gold is all I have."

He gently twisted the key, feeling its ornate double bit scrape roughly against the wards of the lock.

"I could be killed for even holding this," he said.

"You shan't be killed."

"You're awfully sure of that."

Illyria said nothing, but began to weep again, softly. With a little more pressure the heavy lock turned and opened serviceably, and the key came out only a little deformed.

"Why am I doing this?" Ras asked her, or asked himself, as she gently pushed open the gate and he slipped inside.

"It doesn't matter, now," said Illyria. "Come in."

Behind the lavish red curtain were two more rows of curtains, behind those, a massive, hairy beast that almost certainly outweighed him. The dog was chewing on some kind of beef—a choicer cut than Ras himself had ever tried—and that alone kept it quiet as he approached.

"Put down your hand," she said, and he complied. Heward sniffed at it, licked it, sniffed at him, and went back to his meal.

"Speak to him,"

"Well met, Heward," Ras said, feeling rather silly.

"He barks for anyone he's never met," she explains. "Any noise in that passageway at all sets him off. It sets off the guards, and the servants, and everyone. But now that he's met you… he won't bark again if he knows it's only you."

Ras nodded timidly. The great beast, seemingly satisfied with him, took the meat and crept off to the plush Imperial sedan, which sat unlocked and open behind the curtains, and lay within it as any dog might do. It would have been a laughable sight, if Ras had not still felt under threat of execution.

"Why am I here?" he said again. "This is absolutely forbidden. It's the second most forbidden thing I know."

The plain, frail girl with the dazzling eyes smiled at him through her tears. "What's the most forbidden?"

He cast his eyes to the ceiling. "Approaching your father's chambers. The highest treason."

"It was not always so," she said. "Come, come in."

Gold was, indeed, all she had.

There must have been, somewhere beneath it all, the same terrible black iron that made up the rest of the Tower. But the walls themselves were clad in spotless marble and glittering quartz, sheets and mosaics and intricate patterns wrapped and gilded in ribbons of pure yellow gold that covered the panels and borders of every feature of the main chamber. The room was lightly perfumed and opulently furnished; and where Illyria's private shelves in the library had been nearly barren, they rose here to the ceiling, a collection of tomes worth more on their own, perhaps, than a soldier could expect to earn in his lifetime.

"For a girl who is nothing at all like a princess," he said, "you've certainly learned to live like one."

"When I was very small," she said, continuing on oblivious to his awe, "I would climb the tower stair myself. My father was never cordial, you understand, not to me. The Empire has weighed heavily on him his whole life—and my mother's death, it put a shadow upon him I am not sure has ever left him. It must have been a great love story, theirs. I think he has been mourning her ever since. It's why he revived the old Harper's Guild, made the position more than ceremonial. The Imperial Harper is his herald, his only voice in the outside world, now."

"I know," said Rasten. "Everyone knows."

"The world is a terrible place, and he cannot bear it alone."

"That's very sad," said Rasten, hoping it was what she expected him to say. Every sound, every whistling of an insect or crackle of the hearth-fire, commanded his attention for just a moment. If even one of the bloodguards saw him within her chambers…

"The servants are gone," she said suddenly. "They almost never leave me—but they did today. All of them. They've gone to take their orders in the Chapel of Slaves with the other bloodguards, before Lord Ashimar sets out tonight. My grandmother told me so. They'll be with him for some time."

"She tells you many things," Ras said. Illyria's face fell at those words, and she turned away from him.

"Many things," she agreed. She took a steadying breath. "Grandmother says that you and I shall never speak again."

"What?"

"She knows all about us. About our friendship and our stories. Everyone knows."

"Everyone…" Ras felt his stomach plunge within him to make room for the rising panic.

"I don't know how they found out," she said. "I told no one. Only Osgrim…I trusted him. I trusted him! And he…he…but it doesn't matter. My father will decide what's to be done with me. But you…They've already said, you'll be given to Ashimar."

"Ashimar? I'll die by my own hand before his," said Rasten, though he hadn't yet the heart or the resolve to mean it.

"You shan't die at all," Illyria said. "But his ship leaves tonight, and you'll be on it. A fitting end, she says, for your kindness to me. But I'll never—" here she fell to sobbing, and he caught her in his broad arms in spite of himself. He nearly let go of her, at first: if the bloodguards returned to find the girl half-dressed in his arms, a swift beheading might not be so unlikely after all.

"I'll never see you again," she wailed.

"Hey," he said, softly, at a loss. "Hey. You've only just barely seen me now. We are nearly strangers, you and I. Do not weep over a stranger." Still reeling from the dread of these revelations, his legs felt unsteady as wet grass beneath him. He thought of the poor girl, of her life in the Tower, of his own misery at sea under Ashimar's humourless eye. But most of all he thought of Catrine.

"You are here," said Illyria, with sudden determination, "because the theft should be worth the hand, as they say. If I am to lose you because you have dared to see me—then, see me."

He could not resist, but let go of her long enough to step back. It was still bizarre to put a face to her voice.

"Look on my face and do not forget it," she said. "You are my friend, Rasten. You are my *only* friend. And you will be remembered, every day of my life when they take you away, and I want to be remembered, too. I have kept so much from you in the name of obedience. I know you have done the same."

"Obviously not well enough," he said nervously. "How long will they be gone?"

"I would share all I can with you," she said. "Come, you must see my garden."

"Your High—"

"Illyria," she interrupted him. "We are friends."

"Illyria," he breathed. She took his hand and led him through the heart of the Tower to a hidden balcony on the north side.

Her apartment on the north side of the spire must have been a watchtower of sorts, once. From a secure gate on the far wall—a gate she also opened with the makeshift key—a short corridor extended up to a small balcony, enclosed under a dome of twisting, thorny iron vines. Like a black cage it seemed to hang suspended over the northern districts of the city; but at this height Rasten could see all the way to the harbour and beyond, to the stern watchtowers of the Shadewall that jutted out into the sea, and to the traders still coming and going under sail. It was here he saw that the room was not perfumed at all, but rather overlooked a sight he could never have imagined.

There, below her balcony, walled off from the rest of the city and even from the Lornock citadel, lay a flower-garden, lush and thick with blossoms of every colour. A thousand mingled floral scents rose up to meet him, filling his head with thoughts of lost springtimes.

"Impossible," he said. "Nothing grows in this city. Nothing."

"This is my quiet place," she said. "The garden is evergreen. Even the season of the cerulyn lasts the whole year here. In the warmest months, the hummingbirds come, streaking red and green among the blossoms. If I put out a bowl of syrup, they will come right to the balcony."

"This is magical," said Rasten. "Life in a dead city."

"Osgrim—my teacher—has told me that as long as this garden blooms in Travalaith, there is still hope that all shall be restored, and the ancient city will rise again. And I have never seen a single blossom wither, not in my whole life."

"You honour me. It would bring the people hope, I think, to know your garden is still in bloom."

"Oh, you mustn't tell them," said Illyria. "It's a secret." She shivered in the cold.

"Catrine," he breathed. "I should like to tell her. I keep nothing from her."

"All right. Perhaps some day, I shall be free to meet her. She must be—"

From the front chamber, Heward's thunderous bark had returned.

"Already," Illyria breathed. "No. It's too soon!"

"What have I done?" sighed Ras.

"Come!" she called. "Quickly." She took him by one of his broad shoulders and rushed him back into the passage. Heward was up from the sedan, pacing anxiously, hackles raised.

"Olferth," she said. "He hates Olferth. Go, go quickly. Go." She lurched up on her toes to plant a kiss on his cheek; it may have connected, but they parted too quickly to be sure. With a haste tempered only by the need to be silent, he slipped through the half-open gate and pushed it shut, turning the massy golden key roughly in the lock. The head of it bent as it wrenched the lock shut, and when he tried to pass it back to her through the ironwork of the gate, it would not go.

"Keep it," she said. "It does not matter. Keep it. Buy something that makes you happy, if a pound of gold is still worth anything. Wed your lady with a ring worthy of her."

"I—" Rasten's tongue floated helplessly in his mouth as his words tangled round it. Then the karach were in the passageway again, escorting the Imperial Harper himself down the hallway, and he could say no more.

"Never forget me," whispered Illyria, her voice breaking. Rasten's mouth was tight but he was too afraid in that moment to cry.

"Soldier," called the Imperial Harper. "Have you a name?"

"Yes, Your Excellency," Ras said, standing to attention.

Olferth was disarmed, but only for a moment, by the simplicity of the answer.

"…Is that name Rasten?" he prompted impatiently.

Ras swallowed hard. "It is."

"Just the man I've been looking for." He held out a bundled cloak to the soldier.

"What's this?" Ras asked. He knew perfectly well what it was.

"For meritorious service to the Imperator," Olferth muttered quickly, "and for exceptional loyalty and devotion to your duties in serving the strength of Travalaith and the security of the Imperial Family—it's my duty and privilege to exercise the Imperial Will to elevate you to the highest Old Order of Service in all of Travalaith. On behalf of the Imperator, I bestow upon you the formal mantle of the illustrious sovereign bloodguard, with all rights, and so on, and so forth."

"I don't know what to say," muttered Ras, and that was the truth.

"Hand in your cloak," said Olferth, waving the attendant forward. "You have new orders. You will report at once to the *Providence*, moored at Whiteport. You answer now to Ashimar."

"Lord Ashimar is headed west."

"Ah, you've heard. He is."

Catrine. "I'd…I'd like to return home and collect my things."

Olferth was impassive. "The quartermaster in Whiteport will assign you arms and a helm befitting your character, and provide you with all that you need."

"But—Your Excellecy, I—"

"You're a bloodguard, now," Olferth interrupted. "That limits even my powers to deal with your insubordination, so I'll only say that Ashimar meant to depart at sunset, and has been delayed nearly an hour already. Any further delay would be fatal, if you understand me—and we should both stop pretending you don't know why you are going."

Rasten frowned and fastened his new cloak before speaking. "For a man of high esteem, Excellency, you're as black as that trueblack you wear, and half as true. Your good character flakes off too, after too long a day on the hill."

"It's clear the girl's poetry lessons have done you some good," said Olferth, slipping back behind the two motionless karach. His face was impassive but his narrow eyes were like razors of glass. He moved as if to depart, then paused at the top of the stairs.

"Let me be clear," he said. "I've no desire to tamper with you, now that you're Ashimar's personal property. But you will forgo your farewells, or I'll personally arrange there will be no one left to hear them. Report to your post, soldier."

For a tense moment, both men looked to the two karach between them, who clutched their spears expectantly. Rows of viciously sharp teeth blossomed along the edges of their muzzles. Rasten's thoughts were clear on his face, but he held his place until the Imperial Harper had made his exit. To calm his mind—he was not used to such upset—Ras counted the streets from the Lornock Stair to Whiteport, and planned the route.

He would have to run, straight to the boat.

There would be no farewell.

"I'm so sorry," said a gentle voice, far behind him.

He did not give answer.

In the years since he had come to power in the Imperator's service, Ashimar had come by many nicknames. The Red Captain he was called, by those who dealt mostly with the Imperator's bloodguards and knew him to be first and greatest among them. By his proper title, he was the Imperial Scourge, a sanctioned outlaw who answered directly to the Imperator alone and brought swift justice to Travalaith's most notorious criminals and traitors. A few who knew him politically, by the power of his pen and pedigree, called him the Lost Lord or the Lost Kelmor—or the Vasil of Slaves, after his new home in Tamnor's Chapel. But those few who had seen him in the flesh, who had stood in signt of him and lived to tell of it, called him the Weeping Man. It was a title that had come to Rastern's ears by rumour and gossip among the Cerulean Guard, and he had never really understood it. But as night fell, and the Weeping Man came at last to the ship, fully dressed for battle and flanked by his bloodguards, the origin of the name became clear.

Rasten had seen armour like it in Selik, when he had fought there. Only the wealthiest of nobles could afford such a masterpiece; it could take a master smith and his whole smithy a year to forge and shape the intricate steel plates, like the armoured skin of a shellfish, to fit one man and one alone. The precision required to keep the joints from sticking was so great that fathers, he had heard, could not even pass down the suits to their sons. Even without the extensive personal touches of Ashimar's red-enameled suit, such masterpieces were intensely personal creations, unlike the mail-coats of the common soldiers or even the steel breastplates of the Ceruleans.

Sometimes, it was to the taste of one princeling or another to fashion the closed helms of these wonders into the shape of some terrifying beast. The war-helms of Haukmere were given only to the vasils and the generals, though in recent years the bloodguard were permitted to wear them as well. Rasten had seen a few in the likeness of dragons, or sabercats, or bears—perhaps the charge of a man's noble house, if it was a predator of some kind. Elmore swore he had once, long ago, seen a boar's head helm with sharpened tusks of real horn that gored a man in the face when their axes were tangled. The great vasil Janus Veritenh, Illyria's grandfather, had famously worn a visor in the likeness of his own bony face, tremendous moustache and all, as if to warn all who contested him that that no beast of the land was more terrifying than he himself. The general principle, as Rasten understood it, was to choose something fearsome and mighty—a terrifying beast no man would want to meet on the field of battle.

Ashimar's helm bore the face of a crying child.

It was an immaculate and pure face, without blemish or sign of age. It might have been a beautiful boy, or a beautiful girl, or both, or neither, cast as it was well before the bloom of adolescence. Entirely surfaced in a lustrous white metal, gilded at the twisted lips and squinted eyelids, it was exquisite in its expression of suffering; enamelled ribbons of ruby red tears streamed from its impervious meshed eyes, streaking the flawless face like the war paint of the far south and spilling down his gorget to mingle with the blood-red enamel of his armour. The other Ceruleans, in times past, had warned him not to stare if he encountered the Imperial Scourge—and there he was, staring just the same. It was worse than a bear, worse than a dragon. The thought of a wailing child on the battlefield, barely more than a babe, made him sick to his stomach.

"I'm so pleased you could join us." Ashimar's voice was not what Ras expected behind the unsettling visor—surprisingly high and hollow for a man of such fearsome reputation, with the lightest trace of his provincial accent intact.

"I came as fast as I could," said Ras. He hoped the sheen of sweat coating his brow would support his words. "I was only just promoted."

"The Harper sends me two more men than I require," said Ashimar. He indicated, with a nod of his eerie child-face, a towering brute of a man hauling the last of the crates over the wales of the *Providence*. "That one, at least, will lead me to the traitor I seek. Tell me, soldier, what use do you provide?"

Ras had learned, through love and dedication, a gift for writing, but words did not come easily to him. "I—I fight with axe and sword, milord, as well as any man."

Ashimar turned away, unimpressed. "You are strong in the arms."

"I am," Ras said, somewhat proudly. "I wrestle and throw stones. Strongest in my rank."

"Then you will row with the prisoners," said Ashimar, "to relieve my ship of the burden of your weight. We have ballast enough already." He turned and strode up the ramp onto the deck; it was a testament to the craft of his armour that he did so in silence.

Rasten shouldered the heavy bag he had been given by the harbour quartermaster and hustled up the plank himself, onto the central corridor of a mast-deck that lay his full height below the command deck surrounding it from above. On all sides, the whole length of the ship, masses of Travalaithi prisoners were being hastily shackled, three to an oar, onto staggered benches, upper and lower, two oars to a rank. From the ramp, it had been clear there was another oar-deck below. He tried to count on his hands just how much muscle would power the immense warship, and it became clear—in the most inexact terms, for he had no gift for arithmetic—that the town where he was born would easily have fit on board. The prisoners, too, were far more numerous than he expected: there were more than would fit at the oars, and the rest milled about anxiously like livestock under the stern glare of the other bloodguards.

"D'you row, man?" asked a voice. It was the towering bloodguard Ashimar had indicated, who stopped him at the railing as another crate was carried on. The man had donned his own red armour and greathelm—a snarling wolf—but moved his head uneasily, clearly unused to the weight and shape of it.

"Do I row?"

"Do you row regular?" the big man asked. "This don't look like your usual work."

"No," said Rasten. "I'm a Cerulean Guard of the tower."

"Not anymore." The wolf-headed stranger handed him some torn strips of cloth. Ras was so accustomed to the war-gear of the Grand Army that he could tell from touch they were ripped from a soldier's tunic.

"What are these?" he asked.

"Wrap your hands," said the big man. "Wind's calm and he'll want to see a fat wake on departure. You'll bleed at the hands before you're done."

Ras motioned to the prisoners. "There's ample rowers to change out."

"Aye," said the big man, lowering his voice. "Once he's killed off the first lot."

"You're not serious," said Ras.

The big man shrugged. "I've only heard. I don't know from my own eyes. It's my first day as well. More likely, it's the worst tales get told most often. I imagine it depends on his mood."

Ras felt the blood drain from his face and looked to Ashimar, who was ordering the other bloodguards—a dozen or two at most—to herd the prisoners who had no space at the oars into the hold below.

"Is he always in such good cheer?" Ras asked. He smiled nervously, hoping the joke would break the tension and quell his rising panic.

The big man opened his cloak and loosened the strings at his shirt-neck. A tiny scar above his breastbone had been wreathed with fresh wounds, still red and angry, still caked with blackened scabs where the skin had been flogged away to the depth of blood.

"Not always," warned the man.

An uneasy silence hung around them after that, punctuated only by the busy sounds of blue-cloaked tower guards completing rushed preparations while Ashimar's seasoned bloodguards chained the last teams of rowers into position. Most of the Ceruleans had no particular facility with sailing, and were hauling and securing cargo as quickly as possible. Those who had been promoted from the modest Imperial Navy (or, as Rasten suspected, bought their commissions from officials and magistrates as sea-merchants) were changing out some parts of the sea-worn rigging—a demanding task at speed, which might have been the reason for the long delay.

Rasten did not think to look for Elmore among them until it was nearly too late. Night had fallen fully, then, and the view from the mast-deck was not nearly as good as it would have been for the men up above. But standing out as he was from the other Ceruleans with a full beard and greying hair, Elmore was not hard to spot. Ras spied him at last, resting his tired bones down on the wharf, and called out to him, but the sound on deck was too much and the distance too far.

"Come," said Ashimar from the ladder to the lower deck. Ras didn't have to look back to know he was being addressed.

"You... hey, friend," he called to the big man. But the wolf-helm covered his ears, and he did not answer.

"Wolf!" he shouted at last, with desperation cracking his voice. The wolf-headed man turned awkwardly.

"Kellan," said the man. "Kellan's my name."

"That man down there—the grey-bearded Cerulean," said Rasten. "If you can reach him, tell him... tell him to find Catrine. Tell him to tell her, Rasten has shipped out with the bloodguard, only... I didn't mean to. Two weeks at the most, I'll be gone, tell her that. Tell him, I mean. To tell her that."

"You try my patience, soldier," said Ashimar from below with measured coldness. Ras felt himself moving toward the ladder even before he stopped stammering.

"Tell her I'll return," he added. "But don't stay in the house. I don't want anyone to know she can be found there."

"You overestimate the subtlety of my bellowing, I think," said Kellan, but as Ras was set in to row beside one of the prisoners, he could hear the wolf-helmed warrior's deep voice shouted over the rail. The ropes had been loosed from the wharf and the sleek ship was already moving—not under sail, nor under oar, but on the wide harbour currents churned up by the violent and unpredictable motions of a rapid two-moon ebb tide. These were angry moons, and angry reasons for travel; the voyage would not be a pleasant one.

As Ashimar led him into the lower deck, onto a short oar for two men in the murky gloom, he thought again of Catrine—at first in sorrow. But after a moment, when a lion-headed bloodguard rolled out the rowers' drum and the prisoners who knew began to stretch out for the task at hand, he thought instead of her smiling face, and the prospect—however distant—of being a man on campaign who, for the first time in his life, would be far away from a real home, with a faithful woman who loved him to come home to.

He peered into the sack he had been given. Plates of silver armour, gleaming red where the enamel had been baked in, winked back at him in the last sunlight. Despite his years on campaign, despite his time in the Tower, it was the finest armour he had ever owned—and beneath it, the helm whose face rose to meet him was the sleek open-mouthed head of an attacking panther or some other greatcat of the far South.

"A cat," he said, turning over the word—her name—in his mouth. "Cat. Cat. Life could be worse," he reminded himself.

The rower next to him, a wiry, toothless Selikhan prisoner, spat in his face. It caught him completely off-guard.

"*Ai džeb*," the rower barked at him. "*Gakka Traualat'ti*."

"Ai zeb," Ras repeated, though he did not know the words.

With only a moment's pause to collect himself, the man spat in his face again.

"*Ai džeb*," said the man, as if to punctuate the attack. Ras raised a fist, though he had not the heart to use it, and the smaller man cowered, shrinking back in fear.

"Keep your ai-zeb to yourself," said Ras. "The woman I love curses like that, and I'll not stand to hear her words out of your mouth."

On the mast-deck above, waving his arms through a narrow port at the Cerulean guard below, Kellan desperately sought an audience for the tangle of information he had been given, most of which he had quite forgot by the time the guardsman looked up.

"Rasten's gone!" he bellowed over the din of the harbour. "Tell Catrine—Ashimar's taken him away!" It was all he managed to shout, in the end. He was not even sure the phrase had carried, for in the moment that the ship was underway, a cold metal gauntlet seized him by the shoulder and turned him round, not roughly, but with a strength that would not be denied. Unlike most other men aboard the ship, Kellan looked down rather than up onto Ashimar's crying-child visor; but he did not feel his size or strength against that impassive gaze. At Ashimar's hip, where a decent nobleman might have belted a sword, swung the familiar scourge, its cords tightly knotted around a handful of sharpened, rusted iron keys. Meeting the armoured knight's eyes would have been no easier, even without the tails of the scourge swaying dangerously.

"I would congratulate you, soldier," said Ashimar, "on your new promotion."

"I don't expect I please you, milord," said Kellan.

"Have patience," said Ashimar. "In a few days' time you shall delight me, when you lead me to the place where Celithrand bested your whole detachment and somehow eluded you."

Kellan flinched under the weight of those words. The whole of his skin still pained him too sharply to correct the Red Captain on the facts of Celithrand's escape.

"I can't wait," said Kellan.

"Nor can I," said Ashimar. "That is why I am making you my foreman on the lower deck."

"I've done precious little sailing, milord," said Kellan.

Ashimar was unreadable. "The sailing will happen above you. All you need know is this: heed my commands, when I give them, and otherwise keep the men rowing at all costs. We will keep the land in sight. We have one change of rowers aboard, and I should not like to use them until we have crossed the Breakweb Estuary on the borders of my vasily."

Kellan reckoned the distance in his head. "That's three days under oar," he said, "unless the wind picks up."

Ashimar unfastened the scourge from his hip, coiled it neatly, and held it out in a gauntleted hand. Its sharpened keys were too rusted to ring as they clattered together.

"Take this," he said, "and make it two days. We change the prisoners out at Breakweb and ride the coast to Seton. Those who fail us will be put to the sword. Those who give us full oar as far as the Estuary will have a chance to swim for their freedom. You will ensure they are properly motivated."

Kellan felt a sickness in his stomach, but tried not to show it. "A strong man could swim it," he said, "if he's used to the cold and doesn't gasp himself to death in the water. But a prisoner from the Rattle, rowed half to death?" He shook his head.

Ashimar stood motionless in response—silent and unreadable. The golden lips of the weeping child were stretched grotesquely taut in anguish, an expression that lent itself well to displeasure. Perhaps he knew it. Perhaps he knew Kellan could not bear the silence. For a moment it was as if he had gone away entirely, and the whole apparatus were empty inside, like an ornamental guard from some noble's armoury. It was the same stillness that had come just before his own scourging at Ashimar's hands that morning—a scourging it seemed only fitting that he pass on to the next unfortunates.

With a set jaw, Kellan took the weapon from his new master.

"I'll give them all the help I can," he said at last.

"Good," said Ashimar, who canted his head slightly so that Kellan could tell he was looking to the scourge in his hands. "You already know what it means to try my patience, Wolf. But you do not yet know what it means to disappoint me."

"I mean to keep it that way," Kellan answered, hoping he sounded sincere. Ashimar left him to find his own way down, then, striding to the command deck to confer with the other bloodguards—none of whom had offered Kellan so much as a nod in welcome the whole time he had been there. His thoughts again turned to Castor Stannon, the delicate little man whose life he had saved nearly a year ago—who had believed with almost childish certainty that Kellan would be well-rewarded for personally relaying the news that the traitor Celithrand's last whereabouts were finally known.

Every inch of his skin burned him, and the vile weapon that had struck the blows was now in his hand. A small part of him wanted to put it to good use, to take out his frustrations on someone's flesh, as Ashimar had done to him. But Kellan's prudence, then as ever, outweighed his malice: one never knew when the fortunes of prisoners would change, especially when they outnumbered Ashimar's bloodguard nearly ten to one. He had heard stories of slaves who strangled their masters with their own chains—Jordac himself, supposedly, had been one of them—and Kellan had no interest in suffering that sort of poetic justice. He would make do, he decided, with threats and the intimidation of his massive body until it was absolutely necessary to spoil the suspense and bring the scourge to bear. If they revolted then, he reasoned, they'd revolt tired rather than fresh.

When he came down at last to the lower deck, Kellan saw with certainty that such tactics would not be necessary. Among the hundred or so rowers he could see down here, he counted a hundred pairs of defeated eyes staring back at him with something halfway between apathy and cowardice. He stretched gently as he lowered himself to the slavers' drum prepared for the occasion, and felt—maybe even savoured—the centering sting that came from his fresh wounds as he did so. Wounds like the ones Ashimar had dealt him, wounds that were made over the course of seconds or minutes, would heal in time, if he let them. But wounds made over the course of years, he knew, were the slowest to heal.

On the entire deck, only one pair of eyes stared back at him with something more than despair. Among the wretched ranks, among dozens of emaciated prisoners clad in dirty rags, a single bloodguard, immaculately dressed in his new uniform, had settled in at the aisle edge of a long oar. It was Rasten, the man he had spoken to earlier; and the displeasure in his eyes was too fresh to have softened into defeat.

Kellan thumped the drum once, hard, to gain their attention.

"I'm no more pleased to be here than you," he said. "And I wish to my gods and most of yours that I had better news for you. Soon as I'm given the signal from above, you're to row hard and evenly. You'll pace yourselves, but if you want to feel dry land under your feet again, you'll give me your all."

He hoisted the clattering scourge on top of the drum head and the men shuddered. There was no mistaking what it was or from whose hands it came.

"You'll keep rowing until you lose the last of your strength," said Kellan. "Then you'll get flogged until you find it again. And for some for you—for the luckiest among you—that'll be the worst that happens to you today. Have I made myself clear?"

Their grim silence was a sure sign that he had.

"You've all heard what happens to men and women in Ashimar's service," he said at last. "You don't hear such things unless there are some lucky folks who live to tell of it. Perhaps that'll be you." *Or me*, he thought as the prisoners lowered their eyes. Only Rasten held his gaze, with the grim resignation of an ox bound for the plough—but not, if he could help it, to the slaughterhouse.

Kellan laid down the scourge, picked up the mallet that lay beside the drum, and tested its weight in his hand as he waited for some signal from above. But no word came, and for a long time he sat in brooding silence, turning the mallet over in his hand, wishing to one god after another, though he was sure none would hear him, that he had never set eyes on Castor Stannon.

"Ready all, row!" came a bloodguard's cry from the deck above. With a heavy sigh, Kellan hoisted the mallet and brought it down hard.

SIX

WHEN THE SUN WAS GONE, Catrine stoked the fire with fresh wood and cut some more leeks and fennel for the broth. In the narrow space between the licking flames and the stewpot, she suspended a copper grill. When it was good and hot, she lifted the whole hakefish out of the stew and laid it on a wooden board. With practiced fingers accustomed to the blistering heat, she cut off the head and tail, pulled them off, returned them to the stew, and set to work prying the best meat of the fish away from the intricate bones, the way her mother had taught her. The scraps returned to the stew, and the choice filets, two of them, she nestled on the grill to sear. The steam they sent up was sweet and smoky. Soon the great-hall was filled with the smell of fresh herbs, the salt of the sea, seared meat on a cold night, and the Selikhan perfume she had requisitioned from Odi.

She was a fine and precise cook, and it was precision that calmed her nerves and held her churning stomach in check when things went awry. Any deviation from that precision, any variance in the pattern she had learned and practiced with absolute fidelity, was a sign that the storm had come. It was only a matter of time, she knew. And tonight, she was resolved to tell him the truth before time ran out.

She was a moment late in pulling the fish off the grill. It was black on one side, and smelled too much of smoke as she laid it to rest on the board. It would be a little chewy, now.

She would make a fine wife, one day, her mother had said. Even during the famine she had not just fed them, but delighted them with the precision of her cooking. It was that very precision, Baran had told her some years later, that made her indispensable to the Uprising.

The stew was perfect as she lifted it out into two wooden bowls. Perfect, if served immediately. But she was alone.

Six times she had resolved to tell him, to fall upon his mercy and the goodness in his heart. But Rasten had a monstrous appetite, and a full stomach made him agreeable, so she had brought fresh hakefish from the harbour three times—and spiced quince butter cake, twice—and just once, flaky pies stuffed with pork bacon and honey-gilded apples. Without fail, without hesitation, he mistook her efforts to put him at ease for artless expressions of love; and he said to her such sweet things, and took her in his broad arms and carried her to his room, and left her breathless and wordless in his passions. Soon, every time, they were asleep in each other's radiant embrace, each basking in the heat of the other's skin like cats lazing on a stone courtyard in summer. After that, the time for confessions was past, and she would cry so hard when he had gone again that the other men in the boarding-hall wondered if he was cruel to her behind closed doors, in spite of the affection he showed her where it could be seen.

Six times, now, that was how it had been. There was a regular precision to that, too. Each time she applied a few drops of the perfume Odi had issued sparingly to the Vairhurst widows, she wondered if she truly meant to have done with the lie of her affections—or if that, too, was a lie, calculated only to preserve the fantasy of their time together a little while longer.

Fish and stew alike were cold, now, and no light came in at the open windows Only the orange glow of the waning hearth-fire still filled the hall.

Something was wrong.

Rasten would not be coming. But someone would.

She held the thought at bay as long as she dared, but the dread fell upon her all at once as she cut into her fish without him. It was dry, tough, and cold, but she ate it in spite of herself. After a moment's hesitation, Catrine ate Rasten's dinner too, slicing it into small bites and eating until she was on the edge of being too full to run, if it came to that.

It had happened, in the end, just as Baran had warned them it would if they were discovered. He was gone suddenly, instantly, snapped up without word or warning. There was no telling now when she would eat next, when she would have to run. It could be any moment. With the meal finished, the racing of her blood began anew. Catrine slid back from the hearth-fire, huddled in the corner on the verge of tears as the flames began to dwindle.

The heavy hall door, as silent as ever, drifted open. She felt the whole floor beneath her pounding heart give way. They had only sent one man for her—a solitary old veteran whose long, graying beard draped over the front of his mail and made him look more grandfatherly than thuggish. But why should Travalaith expect any fight from her? The women of Travalaith were helpless and mewling in the face of danger; Catrine despised them for that. Perhaps, if cornered, she'd catch him off-guard with her weakness and grovelling long enough to get the sleek arming dagger off his belt—or, failing that, the little Harrod knife off her thigh.

Hesitating in the doorway long enough to consult a scrap of parchment, the stranger flashed the lining of his cloak as he stowed the note away again. Catrine did not fail to notice the telltale glimpse of Cerulean blue, nor the certainty with which he headed up the stairs to Rasten's room—her room.

Against a trained Cerulean, she would have one chance, only one, and then it would be over one way or another. She decided not to risk it. The women of Selik were survivors above all else: she was trained to fight as well as a man, if it came to that, but a burning need to prove it had been the death of many in her village. She resolved to wait for him to enter the room, and slip out through the door in the moment he was out of sight.

The Cerulean stopped at the threshold and drew his arming dagger with caution. She had left the chamber door ajar to come down and prepare supper; now he eased his way in with cautious steps. At once she went for the main doors, shuddering and rushing faster as she heard him softly mouth her name into the dark room. "Catrine…"

"Hullo, Catrine!"

She froze, reeling. The door swung wide as one of the fellow tenants entered with a heavy step, bent low under a bag of vegetables.

"Omund," she said softly.

"Supper smells fantastic," he said, beaming. "If you and Ras can spare—"

Her eyes darted to the gallery landing above the great room. The man had darted back at Omund's sudden mention of her name, and looked straight down at her. Their eyes met. The firelight burned orange on the tongue of his dagger.

For reasons only known to the deer standing before the lion, to the songbird before the lidless snake, her gaze was fixed to his in motionless terror. She could not lift her feet until he had first taken a step toward her, broken the spell of that moment with his terrible intent. Suddenly she was in full flight, shoving past Omund, sprinting across the yard, gown hiked to her knees, tearing down the laneway, knocking baskets and scattering crows as she made for the harbour with the desperate speed of a frightened animal in its last flight.

Omund was not much of a warrior, but took his responsibilities as a tenant of the great-house seriously, particularly where a comely woman was concerned. He interposed himself in the doorway and waited for the rushing soldier.

"It seems she doesn't wish to speak with you, stranger," said Omund. He spread his arms in the doorway. His own fear, in contrast, made him feel larger than he was.

"She's daft, then," said the other man. "You're both daft. I'm here to *help* her."

Omund turned towards the soldier's drawn weapon. "Your naked blade failed to tell her that, somehow."

With a roll of his eyes, the Cerulean stuffed it unceremoniously back into its sheath. A silent curse flashed, then died on his lips before he uttered it. "My blade is naked because I thought she might be in some trouble. Do you know a man called Rasten?"

"I do," said Omund. "Another Cerulean, like yourself."

"Pray, has he spoken to you of Elmore Godshall?"

"No."

The Cerulean thumped his chest. "He should have. He's me. I'm Elmore. We were raised to the blue the same year. Old friends, you might say."

"Might I?" said Omund. He didn't sound convinced.

Elmore stepped backward into the great-hall, moving as if to show he did not mean to pursue the woman. That seemed to put Omund at ease some, but not completely.

"Listen—Rasten's come into some trouble," he said. "I came to warn her, is all. I've heard tell that Ashimar has taken him away—for what, I can't say. I only thought—well, you must know the stories. Sometimes, when the Scourge makes men disappear, I've heard tell their families have a way of going, too, not long after."

Omund took a step back as if the name had struck him in the face. "I want no trouble with Lord Ashimar," he said. "Her room's upstairs. Hers and Rasten's. Do as you please."

Elmore looked at him sourly. "I'm no bloodguard," he said. "Get it through your head, I didn't blow in on an ill wind. I'm just passing unhappy news to an unfortunate man's lover, praying to the Ten she shan't end up an unfortunate herself. If you'll do me the favour of giving her that message yourself, I have no more business here, and I'll be off on my merry way. I never meant to frighten anyone."

"I'll tell her if she comes back," said Omund. "But I've never seen her run like that. You put a mighty fear in her, Master Elmore."

Elmore leaned toward the door as if looking after her. "Strange that she knew trouble was coming," he said. "But I never meant to *be* that trouble. I only thought—the Scourge is not to be trifled with, you know? I fear for my friend. I thought I might do my duty by telling her. Then, at least, I'd not suffer that fear for him alone."

"If he's crossed Lord Ashimar," said Omund, "I've no mind to have any future dealings with him, or admit any past ones. That girl would be wise to do the same."

Elmore had paced down the floor, was studying the food she had left, his hungry curiosity compelling him to see how badly burned it was.

"That's a fine meal," he said, studying the two plates with curiosity. "So fine that she ate his supper when he didn't come." He picked at one of the plates, raised his eyebrows with approval, took a second bite. There was no use in wasting it over a misunderstanding.

Omund walked over, still unsure if he wanted to leave the stranger in the hall alone. "Shame to let it go rotten," said Omund, who was a practical man himself, and took the emptier of the two plates, seeking scraps where he could. "Fine indeed. She must have been wroth with him, to eat his supper as well."

"I mean her no harm," said Elmore. "I swear it on my sword and my life. May I sit, and eat, and see if she comes back?"

Omund sat down beside him. "If it please you," he said. His gaze softened as he sat down, but he would not leave the newcomer alone.

"I was on Shadewall duty once," said Elmore as he ate. "Late one night. I was younger then, mind you. My wife, my Gwen, she'd remembered it was ten years before that very night I'd met her at a wee alehouse near Pickstand. Saw fit to cook me a feast as you've never seen. Jorn himself would've wept and prayed to his own mercy. Three-maiden pie. Roast quail, stuffed in a duck, stuffed in a pheasant. Wine from the Rahastan coast. I was three hours late, sir. Three hours. And do you suppose she ate all her own share, and tore into mine?"

"I would have," said Omund, suddenly jealous he had never married.

"You have a lot to learn about women," said Elmore. "Not a bite. Not one bite of mine, nor any of hers. Stone cold on the table it was, and she was stone cold in the bed. Not a word. And not a bite. I would've sat up and eaten it cold, if I could have. But it might have ended our marriage right there. The whole thing went out in the street, in the end, a royal feast for the bugs and the blackrot. Shame to waste it all, the best feast I'd seen in years, for a fight we carried on only a few days. One of us should have enjoyed it. At least, that's how a man thinks. Women, sir, they don't think like that."

At the mention of wine, Omund had gone looking; miraculously, he found some, and while Catrine had taken care to eat most of both meals, the wine seemed untouched. He poured himself a mug and offered one to Elmore.

"For your stories of happily wedded misery, old man," he said with real appreciation, finally lowering his guard. Elmore held out the empty mug meant for Rasten—surely his old friend wouldn't mind—and let his new friend fill it.

"To women," Omund offered. "To women who don't think like men. Blessings on them for that."

"Aye, women," Elmore toasted, and they drank. The wine was a fine vintage, pleasantly tart and full-bodied to contrast with the sweetness and lightness of the fish. Omund laughed suddenly after a few pulls of the wine.

"Tell me, Elmore the Stranger," he asked at last, "why did you spin me this tale?" Elmore had to ponder the question a long moment—he had, in the good cheer and the memories of Gwen, forgotten the point of his story entirely.

"Right," he said at last. "A lady forsaken without warning has no great appetite. That was the point of it. I've known only two kinds of folk my whole life who stuff their gullets when plans go sideways: soldiers on one hand, and beggars on the other."

"Well, she's no soldier, though she lies with one," said Omund, shaking the last of Catrine's wine from the little bottle. "And you've seen her manners. Her figure too. If a fine lady like that is a beggar, I'm the

Peasant-King of Stonewind."

Elmore nursed his glass, deep in thought. He raised his eyebrows appreciatively.

"Oh, she's definitely not a beggar," he agreed.

Catrine's feet planted the coyest of kisses on the cobblestones as she ran, so light was her step and so fleet her travel. She was no mean study with a short blade, like many of the Selikhan women who had survived the Unrest, but it was always assumed that the Vairhurst Widows, if discovered, would be put to flight, and live or die by their swiftness in the city streets. So it was that she had spent long weeks that year in the guise of a chattel runner, dashing a half-mile length of the Saltway under heavy load on the mornings she could get away. Unburdened now of the training-stones she often carried to the harbour, she moved with an unfettered quickness even in the gathering gloom of night; and as she tore down the Saltway toward the ships, the exertion of running brought back the inner quiet that came with regular training. Although she fled the Storm Quarter as a frightened animal, she came down into the harbour as a soldier of forced calm, back in control of her wits though her heart pounded in her ears and her mouth was still dry with panic.

The tall masts of the *Wyrmsbolt* were already in view, capped with the bright double pennant that erroneously marked the ship as an exotic trading vessel sailed out of distant Seythe. Fluttering in the cold breeze like the forked tongue of a serpent, the bright red pennant caught the firelight of the harbour like a beacon as she dashed through the narrow streets looming over the wharves below. She was nearly there, nearly to the safety of the ship, when she caught herself a few steps from bursting onto the upper wharf and charging headlong toward the plank. Stopping hard on her ankles, she held herself to the shadow of the harbourmaster's yard-house and caught her breath before plunging into view of what little crowd remained. There were still too many to make her way to the ship unnoticed—and far too few, at this late hour, to disappear into the crowd as she had been taught.

Stupid, stupid, she chided herself, when her breath had come back enough to think. *Stupid girl. Don't lead them straight to the boat.* Watching at her heels to see if she'd been followed, it was impossible to know for sure. Her disguise as a chattel-runner was effective precisely because it was so common; the gentle seaward slope of the Saltway was teeming with boys and unfortunate women running full tilt from the city to the sea with coins, messages, or market-wares. In the moments she watched them, heart in her throat, it seemed from one moment to the next as if any or all of them were running her down.

But the Cerulean who had come for her was nowhere to be seen; he had been outfitted and much burdened by the heavy trappings of a tower guard, and could not possibly have kept pace with her, which put her at ease long enough to fight for breath and steady herself against the wall. Shutting her eyes tight, she forced calm into her veins and found a tangible calm in the sounds and smells of the harbour. Great gulls wheeled overhead, occasionally mingling their own shrill cries with the shouted patter of the evening hawkers and vendors, whose voices rose up with the mingled scents of their wares:

> *Fish and flesh o' the sea! O tarry!*
> *Adânasea cod and Banwash humari!*
> *Humari boilt, humari fresh!*
> *Tarry, O tarry, for fish and flesh!*

> *Hot mutton dumplings! Nice dumplings, all hot!*

Mops and hair brooms! Brushes and more!
One for the Rascal, one for the floor!

> *Turnips and carrots! Carrots and navets, aye!*

Five mile milk! Six skatts a pot!
Five miles from the Wall! A fifth of the rot!

There was no use in making her way onto the *Wyrmsbolt* only to be trapped there—to trap Baran and the others, too, without warning. With timid steps, she slipped across the narrow lane between her and the harbour stair, descending to the old stone wharf as she watched for signs of pursuit. She had nothing to tie back or conceal her bouncing golden hair, which fell immodestly over her shoulders as she made her way along the wharf.

The fishermen's wharf was a level below the stone, on a sickly-looking wooden pier that floated far out into the harbour. It was here that she turned her steps, swaying her hips with a brazen but hollow confidence as she crossed one vendor after another. At first the shouts and lewd whistles stung her frightened heart and shook her to the core, as given over to panic as she was. But as the catcalls grew in volume and creativity she took a strange comfort in them: this rotted pier was Odi's stronghold, and these salty men his soldiers, if it came to that. They were none of them freedom fighters, but they were earnest men and hardy, with no love for the Grand Army. Deep in their cups by the hour of dusk, she had no doubt that a few of them would draw steel on the Imperator himself if they thought defending a whore's honour might earn them a private reward.

She found Odi exactly where she thought she would, bent low over his makeshift Kings' Table in a heated game of four-tower with the other men. She cleared her throat, slimy from her sprint down the Saltway, and prayed her voice would not stick hoarsely in it.

"You know what they say about four-tower," she said coyly. "Men who finish quick like to play Fallen. Men who play Risen take pleasure in being thorough."

All of the men, every one, looked up at her with lecherous astonishment—Odi included. He was, as she expected, playing Fallen.

"Is that so?" he asked, holding up his kingpiece thoughtfully. Recognition, then alarm, flashed across his face as his gaze met hers.

"You boys going to play all night?" she asked, her gaze fixed on Odi.

Odi fished for his words and found none, still shocked that she had come to him directly. The men laughed at his awkwardness.

"He's taken moony with her, he is," said one.

"Suppose he don't want his winnings," said another, reaching across the table. Remembering himself, Odi slapped the man's hand away from his meagre pile of mixed coins.

"Go piss on your hands, Loric," he spat. "That's gold enough for you." The men roared with laughter—all except Odi, who didn't feel much like laughing.

"Is all that yours?" Catrine asked with feigned interest. Odi nodded, finally catching on.

"Aye," he said. "T'ain't much, but it's mine. What's your price, lovely?"

She looked away bashfully. "Three riders. And a pint of red ale after. Thirsty work, it is."

"Get off, that's a king's fortune, that," Loric snorted.

The colour drained from Odi's face.

"Three and a red, you say?"

The unlikely price was a code.

She'd been discovered. They were coming.

Odi pushed back his barrel and stood up decisively, sweeping his coins greedily into his hands. "You heard the lady, fellows," he said with a hollow grin. "Past my suppertime, I reckon." A groan of protest came up from the fishermen, most of whom were suddenly eager to win back three riders as fast as he could lose them.

"You're getting fleeced at that price," Loric warned him.

"I haven't got much time," Catrine said, a little desperately. With a nod to the other fishermen, Odi bid them farewell and hustled with her back down the pier amidst a chorus of approval.

"Are you hurt?" he asked, soon as they were out of earshot. She shook her head. He draped his cloak over her and she drew up the hood.

"Can you run? Can you ride, if you have to?"

"If I have to," she said.

"How?" he asked. "How did this happen?"

"I don't know," she said. "I've no idea. He came to the house, dagger drawn. Looking for me by name."

"Impossible," said Odi. "You've been careful…so careful. They couldn't possibly know."

She felt like weeping—he saw it—but she was a soldier, now. She would cry later, perhaps, in great wracking sobs when she was alone and far from him. It was the way all men and women at war cried, though they seldom said so.

"We haven't many friends in the City," he said. "We can't turn to the other Widows. Nor can we risk leading them to Baran. We've got a young message carrier coming with livestock, bound for the market Jornsday next. If you don't mind the stink of goat, I could get you out with him as his wife."

She hesitated a moment. *But Rasten…*

"Yes," she said, nodding. "Yes, that would be best."

They didn't get far up the Saltway before rushing into a private inn. Odi put his night's winnings into a solitary, barred room: they had played out a merry lie for the fishermen that now had to be true. He called for meat and drink, but she turned it away. When they were safely settled, he barred the door. She collected herself and seemed now the picture of calm. His presence gave her surety, not only as her protector, but as a comrade in arms who reminded her of her own strength too.

"You're not hurt."

"No."

"They know your face?"

"Very clearly. He was as close as you to me."

Odi nodded, weighing the facts. "Can you go back to the house?"

She shook her head no.

"Did you leave behind anything of importance?"

Only the man I love.

"Nothing," she said.

"We'll get word to Baran," said Odi. "She'll have some coin, or we'll canvas the bodyguards. Hendec's very free with his purse in the name of the cause. If you can hold out till Jornsday, we can get you gone. I can spare one man for the next room, if it comes to that." He frowned at the sound of heavy boots dropping through the wall. "If it's vacant," he added.

"Thank you," she breathed. "I can't thank you enough."

Odi clapped a hand on her shoulder, man to man. "We're in this together," he said. "You're a man of my quire, as the Imperials say. And I've lost too many friends already—too many altogether. I'll not leave you to the wolves."

She threw her arms around him and hugged him tightly. She even smiled. But he had turned his mind to the friends he had lost, and he stood oblivious for a moment before he returned the embrace, patting her shoulders the way most people seemed to return a hug.

"There, there," he said awkwardly, because that was the thing they usually said. She laughed softly, then sobbed, then laughed again as she let go. She was half-mad with fear, now that it was safe to be.

"There's one other matter," he said. "I'll talk to Baran, see where we can get you to. It won't be far. Maybe Carmac. Maybe we'll have to take you farther than that. But I imagine she'll want you to keep writing those letters."

Confusion flashed over Catrine's face. "Letters…what letters?"

"We've got skilled forgers in Carmac," Odi went on. "We can make those letters come from the Capital. We can put scouts on the road and intercept them that come back. Once you're somewhere safe, we need you to keep writing that Overseer of yours. Keep him talking, as long as you can. We've got plans for that mine."

Catrine shook her head. "That's not me," she said. "You're thinking of Madge. The other widow. Madge, who goes by Lysandra now."

Odi turned the information over in his mind. "Madge is the one with the one-armed chap?"

"Yes."

"Then…who's your mark?"

My mark. The expression brought a sour taste to her mouth.

"Rasten," she said. "The tower guard."

Odi let out a sudden laugh, deep from his round belly.

"What's so funny?"

He puffed out his cheeks and let out a long sigh of relief. "Thank the

Ten. The man they sent for you—a Cerulean guard?"

She nodded. "He was."

"Older fellow? Long grey beard, looked more like a magistrate than a fighter?"

"You know him?"

"No," said Odi, "but I had eyes on him down here, and I know his business. You're all right! He had no mind to hurt you. You're safe, lass! You're safe. It's all right."

Catrine shifted uncomfortably, unready to relax her own guard. "You're sure?"

"Rasten is gone," Odi said. "He shipped out on the *Providence* at sunset. Some big oaf was hollering about it from the top deck. I suppose that old fellow was the messenger he sent to tell you."

She shook her head. "That's impossible. Why? Why would Ras put out with—with *him*?"

"No idea," said Odi. "All he said was, Rasten's gone. Tell Catrine…I s'pose that's you. Tell her Ashimar's taken him away. Sounds as if he didn't have much choice in the matter."

Catrine's hand went to her white face in shock. "Where? Where have they taken him?"

"You might ask that Cerulean who came knocking," said Odi. "I only know what I know. Maybe he heard more than I did. But no mistaking it, he was sent looking for you. By Rasten, no doubt."

"But he came with his weapon drawn."

"Not for you, then. Travalaithi women don't fight. He wouldn't have expected to need it for the likes of you. Unless—"

"Unless what?"

Odi stroked his scruffy chin. "Ashimar's bloodguards have no attachments," he said. "Least none as far as we've been able to determine. Unmarried, no families. They live to serve only the Scourge and the Imperator. Perhaps your new friend feared for your safety. Perhaps he knows something we don't about how Ashimar's bloodguards operate… or how they come to have no loved ones."

"I'm not sure I'd want to know," said Catrine, shivering.

"I know enough for any man to sleep uneasy," said Odi. "But just the same, if you can find out anything about that lot, the Mage would be very grateful. He fears Ashimar, I think, if indeed he fears anyone. But he has an odd fascination with him, too, as I've heard."

"Have you met him?"

"Ashimar?"

Catrine shook her head. "No, Jord—the Mage, I mean."

"We've never spoken," said Odi. "But I've seen him, a few times. Remarkable man. Learn us a thing or two about Ashimar, and you might meet him yourself."

"How? I mean—where do I start?"

"We'll put a couple of men out to find that Cerulean," said Odi. "Won't take long. There's few enough tower guard, and fewer still to match his description. I don't think he means to harm you. But we've got a lot of questions, and it seems to me he was bringing you answers on a platter."

"I could run back to the great-house," said Catrine, "and see if he's still there."

Odi frowned. "You say he had his sword drawn? That'd be for a reason. Even if he hadn't meant to stick you with it…it seemed to cross his mind he might have to stick somebody in your defense. I'd be a poor shepherd indeed to send you back where you're like to be found by whatever wolves he thought were coming."

"If I don't go back," said Catrine, "I'll be missed. The others in the great-house know me, by now."

"It's up to you," said Odi. "If you've got the nerves to keep stationed there a little while longer, it might go best for us. But bear in mind, if the Cerulean Guard truly fear for your safety, then you're a pretty bird under watch by some mighty big cat. In my experience, those birds that survive, they can weather the cat's eye a long time. But when the moment comes to bolt, they take it. Move too soon, move too late, it's all the same."

He cast his gaze out of the single, small window. The night was fully dark now, with the last red rays of sunlight well hidden behind the unbroken curve of the flawless Shadewall. Even here, the pennants of the *Wyrmsbolt* could be seen among the tangle of masts. The criers and hawkers of the fishermen's wharf had finally withdrawn to their hammocks or huts for a few precious hours of sleep before putting out for the dawn fishing. The wind that curled its way westward all evening, against the usual current, had given way to a calm that blanketed the shimmering sea in stillness.

"Aye," said Odi. "The cat's eye is on us all, lass. That's what they call these moments of quiet. Go home tomorrow, if you've got the nerves for it. But do a man a favour, if you would, and stay the night here, just in case. We just lost a Widow in the East a few days ago. It'd break my heart to lose another."

"They'll wonder if I'm suddenly not home the night,"

"Neither is your mark," said Odi. "Both of you gone quite unexpectedly. Make up something romantic, if you have to." With a grunt, he rose to his feet. "It's time I was getting back."

She felt the panic return, momentarily, as he moved to the doorway.

"I was scared, Odi. I'm sorry. I was just—so scared."

Odi nodded with an uneasy smile. "Me too. And here we are, two very scared spies, still breathing. Keep up that fear, if you can. Breathing's the best way to be."

"Do you have to go?"

Her plaintive glance gave him pause. Were he a few years younger, or the Travalaithi Empire a few years kinder, or the knives in the dark a handful fewer, he might have flattered himself to stay in her room and sleep in her bed, though he had no illusions about what it would mean and what it wouldn't. But the time for a lot of things had passed, and would not come again while there was still work to be done.

"I've got my own place to be," he said at last. "You'll be safe here, and you're strong, and in the morning we'll see how things look. I daresay they're better than you think."

"Have you been gone long enough?" she asked.

Odi checked again the colour of the sky. "You said it yourself," he said, smiling. "The men who prefer to play Fallen are over and done, quick as a cricket. Goodnight and good rest, lass."

"Good night, Odi," she said, and barred the window shut.

That night as she drifted into the sea of sleep on an unfamiliar mattress, Catrine turned over in her mind the excuses she might make for staying out all night. She was turning them over still, meticulously shaping the facts and details, when exhaustion took her away into the grey meadow of dream. It was there she saw them together for the first time.

At first, she had dreamt only of Aden, tending their home and their gardens. She dreamt of him all through the long winter; in the most secret parts of her mind they strolled in mournful silence through the pure elm forests south of Selik, lingering on the lush ferny shores of the gleaming Vyazavod in summer, where they spoke not like the ardent lovers they had once been, but like weathered old friends, politely skirting the unpleasant truth that they were now separated by death. It was as if there could be no words of love between the living and the dead—only a civil peace, like the broken stillness of a water unsure of its direction or place under conflicting moons.

When Rasten had first come into her dreams, they were again the visions of a living man, fervid and urgent ones that woke her with nerves tingling, embarrassed in front of him and sick with shame. In time she made peace with him, but still the waves of feeling that whelmed her in the quiet nights left her adrift between her old life and new, like an exile's boat tossed on the stormy seas of dream.

That night in an unfamiliar bed, the place whither she came was unknown to her, a high mournful meadow bathed in mist. She heard their voices first; and while she never remembered their words upon waking, it seemed to her they were words passed in friendship.

There on a grassy heath, hidden in low wet clouds, her lovers old and new made merry as they toiled in the earth, turning up the soil with long iron-handled shovels. It was hard work; Rasten grunted with the effort as his powerful arms hauled up one shovel after another. The weaker of the two men by far was Aden, whose lanky height was not made for digging and was no match for Rasten's shorter, bullish frame. His thinning hair was matted to his round skull in sweaty strands, and though he seemed glad enough in Rasten's company, there was a pallor and tiredness to him, like a ghost whose death finally seemed to be catching up to him.

Indeed, it was then that she saw the grim object of their work, for she had come close by them and cast her eyes down into the soil. With carefree acceptance of his lot, Rasten was hard at work digging a shallow grave in the unwieldy soil that stretched out long and thin before him. Its sides were meticulously cut and tamped with the blade of his shovel—or was it the beard of his brother's axe?—and the whole of it looked so inviting, then, and Aden looked to it with such poignant longing that he nearly forgot his own work: he was digging another grave much like it, but shorter and broader in its dimensions, better suited not for a tall gentle merchant with the frail limbs of an Eastern scholar, but for a barrel-chested warrior brought up in the rude clamour of the West. It was a grave meant for Rasten, as Rasten's was meant for him; yet they went about their business with gaiety and good cheer, and laughed together (Aden softly, Rasten wholeheartedly) at the jokes whose words she could not discern and would never remember.

The discovery of the two graves was not so shocking as to jolt Catrine out of her sleep, as was common in her nightmares. The dream would linger on for some while yet. When at last she drifted free of it, she awoke not in fright, but weighted down by a colossal sadness whose cause, like the conversation of her lovers, was a hair too indistinct to remain with the dreamer on waking. She cried hard, then, and did not know why; and afterward, though it was barely past midnight, she lay there in torpid grief and waited for the sun, sick at heart and alone in the room, in the city, in all the world.

The tapping of the old woman's cane set Heward to growling even before she reached the locked gate. He had never quite grown accustomed to the old woman, nor she to him, and his snarl was not so much an alarm as an expression of distaste. Illyria, still half-awake after crying herself nearly to sleep, started up in a fit of choking at the sound. Her stomach lurched; the soft footfalls and the tapping of the cane called to mind the sickening stink of myrrh and lavender for reasons she could not quite understand—the vile memory of foul incense burned in nights long past.

Gasping, Illyria sprang from her bed toward the latticed ironwork that surrounded the balcony, pushing her lips against the metal toward the fresh air. She dared not open the inner screen, though: the key to that was hidden in the one place even her grandmother would never look. With tight lungs, she sucked in the cold night air and willed herself to calm until the terrible scent had faded from her memory. She did not want to be caught out of her bed, but could not find the will to tear herself away. She was still there, gasping for breath, when a long, hunched shadow fell over the doorway.

"By the Chain, child," said her grandmother, "what are you doing out of bed at this hour?"

The bloodguards who dozed fitfully in the corners of the room snapped up at the sound of the old woman's arrival, raising their unhelmed heads from couches and plush pillows.

"Lady Moriath," one said, and the others rose to attend her.

"Leave us," said Moriath. They rose as one and left the chambers, awaiting orders out by the sedan. She tapped her way to the door, shut it. The door latched with a wide steel bar, but she saw no need to lower it.

"I wanted some fresh air," said Illyria, waiting patiently for Moriath to turn back. "I felt I was choking…"

"The summer is dying," said Moriath, "and the warm nights are well past, whatever hot days may be left. You'll catch your death of cold at that window." *Hardly a window*, thought Illyria, though she dared not utter it. "I'm sorry," she said, shrinking away from the fresh air.

"Gods know, I wish I could be so careless with *my* health," Moriath said. "I'm too old and frail, now, to survive mistakes like yours. Be a good girl and draw the curtains for me."

Illyria reached for the familiar rope and tugged down the heavy tapestries that surrounded the locked gate to the balcony. Without the moonlight streaming in, the quarters were dark; if the room had any warmth left to keep in, Illyria could not feel it.

"Olferth thinks you're safe in this tower," said the old woman, as Illyria made her way back to the bed, clutching her nightclothes tightly about her willowy body. "By all rights, you should be. Yet always you find a way to betray my best intentions for you. I have watched over you, child, your whole life, every day of it. I have seen you through wars without, and wars within. With your poor mother in the ground, did I not surrender my life as the Lady of Lockharme to come and put all that I am into your service? And you reward my sacrifice with what? Recklessness! Betrayal!"

Illyria cast her eyes incredulously to the balcony gate. "Grandmother, it was only a breath of fresh air, that's all."

"Oh, my sweet, foolish duckling," said the old woman. "Breathe or don't as it pleases you, where it pleases you. You know well that's not the betrayal of which I speak."

Illyria's heart fell in her chest and she drew the thick blankets up over herself. Moriath hobbled her way to the bed.

"With Rasten," she said with a sigh. "That's what you mean."

Moriath's mouth was taut, her expression sour. "Of course that's what I mean."

Illyria took a breath, wondering if she should chance a word in the soldier's defense. The old woman watched her with calculating eyes, waiting for her to speak.

"I—"

Moriath slapped her hard across the face.

"A common soldier!" the old woman snapped. "What would your father think?"

"I don't imagine he thinks of me much at all," said Illyria, almost fiercely.

Moriath slapped her again, this time with the back of her bony hand. She whimpered.

"Hush your poisoned tongue!" the old woman scolded.

Good. It was safest to keep her angry.

"Every cotter and lovegoat from here to the Ban pays the Imperator his due respect, though they couldn't tell him from any other stranger. I'll not hear his own daughter fail to keep that standard."

Illyria scowled in youthful defiance, though she quailed within.

"You're right," Moriath added, somewhat surprisingly. "I don't imagine he thinks much of you, the way you degrade yourself with whatever man finds his way into your service. I'm an old dowager at heart, my duckling; high birth and low birth are things of weight and substance to me. His Imperial Majesty, come up as he is, was a man of simple honour for all his trappings. Carrying on with a common soldier, says I? To me, it's like finding you in a barn. But your poor father—it's not so much the trimmings and baubles that hang over the boy's tunic, but those hanging under them, that would most break his heart."

Illyria bristled. "I don't know what you think happened—"

"Yes you do."

"Nothing of the sort," Illyria protested. "You r-raised me well, Grandmother."

"Yes I did. But I extended no such favour to him."

"Rasten is a good man."

"Was he?" Moriath asked, letting the question hang in the air long enough to do its work. "I daresay if you've had your strings loosened, child, we'll know it soon enough, won't we?"

Illyria could no longer hold back her tears, though she did all she could to slow their escape from the prison of her eyes. Her breath came in tight, wheezing gasps, as it often did. At the sounds of her distress, one of the bloodguards opened the door and stood wordlessly in the doorway, though he had been ordered away.

"Medicine," said Moriath with knowing calm. The bloodguard set about fetching the old woman's things, as she shook her head at Illyria with resigned disappointment.

"You bring this on yourself," she said.

It was hard to tell when the weeping ended and the convulsions began. Illyria wailed aloud like a child at their approach, until her sobs were choked to a terrifying silence. Wracked by convulsions, she jerked her spindly arms against the bed. With a practiced shove, Moriath thrust her trembling body to the center of the broad mattress and withdrew to the outer room.

At the opening of the door, Heward nearly bowled her over, rushing into the room to lick and nudge his wide snout at the girl's convulsing body. Moriath brushed the bloodguard away from her satchel, fussing with the contents herself.

"Medicine, I said," she snapped.

"Problem, Lady?"

At the far end of the corridor, through the outer gates, Olferth drummed his clammy fingers against the bars. He was not a man accustomed to waiting.

"We'll know shortly," said Moriath, drawing a phial of thick amber liquid from the bag. "Keep your distance."

Olferth watched the old woman with interest. "Ask her about the Mage."

Old fool. "I will tell you what I know soon enough," said Moriath.

Illyria's fit had calmed itself by the time her grandmother had crossed the wide chamber again.

"Take the dog out and leave us," she said, and the bloodguard complied, joining the others in the entryway. This time, when Moriath closed the door, she barred it tightly. A practiced disinterest guided her motions as she hobbled across the room, breathing against the phial to warm it as Illyria's unsteady breath came in snorts and gasps.

"Troublesome bitch," the old woman spat, in this moment to herself. But she settled in and rolled the girl towards her, holding her gently with a kindness as false as her patience was true.

"No," came Illyria's first slurred, moaned word. "No no no no no."

"Illyria." Moriath's voice was cold and harsh.

"No, no. Go after him."

"Illyria, do you hear me?"

"They're waiting under the moons. In the salty air, they're waiting for him."

"Illyria! Listen to your grandmother!"

The young girl was slack as a rag doll, now. She was trying to push the old woman away, perhaps, but there was no strength left in her.

"No eyes," she moaned. "He has no eyes to see. Go. Go."

"You hush up," said Moriath. It was too soon, perhaps, to force the bitter liquid into the girl's mouth, but she tried anyway, pulling the girl's tight jaw open and nearly choking her all over again on the noxious contents of the phial. Her back spasmed once more; then she was still and spoke no more until Moriath addressed her in a voice as cold and strong as stone.

"What's your name, child?"

"Illyria."

"Good. And who am I?"

"It was a handsome black cat. It was treed by a hunter's hounds—"

"Never you mind that. Who am I?"

"G-grandmother."

"And what is your birthday?"

Illyria let out another low moan. "Seventh. Seventh day. S-seventh day of Idis. Idismaunt."

"And what was your mother's name?" She held Illyria's hand tightly now as the girl began to slip back into herself, drifting into a sleep as weary as any ever woven.

"Althea."

"Althea, my daughter. That's right. Althea Lady Veritenh. And what is your lord father's name?"

Illyria moaned again softly but did not answer.

"Illyria, who is your lord father?"

She hovered on the edge of her senses a long time without speaking. It was impossible to say when she lapsed into sleep. When she was well and truly gone, the old woman cast her hand aside and hobbled to the door. The enormous dog bounded into the room again as Moriath handed what was left of the little phial to one of the bloodguards.

"The girl is sick," she said. "She risks permanent derangement. If she falls into another of her fits, give her the rest of this, and send for me at once."

"My lady," said the servant, who returned to the chamber with the others.

Beyond the outer gate, what little patience Olferth had left was entirely evaporated.

"Speak, woman," he demanded. "Tell me everything."

She clucked her tongue at him in a way that shocked the twin karach who stood guard by the outer doors. "It's no talk for these corridors," she said. "What I've got to say, I wouldn't suffer even the cripple who carries the shitstool to hear."

Olferth frowned. "So there's a problem."

She set her mouth tightly. "There's a complication," she corrected.

"But she knows she's forbidden to talk to the soldiers."

"Oh, she knows it," said Moriath, "though there's still some defiance in her. I'll tell her what end Rasten comes to, when Ashimar's had done with him. That should set her back in line. I would have had some pretty things to say tonight—but she's worked herself into another fit. Another one, already, and the first frost not even struck."

"That's a problem," Olferth admitted.

"It will be soon," said Moriath. "Perhaps as soon as the white moon starts bleeding her. Tûr knows even my strongest potions can't keep that particular red hound at bay forever. She's getting worse, Olferth. Steadily worse as she grows up."

"There's nothing to be done, then?"

"Not for an overpaid pitch-farmer," said Moriath. "But I may be able to manage something. Give me time."

"Time," Olferth repeated. "We have precious little of that left. I used to think I'd grown fat with the passage of time. Now I see it's only that the walls close in a little more with every passing day."

"Perhaps it is both," offered Moriath.

SEVEN

BEYOND THE GREATNESS OF HIS SIZE, Kellan was blessed with arms that never tired from regular use. Never in his long career as a soldier, not in the service of Harrod, nor even that summer he was sent to quell the early revolts on the battlefields of Orrath, had he met a day or night of work that ran his arms to exhaustion—not even when that work had been what he called "wolf's work," the killing of men. But a night and a day of beating the drum, halting only to beat the rowers, had finally done it. He had not been seasick, and descending from the corsair families of Adân, he likely never would be. The fog that clouded his brain was a burden he could manage, for it was witless work to keep the men rowing. But his arms, it seemed, were just about done with him. His work at the drum had split some of his own scourge-marks open again, and those men and women who bristled and whimpered under the weight of his floggings looked up with some pity at the blood that stained his own scarlet uniform a dull brown, and gave him what strength they could. It was their lot, certainly not their choice, to row for Ashimar's whim—and most seemed to understand it was his sorry lot, not his choice, to beat them for it.

But a full day had come and gone with the warship moving at speed. Rowed hard even under sail, with the moons at odds with each other but the winds in agreement, the reckless passage of the *Providence* along the Haukmere coast was so swift that even the sharks that regularly followed the ship in hope of scraps could not keep pace with it for long. In the last hours, though, the ship had slowed considerably as the rowers' stamina began to fail even under the application of Ashimar's particular barbed encouragement. If Kellan's arms were nearing exhaustion, he knew how much more miserable was the plight of the rowers.

Suffering along with the Rattlers and other prisoners-turned-slaves, Rasten bore his burden in silence. When the Esman at his side fell away from the oar in fits of gasping, he doubled his effort and kept the pace of two men alone while the little man recovered himself. Sweat drenched his broad frame and matted his dark hair to his head. But his wrapped hands had not yet bled through, and he kept to his work with greater endurance and will than the raggedy wretches brought up from the Rattle. In the beginning his soldier's conditioning had made little difference, but now he kept at his task with quiet resolve as the rowers around him began to fail.

"I know these waters," Kellan called out to the rowers—but especially to Rasten—not long after the second sunset had passed. "You'll soon have a reprieve, I think. Keep to your task. It won't be long." Indeed, under merciless forced oar, the ship had made better time than even Kellan had imagined. Within an hour of sunset, two of Ashimar's bloodguards had come down to the lower deck with the news.

"Oars up and let her run!"

Rasten looked up with surprise at the command, which had roughly the desired effect as the prisoners hauled their oars out of the water and let the ship glide on smoothly. It was not a smooth transition, with the rowers untrained and exhausted as they were, and the hull creaked as the ship lost more than a little forward momentum.

"We've reached the shoals at Ossiluran," one of the bloodguards said to Kellan, as if he didn't know it. "The water is low and the moons are fickle behind those stormclouds. Wind alone will serve us through the narrows as quick as we can make our way."

Kellan leaned back from the heavy drum with a grunt. "I'm glad for that," he said.

The two men walked the length of the lower deck, taking stock of the rowers, who straightened their backs and did their best to look hale and ready for more rowing. All of them managed it, this time. On their return, they stopped at Rasten's oar and motioned for him to stand.

"You are the new bloodguard," one said.

Rasten shrugged with his bruised and blistered hands. "I thought I was," he said. "But I've rowed for a day with little water and no rest, alongside the worst of the city prisoners. If I've truly joined the special elect of the Grand Army, I certainly don't feel it. I've been treated like one of the enemy's best warriors, not one of our own."

"Your strength had to be tested," said the other bloodguard. "Lord Ashimar suffers none who are weak of limb."

"As soon as you are ready," said the first, unlocking Rasten's shackles, "you can join us on the command deck."

"If it pleases you," Rasten said, forcing a weak smile through his exhaustion. "Though you have strange ways of making a new arrival feel welcome."

The second bloodguard smiled. "It will all be over soon enough." They left him, then, to nurse his sore wrists and endure the scorn of the prisoners who were not, it seemed, about to be granted the same freedom.

"D'you hear that, Kellan?" Ras asked with mixed excitement and relief. But Kellan was nodding softly at the drum, already half-asleep or more as the gently rocking waves carried the *Providence* on into the swift and narrow channel. Rasten might have drifted off entirely, but Kellan seemed like one of those men who never quite slipped all the way under the spell of sleep in an unfamiliar place. Ras chose his steps carefully so as not to wake him as he slipped past.

The mast-deck was above the lower deck, and the command deck above that. It was hardly a climb worth mentioning, but a night and day hard at the oar had brought such woe to Rasten's muscles and joints that it took an effort of his whole body to haul his feet up every narrow step. He pushed himself to hustle as he reached the top, for it seemed that more than a few of the bloodguards had already assembled. Their fearsome helms had come off: here on the sea, they were content with the faces of ordinary men.

"Well met," Rasten said with a disarming smile, "and glad to be among you. Hard errands such as this go much better with good company."

The chilling rain that had begun to fall did much to hide their expressions.

"Should one of us fetch the big fellow?" asked Rasten. "We can't all be new recruits, but I'm certain he is. Has the look about him. We ought not to start without—"

Two of the bloodguards seized his arms and shoved him hard against the rail. In his moment of confusion, a third slammed a steel bracer hard against the foot of his ribcage, knocking the wind from him and doubling him over in helpless surprise. He jerked an arm free, instinctively; but these were hard men too, well-muscled and trained as he was, and they caught him up and thrust his arm against the rail again before he could slip their grasp.

"New recruits," said the largest of the five men. He spat on the deck, though his spittle was quickly lost in the rain. "New recruits? Have you got any Chain-rattling idea how long we've served the Red Captain?"

"He's got no clue," said one.

"No idea what he's in for," said another.

The first man leaned in close, baring his yellow teeth like a dog at the full play of his leash.

"Vosthome born and raised, I was," the sneering man said. "Raised for this since I could walk. Had my first tussle ere that." He nudged the man at his right with a sharp elbow. "Stag here was born with a sword in his hand. Caused his mam some distress, I recall."

"Kil't my twin," added Stag. "Born a killer."

Rasten forced himself to suck in his first full gasp of air. His ribs were on fire and his breath burned hot in the chill of the rain.

"The bloodguard are the oldest order of knights in the Empire," said the sneering man. "Did you know that?"

Rasten had been in pain before—worse pain, many times. "What are you doing?" he asked evenly. "What do you want from me?"

"Older than the Cerulean guard," the other went on. "Older even than the Tower. Knights proper, from the Age of Sun, they say. Protectors of the Oldborn, the first kings of the Vosi."

Rasten frowned at the other men. "And for a history lesson, I need restraining?" The words or the tone of his voice—perhaps both—earned him a backhand from the leading bloodguard.

"Who gives a running shit about history?" said the bloodguard. "What's important is where we're at right now. Bloodguards come up from birth, see. Vosthome born and Vosi bred. Kings, like. 'New recruits,' he says. Are you simple, boy? There's no such thing as new recruits to the red." He punctuated his words with a hard finger to Rasten's face, near the eye.

"No. Such. Thing."

Rasten flinched and turned his head away. "I have no quarrel—"

"You don't call up a knight from the baseborn trash," the bloodguard interrupted. "We all know it. Ashimar knows it. Everyone but you seems to know it. I don't know what magistrate's daughter you sailed up the wrong canal with to get put on this boat. But Ashimar knows plain as we do, it's not because you're a worthy companion." He pulled a long, wickedly edged dagger from his boot.

"Hey," said Ras. "Hey now. You've got the wrong idea."

"Oh, you're the one who's mistaken," said the bloodguard. "We've need of no knights like you. But a fat little squire, aye. You have need of a squire, Stag?"

The one called Stag gave a grinning nod. "Aye, lots of need," he said, cupping his mail-skirt lewdly.

Rasten began to struggle, but his exhaustion at the oars had taken the strength out of him. "You're no knights," he said through gritted teeth. "You're dogs. Dumb ones, too, if you think Ashimar will look kindly on what you do to me. High-born or not, knight or not, I belong to him, now. Not to you."

The bloodguard struck him in the face with a closed fist, but the added power of surprise was now spent: steeled for the blow, Rasten took it almost without flinching as the corded muscles in his bull's neck tightened.

"I don't much like being Ashimar's property," Ras went on, unfazed, "but that's what I am, now. If you lay a finger on what's his, don't expect to get that finger back."

The others broke into a gale of cruel laughter.

"You think Ashimar will protect you?" the bloodguard said. "You really don't know, do you? He doesn't know." A few of the men chuckled. "We are Ashimar's attack dogs. We are his hounds, not his squires an' quires like you Grand Army footmen. We are the vanguard of his cruelty, and that is what pleases him. If we don't put a knife through a bastard-born yantan like you every few days, he'll worry we've gone soft, and it'll be the same for us."

One of the bloodguards who had come belowdecks for him, the one pinning his swordarm, leaned in close. "I told you once, little man, Ashimar does not suffer the weak. You think he'll be angry we've carved you up some? There's more men on his crew than he likes. He'll be glad we've decided amongst our own, and marked the man who's no use to him." He looked to the bloodguard who'd drawn the dagger.

"There's no place for weak men in the bloodguard," he said. "Our first duty's to ensure there are none. The weak must die."

"Is that right?" asked a deep voice.

In the clamour and darkness of the storm, with both moons bashful behind the heavy clouds, Kellan had cast no shadow and made no noise as he drew near. The first they saw of him was a red wolf's head, bright-edged in a sudden flash of lightning, as he took the first man by the top edge of his breastplate. The bloodguard turned, indignant, his open mouth ready to shout, when the big man slipped two gloved fingers past his teeth and clamped his meaty fist shut on the bloodguard's lower jaw. The dagger in the man's hand swung round, but its desperate arc was cut short as Kellan lurched back and tore down with all his strength. The wild slash struck home an instant before the thunder did, into the collar of Kellan's uniform, but there was not much strength behind it. It slit the fabric and drew blood, but the red gash joined the rest of Kellan's reopened scars and was of no more consequence to him. Twisting at the hips, he launched a tight uppercut into the bloodguard's nose, but kept his grip on the jaw. The blow unmade his face and sent him sprawling to the deck choking—well and truly marked for death, but not so dead that he ceased to be a howling spectacle to the other men.

The bloodguard were seasoned and quick to respond, but they had too long relied on the terror of their red armour; the assault on them was more than any reasonable man would dare, and its brutality was more than they were accustomed to. In his last moment of surprise, Kellan seized the hair of a second man and spun him face-first into the mast. Keeping steady eye contact with the others, he gripped the bloodguard by his smashed face and, hoisting him more than a few steps, pitched him headlong over the rail and into the sea. He cried out as the shock of the cold water revived him, but as strong a swimmer as he was, his plate armour was stronger: he thrashed madly for only a moment before it hauled him down like an iron hand, beneath the waves and across the border of the living world.

"No place for weak men in the bloodguard?" Kellan repeated. "I've just done my duty, then. Unless there are any other weak men I need to see to on this deck. Do I see any more weak men?"

The bloodguards looked to each other in alarm, trying and failing to conceal their fear. It was a familiar enough emotion, but they found themselves suddenly on the unfamiliar end of it.

"None," said one of the men at last. "No more weak men."

"Good," said Kellan. "You have a name, son?"

"Stag."

With measured distaste Kellan shook a fistful of teeth from his bloody, gloved hand and clapped it on the man's shoulder, wiping the blood and spittle off on the edge of his cloak. "Stag. Your truename, Stag. Not the name your lady-love there calls you to make you sound like a harder man than you are." He indicated the convulsing body on the deck with a lazy swing of his boot.

"A-Astagar," said the man, gone completely still in Kellan's grip, fighting for composure.

"Astagar, hm," said Kellan. "Good name. Good rugged Vosi stock, no doubt. You'll have to forgive my friend, here. He's a cobblestone child, raised in the Iron City. You know how soft the city-men can get."

"I'm not soft," Rasten protested. "Except when I'm rowed half to death, and then taken by surprise, and *then* outnumbered five to one."

Kellan shrugged. "Excuses," he said. "And soft men with excuses, I'm sure you'll agree, need gentle introductions to a noble company such as ours. I'd like you to see that my friend's introduction is a little more gentle next time."

Astagar nodded and backed away slowly. Kellan clutched Rasten by the shoulder and pulled him free of the other men, leading him cautiously away. They nearly stumbled over the quaking body on the deck: that one was drowning now in an inch of rainwater, or his own blood, or both, jerking and shaking in eerie silence as his flattened nose did nothing to keep his ruined face above the water. One of the bloodguard bent down, as if to right him, but the mangled and shattered jaw gave him pause, and he drew back with what he tried to play off as callous indifference. The others were unreadable as Kellan and Rasten made a cautious retreat toward the ship's sterncastle.

"If you're not gentle in the future," Kellan called as he slipped away, "I'm like to be less gentle next time, too."

"By the Chain," said Rasten when they'd made some distance, "what do you think you're doing?"

"I don't rightly know," said Kellan. "It's not in my nature to get involved. I just had this strange feeling—"

"Those were bloodguards!" Ras breathed. "Ashimar's personal bloodguards!"

"So are we," Kellan reminded him. "Best you start acting like one."

"And what, murder people with my bare hands?"

Kellan shrugged. "If it comes to that, aye. Maybe not when it can be helped. But those men would've killed you. Not today, perhaps, but marked you so you were the first to go."

"You don't know that."

"I have a strong feeling," said Kellan. "Ashimar had two men too many, shipping out of port. We're that two men, or we were; and he was none too pleased about us. Now that we've evened the count, there's a chance he's—"

Kellan fell silent on the first step to the mast-deck. There in the sterncastle, a small door had swung open. The space within was dark as death, but there in the doorway, the gleaming metallic face of a weeping child watched with silent interest. As the red moon slipped from behind the stormclouds, its rays kissed the metal and the face took on a warm and unsettling brilliance. Rasten caught sight of it and fell silent, too, just as he began to speak in answer.

"Come," said Ashimar, and they went.

The cabin within was large enough to be a captain's cabin, but unfurnished and unadorned in any way, save a wooden table on which vast maps of the Travalaithi empire were laid out, painstakingly charted on whole sides of vellum. A naked armour stand stood in the far corner, ready to receive Ashimar's immaculate metal skin if ever he chose to part with it. Over the crossbar of its shoulders hung a greatsword in a red leather scabbard; its jewelled hilt was the only sign of ornament or opulence anywhere in the little room. Ashimar led the two men in and left the door ajar just enough to let the moonlight in with them.

"Those two men were with me a long time," said the Weeping Man.

Kellan bowed his head humbly. "I'm so very sorry that's how things had to go."

"A waste of my best warrior," said Ashimar. "Had you given him but a moment's hesitation, you would have seen."

"Precisely why I didn't," said Kellan. "Not something I wanted to see. Killing's a fine art, aye, but I've no wish to be the canvas."

"This is the second time you have impressed me, soldier," said Ashimar. "You know when to suffer cruelty—and also when to dispense it." He gestured at Kellan's sword. "You were armed. You didn't see fit to use it?"

"Swords aren't much good against this fine armour," he said. "If they hadn't had their helmets off, I would've had a hard time of it. Besides which, these men have seen their friends run through before, no doubt. I'm no match for five of 'em. They had to see something they'd never seen before. Only hope is to make them think twice."

"I expect they will not forget it," said Ashimar. "You may have a place in my bloodguard yet." He gestured to one of the maps on the table with a gauntleted hand. "We have made excellent time. We will change our rowers when we are free of the shoals, and reach Seton within another day. You will lead me south to this place where Celithrand slipped through your fingers, and I will take up his trail. When the traitor is dead, you may consider my offer permanent. Know that it is an offer seldom made to those not born into the life."

Kellan squinted at the grey lines of the map in the darkness. "Thank you, milord. But I've heard tell the druids of old are wise in the ways of the wood," he said. "Even the Havenari couldn't catch him. Suppose he eludes us."

"Then you should consider nothing permanent," said Ashimar. "But I have faith you will not disappoint me."

Kellan nodded and tried his best to look menacing and obedient at the same time. Rasten, at his side the whole time, was silent and cast as small a shadow as he could. Matted with sweat and blood, beginning to tremble with exhaustion, he was a stark contrast to the others' composure. Ashimar stood so motionless, for his part, that when he shifted his crying child's face to look on the weary Cerulean, it seemed as if the whole room shifted to draw him to its centre.

"And you," Ashimar breathed. "Well? What have you to say in your own defense?"

"In my def—" Rasten began with indignance, then caught his words.

"You are a fool," said Ashimar. "You walked into a trap. You owe this man your life."

"They wouldn't have killed me," said Rasten with fragile confidence. "Ordeals of initiation into brutal—"

"They?" said Ashimar. "They wouldn't have had to. You are clumsy, gullible, and weak. I would have killed you myself." He turned away, paced the length of the room.

"I might yet," he added.

Rasten bristled but did not speak.

"I cannot imagine," Ashimar went on, "how you wronged the Imperator or his Harper to be condemned to my care. You lack the spine for insubordination. You lack the ambition for treachery. You took to the oars like a beaten slave, poured out all of your strength and your use to me, and then walked to your own death like a sheep to the block. You seem utterly unremarkable, soldier. One more meaningless face in a sea of a hundred thousand fighting men. Your living and dying are without merit. Perhaps that was your crime."

"I'm *kind*," Rasten said, though he didn't say it kindly.

Ashimar froze, turned. As he advanced, Kellan stepped away from Rasten's side. He had saved the fool's life once, on an impulse he could not fully understand within himself. He would not do so again.

"I was a kind man," said Rasten. "That was my crime. My only crime. And I've had nothing but trouble for it! I was a tower guard—and a strong fighter, too, whatever you think just happened on deck."

"Do not take that tone—"

"I'm dead anyway," said Rasten, his patience gone and his anger driven by fear. "You made up your mind before you brought me out of the rain. One of us is a bloodthirsty monster, which suits your needs perfectly. But one of us was foisted on you for the terrible sin of being kind to a girl who never had kindness from anyone. You already know which one of us is bloodguard material. It's the man who leaves people's blood…and teeth, and jaws…all strewn around your deck. It's not me. You want a new bloodguard? You're right to want a killer, a butcher who murders in the Imperator's name. Not a man who got thrown into exile for making friends with his daughter."

Kellan had heard of no daughter. The news might have shocked him, if he were not already astonished by Ashimar's sudden speed and strength. The table between the two men was now upended; now Ashimar was at his throat; now Rasten, whose bullish frame was hardly light, was off the ground and hard against the wall, his boots dangling, pinned up ferociously where Ashimar's grip held him. The Weeping Man's face was so close to Rasten that the startled soldier could see his true eyes glistening in the shadows behind the fine mesh of the mask.

"You are lying to me," said Ashimar.

"I swear it!" Rasten protested, his voice rising. "I swear it's why I was taken from the citadel. They keep her chained up like a princess in a storybook. Locked away in that awful tower. And I dared to speak to her through the curtain. I dared to become her friend. The only friend of a girl with no friends. For that kindness, I'm stripped of my rank and home, torn away from my wife—from the woman I hope to marry. I'm put on a damned scummy scow of a boat to be chained up like one of Jordac's thugs, rowed half to death for a day straight without a crust of bread, beaten nigh the other half to death by my own comrades, and rescued to my own indignity, only to be beat to death again. All for a woman. It's madness. And not even the woman I mean to lie with, and that's the worst of it. Not even for the woman where they might say, 'he died for true love.' Just for a poor sweet stranger who needed some damned kindness in this miserable age."

He stopped to catch his breath, but found very little of it with Ashimar's hand tightening around his throat. The Weeping Man was motionless and unrelenting.

"Well, I've…had enough," Rasten went on, wheezing. "It's kindness that killed me. If you're going to put…a sword through me, or throw me off to drown like…a ship-born bastard, milord, get it done. And when my wife-to-be…asks why I'm dead, you tell her…I was a friend to Illyria, and cared for a girl…no one else seemed to, and that's why I'm dead."

With a steady calm, Ashimar lowered the soldier back to the cabin floor.

"You will tell no one of the girl," said Ashimar. "You will forget her name now and forever. Both of you."

"What name?" said Kellan—then immediately regretted it.

"There is no living daughter," Ashimar hissed.

Rasten shrugged as bravely as he could. "If there is no daughter," he ventured, "then I could have committed no crime."

Ashimar let go of him and turned back to his pacing. He seemed to turn the words over in his mind for a long time before he spoke again.

"Any man who tries his hand on you has my blessing," said Ashimar. He turned his gaze to Kellan. "My new guide dog will not save you again."

"As you wish, milord," said Kellan.

"You will each take the beds and provisions of the men you killed, if they be better than your own."

"Yes, milord," they said together.

"You will clean your trash off my deck, strip him and dump him over the side. Bring his equipment and personal belongings to me. The bloodguards will show you where to take rations. I want you rested by the time we are free of the shoals. Then you will trade the scourge and the drum until we make landfall."

"Yes, milord."

Ashimar fixed Rasten with what might have been, beneath the bawling child's face, any number of expressions—all of them intense.

"And you will not speak of these matters again," he finished. "Not to any living soul."

Rasten nodded timidly.

"Of course."

"That's all." The Weeping Man turned his back and it was clear they were meant to leave.

Outside above the command deck, the moons were in conflict, and every bit as fickle as the men had said. The rain that was deepening to a downpour when they entered had nearly abated, though the stormclouds off the bow forespoke its return with renewed intensity some time before dawn. The storm seemed almost to wail until Kellan realized the wails were too human to be wind in the sails. On the mast-deck below, where a hatch had been opened, the bloodguards were changing out the rowers, hurling the spent men and women into the icy deep and no doubt bringing up fresh rowers from where they had lain in the ship's narrow hold. One of the bloodguards, the one called Astagar, approached them as they emerged.

"You're both alive," said Astagar. "Seems he's decided to keep you. Welcome aboard."

"Thank you kindly," said Kellan, as both men tried to forget their eagerness to kill each other only a few short minutes past. "We're changing out the prisoners," said Astagar. "You'll come down and join us."

"No. I won't." Kellan shook his head. "One of you's worth ten of those sods, am I right?"

"Twenty," said Astagar, somewhat proudly.

"Then I've thrown my share off already. I'm done throwing men off this boat, and so is my friend here."

"Now listen," Astagar began. Kellan silenced him by clapping his massive hands over the smaller man's biceps, an exaggerated gesture of friendship. The fingers enveloped them nearly all the way round. Kellan's smile was lifeless.

"Ah, second wind," he said. "I suppose I've enough strength left to give the sharks and morays one more course, eh?"

"Come on," Astagar said with the sincerest smile he could muster. "We was only joking."

"I know a good joke about the man in heavy plate who tried to swim for shore," said Kellan, smiling. "You might've already heard how it ends. But I swear, it gets funnier every time I tell it."

Astagar began to back away.

"I'm hungry," said Rasten, matter-of-factly. Kellan raised his eyebrows.

"We'll part out the rations, soon as we're done with the rowers," said Astagar. "I'll come find you." He clambered back down to the mast-deck and slipped out of sight as quickly as he could. When he was gone, Rasten leaned hard against the wall, slid down to a sitting position, and let out an exhausted laugh in spite of himself.

Kellan looked down at him. "What's wrong with you? *Kindness*, he says. You nearly got us both killed. Five or six times over."

Rasten caught his breath and smiled. "I was dead already," he said. "Dead men have no more reason to lie. And I just cheated that death with my kindness, thank you very much."

Kellan shrugged. "How do you figure?" he asked. "Given, I mean, that you'd be meat for the sharks if I hadn't just tore two men apart for you."

"See, that's the difference between you and me," said Rasten. "You won the Weeping Man's favour with brutality. Works well enough, I suppose, but hardly a challenge. Ashimar's the cruellest man in the Empire, they say—worse than Master General Harrod, and I'll tell you, the women in the East name their girdle-knives after him. Cruelty's a short downhill road to his heart, I wager. Now I didn't mean to tell him the whole truth, but I did. Did you see how it changed him in a moment? I haven't shown him a lick of what he wants in a servant, but lo and behold, deep down, even that rusty old statue has a heart. There's a man in that armour, same as anybody else."

"Oh, get off it."

"A lover. A poet and an aesthete."

"*You're* a poet," said Kellan, like it was an insult. "I didn't want to speak up for you, but I did. I didn't want to make enemies over you, but I did. To hear Ashimar speak of it, the worthiest man of us all is the one lying dead on the deck. Some would say that's an injustice. But the world is full of injustice, and today that injustice kept you alive."

"You did no injustice by saving my life," said Rasten. "Thank you."

"Don't thank me for a thing I didn't choose to do," grumbled Kellan. "I was half-asleep at the drum. Not thinking clearly. Poor judgment."

Rasten's smile was benevolent. "Perhaps, deep down, it pains you to see a kind poet murdered too."

Kellan spat on the deck. "I hate men like you."

"Men like me?" Rasten said.

"Soft men. Gentle, pleasant, *kind* men. Poets. No use for 'em."

Rasten laughed at that. "D'you know what I think?"

"I'm about to, amn't I?"

"I think it's men like you who need men like me the most."

Kellan sighed. "If I ever needed men like you, I'd lie with women."

Rasten was quiet for a long moment. "But you don't?"

"Mm."

"So does that mean—"

"I've thrown enough men off this boat for one day," said Kellan, and that was the end of it.

3 Teurmaunt ⟪34⟫3

Derest Lysandra,

Ink and fine paper I had brout to write you when I reached the Fingrun mines, and barely past Carmac I was bifore I broke the seale on the box and thought I would remember me unto you with loving thoughts to you and the baby.

But there has been no peace with these

soldiers, and no moment to write You all these 8 dayes, for we have been hard at the saddle, clamorus and unbearable lowd

as the men had an unexpected chance to fill their wine skins at Carmac, and exawsted their voices and wine together these dayes on the road.

Why, you ask, did we ride east to Carmac when I mean to go west? well the loss of the east mines vexes so the Master of Iron that he made imediate response to the Legions of the Blade. and in Carmac lies the fastest dispatch to Master General Harrod and the front of the war. There being seasoned & hardy Riders & coursers much in demaund who change horses at ten league posts and carry news like the Wind.

Master General Thurmod has gone East to meet him with more men of the Schield. but will be many dayes moving a large force. as I learned from trying to move only these few lazy soldiers on their way that I could reach Fingrun & dispatch to you this letter in all haste.

Not in many yeres have I been eager for this return trip, but owing much to your Praise and Love it is a changed place or I a changed man.

My recolection of a drab and great Keep on the white cliffs withowt lite or warmth is much changed. It is at once both a warmer place and also colder to return to. Colder be cause it is far from you and warmer be cause I see in those mines a wealth of Iron that will provyde much more glad a future for you, for our child and no less for me.

& I again am happy to imagine myself some day rich. Miserible lords and vasils I have known many & perhaps I had been one of them. but your love kinddles in me such joy in my povertie that can only wax greater in prosperitie. Both palaces and barrows are filled with treasures & gold, they say. Though I might in good fortune fill the barrow of my days with gold, it remains a barrow still. Only you have made it a palace full of lyfe.

So from Carmac we set out west by the olde Vosthome road, where was no way to reach my letter to you. When we passed through Kelms Cott there had been much news to send of the traytor Celithrand in the West and so there was no ryder for to send you on my letter. At last I am arrived at the Mine and can dispatch a man from my escort to bring my words to the messengers and so to you.

 I rejoyce I can aquaint you my Health is well & spirit high. The season will pass quickly and the winter I will be warm in your love. I expect to riturn with the thaw & Tur willing will stay from then to see my son or dauter, and bestow on him in equal share what love I have each day for you. Keep well yourself, and do not worry your heart over much about the price of goods. If you want for any thing, see to the Warden I have furnished him with some silver for you. He will look to your wellfare.

 He also knows how to reach me bc Grand Army dispatch now that I am arrived. If you would write me, please send on another sheaf of something for my pen whatever the cost. I feel I shal write you often as I can. As you can see I lack practise but hope by the time I riturn I shal write as well with my West hand as ever I did with the East. I subscribe myself your loving servant and worshipfull man

       Rendon.

The letter was, indeed, scrawled on a smooth, stone-polished linen paper that was more often the province of men twice as wealthy and thrice as literate. But where the words were weak, the letters themselves were elegantly drawn, owing not to the laziness of experience, but meticulously measured as Rendon strained to make them legible with his remaining hand. The scroll had survived its passage and the storm through which it had come in pristine condition, as if the ink and seal had been wet mere moments ago.

With delicate hands, she turned it over, and could not contain her smile. Looking up at Lysandra—that is, at Madge Dunny—with great admiration, Baran simply said: "This will do nicely."

Madge's mouth was tight with pride, though it was not quite a smile. "The couriers are fast," she said, "and that news is fresh. The third, it was written. Three days ago."

"The location of their fastest couriers," said Baran. "News of what they carry. Movements of the Legions. All this will be useful. And the loss of the eastern mines has been deeply felt. That should cheer the hearts of the men who lost friends and brothers taking it."

In the shadows, Catrine shifted uncomfortably. It had been thirteen days since the morning they'd last met—since the evening Rasten vanished aboard the *Providence*, stolen away by the enemy, perhaps never to be seen again. That Madge was eager to be rid of her lover was abundantly clear. The resentment between them pained her so upon hearing his words, which were not so well-formed as Rasten's, but seemed no less sincere. She found herself wondering if he, too, was a good man, in spite of the ill deeds she knew he had done.

"I will write back tonight and send it tomorrow," said Madge. "If there is anything you would like to draw out of him—"

"Too soon to tell, I think," said Baran. "We'll bring this information to the Mage directly. With both Master Generals and both Legions in the East, an under-guarded and over-staffed prison mine in the West may prove a tempting target, if we can cross the countryside quietly. But I am loath to make assumptions. I've been wrong about his plans before. This man will be a wealth of information—as fine a success as the Vairhurst Widows have ever had—and if we storm the mine we cannot guarantee his safety."

"He means nothing to me," said Madge. "Let him be slaughtered, if it please the Mage."

"I will pass on the sentiment," said Baran. "Keep up your letters in the meantime. The state of the prisoners and the movements of the troops are most important to us now."

"What of Celithrand?" asked Madge. "Rumour has it he eluded them in the West, quite spectacularly. Summoned a pack of wild wolves from the wood who tore the soldiers to pieces and carried him to safety."

"Easy," said Baran. "The old Owl does not concern us. He has nothing to do with the Uprising—not with any of us, at least. He's a champion of the people—especially to the Oldborn who remember—and he'd be the strongest rival claimant to the Spire, if he gave a damn about such things. I suppose he'd be some use as a figurehead, but the Mage seems to have the hearts of the people well in hand already. Hunting down Celithrand is little more than due diligence for the Imperator right now. Frankly, we can use the distraction. We think, but don't know for certain, that's why Ashimar sailed west." She fixed her eyes on Catrine. "We'd be more sure what the Scourge was up to, if your own dear lover wrote letters home."

Catrine opened her mouth to answer, but a dozen competing phrases collided in the doorway of her pursed lips, and none could pass all the way through.

"Anything that takes Ashimar out of warring alongside the Legions is welcome," said Madge. "But this does put him closer to Fingrun, which could go badly for any attack on the Mines."

"I don't expect that attack to come before Yearsend," said Baran. "If it comes at all. If Rendon continues to give us sweet wine like this, his success may be more useful to us than his failure."

"Give us wine, Lady?" asked Madge.

"One of the Mage's proverbs," said Baran. "How do you tell a wise man from a fool?"

Madge shook her head, and Baran looked to Catrine.

"Give each of them a magic cow that gives wine for milk," said Catrine, "and return the next week to see who is eating beef."

"Just so," said Baran. "As long as the lady Lysandra can keep Rendon's obedient little pen flowing, he's worth more for the wine than the flesh."

Madge frowned. "I grow tired of him. I thought the attack on the mines would be the end of my—service. And the end, perhaps, of our worries about a baby that does not exist."

"Be not so quick to dismiss him," said Baran. "I need not tell you what misfortunes the Vairhurst Widows have endured for the cause. The two of you are among the luckiest women I have known—she, because she loves her target, and you, because you need have very little contact with him. There are widows with brutish men, ugly or cruel, who would give anything for your kind of luck. Keep up your letters as long as you can, count your favours and fortunes, and let us worry about the rest."

"And what should I do about Rasten?" asked Catrine.

"Be patient and keep up appearances," said Baran. "He has been gone nearly a fortnight with no word. The *Providence* will be slower by far coming home under sail than she was going with a belly full of slaves—but she's a fast ship, and Haveïl is not far. If they are swift in their errand, he may come home any day. Give him one more week."

"And if—if he does not return?" Catrine's mind flooded with reasons why she might never see him again.

"I will speak to the Mage and see," said Baran. "Most likely he will send you back to the graveyard to start again. I hope, for your sake and ours, you are as lucky the second time as you were the first."

There was little enough to be said after that. All three women were dissatisfied with their lots, all three had much to say about the nature of duty, and each wondered to herself in her own way whether duty was an inherently manly virtue—that is to say, a foolish one. But war had a way of making men out of children in very short order; and if even they were not immune to such a fate, no woman of Selik could expect much more.

By the light of three candles alone, hedged in by bolts of fabric stacked on shelves high as the hold, the passage of time aboard the *Wyrmsbolt* was hard to reckon. The women dined on soft cheese and a fresh cake Catrine had baked that morning at the great-house—a desperate concession on her part to make the conspiracy feel more familial. Necessity had made them sisters, she thought; only they didn't feel very sisterly. Owing to the lateness of the hour, and the early sunset of a late season, the women were still planning the time for their next meeting when Hendec came down through the hatch, lowering himself into the hold with a pigeon-scroll clenched between his rolled lips. The three women fell instantly silent.

"He's set the place," Baran breathed.

"I imagine so," said Hendec. "I can't read a word of it, of course. But there's no mistaking his mark." He passed the tiny slip of parchment to Baran, his hands dwarfing hers; as she unrolled it to read its contents, the other women saw only a single rune, marked in the old Selikhan style on the outward side of the scroll.

"What does it say?" asked Catrine.

Baran took a breath to steady herself. "He wants to meet. Tonight. Now."

"How is that possible?" asked Madge. "Would he dare come himself, within a day's ride of the city?"

"Of course not," Baran said hastily. "He leads the forces in the East against the Legions of the Blade. He will send a rider, his fastest rider." But it was too late; both women knew in that moment that Jordac was come to the heart of the Empire itself—though for what purpose, none could guess.

"I should like to meet him one day," offered Catrine.

"Out of the question," said Baran. "Hendec, see the girls safely ashore. Send this one with Odi—" here she gestured to Catrine— "but I'd be obliged if you'd take the lovely Lysandra home yourself."

"We can take care of ourselves," said Catrine.

"You, Catrine, live among lords and merchants," said Hendec. "Go alone if it pleases you. But Greymantlehouse is smack in the heart of the Westle. Beggars' Alley is no place for a young woman after dark."

"I'll be glad," said Madge, "for the company of a man with no designs on me, after all these false husbands, rakish neighbours, sailors who watch me come and go to this boat like a common doxy."

"I'm your man, then," said Hendec. "Let's go. Not—not that you're any less than pretty, mind you."

"I'm sick of being pretty," said Madge, "and sicker still of being told it."

"Your flirtations can happen elsewhere," snapped Baran. "All of you, get out. Out with you." She made no movement from her seat at the small table, made no indication of what she was about to do or which direction she was headed, until Hendec had led the two women out of the hold and down to the dock. Odi met them on the wharf; his usual friends would be expecting him soon, but they were alone just long enough to speak freely. Hendec handed off Catrine, who seemed truly grateful for the company of the grubby little man, and he took Madge's arm like a proud escort as they strode at their own pace up the Saltway. Only then did Baran slip away to prepare for her meeting.

In the shadow of the tall ships as they came up from the harbour, Hendec cast a glance backwards toward the *Wyrmsbolt*.

"She seems happy enough," he said.

"I'm glad for that," said Madge, keeping pace with his long strides through hurried steps. "But I could stand to hear less of it. Makes my work all the harder."

"I can't even begin to imagine," said Hendec. "It's a stroke of genius, if you ask me. But something about the whole business doesn't sit right with me."

Madge sized him up shrewdly. "You're a romantic at heart," she said, "though you're a soldier and you don't like your man-friends to know it."

Hendec shrugged. "I'm a man with old-fashioned ideas about women, that's all."

"No," said Madge. "It's not just that. You know you can be trusted with me, for instance, because you love another."

"That's not fair," said Hendec.

"Of course it's not fair," said Madge. "But I'm a spy. It's part of what I do."

"And a good one."

"I'm better than doe-eyed Catrine, at least," said Madge, smiling for perhaps the first time since Rendon had left. "So, who is she?"

Hendec shrugged. "No one."

"Not to you."

"She may as well be," said Hendec. "A village girl who loves another."

Madge smiled. "And you are a long way from your village. What's her name?"

Hendec hesitated, waited until they had passed off the Saltway onto a less busy street, as if he did not trust the city itself to hear her name. "Melia," he said at last. "Melia, the miller's daughter back home."

"The miller's daughter," Madge echoed. "I've heard a good merry tale that starts off with one of those." But the way his face fell, she saw that she had wounded him.

"It doesn't matter," said Hendec. "I rode with the Havenari in days before this. We kept the peace in the Outlands. We'd ride home in the fall, just when the leaves started turning. We wintered there, more than a few years. The trails get snowed out and it'd be 'round to Romaunt, some years, before we'd be gone again. But the thaw always came, and I'd always leave again."

"It's none of my business," said Madge.

"A woman gets tired of waiting through the seasons," he said. "The year after our last true Captain left us, we didn't even make it home. She took up with a mere boy, a farmer's son, Ard. I can't say I blame her, and I shouldn't be surprised. A farmer, what does that tell you? A man rooted, year-round, to the same little patch of soil. Never was much hope for me.

So, aye. My heart's in another place. That's why they trust a new recruit with an unaccompanied lady."

"Perhaps it's for the best," she said. "I'm sad to say your story still affects me. But you're a part of the cause, now, for good or ill. Best to keep all that you love far away from the fight, if you can."

They kept the Lornock hedge on their right as they skirted the tower, and made their way in silence for a time as processions of black-armoured soldiers made their way from company halls and barracks onto the wide cobbled Iron Road. Where the Ceruleans and many of the city guard carried sword and dagger alone, the men (for the Travalaithi soldiers were all men) who mustered to march east were carrying the broad-boarded shields and clattering longspears of foot soldiers who expected a hard fight ahead of them.

"The geese are on the wing," observed Hendec, once they had passed over the Iron Road and come into the dodgy streets behind the Tavern District. "Perhaps you are right. Things are changing too fast. Have you family?"

"I do," said Madge. "An old, blind father, and two sisters living. One younger than some of the Hedge-girls with their flowers. And also two brothers and a third sister, all dead in the fighting."

"I'm sorry," said Hendec.

"It's the living ones I keep in mind," said Madge. "Not much to be done for the dead. But I don't ever want my youngest to learn what a Harrod knife is, or to lay eyes on him it's named for."

"Gods," said Hendec. "I hadn't even thought of that. Thank you for putting that into my head."

"It's the way of things, now, in the East. Is your lady-love in the East?" Hendec shook his head. "West," he said. "Some nothing village in Haveïl. Far side of the Empire from Harrod and his men, small blessings."

"That's the best place for her, then," said Madge. "Safest place to be in the whole Empire right now, unless your name is Celithrand."

Hendec stopped in his tracks.

"Celithrand? What about him?"

"He's guilty of treason, supposedly," said Madge. "They're saying he taught his sorcery to the Mage, which we know just isn't true. If you ask me, the Imperator simply wants no one left alive with the clout to contest his rule."

"Aye, I know that. But you had something specific on your mind, just now."

Madge shrugged. "Word just came he was seen, somewhere in the West. The Imperator has let Ashimar and his bloodguard off the post to hunt him down and wipe out all those who gave him shelter. That's where Catrine's stupid lover has gone off to; you should hear her whinge about it."

Hendec's face darkened as he seized her by the wrist with no great gentleness and prepared to bolt. "Come on," he snapped. "Quickly."

He set off at a run, ducking through alleys whose twists and bends he was still learning. It was not hard to find Greymantlehouse, which towered in the profane shadow of the Shadewall and stood watch over most of the slums in the area. Her room was accessed through the building's small inner court; true to his duty, he took her as far as the tarnished copper gate that opened to the rooms within.

"There, you're home," he said. "I have to go."

"Go?" said Madge. "Where?"

"Home."

"What?"

"I have to warn them. I saw him. I know where he's going."

It was her turn to grip his arm tightly. "Slow down," she said. "What's happening? Saw him, who?"

Hendec took a deep breath, and willed himself to be calm, but the racing blood that thundered in his ears would not be slowed.

"Widowvale is the village," he breathed. "It's Melia's village. It's where Ashimar's headed. I have to go."

"They've been gone a fortnight," said Madge. "You won't catch them."

"I may yet," said Hendec, "if I can get one of their coursers."

"Steal a post-horse? From the Grand Army? Are you mad?"

"They're the fastest horses in the Empire, and branded for the couriers," he said. "I might be able to get a fresh one at every post, if they don't look too close—or if I'm willing to fight for one."

Madge pulled at his arm. "This is nonsense. You'll be caught, you'll be tortured, you'll give up everything. It's not your own life you're playing with!"

Hendec turned back long enough to wrest her fingers off his arm with apologetic force. "I'm going," he said. "I joined the Havenari to protect the people I love. I thought the Havenari would stand up to them, but it seems they're just one more branch of the Grand Army after all. So I joined the Uprising, to do the fighting the Havenari won't. And if I abandon the people I love to the Grand Army, or to whatever damned thing Ashimar's bloodguard is, if I fail to protect the commonfolk from the cruelty of powerful men—well, that's what this whole revolt is about, isn't it?"

He clutched her hands in a gentle way that nevertheless made clear his immovable strength to her. "I'm going," he said again. "I'm sorry."

Madge's face clouded with terror, then anger; but long weeks with Rendon had taught her composure, and she calmed herself with a sigh.

"Wait," she said, a little reluctantly.

"I'm done waiting."

"If I can't stop you," she urged, "I can help."

Hendec was already poised to run; his head was leaning in that direction even as he turned.

"I'm listening."

"One of the Widows, she has a key to the coursers' stablehouse," she said hastily. "The one on the East Road, mind you…bottom of the hill after you've left the Gate. You know where it is?"

"I know where," said Hendec, a little suspiciously.

"The guards change shift just before sunrise. Make yourself ready, gather your things, and I'll go for the key."

"What things?" he asked. "My sword. Maybe some water, or a flask of wineseed for the road. No other things."

"We'll meet at the stables just before dawn," she said. "You take the key, you slip in, leave no damage, leave no dead men. If you fight for a horse, they'll have riders behind you in minutes. Go by stealth, and it could be hours or days before they count a horse missing."

"Why now are you—"

"Go! There's not much time." For all Baran had said about an unaccompanied woman, Madge seemed ready and willing to brave the trip back down Beggars' Alley alone.

Hendec nodded. "Tell Baran and the others I'm sorry. Tell them it's all for the same cause."

She offered him one more grave, hasty nod, before she turned and ran. He did the same, though he had not far to go, and not much to gather. It was clear she had rushed him for her own sake, not for his. He knew all too well what value a military key would have to Jordac—securing one might be the whole purpose of another Vairhurst widow—and he could only imagine the hard time Madge would have convincing them to hand it over. He resolved to leave at dawn, whether or not she could help him.

With time and silence to think, he had his doubts Madge would succeed—but it brought him comfort, at least, that she was willing to try. He had made his way alone in the world for a long time, and faith in others was a thing that came only reluctantly to him. But there in the dark he did his best to stay hopeful. Perhaps she really could get it, after all. She had served the Uprising now for longer than he had; she knew the measure of its operatives and knew more about them than he did. And while he hoped in the end she would do nothing to jeopardize her own position, he had to admit she was a smooth talker and a fine liar, if it came to that.

EIGHT

BARAN'S KNUCKLES WERE WHITE on the tiller as she ran the boat into the reeds. The unnaturally perfect circle of the Shadewall extended well out into the bay, its flawless black outline broken only by a single gap several hundred yards across. It was here that the city's entire naval traffic came and went, and where ships could sometimes jam together in long queues when the Imperial fleet was in harbour, while the fishing boats sailed lazily through the yawning Seagate. In the starry hours of early night, it was mostly emptied of traffic, and the tiny flat-bottomed skiff had made its way easily out and around the westernmost gate tower, close to the wall and far beyond the reach of the knarrs and cogs that passed cordially across the center of the gate channel.

Beyond the Shadewall, all along the silty promontory that chased it out into the bay, a squalid little town of fishermen's hovels and floating slums had sprung up. While good land close to the city was more than these rude folk could afford, the sodden strip of marsh grass and stagnant water that ran along the wall's base was barely considered solid ground at all. It was here, to the shack city popularly known as Mudtown, that that Baran had brought her little skiff, bouncing uncomfortably across the waves that wracked the shore beyond the city's ironclad heart. Although there was more strength in her lean arms than met the eye, no amount of it could steady the light craft in the tumult of the fickle tide, tugged greedily back and forth under two jealous moons. Shallow as the boat was, she had brought it to rest quite accidentally in the briny mud, surrounded by salt-choked grasses and hardy stalks of coastal ashweed. She had come, as requested, in the garb of a fishwife, and in coarse throwaway shoes so that she might not track the telltale mud of Mudtown back to the *Wyrmsbolt*.

A little ways inland on the narrow spit, past the first long row of wind-creaking shacks, a wide stagnant pond had pooled in a sunken hollow on the rare occasion of a perfectly aligned double-tide, and lay in perfect stillness until the proper alignment of the moons came again to wash it out. The bogflowers of Haukmere had crept their way along the coast and seemed almost eager to surround the brackish pond, their sickly ivory blossoms crowding at the water's edge and sending up a foul stink that overwhelmed with ease the cool, musty scent of the still pondwater. It was here, Baran knew, that her master had lately come to take his ease, no doubt to unburden himself of the terrible weights and pressures of greatness.

Jordac of Travalaith, the chief architect and driving force of the Mages' Uprising, sat like a motionless stone in the muddy soil, hidden beneath a heavy cloak so that only the points of his dark eyes glistened. Before his lowered face, inches above the still water, a cloud of fireflies danced in the fading light, playing and flickering over the pond. With stillness and patience, Jordac had lowered his face so close to the water that their signals in the night sparked in his glassy eyes like tiny motes of eerie gold flame.

Jordac did not lift his eyes to look upon her as she approached—only raised his heavy eyebrows in acknowledgement.

"And lo, when the thanes came to Sarvalen," he said, "they found him splayed upon the ground, undone at the belly by the kiss of Gritiam the Harvester. And he called for their hands, and they put him up on his feet, though the red yawning of war was upon his breath. And in the last refrain of his life, rejoiced he then upon the grass, and danced until the meadow was bloody with his joy. For at the last when death had come, he was no lord of war, nor tyrant of the great Verdant Waste, but only a man, a conqueror who had ruled too long without dancing."

Baran listened with absolute deference to his words, though she knew not what to make of them. The popular Saga of Sarvalen was well-known among skalds and scholars—but the old tales of heroes were not what she had come to study.

"They're dying, you know," said Jordac. "The fireflies."

"As you say, sire," she said, following his unbroken gaze to the flickering insects upon the water.

"They're warm-weather insects," he said. "Hardier than their southern cousins, perhaps. But they won't survive the winter here. Their eggs hatch in summer, and the little ones hibernate, like tiny bears. The next year, having grown, they mate and then die. They don't feed as adults, not these ones. They reproduce and then die, and that is their whole purpose."

"Sire, we need to speak of the Widows—"

"Shh." He silenced her with a wave of his broad hand, snatched at one of the fireflies as it eluded him. "This is important if you are to learn."

"If you say so, sire."

"They dwindle in autumn," he said. "They diminish and die as the hoarfrost creeps over the marsh. Having spawned, their life's purpose is fulfilled. They need do no more. And yet as they freeze, as they starve, they are unburdened of all that they were. All they were called on to be, for the good of their crawling kin. And in their last days, with their mating displays long behind them, they dance only for the sake of dancing."

"They're quite beautiful."

"They are more beautiful," said Jordac, "when you know what it is they do. But why do kings and insects alike dance upon their deathbeds? That, Baran, is a mystery to me."

He pulled himself up from muddy knees and, reaching down, retrieved a corked bottle from the mud. The glass was cloudy and crudely made—no work of an artisan—but the inside of the bottle pulsed and glowed with an inner fire from the insects trapped within.

"Why did Sarvalen dance himself to death?" asked Baran. Jordac smiled beneath his hood and pointed approvingly.

"Exactly," he said. "The world is full of echoes."

"My lord—" she protested.

"I'm not your lord," said Jordac.

"The Vairhurst Widows—"

"Do you know the song of the Fire-bug and the Ember?" he asked. "They sing it in the North."

Baran frowned. "No."

"More's the pity," said Jordac. "I've quite forgotten all the words, myself. It's a Banlanders' song. A little firefly of some kind has lost its way into the frost fields, and sees the last glowing ember of a dying fire, and falls in love with it. Sentimental stuff, but buried in it are the secrets of navigating the Northern roads." He hummed a few notes absently, in a singing voice that was on pitch but not altogether pleasant. "I should dearly love to hear it again someday."

"I'll make a note of it, sire," she said. "Perhaps one of the men knows it. Calvon, the blind man who sometimes plays Odi at the king's table, is a Northerner, a skald. Perhaps he's heard it."

Jordac smiled at the thought. "Perhaps he has. But—you had a report to deliver, Commander?"

Baran took the pause of a full breath to re-center her thoughts, and then told him all that had happened with the Vairhurst Widows—which pairs had found mates and which had been forced to leave them, which troop movements had been reported, whither the soldiers being deployed that very night were being sent. She saved the difficult matter of Madge and Catrine for the very end, handing over Rendon's letter to him at last, and upon reading it he listened to the whole problem of Catrine and Rasten with patient silence. On the matter of the dancing insects, he had been aggressive in his interruptions; here, on the matter of the civil insurrection he supposedly led, he had little to say.

"I expected this," he said at last. "You ought to have foreseen it."

"There was no sign—"

"Does Catrine use her truename with him?"

"She does."

Jordac jabbed with a finger again for emphasis. "There. That is how you know. She uses her true soul with him, then. Language is nothing but heart made breath. Things like this—in the play of true souls, they happen. It is inevitable."

"It doesn't worry you?"

Jordac frowned and seemed to stare through her, past her to the horizon. "It merely forces certain adjustments," he said. "The only thing that worries me…is that boat."

She followed his gaze to the edge of the marsh, where a familiar cinnamon-haired woman was charging inland from a small fishing boat as fast as she could hoist her legs through the muddy ground, much to the astonishment—and the notice—of the man who had brought her.

"Madge," Baran breathed.

"You were followed," said Jordac. He lowered his bottle of fireflies back into the mud and freed both hands from the rumpled sleeves of his cloak. His eyes flashed with anger, but he frowned as if in pain and hunched his back as she approached.

"Commander," said Madge, gasping between breaths. "We have a serious problem."

She stopped short, her words tight in her throat. The hunched man before her had the appearance of a beggar; but from Baran's silent and furious reaction, from the wild terror in her eyes, Madge knew at once in whose presence she stood.

"My lord," she began, and made to bow as best she could in the mud, but he was on her as quick as if she had pulled a knife. He wrapped her in a tight embrace and held her close as she began to lower, holding her on her feet.

"Madge!" Jordac said loudly, as if greeting a friend who had been too many seasons away—then, softly against her ear: "I am no one of importance. Do not bow."

Madge backed away and nodded, a quick learner. "It's a true honour to meet a man of such little importance," she whispered. "Forgive me. I did not know—"

"How did you find us?" Baran asked.

"I have seen your little boat before," said Madge. "I saw its sail and followed the wake in the stillness of the harbour."

"Sell the boat," said Jordac. "We will not meet again here."

"As you say," said Baran.

"I can never return to this place." At this Jordac cast such a human look at the fireflies that he seemed smaller to Madge, somehow—less heroic. He was not a large man, now that she looked upon him, eye to eye.

Baran's anger was uncommonly easy to read in the shape of her usually stoic face. "You knew not to follow me."

"I—I had no choice," she said at last. "We are in trouble."

Jordac narrowed his dark eyes and turned to the water. "Were *you* followed?"

"Not that I could see."

"Out with it, girl," said Baran.

"It's Hendec…the new recruit."

"What of him?"

"He plans to steal a horse. A courser from the Imperial couriers."

Jordac frowned sternly. Baran's eyes went wide with disbelief.

"What? Why?" she asked. "It makes no sense."

"Have we no horses?" asked Jordac. "None of our own?"

"Six of them within a day's ride," said Baran. "We could have spared one for him."

"He races the *Providence*," said Madge. "Unwed he may be, as he swore to us, but unattached he is not. He is in love, or he thinks he is, with some frontier wench in the village where Celithrand was seen."

"And you told him of Ashimar's errand," Baran surmised.

"Celithrand was of no importance to us," said Jordac. "A nice distraction, that's all. It is good to have Ashimar out of the city."

"It's perilous to have him off the Imperator's leash," said Baran. "We all know what he'll do if he thinks the villagers are covering for a personal traitor to Valithar. No doubt Hendec knows too."

"Hendec is riding wet-kneed and steed-weary," said Madge. "I think he plans to seek out the courier posts and steal a fresh horse at every post."

Baran cursed under her breath. "One man? There's no way. There's a quire of soldiers at every station, at least. The couriers are expert riders. If he's in a panic, he'll push his horse too hard and they'll take him over distance, probably alive."

Jordac shook his head. "That cannot happen."

"I told you he was impulsive," said Baran. "I didn't know he was *this* impulsive."

"He's an idealist," said Jordac. "I bear a special love for idealists. This is my failing, my fault. I am a fool who should have foreseen it."

"You had no way of knowing," said Baran gently.

"I *always* have ways of knowing," said Jordac. Then, to Madge, "you were right to come to me with this. We cannot allow him to be captured."

Baran's mind was already working. "How long since he went?"

"He hasn't, yet," said Madge. "I told him—I told him I would help him. I told him we had a key for the stables."

Baran scoffed. "Is there a locked gate on the stables?"

"No," said Madge. "He'll find that out just before dawn, when I meet him."

Jordac nodded his approval. "Well played. His affections for this girl—are they genuine?"

"Yes," said Madge—then, with some disdain, "he's completely stupid for her."

"He was a poor choice for the *Wyrmsbolt*," said Jordac. "I should have sent him to join the fighters in Estelonne."

"We can give him new orders…"

"That time is past," said Jordac. "He'll desert us at the first post. He deserted the Havenari—beloved by idealists, that lot. He'll desert us too, in half a moment, for the sake of his lady love. When did my Uprising become a honeyed Hanic romance, Baran? When?"

Baran nodded solemnly. "I had hoped better for him. He's a good fighter with a good heart. But he's going to cost nine of us their lives— the six active Widows, you, me, Odi, at the very least. "

"We can't have a murder," said Jordac. "Not of an independent fighting man come suddenly to the Capital. The Shield has a thousand Inquisitors, waiting for such a clumsy mistake. We know not all of the bloodguard are with Ashimar. And they have Mardon Black, besides."

"Mardon Black?" asked Baran. "That fat old Master of Iron?"

"He's no warrior," said Jordac. "But he's better versed than many in the ways of death. The stories I could tell you, when the time for stories is come. But that night is not tonight."

"What, then?" asked Baran.

Jordac stroked the short beard at the front of his face, deep in thought.

"How much coin have the flower-girls taken in?"

"Not much," said Baran. "Shavings, really."

Jordac nodded. "We have to use Alethir," he said.

Even Baran's iridescent skin blanched at the name. "Is that necessary?"

"I'd hoped to save him for late in the war," said Jordac. "I'd hoped to save the gold, too. But we have to be sure."

Baran sighed, and cast another disparaging glance at Madge because there was no one else to blame. "What must we do?"

"You," said Jordac, "must go to Odi. Tell him you need eleven sovereigns"—here Baran whistled audibly—"under cover of minters' wax. Made up to look like a payment of wax iron. He'll know at once for whom it's meant. You'll find Alethir in the aeril quarter. He won't be in hiding yet, not until we activate him. Can you do this?"

"By dawn? If I can find him."

"Good. You, Madge, should return to Vairhurst and start the game again. I've heard your complaints of Rendon, and you are free of your wicked lover. I'll write his letters myself until we're finished with him."

Madge nodded, suddenly uneasy. "I promised Hendec I would see him off myself. I could be useful—"

"You have been very useful indeed," said Jordac, "and that time is now done. If he sees you again, he will know you betrayed him. I cannot protect you in close quarters, and we cannot afford to lose you."

"Will Alethir fight me on the price," asked Baran, "if he knows our desperation?"

"No," said Jordac. "Eleven sovereigns is the cost. Waste no time haggling. I know not what his methods are, but he may be hard pressed to see it done by dawn in the manner we require. Eleven sovereigns, and say no more of it."

"Eleven's an unlucky number," said Madge.

Jordac offered the ghost of a smile, though he wasn't happy. "It's about to be," he said.

In the blue light of the early morning, Hendec waited for Madge in growing frustration as he shrugged off the half-dreams of a long sleepless night. Down the hill, some half-dozen horses nudged at the grass in their paddock, carelessly left to graze outside the Imperial stables while the prized coursers were kept inside.

It was a strange kind of deterrent, leaving them in plain sight for any horse thief foolish enough to try and sneak one out of the enclosure, while leaving more than enough light racers to run a horse thief down on the road, if it came to that. It was poor treatment for the fat horses, though: the grass that was hardy enough to grow just beyond the Shadewall retained its green, and its sweetness, well into the cold months. It was bad enough that they had run to fat by comparison; Hendec could still hear the bitter complaints of old Orin that horses left to graze on sweet grass too long were prone to terrible cases of founder that ravaged their hooves and left them too damaged to run.

Or perhaps that was part of the trap as well: catch a horse thief with a heavy horse unfit to ride, and run him down with the coursers. The thought would have disgusted Orin, and it disgusted Hendec on his behalf.

Long before the more glorious songs of his Rahastan ancestors had led his hand onto a sword-hilt with almost melodramatic purpose, Hendec had grown up the son of a free miner in the hills of Haveïl. He learned the learned the tracks of the woodland deer and foxes, catching glimpses of them on far hills as their curiosity brought them nigh to the mining camps, but the clamour of men hard at work and the various human scents of the place kept them at bay. When first he had met Orin, the village groom of Silver, on one of his father's trips in to the village, he had been mystified by the man's talent for drawing gentleness and trust out of the horses and sheep. He recalled now the long hours he spent as a boy in Orin's company, asking one question after another in the manner of any insufferably wise child. It was from Orin that he learned how to feed and water and groom and shoe—skills that put him in high demand when he was old enough, at last, to ride out with the Havenari.

It had made him, in the end, an expert rider, a fine judge of horses, and wise in their ways for a young man. He could tell from the condition of the Travalaithi coursers just how far they could carry him, and how much of it at a steady canter. He had made in his mind a plan to push the horses to exhaustion, to ride each past the next station and steal a fresh horse at every other post. Despite Madge's foolish assurances that the horse would not be missed for hours or days, he knew better; his theft would be marked almost immediately. But it was his hope that avoiding every other post, his direction would not be so clear—or better yet, that his pursuers would check in at the next station and lose valuable time explaining the matter to confused frontier guards who had not heard nor seen anything out of the ordinary.

Hendec had a long time—too long a time—to think on these matters, to call back all he had ever learned that might now empower him to reach the village before Ashimar and his men worked their way in from the coast. The sky was brushed with gold when the first soldiers came out of the long stablehouse, trading friendly words with the nine men who had come down the hill to relieve them. Outnumbered as he was, the brief exchange was his only chance, with or without Madge and her dubious help. As a creaking wagon of dry goods trundled past them on the main road, he slid down the embankment with the ease of a man accustomed to slipping silently and quickly over rough terrain.

His concerns about the back gate of the stable, concealed by a winding fence, were set at ease when he found it left nearly wide open, with none but a few unattended, fat horses to guard it. The nature of the building sent up a particular stench, and it was well-ventilated, surrounded on all sides by unshuttered windows. The pens themselves, he could see already, were insulated, but the stablehouse's main corridor was left nearly open to the elements, but for a long thatched roof that covered the length of the stone building.

Wary of the shadow he might cast, and the impression he might leave on dawdling soldiers if he came in at the window like a common burglar, Hendec slipped through the rear doorway as quietly as he could while affecting a confident gait in case he was spotted. It was easier to talk your way out of a purposeful stride, he thought, than to talk your way out of skulking.

The Travalaithi coursers were magnificent animals, larger than he expected for light horses, sleek and well-muscled and bred for the same blackness of coat as their armoured masters. They awaited him with a steely patience, and he wasted no time among them but moved to the first of their pens: it would not matter much, he thought, which horse he took. But there among them he saw one horse that had been made ready to ride, standing already saddled for the morning courier. He cast his eyes over the other pens and found, to his relief, that none of the others were so readied. It was one more delay to their pursuit, even if they caught him in plain sight the moment he mounted up.

The dread came suddenly, but set in so gently that Hendec could not tell where it came from. Perhaps, in the back of his shrewd mind, it twigged him that a single horse had been made ready, or that Madge's lie about the key was oddly specific to have been a mistake. Perhaps it was something about the proximity of the guards, or the whirling fear that his theft might bring even more trouble upon his lady-love. Perhaps it was even the rats that unsettled him so: Hendec kicked one away from the front of the horse's pen, and saw they had come into the stables and were nesting in the hay in a manner most unbecoming a military building.

At first, it felt as if one of the rats had dropped down and bitten him. High up on his shoulder, he felt the weight come down as if a fat rat had come from the rafters, felt the cold sharp prick of its little fangs in the flesh just behind his collarbone. Forcing calmness, steeling himself not to cry out in alarm or disgust, he reached up with both hands to seize the rat and throw it away, only to find that his left hand closed on thin air—and his right hand, his sword-hand, did not answer his call, but dangled helplessly at his side. The wound was wet, hot, and slick to the touch; as he clutched his fingers over the wound, Hendec felt his rushing blood pound hard, then hard again, like a siege engine against the flimsy gate of his fingers. His whole hand came away so thick with blood that the lines of his palm could not be seen, and he knew then it was no mere rat that had opened him to the cold air.

He had sunk to the floor somehow, and the scrape of wood beside him as something—a weapon—was hoisted, brought him halfway back to his senses. In the dimness he could make out a broad iron horseshoe, fixed onto a heavy sledgehammer in the hands of a slim figure whose face was lost in shadow. A slender dagger flashed in the stranger's hand, but he slipped it away into his cloak and took a heavy, crude grip on the sledgehammer with both hands.

Hendec tried to cry out as the horseshoe-headed hammer floated away from him in the blackness, but no breath or sound came. It swung back in a terrible arc, coming down full force on his wounded shoulder, and the shock of the first blow was so complete that it spared him from suffering the second.

The killing blow was not long in coming, nor was Hendec long in going. His story ended in the hay and manure of the stablehouse floor, and there is no more to be said of him. The change of the guards came, as Madge had said it would; and when the alarm was raised, it was over a horse thief too far gone to be questioned. The death was relayed at once to the Master of the East Gate, who came down personally to see the body and chide the guards for letting him slip past so easily. He was satisfied to find the man with his head and shoulder stove in by a monstrous double-kick from the agitated warhorse that now paced back and forth, half-saddled and nickering, through the blood-spattered hay around the corpse.

"We heard nothing," one of the guards insisted. "He must have come in like a ghost."

"You and your whole quire are very lucky men," said the Master of the East Gate. "It looks as if he went out a ghost as well."

The guards had a good laugh at that; the dawn had come in force, and laughing at ghosts was easier now than before. The body was laid to rest, not in a pauper's field, but in the nearby field of honour where thousands had died in the Siege of Shadow. It was a place properly reserved, under Imperial edict, for military burials; but they were none of them too eager to haul the grisly body, smashed head and all, into the town and up the hill to Vairhurst, or all the way out into the pauper's fields. There was just too much to be done, and the soldiers decided with equal measures of pity and charity that perhaps the unfortunate thief had fallen harder on his luck than the well-fed men of the Grand Army. His true story, whatever it might have been, was lost forever with his death, and they decided it was best to treat the poor wretch with respect. The soldiers, even the Master of the Gate, imagined themselves to be only a single crippling wound away from sharing his beggar's fate; they were at war, after all, and times were hard for everyone.

"What's your name, lass?"

The little girl blushed at Elmore's smile. "Maddie," she said with a curtsy.

"Those are lovely flowers you have there, Maddie."

"Thank you, m'lord."

"Are they for sale?"

The girl paused, uncertain how to respond. "These are winter violets, m'lord. Meant for the Hedge. Me and my sister hang them on the long stair."

There was no impatience in Elmore's smile—only warmth. "I know what they are," he said. "Will you sell me some?"

"They's forbidden in the City," she said, a little proudly.

"Not to you and me," said Elmore with a smile, showing her the inside of his cloak. "The servants of the Tower are given special exemption, isn't that right?"

Maddie nodded, backing away a step as she noted his rank.

"And aren't the flower-girls servants of the Tower too?"

She kept nodding her head in silence.

"You're little Cerulean Guards yourselves, I think," he said, casting an admiring glance toward the blossoms adorning the thorny walls of the Lornock Stair. "You've done more for the Imperator and the Tower than I ever have. A pretty maiden with a basket of Maidens must warm his stony old heart, I think."

She blushed as a handful of silver jangled in his hand.

"Now, I'm headed up Vairhurst way for a friend of mine," he said.

"Is he dead?" she asked. Her knowing concern wounded him to the heart.

"No, no," said Elmore. "He's not dead. He had a brother who died, and he pays his respects. Only now he's away on a trip, and he would want me to go in his stead."

The little girl nodded.

"I'd very much like to take some violets up," Elmore explained, "before the cold steals them all away. You give me some—there's a good girl—and you take this home to your mama. You tell her soon as the day's meat and drink are paid for, you tell her to buy you a pretty blue dress. And if she tries to tell you that your kind can't wear blue in the city, lass, you tell her: you're a servant of the Tower, technically speaking, and you've earned the damned blue as much as I have."

The girl beamed at him and took the silver, handing her whole basket to him. He gathered a few of the best flowers into a small bouquet, but left her with the greater half of them. He could have bought the whole basket thrice over for what he gave her, he knew; but it wasn't *his* brother who died, after all. It seemed strange and wrong, somehow, to bring too many flowers—to make too big a show for a man he had never met.

The Iron Road itself was Elmore's preferred route to the hill. The streets were lively and crowded, but all who dwelt here at the heart of the Empire treated him with respect and cleared out of his path as he came. Even fellow mourners, of whom there were many, seemed to take special care not to obstruct him. He forgot, quite often, that he was of real rank and clout now: the pay was not quite good enough to remind him how important he was, though it sufficed to keep his wife in fine linens, if not quite silks. He looked forward to the day the whole of Selik fell back under Imperial control, if only so that its textile mills did, that he might clothe her again in colours and weaves worthy of her ready smile.

He made his way swiftly up the parade route, smiling mostly to himself as even the purple-cloaked officers of the regular Grand Army moved out of his way with a begrudging deference. Reaching the narrow, cobbled way called Torgirdle, he skirted the hill to the shortest of the stairs to the Vairhurst memorial. He was nimble enough on level ground, but a little too much standing at attention for a man his age had wrought havoc on his knees and made nearly any climb a torturous affair.

With a few unseemly grunts, Elmore mounted the hill and came to a place of still packed earth and towering memory stones whose imperious southward gaze seemed to take in the whole Empire with a stern and solemn anger. It was not Elmore's way to come here: the silent and barren field filled him with a restless worry as he moved among the stones.

The place was empty, for most of the soldiers had died on campaign, and few had ever been brought home to rest in the grassless earth behind the Shadewall. That emptiness made it worse, somehow. Elmore was many things after his years in the library, and he was a lover of ghost-stories and improbable tales most of all. He didn't mind the stillness of a true graveyard, filled with the bodies and maybe the ghosts of good folk who had come and gone. But here, in a false graveyard empty of spirits, anathema even to the restless dead, he was unsettled and on his guard, eager to be gone even as he searched in vain among the towering monuments.

With his senses buzzing and his heart already unquiet, it did not take him long to hear the sound of eerie weeping among the pillars of the dead. Clutching his bouquet and pursing his lips, Elmore waited as long as he dared before abandoning his errand to seek out the unmistakable sound of a woman stricken with grief. He found her some rows down before an immense monument, clad in the black cowl of a wife at mourning, an overturned basket of scattered cerulyns at her feet.

"A thousand pardons," he said. "I heard you among the stones. I thought—I don't mean to intrude, dear lady. Are you all right?"

"No, it's good of you," she choked. She turned at last and drew back her hood to look at him. Her curly hair tumbled free like a summer sunrise of red and gold; Elmore found himself stunned by the marred beauty of her immaculate but troubled face.

"A woman's grief is a very private place," he said. "I shouldn't have bothered—"

"No," she said hastily. "It's no bother. I'm simply paying my respects. That's all."

Her voice rang false and Elmore knew it. At first, he did not press the issue.

"I'm laying flowers for a friend," he said. "Poor fellow comes nearly every week, leaves them for his brother Jalen. Have you seen his marker? Jalen Varhame would be the name, I suppose. He was with the Fifth Legion of the Blade. Harrod's Hammer, they called them."

She shook her head abruptly and looked away; whether in shyness or in shame was impossible to tell. As she turned from him, he saw the outline of an open Mother's Drop pressed in her little hand, and the sight smote him to the heart. The little drop of liquid at its glass heart was bluer than the tears in his sad blue eyes.

"Oh, lass…" Forgetting himself, he came to her, clutched her delicate hands in his. "No, lass, no." She looked at him with a piercing sorrow as he pried the little pendant from her shaking fingers and fixed its crystal stopper as hard as he dared.

"Give that back," she said with exhausted anger. "It belonged to my husband."

"And you mean to follow him, I suppose?"

"I mean to…" she sighed. "No. Now that it comes to it…I'm a false and faithless wife, sir. I swore today I would see him in the next world, only now that it comes to it…I haven't the courage. I'm afraid. For pity's sake, my lord, if you've a blade at your belt…I beg you, be my valour, for my own valour has deserted me."

"Valour?" Elmore echoed. "What kind of talk is that? You speak of surrender, dear lady. Valour's in the fighting." He turned the Mother's Drop over in his hand; the thing was genuine. He wore one at his own neck, like all the Cerulean guards.

"I cannot go on," she said.

"That's naught but your grief speaking," said Elmore.

"Aye, my grief," sighed the woman. "And what can a decorated man, a mighty warrior with a pension and fine commission, know of a poor woman's grief, wretched and poor as I am, and alone in all the world?"

Elmore smiled in spite of himself. "I'm hardly mighty," he said.

"Do not take this poor woman for a fool, sir."

"I'm not," he insisted. "I'm not even properly a veteran. D'you know how I won the Blue?"

She shook her head.

"I was a curator in the library at Lornock," said Elmore. "I served the Master of Scrolls in the preservation of Imperial records. I was a scribe and a binder, and I wrote moral fables for the spoiled children of the Magistrates. In the Battle of Lornock, when the First Uprising began, Jordac and Aric's men broke the Banlanders out of the Rattle. They set fire to the whole back wing, and the fires spread to the library. I saved a few books, that's all. A few beautiful old books I couldn't bear to see consumed."

The woman watched him with rapt attention, studying his face with wide, inquisitive eyes as he spoke. He fumbled for words as thought of what else he might say: he searched for anything at all to keep her occupied, until all designs of suicide had left her behind.

"My lungs haven't been much good ever since," he said. "I took in so much smoke and ash that day, I came out with a beard whiter than this one. But I saved a dozen books in the blaze. Just a dozen. That's all. Old poems, legends from the Age of Sun. Bestiaries. But I'd also saved the whole genealogical history of the Baron-Kings, the lineage of the old royal families of Travost. Ancient, irreplaceable things. The kind of things wealthy men care about, so they can keep on feeling entitled to their wealth." He sighed with some resentment. "Not silly old things like poems. But there I was, hailed as a hero of the Empire, a civilian done right. Olferth, he was a young man then, just coming to power—he appointed me to the Ceruleans for life. Now I'm rich enough, aye, and I'm a commissioned man, aye, with a fine cloak and more fine food than I've any right to. But I'm no soldier, lass, not like the others. Not even like your—your brave husband here."

At the mention of her husband, she burst into sobs again, and Elmore cursed himself and his clumsy words. He tried again.

"What do I know of grief?" he asked. "I know it makes fools of us all. I know that good folk in despair carry a special madness. I may be nothing more than an old bookworm, lass, but I know my stories. Have you read the Hanes?"

"My husband could read," she said. "He was to teach me, before…" But as she fell to sobs again, Elmore put his cloak and a warm arm around her, and sang in a voice that was deep, tremulous, and tinged with a little rust:

> *"Come, grief, to me, and be my dagger's point,*
> *O come and give my rogue and rebel hand*
> *The strength it had, and seeks, thus to anoint*
> *My pov'rished flesh with fare to Dagan's land,*
>
> *That is no thunder on the fated wind:*
> *It is the hoofbeat of my hated foe,*
> *Who'll take the way, but find his vict'ry thinned*
> *Like wet-wine by my lifeblood, to his woe."*
>
> *So spake the vasil; taking up his knife*
> *Upon the crest of Muleth, at the dawn,*
> *He brought forth rain: the waters of his life*
> *Stained red the ridge's earth from that day on.*
>
> *The thunder waxed upon the morning air,*
> *As through the canyon sped the vasil's son*
> *With word of victory, found him lying there,*
> *And knew the cost with which the day was won.*

It was only one piece of a vast lay, and Elmore had forgotten much of the rest. But it seemed to have an effect, for the woman calmed herself and fixed her brilliant green eyes on him throughout the stanzas. With some measure of pride, Elmore gestured down to the ruddy earth at her feet. It was almost the colour of dried blood.

"And that's the story of how the soil up here on the hill got to be so red," said Elmore. "So say the Hanes."

"It's... a rather grisly story," said the woman, with the hint of a smile breaking through her sorrow.

"Oh, all the best stories are," said Elmore with pride. "Ripping adventure yarns. Full to the margins with heroes of might and deeds of great renown. Kings and vasils, fierce Horrors from beyond the night. Great bloody affairs, the lot of them. But a few fair maids in them, I'll admit, maidens of such solar beauty they'd give even you a touch of competition, I think."

Her smile beamed all the more brightly. "An awful shame it would be," she said, "to leave the world with such poetry still unheard."

"Well, I'm full of it," he chuckled. "Poetry, I mean. Great long years I spent curating that library. The Mysteries of the Unwatchers, what they call the *Uliri Imidactuai*, I know well. The sagas of the Banlanders, too. And a few crass little verses by no one of note—myself included."

The woman cleared her throat. "If I swear an oath not to kill myself tonight," she asked, "will you come back with me to the inn, and tell me more of your tales?"

Elmore hesitated; the hour was late and his errand unfinished. But at last he nodded and helped the woman collect her cerulyns and lay them reverently before her husband's stone. She seemed to know the Vairhurst monuments very well indeed, and she helped him find the stone for Jalen—Rasten's brother—without too much trouble. Then they were off and down the hill together, her step lightened by his presence and Elmore's pride glowing in him.

They spoke all the way down the hill of myths and legends, the sorts of things that had enthralled Elmore since his youth. She was wise especially in the stories of the eastern reaches; Creslyn and Selik were familiar places to her, and her accent slipped over the strange foreign names so easily that it was clear she'd travelled far in her old life. The inn she'd found for herself was hardly more than a dingy private house with a few vacant beds along the narrow loft. The whole structure leaned like a drunkard against the wall of an abandoned temple, in an effort to keep upright at any cost to its dignity.

A low fence of wood, rotted nearly through like all old wood in the capital, surrounded the front yard of the inn where a few sickly chickens plucked in vain at the barren soil. Like a gentleman, Elmore let the lady pass first through the narrow gate, but as he followed her under the low wooden arch, she stumbled as her cloak tripped her up. He reached for her as she fell, and found her in his arms, pressed hard between the edge of the fence and the broad expanse of his chest.

She fixed him with emerald eyes in that moment that seemed to light with hidden fire; and whether from desperation or gratitude or something more, she leaned in to kiss him. A little baffled at the woman's brazenness, he turned his head at the last moment, and her lips met nothing but the jagged line where his cheek met his long grey beard.

"Hm," he smiled kindly. "What was that for?"

But when she moved to kiss him again, he stepped back out of the gate and let go her arm gently. "I think you misunderstand my intentions," he said, choosing his words carefully.

She looked as confused as he felt. "Don't you want this?"

"This," Elmore echoed, tugging at his beard. "Ah, *this*. Do *I* want this, I mean, that?"

She opened her arms with her hands held low. There was no pretense.

"That's a many-layered question," he said. "But I'm not the sort of man you think—"

"Do not fear for your honour," she said, "nor for mine. I died on that hill tonight, sir. I died, but for your kindness. The maid Lysandra passed from this world tonight. She is gone. All that is left of her is this wretched ghost before you, left haunting this cold world alone."

"Lysandra," Elmore breathed. "It's not that I…I'm old enough to be your father."

"If that is what you wish," she said coyly. But then she took his hand with candour. "You are a good man, Cerulean. There are so few of them left. You would not stain a woman's virtue. But know I speak the truth when I tell you, I have been no right woman since my husband died. I am but a ghost in this world. I am but a *draugur*, if you will indulge me. A spirit of the restless dead, imprisoned like the old tales say in a dead body no longer my own. Forget your courtesy with me, my lord. I am broken. I am no more a woman."

"W-well," stammered Elmore as she stroked his hand, "just the same, I am still very much a man."

"Of that I've no doubt," she whispered. She was close enough, now, to whisper.

"And there's more to manhood than—well, hmm—manhood, if you follow me," he said. He took her by the shoulders and gently pushed her away. "I've a wife, Lysandra. A very particular, very good wife, thank you." He laughed nervously. "A very fierce wife."

"In the tribes of Adân—" she began.

"Ah, yes, I know all about how they do it out West," he said. "My wife and I—ah—we are from the East."

She smiled at that. "You're a good man, Cerulean," she said again.

He laughed nervously. "And trying damned hard to stay that way."

"You do remind me of my husband," she said.

"You must miss him terribly. What was he like?"

She shrugged, but thought hard about it. "Noble to the end. He believed too much in the Hanes, like you. He liked to imagine, I think, that war had more to do with war-poems than it does."

Elmore nodded. "Soldiers at war need heroes' tales most of all," he said. "Helps them forget what war really is. It's a hard thing to do, once you know."

"Harder than many will ever understand," she said.

She was still, now, and kept her distance. But the look that passed between them was so genuine, in that moment, that it proved by its very purity the whole falseness of all that had come before it. Wary again of the time, Elmore bowed with recovered dignity, and only the lightest twinkle of flirtation in his eye (for he'd been, after all, quite a rascal in different times).

"This is really your home?" asked Elmore. "That much is true?"

"For a time," Lysandra said. "But yes, Cerulean. You have seen me safely to my door."

"Then good night, my lady," he said, "and I wish you better fortune on future nights." She did not have to ask with what.

The stars would have been well out and burning brightly by the time he made his way home. But new clouds had come in from the water, and the first real snowfall dusted his cloak and turned his grey beard white as he rushed through the city streets. Aching-legged and out of breath, he was nearly knocked over by the heat and scent when he tore open the little door. There in the bright glow of a blazing fire, little old Gwen sat up with one of the many old books into which they'd sunk most of their small wealth—and some of which had come to them by more than a few lapses of conscience in the Imperial Library.

"I expected I'd marry a husband who'd stay out all night," said Gwen laconically. She didn't look up from her book. "Didn't expect one who'd go out for a single watchman's shift in the autumn, and stay out till winter."

"I was waylaid, you might say," he said. At their age, they'd moved on from rote apologies to explanations.

"Guard duty in the Great Library?"

"Pretty girl," he beamed, taking down his heavy cloak. "Seemed quite taken with me."

"Pretty girls can't make a beef and almond brewet like I can," said Gwen. Elmore sniffed the air, let the thick aroma of the hot stew fill him completely.

"You didn't," he said.

"I did."

Elmore approached the cauldron over the fire. "By the Ten, woman. It's thick as cement, in the best way."

"It's been on long enough," she said with a shrug. "Simmering for hours. Nothing fancy. But I learned long ago not to count the hours by your comings and goings."

"Have you eaten?"

"Aye," she said. "But long enough ago to eat again."

As the night wore on they dined together and spoke of things that are not recorded here. In time, Elmore unravelled the story of Lysandra, whom he now knew he could not possibly have saved from an early death.

"She spoke of her husband with such sadness," he said. "I think that part was true. That's always the best way with a lie. Such a pretty little lie she peddled too."

Gwen shrugged. "So many women have sad stories to tell," she said. "Sometimes lies suit them better. Can you blame them?"

"Oh, this was no woman's lie," he said. "Not one for herself. This lie was woven purely for a man's benefit, I swear. A poor widowed lass, alone in all the world, wailing around the memory stones like a lost soul, waiting to be saved by the wits of a man who thinks he's clever, or by the strength of a man who fancies himself strong. Or maybe by the long, swinging—"

"Don't be vulgar," said Gwen.

Elmore laughed. "Chain of office," he finished. "Of a Magistrate Councillor or other rich greatfellow, with too much gold and nowhere to put it—so to speak."

"You think she was a whore?"

"Hard to imagine much else," said Elmore. "Women like her don't much fancy an old gnarled sage like me. Lucky for you, of course."

"Lucky for me," she said; then, after a mouthful of stew, "No. She's no whore."

"Are you saying my charms are still genuine?" Elmore asked with the hint of a leering smile.

"Oh, I wouldn't go that far," said Gwen, a little too quickly. "But she sold you a story. An experience. You've saved a girl's life with your cleverness, and all that. That's the fantasy, isn't it?"

"Aye," said Elmore. "The part that mattered most to me, of course."

"Whores don't just sell a man their bodies," said Gwen. "They sell him a *fantasy*. And that lass gave up far too much of her little fantasy for free."

"It did feel good," Elmore admitted. "Even if I knew it was false. It did feel good to think I might have helped her."

Gwen nodded. "Then it ought to have cost you something."

Elmore checked his purse and found it exactly where he had left it, with the same heft and satisfying jingle.

"It cost me no coin, at least," he said.

Gwen unfastened her hair and made a spectacle of her yawn. "Then you ought to figure out what she took, I suppose. But it's a late hour for such espionage. Come to bed, El. Rest those old bones, and leave off the chasing of doxies 'round the memory stones to men of Rasten's age."

Elmore paused in his snuffing of the lights.

"What did you say?"

Gwen shrugged. "Your friend from the Ceruleans. That's how he met his girl-thing, wasn't it? Up on Vairhurst, laying flowers on his brother's stone?"

"I suppose it is," said Elmore as he quenched the last of the candle-flames. "Exactly the same way."

"It's a young man's business, that is. Come to bed, El."

They had been married long enough that Elmore did not need to voice his agreement. They retired to a whole separate bedchamber where Gwen doffed her expensive silks and slept naked and warm under skins of wolf and bear, while Elmore lay awake and thought of the mysterious woman, unsettled by his wife's shrewd words as they echoed now and again in his troubled mind.

NINE

ALL SOUND AND CHATTER STOPPED as two clay pitchers tumbled to the threshed floor and shattered on the straw-covered stone. Rich, dark wine poured out over the straw like blood, splashing back over the serving girl's sandaled feet. She looked to Ursula, the matron of the alehouse, with frightened eyes, but there was nothing but compassion in the old woman's face. Ursula motioned the young girl to her as conversation resumed.

"I'm sorry, I'm sorry," she whispered. "I'm so sorry."

"Shh, child." Ursula took the girl's hands in her own. The pretty maid was shaking to the very core with terror—she had been all night. Ursula's hands shook with the palsy, but beneath her wrinkled skin she was hard as steel. Of the two of them, her gnarled hands were stronger and steadier, now.

"I didn't mean—I'll be careful—"

"It's all right," said Ursula. "You've done enough. Go on home, if you can make it."

"But this many—in this storm—how will you manage?"

Ursula cast her deep grey eyes over the great-hall of the Sunderhouse. It was full to bursting with travelers seeking shelter from the storm. But these were no ordinary travelers: the room was bristling with steel, from the mud-caked Havenari outriders to the red-armoured bloodguard and their singular commander. It was they who had put the locals on edge, and the young maid most of all.

"I'll manage," she said. "Now get you home."

"But Ursula—"

"Mind your way in the snows, child. It's a terrible storm, and like to get worse. Keep to the fence, then one hand on the wall, all the way home. Methinks the Woman of the Wood doesn't like this company any more than we do."

"The Woman of the Wood's a myth."

"Never you mind what's a myth," said Ursula. "Off with you, before I change my mind." She shooed the girl away home with a weathered hand, and set to filling another jug with wine.

The bloodguard were served first, of course. She knew better than to keep them waiting. They drank with relish but not to excess, she saw—men with more discipline than common soldiers to be sure, or else men under a tighter yoke. Only one ate and drank with the appetite of a real fighting man, a man nearly as long in the shanks as two little Ursulas laid end to end, who was trying and failing to get himself drunk. He was seated as far as possible from Ashimar himself—it could have been no other—who took no food or drink among the common men.

"Keep it coming," barked the tall one, and she did. Only when he had a pitcher all to himself did she turn to the other guests. The traders and mercers clustered around the fire-pit, all of them crowded in tightly, were her next patrons.

"Apologies for the wait, gentlemen," she sighed with stony patience, but they met her with smiles.

"Tûr's blessing on ye, Ursula," said one of the merchants. "Pay us no mind. We're glad for a roof in all this winter, is all. See to the strangers first."

She made her way through the outriders next, seat by seat. At the far end of the table, another pair of hands was shaking, too.

"Damn this blasted storm," he said. "And damn the backborn yantans at Seton and their false forecasts. An alehouse. Not even a proper bedded inn. An alehouse wet as a Carmacen wedding. Robyn, I'm having a time of it, a real time."

The tall woman at his side put a comforting arm around her brother—a gesture he shook off before the other men saw it.

"We need you, Bram," she said softly, close to his ear. "We need you, and you need yourself."

"Wine for the man and his missus?" asked the old matron, approaching their end of the table. Robyn's icy glare at the woman was fierce enough to send her away without a word.

"It's been more than a red month since I've had a drink," said Bram. "I'm shot, slow and shaken. I'm half the fighting man I ought to be. I'm not much good to you, whatever we find on the trail. I'm especially no good to you here."

Robyn looked back to the others, drinking merrily, their faces red with relief after a hard ride through trails nearly blocked with snow—and certainly blocked now.

"If you can't handle it," she said, her jaw set, "I can tell the men to push on. We can make camp in the wild. We have a dryad now, after all, don't we? Aewyn's a little wonder with fires and shelters."

"And not so little anymore," said Bram with pride.

The two looked up as one more traveller stumbled in from the blizzard. The swirling sky was nearly black at his back, though it was still late afternoon. The merchants sent up a cheer, recognizing one of their own.

"Not in this storm," Bram decided. "We can't risk the horses. And I'll not put the others out in this cold just because I—I can't—"

"The men would understand—"

"They can't know," said Bram. "I'm fine."

"Trust me," said Robyn. "They know."

The two of them sat in miserable silence as the wind wailed against the roof. Drops of water had begun slipping down the timbers, and the old alewife, Ursula, watched the roof-beams with endless worry as she bustled around the tables. Most of the patrons paid her no mind until their cups were empty. To a few, lost in troubled thoughts, her constant movement was a pleasant enough distraction.

On the far side of the room, Kellan emptied his jug and shook it distastefully.

"Still nothing," he said with disappointment. "D'you think they water it?"

"Sorry, what?"

Kellan turned to Rasten and shook him out of his trance.

"The wine," he said. "Seems watered down to me."

"Do you see that old woman?" said Rasten. "I've been watching her. She's worried this whole roof's going to come down."

"You haven't heard a word I've said."

Rasten looked up to the roof. "This place might cave in if the storm gets worse. That doesn't bother you?"

Kellan shrugged. "Freezing to death's as a good a way as any."

Rasten slapped him on the back, and—charitable soul that he was—passed over his mug of ale.

"Here," he said. "The ale might do it, if the wine won't. And I very much doubt you're going to freeze to death."

From the corner of his eye, Kellan glanced down the table at Ashimar, who had fixed him with an unreadable gaze since they sat down. The shining mask, the little child bawling its enamelled tears, caught the candlelight in an eerie way, as if the child were burning.

"Oh, I won't freeze to death," said Kellan. "The Weeping Man there will find me a worse end, trust me."

"What, him? He needs you. He needs you a fair sight more than he needs me."

"He needs me only because I'm the one who's supposed to know the way," said Kellan. "More than three weeks, now, we've been on this fruitless search. We *flew* up the coast, Ras. Flew like the wind. And then, here we are, bogged down in the worst early snow I ever heard of, all the trails covered. We're charged with tracking a druid through the woods, mind you, which is the kind of stupid you only get from Imperial papermen. Impossible at the best of times. And now the whole forest seems to conspire against us. I swear to the Ten I've taken you by the same roads—but they spin us around, take us in circles, lead us places I don't recall. There's some curse to these woods, I swear it. Some old power in these woods that aims to lead me astray."

"Don't be superstitious," said Rasten.

"Celithrand's long gone," said Kellan. "You haven't ever met a man like that. He was gone the minute we took our eyes off him. He was twice that gone in an hour. He was tenfold gone in a day. Weeks and months have passed, now. We are doomed to fail. Ashimar is doomed to fail, Ras, and that's on *my* head." He drained Rasten's ale with one pull and wiped sloppily at his mouth. "My head will be clean off, the minute he figures that out."

"The storm will lift," said Rasten. "We'll find our way."

"You and that bloody optimism," said Kellan. "I'm telling you, I can't find the damned place."

"Soon as the sky is clear, you'll have us on the right path," Rasten replied. "Every place we've stopped, I talk to the innkeepers, the woodsmen, the farmers. A squall like this is well out of season. It can't possibly last. There haven't been storms like this in Haveïl, in Teurmanunt, for fifty years."

"And that's supposed to make me *less* edgy?"

"Nothing makes you less edgy," said Rasten. "I'm starting to think that's how you stay alive. I only mean to tell you, the village won't be lost for much longer. I can feel it."

Kellan refilled his mug—Rasten's mug--with an impatient snort. "Do other men grow weary of your certainty," he asked, "or is it just me?"

Rasten shrugged, his mood fading. "I'm certain because I have to be," he said. "Because I fall asleep every night in a room of men who'd like very much to slit my throat, only you and Ashimar have made them afraid to. And every day they forget, little by little, why they're afraid. You think you're the only one in danger out here? You *have* to find your way, for both of us. Blizzard or no blizzard. I'll do everything I can to help you. I'll do anything you say. The sooner you find this blasted village, the sooner we catch our traitor, the sooner I can go home to Cat and see the end of this fool's errand."

"I'm not going to find your blasted village," said Kellan wearily.

"You find it," Rasten commanded, "or we're both dead men." He slumped back in exasperation. "I just want to go home, Kellan. I'm heartsick and want to go home."

Kellan nodded. "A little weariness looks good on you," he said. "You're a kind man. But this is the first time I ever felt you were honest."

"I'm sorry I gave you my ale," said Rasten. The two shared a laugh, if only for a moment.

While the two were thus engaged, Ashimar had slipped away from the others. He had taken a room for himself, putting Ursula out of hers: the Sunderhouse was never meant to be a proper inn, being instead a simple tavern built from a ruined Sundrist monastery. It was a watering hole and stopping point halfway between the village of Aslea and the Wagon Wheel, the proper full-size inn a half-day's ride to the south. The sudden squall and ferocious cold had driven everyone off the road hours earlier than anticipated: travelers from all corners had crowded the only shelter for miles. There were no rooms for overnight guests, but they would drink in the great-hall and then sleep in it, as the Vosi of old did in the ancient tales. And Ursula, the hall-matron of that old tradition, had been put out by an agent of the Imperator whose disregard for traditions of hospitality was well known.

"Look," said Robyn. "Ashimar's gone. Up to the old woman's room, probably."

Bram looked up from his feet, where he had kept his gaze resting in stony meditation. "Are you sure?" he asked.

"I'm sure," she said. "He's not hard to miss. It could be no one else. I've heard the stories. That's him."

Bram nodded. He could feel the Scourge's identity in his bones. "What's he doing this far out, I wonder?"

Robyn drained a mug of clouded water with distaste. "Nothing good."

"We ought to find out."

"How?"

"I could go and listen in."

"Too dangerous."

"We could send Aewyn. Where is she? Out with the horses, still? She has a way of not being seen—"

"Out of the question," said Robyn. "She's still too green. I've an idea. Are the Havenari not sworn to protect the travelers of this wood?"

Bram frowned. "I don't like where this is going."

"Are we not agents of the Imperator ourselves? Charged with keeping the way safe and seeing riders unhindered to their destination? There are horrors in these woods such as most living men have never seen."

"You can't be serious."

"I'll talk to Ashimar myself. I'll offer our services as guides. It makes perfect sense, in this storm. We'll find out where they're headed. We know he's headed south, if rumours of the *Providence* moored at Seton are true."

"If the rumours are true," said Bram, "they've hauled two dozen bodies off that ship, men flayed to death, or dead from exhaustion or worse. Sister—"

"I don't want him in my wood," said Robyn, her resolve firm. "You wanted me to lead. Now I'm leading. Don't gainsay what's already happening."

Bram meant to stop her. But she rose in silence, unopposed, and followed Ashimar back into the darkness of the alehouse.

Robyn was tall, even by the standards of some men; as she stood up and motioned the Havenari out of her way, she cast an unusual bearing for a woman. Kellan was not so sure of her features at first—not after the very short time he had seen her—but that bearing was unmistakeable, and his desperation had made his senses sharp.

"There," he said simply.

"Where?" asked Rasten. "What?"

"That woman. I've seen her before, I know it. I saw her in Widowvale."

"The town?"

"Aye. Damnedest thing you ever saw. A woman in full armour, like a Sister of the Shroud. Led a dozen men or more. I'd know her anywhere. She was in Widowvale." He paused. "When Celithrand was there."

"And she's gone to talk to Ashimar?" asked Rasten. "Why?"

"No idea," said Kellan. "But I mean to find out. These bastards are my way back there. Maybe my last chance to find it, if this storm doesn't let up."

Rasten nodded. "Anything's worth trying," he said. "But suppose they lead us back, and still you can't catch Celithrand? What then? Ashimar won't kill you once you've done your job?"

Kellan shrugged as he stood up to his full height. "He'll kill me first if I *don't* lead him to Widowvale. I've cheated death before, Ras. I may yet again. But I can only cheat it one death at a time."

He didn't wait to hear Rasten's further questions. With grit that comes only from desperation, he shoved the sitting merchants out of his way as he crossed the room for the woman's companion, who was staring mournfully at his feet.

"Hello, stranger," he said in a voice of some authority. "Can I buy you a drink?"

Bram's sneer of disdain was more than he bargained for.

"All right, then," said Kellan. "No drink. I can see you're not a polite man. Good. It's not my natural way. I've got some questions."

"I'm not a seer," said Bram.

Kellan looked over his shoulder at the bloodguards packing the room. "If I start a fight in here, I'll get no answers out of you till it's all over and you lot are on the floor. But I will, if I have to."

Bram's shaking hands steadied themselves.

"Speak in the language of your choosing," he said evenly, "and I will give answer in the same."

"I know your lady captain," said Kellan. "I saw her in Widowvale some months back. I presume you were there too."

Bram's eyes went wide. "You…you were the soldier. One of Castor Stannon's men."

"Doesn't matter who I was then," said Kellan. "I'm a bloodguard now. Your lady captain has some business with Lord Ashimar. I very much want to know what it is."

"Perhaps you can ask him," said Bram. "I hear he's a talkative fellow."

Furious and frustrated, Kellan made a move to throttle him—or to hoist him by the neck—or to shake the little man like a rag doll till he spit out a better answer. In honesty, the ale was finally setting in and he wasn't sure what his hands would have done if they'd got there. But the pommel of a sword struck his nose and smashed it on the way out of its scabbard, and before the flash of pain cleared there was a length of steel at the side of his neck. Bram hadn't quite drawn his sword—maybe four inches of live steel shone between the hilt and the scabbard—but the perfect stillness in the smaller man's eyes made it clear it was two inches more than he needed. There was a narrow strip of exposed neck between Kellan's jawline and the iron gorget of his armour: that space was now filled by a cold edge. Kellan had the sense to freeze before the motion of the draw did its work.

To the Havenari on Bram's other side, Kellan's height and bulk obscured the action. They looked up with concern briefly, as both men sat down together, but went back to their cups in moments. They were already deep in the drink, most of them, and they knew after an eventful autumn that Bram could still take care of himself.

"Let's start this talk again," said Kellan, eager to have the steel off his neck. "I need to know your business. It's a serious matter. You've taken quite an interest in us. I'm sure you know who you're dealing with. I'm sure we're not the sort of folk you like to see out here in the thick. So tell me your business, and I'll tell you what I can of ours." He wiped gently at the blood that now poured over his moustache, held a hand there to staunch the flow.

Bram pushed the hilt of his sword back down to the scabbard and sighed.

"She's decided to offer you the services of the Havenari," he said. "It's our sworn duty to protect travelers from all dangers of these woods, mundane and otherwise. We keep the peace, and we preserve the life and limb of the Imperator and his subjects. Wherever you are going, we will be your guides. We'll see you to your destination, quick as we can, in the hopes that we'll be rid of you soon after you're done with your business. At least, that's the offer she's making."

In moments of light peril, like many men, Kellan was prone to cursing. He was surprisingly well-read for a soldier, and had a creative gift for profanity that was seldom exceeded. But in the forced calmness of the moment, he received the news with silence and a respectful nod. He moved now like one predator in the eyes of another, backing away slowly.

"If I'm going to be doing that work," Bram added, "and, I must say, completely against my will—I'd dearly love to know where we're taking you."

Kellan pushed himself back from the bench and turned toward the stable door.

"No deal," he said, and was gone. Bram moved to follow him, but turned back, nervously eyeing the stairs, at the top of which his sister was sequestered with one of the most feared men in the Travalaithi Empire. Clutching his sword, he moved instead to the end of the bench nearest the doorway, but kept his gaze on the stairs; and there he waited in fear, confusion, and more than a little thirst.

"I don't know how you can sweat so much in this cold, Melia."

With patient hands, Aewyn brushed and groomed the tall mare. Unlike the miller's daughter after whom she was named, Melia the horse was patient and mild in temperament, and suited Aewyn well as a beginning rider. Her hands were near frozen as she completed the work and debated blanketing the horses now that they were tended to. She was loath to do it—"their cold is not your cold," as Orin the groom had once said. But the storm was just too severe, and even the best stabling available was little more than a drafty old building adjoining the main alehouse. As the other horses awaited her care, she sang softly to Hendec's abandoned mare in a little song of her own making:

> *Horse, horse, horse,*
> *Niel, niel, niel,*
> *Black is your coat*
> *And your mane as well,*
>
> *Black are your hooves*
> *And black your eyes,*
> *But bright is your heart,*
> *It tells no lies.*
>
> *Horse, horse, horse…*

The stable door creaked suddenly as a looming figure filled the frame. He was not one of the Havenari, but in the light streaming from the warm alehouse she could not make out his features. She stopped her song, suddenly ashamed of her childish verse, but otherwise paid him no mind—until he untethered Robyn's horse, Acorn, who snorted haughtily and showed no signs of eagerness to take a new rider.

"Begging your pardon, sir," she said, catching his attention for the first time. "She's not your horse."

Kellan jumped as the girl slipped into view around the mare. "What, this horse?"

He meant to loom over her, to use his natural presence and a fierce glare to put the girl off without doing any real harm. But as their faces met in the dim light, he was too shaken to put on the airs of a threat.

Her hair was white as snow, like an old woman's, but there was no mistaking her face. It had run leaner and she had grown some, but her wide, round eyes were exactly as they had been in Silver. He brought a hand up in surprise, stroking the thick muscle of his chest where her little arrow had nearly ended him.

Aewyn, if anything, was all the more shaken. She had seen him clearly that day, and ever after in nightmares that came to her when she was overtired on the road. He was one of only two men she had ever tried to kill, before she understood what killing really meant; and if Castor Stannon's haunting, one-eyed face was the chiefest terror of her fitful dreams, the giant with a scarred chest and a horrible scowl was not far behind.

"You," she breathed.

"The girl," he said.

She was fast, to be sure. If the delay between Kellan's wits and his brutality had been as long as a normal man's, she might have dodged the punch. But his mailed fist shot out hard on raw instinct, as if he'd held it at the ready ever since the day he'd been shot. There was nothing much to her; she was small even on the edge of adulthood, and his fist slammed against the side of her head and lifted her clean off the ground. She hit the stable doors hard enough to rock them on their hinges, and crumpled to the floor in a motionless heap.

"Murdering bitch," Kellan spat. "That's for taking Castor's eye!"

"Pots and tossers!" Rasten cursed. "What's going on out here?"

Kellan spun on his heels. Rasten had followed him to the door, stood there in alarm, his hands on the hilts of his weapons.

"What are you doing here?" Kellan barked.

"What does it look like?" said Rasten. "I'm here to stop you from making a terrible mistake." He looked at the girl's body, moving restlessly at his feet as she tried to rise. "Seems I'm too late."

"This little bitch put an arrow in me," said Kellan. "Meant to kill me. Castor Stannon, too. She attacked us at the hanging." As he pulled his dagger out of his belt, Rasten fought desperately to find more words in time to halt its descent.

"No, no!" he said, waving his big hands protectively. "She's just a girl!"

"Aye, a girl cruel enough to kill two men who never meant her no harm—and then dumb enough to do it only halfway."

"Revenge will get you nothing," said Rasten.

"Not revenge," said Kellan with a shrug. "Precaution." He took a deep breath to steady himself, as if to be sure it was prudence, not rage, guiding his hand.

Rasten snapped out his weapons. Sword and axe gleamed in the lamplight.

"Listen to me, if you want to live," he urged.

Kellan looked at his friend with a mixture of sadness, pity, and exhausted obligation. "Don't wag those toys at me, boy. You know I'm a harder man than you. I'm already leaving. Don't make me leave with regret on my hands."

Rasten jerked his head toward the big mare untethered beside him, backing away in confusion and shuffling its hooves. "So what did you think you would do, steal a horse? Ride out in this storm alone? No blankets or bedrolls?"

"Aye, if it comes to that. Old tin-britches would be mad to follow me."

"He wouldn't have to. You'd be frozen dead in three hours without warm bodies next to you."

Aewyn moaned softly and put her hands under her, trying to get to her knees. She seemed so very small now that Kellan sheathed his dagger with disgust and pity as he bent down, seizing her hard by her white locks.

"My friend here has a delicate stomach," he said. "For his sake, instead of me cracking your skull open, let's just pretend I did. Put your face on the ground and don't move."

With a whimper, the girl did as she was told.

"You're a monster," said Rasten.

"You're the one with killing weapons drawn," said Kellan. "You don't understand what's about to happen. Those woodsmen in there—those Havenari—they're going to take Ashimar straight to Widowvale. They know these woods inside out. They know exactly where it is. They'll make me look like I've been pissing around for weeks just to spite him. Soon as he's got a better guide—and that could be five minutes from now—he's done with me for good. I'm leaving now, while my head's attached. I'll take my chances in the cold."

"He offered to make you a permanent bloodguard," Rasten protested.

"Of course he did," said Kellan. "And you believed it? He's never had a bloodguard who wasn't born to the life. They're trained from birth for it. He's keeping me in line until he's done with me."

"You won't make it five miles alone in this storm. When those Havenari see what you've done to that girl, they'll be on you from one side, and we'll be on you from the other. I'm begging you, don't be stupid."

"What would you have me do?" Kellan asked, as loud as he dared with the Havenari just through the wall. "Stand and wait while my usefulness to Ashimar runs out? Let those backwoods pig-stickers run me through when they see what I've done to her?"

Rasten gestured incredulously to Aewyn. "Yes, about that. Was that necessary? Really?"

Kellan shook his head. "We seem to keep forgetting the part where she tried to murder me!"

Suddenly, Rasten grew quiet and shouldered his weapons.

"Wait. She shot you…at the hanging," he said softly.

"Aye."

"In Widowvale."

Kellan looked down at the girl disdainfully. "Aye."

"Wait here," said Rasten. "Just don't hurt her. I've got an idea. I may get you out of this alive."

"Oh, '*may*,' there's a word I love to hear," said Kellan.

Rasten pointed to Aewyn. "Listen: after all this searching, you found her. You finally found the girl who would lead us straight to Widowvale…*if* you keep her alive."

"The Havenari will lead you there just the same," said Kellan. "I've still got nothing."

"You've got everything," Rasten protested. "You're the cynic here.

You know how Ashimar works. He doesn't compromise. He doesn't bargain. He doesn't even work with the Grand Army. You think he'll trust himself and his men to the mercy of these country squires on their own soil? Right now, he'll work with the Havenari because he thinks he needs them. You keep her alive, you bring her with us, and that all changes. He's not a patient man. He'll ride out of here right now, tonight, if you tell him you know where you're going, and we don't need to rely on the rest of them."

"Those Havenari will be on our tails if we take her," said Kellan. "There may be blood. Maybe yours."

"Bar this door. Pile up whatever you must to keep it closed. And for the Fool's sake, don't kill her. I'll bring the men out around the back. If we can get twenty minutes out, in this storm, there'll be no trail for them to track."

Kellan nodded approvingly. "That almost sounds like the start of a plan. You're a good man. Never thought you'd stoop to kidnapping."

Rasten sighed. "I'd rather not think about that till it's too late."

There was a viciously sharp dirk hidden away in the gauntlet of Ashimar's dreadful armour. Robyn waited a long time on the darkness of the narrow stair, gathering her courage; and when she came to him at last, it was the point of the dirk that met her face to face as she mounted the top landing. She did not flinch as he levelled it at her; that seemed to impress him.

"I know who you are, my lord Scourge," she said.

"Then you have me at a disadvantage," replied Ashimar, in a way that reminded her who really held all the power in the little room.

"My name is Robyn," she said. "I am First Spear of the Havenari of Haveïl, and I am at your service."

Ashimar sheathed his weapon. "I have no need of your service."

"My lord, in a storm such as this, there are none whose travels do not go easier with the Havenari to guide them. Our sworn duty—"

"Do not speak to me of duty, Captain. I have come to your woods for one errand alone. When it is done, I will leave you. I pray you will not complicate my work."

"Oh no, my lord," said Robyn. "Truly, I mean to help you achieve it as quickly as possible."

"Why?"

"As you say, my lord," Robyn said, chancing a smile. "When it is done, you will leave us."

"I seek a traitor to the Imperator," Ashimar said, wasting no time. "He is called Celithrand, though he has many other names. He was sentenced to die, but slipped through the fingers of lesser men."

"I have heard of him," said Robyn.

"He was last seen in a farming village. Widowvale. Not far off the Iron Road."

Robyn had guessed, of course, the nature of his business; but to hear it in his eerily soft voice still unsettled her. The thought of him there, among the people, seeking answers…

"It's a long way hence, my lord," said Robyn. "Or so I've heard."

Ashimar folded his hands. "Don't toy with me. My own men have exhausted my patience. I have none left for you. You will lead me to Widowvale, I will finish what the censor began, and we will be on our way the same day."

"If he's still there," said Robyn hastily. "But suppose he's moved on." She'd come with ample resolve, for she was always forceful in her dealings with forest criminals, bandits, murderous men. But her composure was fast slipping away from her for reasons she could not quite understand.

"The traitor knows the ways of the old woods," said Ashimar. "He will be hard to track. But if the trees and grass do not betray his direction of travel to me, I am sure the villagers will. I have that feeling." He paused for a moment as Robyn's face whitened.

"My lord," came a voice from below. It was Rasten on the narrow stair, eyes wide.

"My chamber is not a common-room," said Ashimar. Laying an armoured hand on Robyn's shoulder with sudden impatience, he pushed her effortlessly back out of the room and sheathed his weapon. Despite his presence, Robyn realized he was no taller than she was; but the strength of his arm would not be denied and she found herself shoved back against the broad-shouldered bloodguard behind her.

"My lord," said the man, "we have found our way! No need to trouble with these country squires."

"Impossible," said Ashimar. "How? When?"

"It seems your overgrown guide dog has come through after all," Rasten beamed. He looked eager to say more, but regarded Robyn with an awkward suspicion.

Ashimar turned to her suddenly as he came forward. "Was your offer sincere?" he asked.

"M-most sincere," she said, her face inches from his weeping mask.

"Do not depart this place until you are given leave," he said. "I may yet have need of you." He pushed past her, then, following his obedient bloodguard down the creaking steps. Although she meant to follow them, she leaned first against the jamb of the door and drew deep breaths as she willed her innards back to calm.

"I hope for your sake you are not deceived," said Ashimar, close to Rasten's shoulder; then, with perhaps the first note of genuine surprise Rasten had ever heard from him, "where are my men?"

The alehouse did not really seem emptier; in the absence of the terrifying bloodguard the merchants had spread out their bodies and bedrolls across the unoccupied space. Most had drunk their fill and many were ready to sleep—including most of the Havenari, who lay grain-weary in their cups—all save one, who watched them intently as they came.

"They're out moving our gear up onto the horses," said Rasten.

"We came with no horses," Ashimar reminded him.

Ras shrugged. "That's about to change. Imperial business, and all."

They went out the way they came in, through the front door into the cold, and already Rasten felt only a fool would follow them. The blizzard caught him full in the face, stung his cheeks and blasted tiny crystals of ice through his eyelashes as he squinted against the wind and cold. Ashimar took the lead now, tireless in the snow; it was easy enough to tell where the men had come only minutes before. More men had come on this thankless quest than had stayed with the ship, and even in this fast snowfall there were easy traces of their passage.

There were many worn-out stable-buildings, but the barnlike structure adorning the outside of the alehouse was by far the best suited to weather the storm, on account of sharing a thick stone wall with the radiant hearth-hall. It was here that the Havenari had been given the choicest stabling for their mounts, and it was here the bloodguard now made ready to travel, loading their own kits onto the horses. Few trusted Rasten, and fewer still welcomed his direction, but all were relieved that there would be no more trudging through the snow with such weight. Kellan, easing up onto the largest of the horses, was loading a groggy-looking white-haired girl whose hands were tightly bound.

"I see our ranks have grown yet again," Ashimar said—and not happily.

"I've found her," said Kellan. "This girl comes straight from the village. She's the one who shot Castor Stannon's eye out."

"What, *her*?"

"I swear it," said Kellan, with his desperation a little too transparent. "She'll lead us straight there."

"Unh," Aewyn moaned softly.

"Well, soon as she's back to her right senses."

"She wears the green of the Havenari," said Ashimar.

"She does," said Rasten. "That's why we're taking the horses. They'll not let her go lightly."

"Then I will conscript her as I have conscripted you," Ashimar said.

"They may not take kindly to that," said Rasten. "But if we take the horses, we'll have no chase from them, especially not in this weather."

Ashimar nodded. "Our duty to the Imperator dwarfs all else. Take them. Do it quietly."

"There's more horses than we've got riders," said one of the bloodguards.

"Take a horse for every man," said Ashimar. "Ride them well away from the stable. When they're far enough out not to be alarmed by the others, break the legs of the rest and we'll be on our way."

At first, the horses steadfastly refused to cooperate. They knew their riders by sight and scent, and though they were trained to take armoured riders on cue, they bristled nervously at the prospect of strange men. Ashimar's new horse, the sleek black mare Aewyn had been brushing, started most of all, sending up such snorts and stamps of discontent that he was compelled to stand well back from the lot of them until the bloodguard had them moving. They were none too eager to brave the storm again at the best of times, but Rasten gently led and coaxed a mild-tempered gelding out of the stable on foot; soon a second horse was made to follow it, then a third, at which point the others began to fall in with the natural obedience of herd animals in spite of their misgivings. Cold though it might have been, they much preferred the night sky and open field to being tightly closed in with so many unfamiliar men.

"You are sure she will lead us," said Ashimar. "You are staking your life on this girl, you know." Ahead of him, the horses and riders moving back toward the main road disappeared into a curtain of snow. They had scarcely stepped out of their own footprints when the blowing snow began to fill them.

Kellan held his mount in check as the others cleared out around him. "Aye. She'd lead us to the Banlands and back with the right encouragement."

"Put her down," said a voice.

Kellan jerked sharply around. The main door to the alehouse was still tightly barred, but one of the Havenari, the quick-handed one, had slipped out the back door and followed them around the long way. Kellan tasted the blood still crusted in his moustache and thought better of responding with sudden brutality. But he no longer stood against the stranger alone.

"Out of our way," he spat. "This is the Imperator's business."

Bram stepped back for a moment, thought of going back for the rest of the Havenari. But all save Robyn were deep in their cups, more than half-asleep around the hearth. The snow was falling in thick, fat flakes; it was the kind of storm you could lose a whole village in, let alone a single young woman.

"If the Imperator enlists common horse thieves," said Bram, "so be it. But that girl stays where she is."

In the narrow space of the stable, Ashimar motioned for three of the remaining men to dismount.

"Do you know who I am, stranger?" he said.

Bram's hand went to the hilt of his sword. "You're a man pushing sixty, slowed by sixty pounds of plate," he said, "with nothing to show for it but two dozen exposed joints." But the Weeping Man would not be baited.

"Go," Ashimar said to Kellan. "Take her. Get the others moving. You three, see to him."

"He's quick," warned Kellan. "Watch yourselves." He kicked his horse and sped from the barn as the three bloodguards surrounded the stranger and reached for their weapons. The last man, the smartest of them, secured his bull-headed great helm before moving in to flank, and Bram stepped back warily, reconsidering his strokes as the exposed face and throat vanished.

In the end, to his credit, one of the bloodguards did manage to get his sword-point free. The first of them, the slowest, had just put his hand to his hilt when the very tip of Bram's sword, flicking out on the draw, opened his throat and put him down. The second man, probably the fastest, had nearly pulled his weapon free from its his belted scabbard when Bram seized the weapon's hilt with his free hand, the scabbard with his sword-hand, and twisted hard on the long rigid bar made by sword and scabbard together, as if turning the wheel of a ship. Fastened as it was to his hip, the man soon followed, his head tumbling down hard into the path of the third man's blade as he drew.

Faced with the prospect of fighting unarmed if he could not get his weapon out in time, the bull-helmed warrior finished his stroke in spite of the fatal blow it dealt to his companion; he was, then, the only one of the three whose sword was live and free in his hand when he was cut down. He even lived long enough to cry out in agony as he went down, though this, too, was by design. There are few things that call attention like the scream of a dying man, and so Bram killed him at the inside of both thighs, so that he might fall with the whole structure of his chest intact, and give some real breath and strength to his dying screams for long enough to alert the others. Beneath the steel of his great helm, the screams echoed like the sound of a bull at slaughter. With his free hand, Bram shoved the bar off the door and waited for the others.

"You are a master, then," Ashimar noted with dispassionate approval as three of his bloodguards spilled out onto the frozen earth between them. Bram looked to him, then to the horse darting away into the snow with Aewyn slung across it. In the moment it took him to make his decision, Ashimar had retrieved his immense greatsword from the side of the horse he had attempted to ride. He was coming fast, but Bram sprinted for the retreating horse instead, trusting that Ashimar's armour would weigh him down in the snow. If he fled the fight, he could always return to it. If he lost Aewyn, he knew he might not find her again.

The drifts were up to Bram's knees as he chased desperately after the rider. The surface of the snow here was already broken, and for now a scattered set of tracks led the way to the other horses. But Bram could not hope to keep pace with the horse as Kellan kicked it recklessly to a gallop through the treacherous snow. He reached for it in vain as it sped away from him; then, without sound and almost without warning, Ashimar was on him, greatsword flashing with uncanny speed for such a heavy weapon. Bram caught the stroke with his own blade and turned it, though the force shook his arm; he tapped his sword-point in twice against joints too well-made to give way to such light strokes. Ashimar cut back, catching nothing but thin air, then seized the blade of his sword with his gauntleted hand and thrust it forward like a spear. Bram planted a foot on the flat of the immense blade as it pierced the air, and launched a vicious kick against the weeping visage of Ashimar's helmet, snapping his head back and stealing the force from the thrust. Bram's sword darted in twice more, licking at the edges of the Weeping Man's breastplate, but Ashimar turned his shoulders and it could find no purchase in the weaker mail that covered the joints.

They were well away from the alehouse now as their swords crossed, far from the light, caught up to their knees in caking snow as more of it fell around them. Bram, with no armour but the heavy fur cloak he quickly doffed in the fighting, twisted away from Ashimar's swings time and time again. The Weeping Man threw his greatsword about as if it were a weapon of half its size; the weight of his exquisite plate seemed of little consequence to him, and he showed no sign of tiring. The question of catching Aewyn and the horse was moot, now; there was only the flash of steel, the steaming clouds of Bram's laboured breath, and the steady ring of his blows as they rained home but did not penetrate.

"Sister!" Bram called into the night as he ducked one swing after another. "Robyn! Sister!"

"Your technique betrays you," said Ashimar, his voice emotionless despite the exertion of the fight. "I thought for certain Master General Harrod had wiped out the last of Draden's honour guards myself."

"With what army?" Bram spat back; but the words cost him too much breath and he was forced to take another slash on his blade, nicking its fine edge even as it spared his arm.

"Now I see he was as sloppy in his execution as you are," cooed Ashimar. "Tysen's style was a quaint relic even in my youth—and I am an old man, now."

In quieter moments, Bram might have had a retort for that, too; but all his thought was turned to the problem of the armour, and how he might overcome it without a mace or crushing weapon to make short work of its occupant. Ashimar seemed spry enough and unhindered by it, so fine was its craftsmanship, and here in the darkness of the field it was hard to spot its flaws, of which he had taken only brief stock in the lamplit stable. That Bram was the superior swordsman was not in doubt; but the odds were tightly stacked against him. He was working harder to do less, and he was caught off-guard by the uncanny strength of his opponent, who foiled his strokes one after another with deft turns of his heavy armour, then struck one riposte after the next with the grace and speed of a man in jesters' hose rather than heavy plate.

They dueled, if a fight without niceties can be deemed as such, for what felt like a year passing in the space of a half-minute. The hits went to Bram, but counted for little, and a single mistake against Ashimar's flashing greatsword would have taken an arm or a leg in payment. In time, though, the fatal moment came: finding the stable door still blocked, Robyn had come around the back as well with some of the men. Her voice sent up a shrill curse as she stumbled on the stable doors thrown wide, and most of the horses missing. Some of the others were there with her, too, from the sounds of it.

Bram heard it, as he knew he soon must. Ashimar heard it, too, and in a moment of vulnerable surprise he glanced back to see how many reinforcements stood at his back. In that briefest of beats between swings of the sword, Bram gripped the Weeping Man's shoulder with frozen fingers, wrenched the pauldron desperately forward to expose a narrow crevice in the nearly seamless armpit of the suit, and plunged the tip of his sword home.

The sword did not slide smoothly or thrust deep, but there was no mistaking the familiar feel of steel piercing mail and meeting with flesh. Ashimar roared out in anger and pain, and his greatsword fell free of his hands. Bram jerked the blade and tried to twist it, widening both the wound and the split in the mail, but the sword was stuck fast—more so, now, as Ashimar twisted his arm down over the wound, clamping the blade in place. Unexpectedly snared, Bram tried for an instant too long to pry his weapon free, planting his boot atop Ashimar's turned knee as he pulled the blade back—then Ashimar's hand flashed out with the dirk hidden in his gauntlet, and the inside of Bram's thigh was suddenly hot and slick as his blood streamed over it.

His piercing cry called Robyn's attention to the field, where he jerked his sword free with a last desperate surge of strength and fell backwards into the snow, rolling back just out of reach. He came up on both feet, but the right leg could not hold its full share of his weight for long: now that his blood was up, the pain was bearable, but the wound was deep and he knew it. He took a defensive stance as his opponent picked up his greatsword again, but to his surprise, Ashimar looked back to the Havenari streaming out of the alehouse and charged away, dashing off into the raging storm. Bram took a few steps, tried to give chase, but knew in an instant it was not to be. He screamed in frustration and agony, and fell to a knee, holding his sword low in the Fool's Guard in case he could lure his opponent back to finish the job. But it was too late, now. Ashimar was gone, Aewyn was gone, and the fight was lost.

Robyn was first to reach him, springing nimbly through the snow as the drunken Havenari staggered behind her.

"They've taken her," he gasped. "They've taken Aewyn."

Robyn looked after them, her eyes burning. "Can you run?"

Bram shook his head. "No."

"Can you ride?"

Bram clutched her hand, led it to the streaming wound in his leg. She felt it again and again in disbelief, as if she could not quite comprehend that he had really been touched by steel.

"This…this is bad," she breathed.

"Go. Go after her. We've still… they left horses. Take Roald, he's… fast rider…"

"Help me!" Robyn cried. "Help me with him!"

Big Venser was the next to reach them, tromping through the red snow with long strides, and then Roald, who was smaller but quick on his feet. Between the two of them, they hoisted Bram up and hauled him back toward the alehouse. Robyn took up his cloak and followed them back, for he had begun to shiver without it.

"They've got Aewyn," he said, softly. "I'm sorry."

"Hush up," his sister said. "We'll find her."

"The horses. The supplies."

"Never you mind," said Robyn. "We'll see to you first. You're in a bad way."

"Never catch them," Bram wheezed. "Too much…head start."

"Don't gainsay what's been decided," Robyn told him again. "He won't get far."

They laid him out in the stable where the last few horses milled about on their tethers, nervous but still unharmed. Robyn laid both hands over his leg and sent Venser in for bandages and hot coals from the hearth.

"Did you make him pay for this?" she asked. Bram gestured around the stable to the bodies he had left there.

"Three men, I cost him. And I put a hole in him…he'll not soon forget," he said. "He's sore wounded, too. Close by the lung."

"That should slow him up some," said Robyn.

"Won't matter," said Bram. "Not if we lose them in this storm. Forget me. Leave me with the alewife. Get to the horses. We'll never track him if you wait until those tracks fill in."

"We don't have to track him," said Robyn. "I know where he's going. Tsúla, can you ride?"

A lithe but well-muscled Esman raised his head with his jaw firmly set. "One of them took Rascal. But I can ride faster in anger than any man alive in fear."

"Saddle up Meioc or Jumper, then. You're going. The rusty old fool told me right where he's headed."

TEN

OSGRIM FROWNED as only a schoolmaster could. "If you are feeling so miserably unwell," he said, "perhaps we should leave off until tomorrow, and return you to your chambers."

The lesson was not going well. Outside across the courtyard, the Imperial Harper's masons had spent most of the day hammering and chipping away at the immense mural of the Company of the Owl that covered the twisted, wailing faces carved into the Inner Wall. The sun had set some time ago, but the tradesmen had clanged and cracked and rattled well into the night, as if something about their work were too shameful for the light of day. Illyria's lessons on poetry, the Viluri and old Vosi languages, and even duller things had been entirely spoilt by the clamour of their tools and their rowdy work-songs. Now that she was on to the weird histories of far-off places and the strange laws of king-ruled lands, she had become her own worst enemy.

Far from her books, farther still from her lessons, she lay whimpering on a pillowed divan in her private study, complaining of a sharp pain in her ribs—a pain that had arisen, as if by marvellous coincidence, just as she was about to turn to the dull subject of border treaties and the legislative burdens of sovereign nations.

"I'm not lying," she groaned. "It really hurts again." She winced as only a young girl tired of her studies could.

"Something you ate, perhaps," said Osgrim. "Or too long lying abed can upset the breathing. Shall I call for the sedan?"

"No," Illyria said. "No. Please don't send me back yet."

"You're in no condition to study. We should get you back—"

"No. No, I'm fine."

"Well, then." Osgrim motioned to the table, and Illyria hoisted herself up with some difficulty and began to shuffle back toward the books.

"I have noticed," said Osgrim, "that the excuse of your frailty seems to align itself with the dullest of your lessons. The romances of Ithuriel, I hear no complaints, beside your usual shortness of breath. But when we discuss the treaties that bind the Protectorates—or just last week, the Banland migrations of the Vosi—you suffer from an attack of the joints or some other distraction. Discussing the diplomatic process of the Rahastan court is a sure way to give you a fierce headache. And today, searing chest pains close by the heart as we turn to the Scorvanian border-disputes. History is not your enemy, Illyra. A few dull, dry documents can't truly bore a young girl to death. If they could, Olferth would have every censor flogged and every ledger burned upon their entry to the city."

Illyria smiled in spite of herself. "Olferth doesn't really care about me," she said. "He only knows my father would have his head up on Lornock Gate if anything were to happen to me."

"Are you really in pain?"

She nodded. "But I'm a sickly girl, Osgrim. I've had worse. It will pass. Please don't send me back to my chambers."

Osgrim cast his troubled gaze up through the coloured glass dome of the rotunda, to where the mottled black shadow of the Cîr-Valithar loomed overhead. "I am sorry you are unwell," he said, with the weight of a man starting to take her seriously. "Perhaps instead of endless border-treatises, you would prefer to hear the tragic tale of Karm Parvis of Seythe—and of the fatal woman who loved him."

Illyria smiled, but with the hesitation that comes from suspicion.

"I should like that very much," she said.

Osgrim shut the wooden lid on an enormous board-backed tome of charters and cartularies. "The twin isles of Nalsin and Seythe," he began, "were settled not by charter, but by wars great and terrible in days of old. Scorvan was the southmost capital of Nalsin, instrumental in the Seythan Conquest and the Suther Wars. For some time, it was a neutral city to which refugees of both sides fled. Neutral parties flourished there, and assassins or spies or even knights could be bought and sold as cheaply as vegetables at market. It lay on the Bastrien River, and it was—and still is, mind you—the only reliable ford between the south coast and Nalsin proper."

Illyria yawned, but made an effort to pay attention, knowing full well she had drawn special privilege out of the old man.

"Parvis was an anointed Karm, a Seythan knight and a hero of the war. He was also, at least as the Hanes tell, the fastest rider in the Near West. His stallion Fleetwind was the hero of many songs even without his rider."

"I wish I could ride a horse," said Illyria. "Perhaps someday I'll learn."

"So thirteen years the Suther Wars had raged on," said Osgrim, "and the Seythans, too eager for the land across the channel, had come off the worst for it. The Aeril King of Nalsin, Zaran the Second, called Spurnsea, had driven the Seythan invaders back nearly to the coast. Only one Seythan general, Baigan the Bold, remained in the forests of Nalsin. With almost the whole of the Seythan army, they wintered on the coast, looking over the sea to Daer Móran, cut off from their countrymen."

"Old Mardon would love this story," said Illyria, though it was clear that war-stories were not entirely to her own tastes.

"In time," said Osgrim, "the Seythan king could hold out no longer. He called Zaran to the isle of Seythe, where they signed a peace treaty. The south isle was to be abandoned and returned to Nalsin, and in return the wars would cease and the Seythans would be given three years to settle and marry according to laws I've outlined in this book—laws you ought to have read by now—or to salvage what could be had of their fortunes and return home across the sea in disgrace."

"But the Seythans won the war," Illyria said.

"Only because they did not know they had lost," said Osgrim. "The message to lay down arms was trusted to Karm Parvis, who rode day and night from the channel with a copy of the treaty for Baigan's encampment. Karm Baigan was duty-bound to disband his forces and walk them back to the coast to begin the withdrawal. Zaran was ready to wipe them out, and the Seythans did not want the deaths of thirty thousand men on their hands."

"So what happened to those thirty thousand men?" asked Illyria.

"One woman did," said Osgrim. "As is often the way. Karm Parvis was a man of many appetites, and he frequently indulged them at Scorford Bridge, where the city crossed the Bastrien. It was there in the bloom of summer he met a woman of exquisite beauty, a siren who enchanted him so completely that he lost his soul to her. Perhaps she was a fairy queen of Daer Móran. Perhaps she was one of the druid lords, whose women rose as high in the ranks as any of the men. Perhaps she was a common tavern-wench, or something in between; the stories differ. But they all agree that for nine days, Karm Parvis lingered on the banks of the Bastrien and took his ease in the arms of a foreign lover. And for those nine days, the order never came to Karm Baigan; and when the Nalsian forces entered the wood, he fell upon them with guile and ferocity. They did not expect it, you see, for they knew the surrender had been issued. They outnumbered him three to one, yet he much reduced their strength and fled into the woods with his men. For a whole year after that, even his own king could not find him. And when summer came again, the tides of war had much turned. So much fighting had gone on that Zaran tore up his own treaty and considered it betrayed. The war went on another twelve years after that, and when at last a treaty was made again, it was under different skies, and the Seythans kept their new homeland, right to the coastline. They demanded all lands south of the Bastrien, and this was denied them; but all of Seythe would have been lost to them if their king's letter of surrender had gone through."

"That's a war-story," said Illyria. "Not a love story."

"I like to think it's both," said Osgrim. A rare wistful look crept across his stony features.

"What became of the lovers?"

"Oh, they were put to death, of course," said Osgrim. "Karm Parvis for certain, by the Seythan King, for desertion and failing in his duty."

"And the woman? What was her name?"

"The Hanes do not say," said Osgrim. "War-poets are careless with the names of women, in my experience. But the story I have heard, the one I like to believe, is that she was Karm Baigan's wife, who never lost faith in him even when his own king had done. It was she who seduced the messenger and kept the surrender from reaching her husband's hands."

"But…did she love him so little, that she would lie with another man?" Illyria asked.

Osgrim only smiled. "In the great lays," he said, "those matters are complicated. I imagine in the histories, they are even more so. My point with this tale, is that all those Scorvanian border-disputes, civic matters that seem so dull to you, have their origin in a love-story. And no doubt many love-stories, too, have their origin in civil disputes. Great successes and failures in diplomacy, Illyria, have forged or broken loves and treaties like. Affairs of the heart are in want of a diplomat, sometimes to a far greater extent than affairs of the sword. All the more reason why a comely young girl with a romantic heart ought to know the Scorvanian cartularies more thoroughly—not less—than any general."

"You will say any old thing," she said, "to keep me at my studies."

"I will," said Osgrim. "One day these things will become important."

"I should hope so," said Illyria. "Idleness does not become me. Do you suppose—when the war is over—when I can see my father again—do you suppose he would make me a diplomat? My family is of no small nobility, even notwithstanding the Siege and the Annexation. If I study the treaties of far lands, if I read and write as well as any Magistrate, I could be an ambassador or a diplomat, couldn't I?"

Osgrim nodded in spite of himself. "I think you would make a fine ambassador," he said.

"Do you think he'll let me? When the war's over?"

Osgrim was silent a long moment. "One thing only is certain," he said. "Such work could never come to a young woman who was unprepared for the adventure, and too unlearned about foreign lands to be trusted beyond their borders."

That, at least, seemed to have its desired effect. She smiled at him and resumed her seat dutifully.

"I'll try," she said.

Osgrim hoisted up one of the heavy codices and slid it back across the polished table. "Good," he said. "Read."

She opened the book, if not with relish, with less boredom than before, and Osgrim slipped away from the table and toward the chamber door. He glanced back again, as if to ensure it was not a posturing, then slipped out into the anteroom.

"You should not be here," he said.

There in the shadow of Illyria's sedan, with his old curator's robes draped over his Cerulean cloak, Elmore Godshall stood patiently in wait.

"Well met, Osgrim," he said. "I must speak with you on a matter of—"

"The rules are clear, soldier."

"Soldier?" Elmore looked pained. "Do you so soon forget a fellow Curator of this library?"

"Lower your voice," said Osgrim. "Of course I remember you. But there is a protocol to be followed when you escort this young lady. You put yourself, and much else, at risk by breaching it. The last man who did so—"

"Rasten, I know," said Elmore. "Sent off with the Scourge. Promoted to the Bloodguard. If you can call it a promotion."

Osgrim took Elmore by the arm and led him farther away from Illyria's study.

"So you know what happened to him. You know, then, what a risk you take by coming too close to her, especially after another of your rank has done the same."

"I've never understood the importance of her," said Elmore. "Strategically, I mean. Valithar is no Baron-King of old. He did not inherit the Throne Tower, and when his deathday comes, it will not pass to her."

"Won't it?" Osgrim said, like a man who already knew it wouldn't.

"I don't know what will rightly happen," said Elmore. "I imagine that'll be a matter for the Magistrates to decide—yourself included, my lord. Maybe the title will pass, and Travalaith will come under some other rule. Or maybe Lord Olferth has got the Master Generals under his thumb, and will push to become Imperator himself. Fool knows he's already running the Empire. Mouth of Travalaith indeed! If he's the voice of the Imperator, I'm sure Valithar doesn't know half of what he's truly speaking."

"There is some disagreement over what will come," said Osgrim.

"Either way," said Elmore, "that sheltered child will not take command of an Empire at war. I'm surprised Olferth hasn't shipped her off to Vostarban, or married her off to some pig-farmer as a foundling, just to ensure his hold on Valithar's legacy is absolute."

"It is not as simple as all that," said Osgrim. "But you did not interrupt us at great risk to twaddle on about matters of succession."

Elmore, having genuinely lost himself in these matters, stuttered momentarily as he recalled his original purpose.

"I...I seek your advice, old man."

"Regarding what?"

"Regarding a woman."

They had come now to a quiet place far from Illyria's study, through winding aisles of scrolls and codices that kept their voices from echoing back to the solarium. Even so, Osgrim was not given to laughter; the broad white smile that suddenly capped his dark beard was as silent as the still air itself.

"You are an old man for such lessons," said Osgrim, "and on those matters I would be a poor tutor."

Elmore cleared his throat and, in spite of his seriousness, embraced the spark of humour. "Regarding two women, then, I should say. Perhaps more than two, before all is said and done."

"Now you have my full attention," said Osgrim dryly. Elmore composed himself and lowered his voice.

"I would bring this matter to the Imperial Harper himself," he said, "if I could trust his interest was for the good of the Empire, and not for his own trueblacked purse. But I don't know whom to trust, save another fellow of the Library. This city, that was supposed to be proof from spies, has been breached. These walls, supposed to have been impregnable, are of no consequence. There are spies in the city, Osgrim; I have found them. You know how little I care for the war effort. You of all people know I should never have been made a soldier. But I care a great deal about that young lady you have in there. The tighter she's guarded, the more the enemy will want her. And she's in worse danger than you know. The enemy knows of her; I'm certain of it. They know she's here. They know everything about her."

Osgrim was no longer smiling. "This is a matter for the Imperial Harper and the Ceruleans," he said. "For Master General Thurmod and the Legions of the Shield."

"It is a matter for you, Osgrim!" said Elmore, his voice low but his blue eyes desperate. "You are the only one I trust."

"I understand your misgivings," sighed the old man. "Those who hold power here do not always have the will of the people at heart. But I cannot interfere in Illyria's upbringing beyond my very limited capacity as her tutor. Not even to protect her. Do you understand?"

"She's in terrible danger," sad Elmore. "If Jordac knows of her existence, her life is forfeit. I cannot warn her—but you can. Please, Osgrim…"

The old man waved his hands. "Her personal security, above all, is a matter for the Cerulean Guard. For you, if I understand correctly. You and your friend Rasten."

Elmore cleared his throat. "It is Rasten who has betrayed us," he sighed.

"What?"

"Betrayed us without knowing it," Elmore was quick to finish. "Betrayed us to a false and fatal woman who has snared the poor fool's heart and turned him into the eyes and ears of Jordac."

"How do you know this?"

"There are more of them," said Elmore. "These women. How many more, I don't know. They find us up on Vairhurst, among the shrines of the fallen. Ruined men, grieving men. Veterans who come home from war broken and loveless, whose honours and infirmities both win them rare positions of power and influence. They tried to snare me as well! They take good men, good men like Rasten, poor stupid innocent men, and—Myrine's tears, Osgrim! That boy! If the Imperator finds out what Rasten's done—the true extent of it—he'll kill him!" The old man wiped an eye. "He was a good fellow, Rasten. He doesn't deserve that."

Osgrim's gaze was fixed, like a hawk's.

"Tell me everything," he said.

In the dream, Rasten and Jalen always stood back-to-back, four weapons at the ready, waiting atop the hill for the faceless hordes of masked Selikhan raiders that would never come. Rasten had no love for the danger of battle—few men too well-acquainted with it do—but it vexed him sorely, once he came to know the dream, that he would wake just before they reached him. He and Jalen had been unstoppable together, once. It would have been glorious.

Instead, they stood in tense silence, awaiting the fight that never came. It was not a frequent dream, and it had grown less frequent since Catrine had become his lover and confidante. But here, on the frontier, the dream came again.

"Here they come," said Jalen, unconcerned.

"I miss you," said Rasten. It was the first thing he said, every time, when he had control of his own voice in the dream. It was usually a sign that he was waking—that they had only moments left.

"I know it," said Jalen. "You're worried about the girl, aren't you?"

"I'm worried about everything," said Rasten. "I don't know what we're doing out here. I don't know what's happening back home. I know we're on a fool's errand; I just can't believe Ashimar has taken the bait. We're all going to die in the snow if we're not careful."

Jalen glanced down the hill at the cloaked men, spectres of some fear Rasten could not yet place.

"You'll die sooner than most," he said, "if you don't go back."

At those very words, Rasten felt the chill return to his bones. It was like being trapped underwater, this dream, and the surface was drawing ever closer.

"It's not time yet," said Rasten, though he knew it was.

They didn't touch or embrace each other. They never did. But for a moment, in his brother's eyes, Ras was a child again, carefree in his brother's arms; then they were young men, too eager for battle and proud of their glorious place in the wars to come. Then, there was only one brother, Rasten, who found himself flat on his back in the snow, half-covered by it, as one of the bloodguards shook him awake. The snow was still falling, still thick enough to coat the ruddy skin of his face and mask the tears that welled there as he was pulled out of the temperate green fields of his brother's company, back into the frozen and barren world of living men.

"On your feet," said the bloodguard. "He's caught up with us."

They'd taken what shelter they could in a copse of alder trees blasted prematurely barren by the storm. The horses, uneasy and uncomfortable at being separated from their usual riders and the rest of their herd, were proving difficult to control. The girl they had taken had come back to her senses, and was sitting by a little heap of kindling as the men tried in vain to get a fire going. There was no need to bind her hands or feet: she shook with fear in Kellan's shadow and dared not test his patience.

In the dark of night and covered as he was with snow, Ashimar was nearly on top of them before they could make him out. With steady, plodding steps, he approached the defensive drift they had raised around their little camp and ploughed his way through it without breaking pace. Still in his hands, his greatsword dragged and bounced its way across the snowy field. For the first time, Rasten saw a tiredness in his step and wondered, now, what might have happened.

The bloodguard met him not with eagerness, exactly, but with promptness. Ashimar passed through them, too, toward that part of the copse where the branches hung thickest.

"*Report*," was all he said. His voice had a chilling hollowness to it.

"We await your command," said the bloodguard. "The horses will serve, for a while, at least. The girl is awake, and we're ready to keep moving. We've taken down a tent to try and get a fire going, but there's little hope for it in this storm. If you mean to push on through the night, we may as well keep moving to stay warm. We could be ready in five minutes if we pack up now."

"Do it," said Ashimar. "And light no fires. Our hunters are seasoned trackers, and the last thing we need is to leave them a beacon."

Rasten watched as the words brought back a mote of concern to the bloodguard's face; even he could not conceal it. He was surprised, perhaps, to hear that they might be pursued.

"And the others…" he said.

"The others are not coming," Ashimar confirmed.

"And the Havenari, my lord?"

"Load the horses," said Ashimar. "You—Rasten—come with me. Bring the bandages."

It was the first time Rasten had heard his name spoken through that metal helm, and the sound of it was not pleasant. Rasten brushed the snow from his uniform, took down a satchel from one of the saddlebags, and followed the Weeping Man away from the others.

"Come closer. Unarm me."

"My lord?"

With a gauntleted hand, Ashimar tugged at the shoulder of his armour and lifted a tiny, hinged flap of steel away from his gorget. A threaded fastener beneath in the shape of the House Kelmor double-crescent held the plates tightly together; with a gentle turn, the tension in the steel relaxed, gaps between the plates widened, and the loose edges of other hinged panels inched into view from beneath their protective shell.

"Unarm me," he said again.

With thick fingers numbed from cold, Rasten explored the puzzle of his commander's ingenious armour, whose carvings concealed an intricate array of fasteners and straps. With as much haste as he could, he loosened the individual plates and set them aside. When the gorget was unlatched and pried open, the buckles of the closed helm exposed themselves and the man within seemed, at long last, vulnerable.

It was the darkest hour of night when the weeping visor was set aside. Even so, the disfigurement was clear. Ashimar's face was lean and strong-jawed, but his flesh had been badly burned, long ago—healed, if it had been healed at all, by clumsy hands that left his face puckered, purpled and scarred from forehead to jaw. A few wisps of white hair that might have once been golden hid the worst of it, and his piercing eyes still shone like the ice mountains of the far North; but the rumours at Lornock that he was a man of delicate beauty and extreme vanity, who remained masked because he dared not expose his perfect face to the unclean world, were now thoroughly quashed.

Rasten cast his eyes down, doing his best not to stare, and saw that the wounds did not stop there. A grisly cut down the side of his neck, likewise poorly healed, marked him as a man lucky to have survived some ancient battle or other—and now, as the pauldrons came loose, and the mail beneath shed, it became clear that a serious new wound had joined the company of the old. With naked hands already blue from the cold, Ashimar stripped the tattered layers of fabric away from the hole that had been carved into his side.

"Watchers deny it," Rasten cursed. "You're hurt bad."

"We shall see," said Ashimar. He brushed Rasten away, narrowed his icy eyes as he inspected the wound beneath his arm, testing its depth with a finger, eyeing the dried blood with concern.

"That's too big to stay stanched under hard riding," said Rasten. "You push on with us, that'll open up on you at a trot. I'd sear it shut, if we had the means." He paused awkwardly. "Begging your pardon, my lord. I have only your safety in mind." He thought briefly of Jalen's fatal wound, which was no bigger—might even have been smaller than that. The thought chilled him, and he wished for a moment he had never awoken from that dream.

"You are an expert in these matters?" Ashimar asked.

"I'm no field surgeon," said Rasten, "but I've seen men fall to lesser wounds."

"And survive greater ones," Ashimar reminded him.

Rasten looked to the exquisite mail-coat where a tiny hole, wide as a sword-point, had been punched through the riveted steel. "Looks like you ran afoul of a field surgeon already. This is some real precision."

"I did not call on you for your craft at medicine," said Ashimar.

"My lord?"

The Weeping Man opened the satchel and set about winding some herbs and linen into a poultice. "Tell me about the girl," he said.

Rasten's heart leapt in him. "She's awake now," he said. "Kellan gave her a terrible knock, though. The others told you—"

"Not *that* girl. You know of whom I speak."

Rasten swallowed hard. "My lord?"

Ashimar did not need to turn back to show his displeasure.

"You are here for a reason, Cerulean," said Ashimar. "You have been thrown into my service, against your will and against mine, because you dared to speak to the lady Illyria."

Rasten could only shake his head. "As you told me once," he said, "under pain of death…I know of no such girl."

Ashimar grit his teeth as he packed the small poultice into the wound at his side.

"Lies do not suit you," he said.

"But you asked me to lie—"

"You looked on her, and you spoke to her, more than once. Tell *me*, and no other. Tell *me* what you spoke of. Defy me again, and your punishment will be so exquisite that Master General Harrod will weep his first tear to have missed it."

"Nothing, really," Rasten said, then hastily tried to recall something more satisfying. He could think of no one but Catrine…the poem…

"Poetry," he spat out.

"Poetry?" Ashimar turned round at that, though there was no light to catch his face.

"I-I couldn't read," Rasten stammered. "Not well. Reports and pigeon-squawk, mostly. Things for a soldier's eyes. She read me poetry from the Hanes, old court verses. That's all, truly. Nothing untoward, you understand. And no great secrets. She told me nothing of the Tower or her father—truth be told, my lord, I don't imagine she sees any more of him than you or I."

Ashimar sat in silence for what felt like an age. Quietly, he began sealing his armour again.

"You speak the truth," he said.

"I don't like exquisite punishments," said Rasten, trying to smile.

"You risked your life—indeed, you sacrificed it—for nothing more than obsolete poetry of a bygone age."

Rasten considered his words carefully.

"I risked my life to be kind to a young girl with no friends," he said.

"Fasten my shoulders," said Ashimar.

"My lord, you can't ride with that wound."

"I can and will," said Ashimar. "We need to put some distance between ourselves and the Havenari while the horses endure. We'll rest at first light, and then I will extract the location of Celithrand's village from the girl. We will see then if your friend remembers the way himself."

"If Kellan remembers the way," Rasten offered, still uneasy about the kidnapping, "we can find our way there without her."

"You have a soft heart," said Ashimar, though not as disapprovingly as Rasten expected. "When the time comes to be rid of her, I will kill her myself. You need have no part of it." He fixed his helmet into place and buckled again the weeping-child visor.

"We need to keep her alive," Rasten blurted out. "She may not jog

Kellan's memory after all. If he's truly forgotten, we'll need her."

"That will serve as well," said Ashimar. "She is his last chance. If he cannot remember, he has failed me, and maintaining her will take half the rations of maintaining him. But make no mistake: either the girl or your friend will outlive their usefulness by nightfall. You impress me, Cerulean, but I will not spare their lives to appease you."

Rasten shuddered at the coldness of his tone. Any hope he might have held out for friendship, any faith that a reasonable man had come out of the armour to meet him, was lost in the falling snow as the two headed back to the others.

"I pray I may still be of some use to you, then," said Rasten.

"I had meant to end your life by now," said Ashimar casually. "That is clearly what the bureaucrats who assigned you to me expected. But I have changed my mind. If you care so much for the innocents, see to the girl. Be sure your friend doesn't cave in her skull before we have what we need from her."

Rasten needed no further encouragement to get out from under his commander's gaze. He hustled toward camp, where the girl was propped against a tree. An ugly welt had risen to mar her cherubic face, and one eye was swollen nearly shut. Neither her hands nor feet were bound, but Kellan towered over her, waiting for an excuse to beat her again.

"Are you all right?" he asked her. She turned her eyes on him with a foul look.

"Any news?" asked Kellan.

"We're not making camp," Rasten replied. "We'll ride south till the horses are done, and then—" he looked to the girl— "sort out where we're going from there."

"Desperate times," Kellan said with a shrug. "Don't look at me like I meant this. But we're on the right track, again."

Rasten nodded but didn't look convinced. "I'm here to take over guard duty while you pack everything back up."

Kellan grunted and walked away. "No need," he said over his shoulder. "I've already told her what'll happen if she moves."

Rasten knelt down beside her and brushed a strand of her hair away from the bruise. It was as white as the face of the little moon above them.

"Let me take a look at that," he said, but she flinched away from him.

"All right, then," he said. "Have you got a name?"

"Not for the likes of you," she said. Her spirit was strong—but he had spent a hard month with even harder men, her best efforts to appear threatening were wasted on him.

"I'm not going to hurt you," he said.

She spit blood-red into the snow and locked eyes with him. "I don't believe you," she said.

"Do you know what I am?" Rasten asked. "I'm a Cerulean Guard. It's my job to keep the peace, anywhere I go in the whole Empire. I make war against the enemies of the Imperator, and I kill the rebels in the East. But everybody else is an Imperial subject, and it's my duty to protect them. Even you. Do you understand?"

"I could get away," she said.

"What?"

She stretched her legs out and flexed her ankles in the snow. "Those trees. If I could get to those trees, I'd get away and you would never find me. Not if you had a thousand men, not if you searched a thousand years."

Rasten followed her gaze to the tree line. It was close enough to make out a row or two of trunks even in the blizzard that had raged most of the day and into night.

"Please don't run away," he said.

She kept watching the trees. "Why not?"

"Because we'd never find you. Not if we searched a thousand years. And you wouldn't last the night in this storm."

She smiled then, with a weird confidence, but with something more than confidence.

"Please don't run," he asked again, "because if you do get away, they'll kill me. And if you don't, they'll kill you."

"My name is Aewyn," she said. "I'm an outrider with the Havenari. And whoever you are, they'll catch you and they'll stop you."

"Do you know who that is?" Rasten asked, gesturing off into the snow. "That's Lord Ashimar, the Red Captain of Travalaith, the Imperial Scourge. You're right to fear him. He answers to no one save the Imperator himself. I've seen how ruthless he can be. The next time we stop to rest, he's going to ask you some questions. And if you value your life, Aewyn, if you want to go on living, please, please tell him everything he wants to know."

"You're not a Cerulean Guard," she said.

"What?"

"The Cerulean Guard are peacekeepers. Ashimar rides only with the bloodguard. Everyone knows that. In the name of the Imperator, they ride through the country, going wherever they please on their secret missions, burning villages and killing anyone who stands in their way. Even me." She shook her head. "If you ride with them, you're no Cerulean."

Rasten had no answer for that—not even to himself.

"See to it you do as he says," he warned her.

"I won't," she said defiantly. Rasten threw up his hands in frustration as Kellan came back to fetch him.

"You won't right away, then," he snapped—then, to Kellan, "What now?"

"One of the horses is already down," he said. "Fool thing just lamed itself starting at Ashimar. Broke its own damn leg. Figured a man like you would want to see to its suffering before we go. Hurry up; it's making the other horses twitchy. I'll bring her."

Numbed, Rasten abandoned the girl, shut out whatever she might have cried after him. The blizzard here was fierce and howling. It was impossible to make out.

"Not the horses! Please! Please don't hurt the horses!"

It was something like that.

The mare was on her side in a tremendous panic, legs thrashing, mouth foaming. Rasten knelt at her head. He brought her little comfort; she brought him none. Some of the bloodguard might have been jeering his compassion, but it was all lost in the wind. His sword was a dancer's weapon, but his axe—Jalen's axe—was a savage tool. He found it in his hand. Aewyn was screaming. The wind was screaming. Orders were shouted overhead. The little caravan of death was already moving.

Rasten had been spared the massacre at the Danhorn: by then, he was already a tower guard. But the order of merit that had put him there came from other fields made muddy with war-sweat. The strength of his bullish shoulders and thick, powerful arms had come from long and grisly harvest seasons there, and the strength in his jaw, too, which tightened so hard when the moment came that it sometimes took days to go loose again. He had made tactical use, advancing and retreating, of the dying men whose last service to their Empire was to serve as a spiteful obstacle to the enemy, gripping at ankles that passed, striking up with their daggers at the trampling legs of the hated foe. He pushed down the horse's head with one meaty palm, almost angrily, and raised the axe.

Rasten had never considered himself particularly afraid of death. The loss of a head did not seem like much, in the end; and on the plains of Selik he had known men who in an hour's work had passed from boasting and the singing of war-songs into another realm. To Rasten, it was an adventure to die, if anything was. But to *be* dying, to lie on the ground, caught in a net of agony spread halfway between one world and the next—that, to him, was the worst of it. It was worst by far to wait, as indeed he waited now. As Jalen had waited week upon week.

Rasten tightened his mouth, having found his anger at last.

He was skilled enough, and ferociously strong, so that the first swing of his brother's war-axe did the job: death was instant and painless. That small mercy was his duty and his compassion. But he did not weep, nor stain his cheek with tears—only landed a second furious swing, then a third, then a rain of savage blows that did some real indignity to the body, though he had been careful to end the poor creature's suffering humanely at the first blow.

No fully civilized onlooker would have taken him, in that moment, for a gentle man, so furious and violent was his assault. But Kellan watched him knowingly, with a keening heart, as the insufferable girl wailed helplessly beside him. Wiping the blood from his axe, from his gauntlets, from his forehead, Rasten stood, looking down at his own brutality for only a moment, before falling in line with the others. Kellan knew only too well the brutality to which men turned when weeping was forbidden.

Rasten was one of the last to enter formation. Kellan, with lead in his feet, was dead last, but there was no more use in delaying. He hauled the girl to her feet and silenced her crying with a threatening shake of his fist.

"That man," he said, pointing, "is the kindest, gentlest man in this whole company. When the time comes to start answering questions, you just remember that. Every one of us is a crueller man than he. If you remember that, you might just make it out alive."

Aewyn looked at him with loathing in her eyes.

"You're afraid," Aewyn said with cold strength. "You're afraid I won't tell them anything. And then you've turned all the Havenari against them for no good reason at all."

Kellan shrugged and hoisted her forward. "I'm afraid of a hundred damn things," he said. "It's why I'm still alive. If you can't get that through your thick skull, you're dead already, as sure as if I'd got my hands on you back in Widowvale."

At the mention of the village, Aewyn's eyes widened, but her resolve was only strengthened.

"I don't want to die," said Aewyn, "but I will never fear you. Not any of you."

"Then I've done all I can to save you," he said, and swatted her in the back of the head to get her marching.

The afternoon had been surprisingly warm. From his chambers in the west corner tower of Lornock, sheltered from the sun in the shadow of the looming Cîr-Valithar, Mardon Black had spent the morning watching the storm as it churned in troubled skies far to the west. He had anticipated a heavy snowfall and a chill in the air as the storm raged across the south plains of Haukmere and the forest of Vosthome, then swung up over the promontory to blanket Travalaith in its poetic last words before crawling out over the Sea of Garulf to die. He was sure for the longest time that he would have to cover his trueblacked robes with a heavy wolfskin cloak to make the ascent, and was pleasantly surprised when the storm came no farther east, but hung with unseasonal spite over the eastern arm of Haveil and spent its fury there.

It was shaping up to be a beautiful evening.

There was no denying the bulk of his work for long. He was tired of people pestering him to get the books done, but could hardly fault them: the Master of Iron held an important post, especially in wartime when poor men went off to war with a year's wages draped over their back; and the adoption of an Imperial iron standard alongside the standard of gold and silver had only deepened that importance. What was at once merely the oversight of an industry—an industry of war, and thus, to Mardon, of history—had become so embroiled in the vulgar world of economy that men of greed had involved themselves in the sacred enterprise of statecraft. He thought of these high-minded things often, for he was at heart a philosopher, and he dwelt on them all through the afternoon as his excitement grew, though he was sure not to let them reflect in the facts and figures of his audits of the Empire's iron stores.

When the afternoon had grown out its whiskers, as they used to say in Carmac, an Inquisitor from the Sixth Legion of the Shield came to the tower, and told him the preparations had been made. It was a relief to be done with arithmetic for the day, and as he brought out the ornate, finely wrought steel dagger from a pigeonhole beneath his desk, Mardon felt again in his hand the reliable weight of history—the true weight of iron, not as numbers on a page, but as a good sharp blade in the hand.

"It would be no trouble," said the Inquisitor, "to put a senior officer to the task."

"Nonsense," said Mardon, testing the breeze by the window, weighing the need for his heavy cloak. "I'm a rare prize, and I've got nothing better to do with my afternoon. What's the matter? You think I've grown too fat for soldier's work?"

"No, my lord."

"Of course you do," said Mardon. "There's no shame in the truth. You're wrong, for what it's worth. But I'm not a fool. There's a reason I've got your men lining the harbour in their plain-hose, waiting like cats for their supper. It'd reflect poorly on the public faith to watch an old man like me waddle his way down the Saltway in hot pursuit with a battle-cry on his lips. Rest assured, I'm in no danger—and you're in no danger of being robbed of the credit."

"As you say, sir," said the Inquisitor.

"I expect when the whole cloth unravels, you'll have an order of merit for your work."

"As you say, sir."

Mardon led the Inquisitor down the stairs with an almost youthful energy that did not abate until he had crossed the Iron Road, passed through the noisome inns and shops along the busy thoroughfare, and found himself below the Vairhurst memorial as the sun lowered behind the hill.

"And here," he said, "I will take my leave."

"Gods protect you," said the Inquisitor.

"They always have," said Mardon. "Be ready."

The climb was farther and harder than he anticipated, but in his eagerness he made it without stopping. At the top of the stairs, among the first memory stones, he forced himself to a halt, collecting his wits and his breath. With careless disdain, he scooped up a handful of flowers from one of the lesser stones—wildflowers which had already begun to wither in the weird sickness of the place—and made his way to the center of the memorial, where the tallest stones were clustered.

Madge's hearing had always been keen, and she heard him puffing up the trail before she saw him. When he came into view, she was already on the verge of tears. They came easily in this mournful place; with every lover that had come and gone, they came more easily still. She thought of her husband, as she always did, and how little he had thought of the war, and what he would think, now, to see her in this place, with these men, spiteful and cruel. In those crucial first moments, she was nearly sick with self-loathing. It was, as Baran told her, the secret to the spell she wove. And of all the Widows, she wove it best.

"Are you all right, lass?" the man asked. His old voice was higher than expected. He loomed over her like a shadow, draped in flowing robes that stood out stark and black as night against the faded dull grey of her mourner's robes. He was grossly well-fed, but moved with hidden grace and stank of money.

"I am sorry, my lord," she said, "if my grief has disturbed you." She drew back her hood to wipe at the tears streaming down her exquisite face.

"Nonsense," he said. He came over, into the shadow of the stone, and she saw his face. His wide beard had greyed some, but there was no mistaking him.

"My lord Magister," she gasped, bowing to hide the flush in her cheeks. Her excitement, too, was genuine.

"We'll have none of that," he said. "None of that 'my lord' business up here. We're naught but a man and a woman here. Neither high-born nor low, neither rich nor poor. Just two friends come to pay our respects to the fallen." He shook his little bouquet with an apologetic smile. She almost laughed. But it was too soon for the laugh.

"Yes," she sighed. "To pay our respects." She turned away from him coldly and sharply. A single ringlet of cinnamon hair tumbled loose before it was hidden by the cowl of her cloak.

"The loss is fresh, then," he said. "Or some losses, I suppose, are always fresh."

She nodded without turning round. "He was my husband," she said.

The old man nodded solemnly. "Too sad, too sad indeed," he said. "How did he die?"

She turned, met his eyes for a moment, surprised he would ask.

"Killed in the fighting," she said.

"Aye," said the old man. "It's unbearable on the frontier, now. Did he speak of it much?"

She hesitated, just for a moment. "No," she said.

"Then I suppose you wouldn't know," he said at last. "I'm Mardon Black, the Master of Iron. I hear all sorts of things from the front. Things a lady like you should never have to hear."

"I'm—Lysandra," said the woman. He offered his hand, and she turned back around to shake it, taking care to let the dagger in her hand fall into the grass with a rustle, as if trying to conceal it.

Mardon ignored it.

"Forgive me," he said. "It's unkind of me to dwell on the specifics of military business. Not very sensitive, to a woman freshly widowed." He watched her eyes. "The pain is still fresh?"

She nodded. "V-very."

He looked up to the memory stone towering over them, looked down to the blue flowers piled around its base.

"Hm. A Cerulean Guard," he said approvingly. "Second Legion of the Shield. You're practically a nobleman's wife."

She nodded absently. "I'm a nobleman's widow," she said, "if—indeed I'm anything at all."

Mardon clucked his tongue. "What kind of talk is that?" he asked.

The tears returned to her eyes with sudden fierceness. "I—am nothing, now," she said. "I—I cannot go on. Forgive me, my lord, but you cannot know. What can a decorated—what can an Imperial Magister, with the ear of the Imperator himself, know of a poor woman's grief, wretched and poor as I am, and alone in all the world?"

"I wasn't always a rich man," said Mardon.

"Nor I a poor woman," she replied, "except in coin. It's just as well, now. I've nothing left, and no one to leave it to, when—when I—"

She looked down in shame at the dagger lying at her feet. He ignored the cue and did not comfort her.

"He must have been very brave, your husband," he said.

She nodded patiently. She unlaced her collar a bit.

"It's the bravest men who fall in the fighting," he went on. "I've known many Frontier Ceruleans. There's only a thousand in the whole army, did you know that?"

"I—"

"Of course you didn't," he interrupted her. "We keep that number a secret. They're still tower guards, as such, only the Frontier Ceruleans go out and hold the watchtowers and border keeps for us. Unless the Legions of the Blade send for reinforcements—as they have done, this past week—they're the only men of the Shield within a hundred miles of the frontier. Brave men, every one of them." He looked up at the memory stone. "Not like the cowards who hide in the City, far from the fighting."

"My lord—"

"Mardon," he said. "I'm not one for flattery."

"Mardon," she repeated, taking the name as a cue to move a step closer. He took her delicate hand gently between his palms, which were clammy and soft.

"Let me show you something," he said with a smile.

He led her away from her little dagger, away from the memory stone to a towering pillar some thirty feet away.

"You see this one?" he said, looking up with a smile at the smooth limestone.

She nodded, lost for words.

"Third Legion of the Shield," he said. "These men, here, are the Frontier Ceruleans. The men who hold the borderlands against the vile Selikhan hordes at any cost. The men who stand up to sieges. The men who turn back catapults from their walls—the men who sniff out spies among their own troops and burn them alive for the amusement of locals."

She looked on with feigned interest and barely concealed horror. He waved his hand at the stone where they had been standing and scoffed dismissively.

"Those men?" he said. "Second Legion. The Cerulean Guard proper. Same cloaks, same pay. Mostly made up of men who had some success in the field. Brave at one time, maybe, but considered too valuable to trust to Dagan's whim on the battlefield. They guard the Tower, now, and maybe the Lornock. That's all. Their names are few not because they're elite, but because the Tower is unassailable. There are illnesses, accidents, to be sure. Men die in service everywhere. But I've never known a one of them to die in battle."

She made to turn away, to gather her thoughts and settle her sudden dread, but found herself held fast. His grip, quietly, had tightened around her wrist. When she looked up her fear was too much to hide.

"Maybe they're still brave," he said. "I'm sure some are. But some are cowards, too, grown fat and soft in the city. Like me." He jerked hard on her arm with hidden strength for a fat little man.

"You're hurting me," she said.

"Aye," said Mardon. "You can't really tell the brave soldiers from the lying cowards, can you?"

"Stop it—"

"Not until you see how well they handle the sight of their own blood."

With a sharp jerk of her arm, Mardon hauled her forward, hard. As she stumbled, he flicked his dagger out of his robes with surprising deftness and sliced a deep cut across her leg. She screamed, once, in shock, and fell silent as death as the blood welled up and began to spill. Mardon released her with careless disgust, as if throwing away an apple core.

"Even the enemy deserves a better class of spy than you," he said. "Out of pity, I'll give you a count of twenty before I call out your so-called husband's Legion, and we find out just how good at killing they still are."

She clutched the front of her burning thigh with both hands, felt the warmth of the blood oozing against her palms. It did not surge with the desperate pounding of her heart, but still the agony and shock of the blow left her reeling. Her mouth and eyes hung open in horror as Mardon reached out, again with quick hands, and seized the hem of her cloak to wipe his dagger clean.

"One," he said, raising the dagger as if making a farewell toast. "Two."

It took her a dozen strides to realize fully that her leg would take more of her weight than she had first thought. The muscle was cut, but not all the way through; she was hobbled but could move well enough for now. The blood poured forth and the sight of it made her sick, but she had been taught enough to know it would not be the end of her with immediate rest and care.

"Three," Mardon called, with seeming glee.

It was no time for rest.

How did they find out? How much did they know? The logistical questions, questions of the operation, spun in her mind with the unrelenting pain and the searing heat of her own blood pouring over her cold skin. She wanted nothing more than to escape, but could not trust her safe havens. If Rendon had found out—if he had somehow discovered her and reported her—his place in Greymantlehouse was a trap waiting to spring shut on her.

She resolved to make for the harbour and the *Wyrmsbolt* as best she could, though the pounding ache of descending the Vairhurst steps nearly knocked her out before her run even began. The ship was ready to leave at a moment's notice, and with Ashimar's warship out of the city, there were not many vessels that could catch it in open water if the wind was right. They were trained to run, if it came to that; even wounded, Madge thought her chances were fair.

With detached interest, the Inquisitors of the Sixth Legion throughout the city watched the passersby for a young woman in mourner's attire, rushing hastily to some unknown destination with a pronounced limp. Most were disappointed, and watched the milling about of the winter market's merchants, the stewards and support officials of the trade guilds, until the sky was dark and there was no more to be done. For two dozen men, though, quietly stationed along the Torgirdle, the parade route of the Iron Road, and the gentle downward slope of the Saltway, her passage was not hard to note. One by one, they watched her pass; one by one, as Mardon had taught them, they let loose at the top of their lungs with hawking cries for goods they had no mind to sell: salt from the Pale Sea in the north, lead and silver from the mines to the west, exotic spices from the south, rare silks from the east. In this manner, they confused many who asked after their goods and found none, but so too did they alert the men east and north of them, who followed Madge to the harbour without giving pursuit, tracking her mostly by cries of *coarse salt* and *silk dyed red* until she had come at last into the harbour, dizzy from the loss of blood and desperate for aid.

Far out in the harbour, hidden among the largest fishing boats headed out to meet the baitfish brought in toward the Shadewall by the powerful inland tide, the *Wyrmsbolt* made its way gently toward the gate-channel, shallow-sailed and moving well below its cruising speed to keep pace with the fishing boats. On the aft deck, in the garish concealment of wealthy merchants' garb, Baran watched the shoreline with Odi at her side.

"You're sure about this?" she asked.

"No," he said. "But I haven't kept us alive this long by waiting around to be sure."

The water churned and they rocked unsteadily among the fishing boats.

"Storms in the west," said Odi. "Quite early in the season. Is that the Mage's doing?"

Baran shook her head. "He's here in the city."

"Gods blind me," Odi said. "Here? To what end?"

"Something of great importance," Baran replied. "I don't know what. It has something to do with the Tower."

"If you ask me, nothing good ever came from that tower," said Odi. "It's Tamnor's tower. It's cursed. If you can't tear it down, build a high wall with no door and put it to sleep till the end of days, like him. Don't build a throne room of your own and move in all the Magistrates. Just the thought of him meddling with—"

"There," Baran snapped, directing Odi's gaze with a pale hand.

In a grey mourner's robe stained brown with blood, Madge Dunny had come to end of the Saltway, staggering under her own weight as she lurched forward, nearly tumbling over the upper boardwalk's edge.

"That's one of the Widows," she said.

The words under Odi's breath would have turned a sailor's head. Inquisitors of the Sixth Legion he had thought them, and Inquisitors they were, these strange merchants with muscled arms but soft hands, these supposed seafarers with pale faces who wound their genteel Vosthome accents around the colourful language of the sea. All afternoon they had been coming down the way, swelling the crowds even as the merchant ships set out for the Pale Sea on a favourable wind. They were amateurs, of course—little more than thugs playing at spycraft—but he knew only too well that in the circumstances, they would serve.

There was no pursuit—indeed, there would not have to be. The evening crowd caught side of her and watched with a mixture of interest and horror as she stumbled, then careened down the steps to the lower harbour, making her way out to where the *Wyrmsbolt* was usually moored.

"Now," Odi mouthed. "Take her now. Don't let her get to the pier."

But the Inquisitors were unhurried. The only sign of her passing was a single unfamiliar vendor who began to cry his trade in red silk as she passed, though he had been selling pickled herrings all day. With strength born of desperation, and the genuine belief that she might outrun them, Madge dashed out onto the wooden planks, running blindly until she looked up and saw that the ship was not there.

Baran's eyes were keen, and even at this great distance she could see the colour drain from Madge's face as the young woman looked up to where the familiar masts and the well-armed ship should have been, and saw nothing but churning waves and a dull red sky. She watched the girl's shock and sudden astonishment like the drop of a first fruit in autumn, and then the gradual passing of the season in her terrified face as the colours of betrayal began to set in.

"Poor girl," said Baran. Perhaps, Odi thought, she even meant it.

At the end of the pier, Madge collapsed in despair at last, crying out so loudly that the true merchants shuddered and looked away in awkward revulsion. Only a handful of unfamiliar men in merchants' garb paid her direct heed, and here they earned the silent admiration of the crowd as four of them approached the woman gently, dried her tears, spoke gently to her as they put a fresh blanket over her for warmth. They came for her at the dead end of the pier, and there they whispered sweet words to her, before leading her away with firm but gentle hands to discuss the matter of her grief in private. Only Baran could see the terror wash over her as they whispered softly to her. Odi could not make out such details, but he had no need even to look. He knew what manner of things such men said.

"We're done," Odi murmured. "That's it. We're done. It's over."

The wind had died away and left a pall of eerie silence hanging over the boat as the waves rippled down into a mournful stillness. The two figures stood wordlessly at the wale. There was not much to say.

"Which girl was it?" asked Odi at last.

"Madge," said Baran.

"How much did she know?"

"Enough."

"They'll be looking for the others, ere long."

"I imagine they will."

"How can we get them out of the city?"

Baran paused. "Many things are in short supply in the East," she said. "Widows are not one of them."

Odi screwed up his face. "We have to go back," he said. "These women are soldiers."

"You know that's not how it works."

"How many ships do we have?" asked Odi.

Baran began counting, then stopped. "Not many," she said.

"I suppose you'll have to tell Jordac you lost him one," Odi said, letting the Mage's name hang with weight in the air. Baran glared at him with shock and, for a moment, had no answer.

"You saw how far down the pier she ran," said Odi. "The Inquisitors aren't fools. A pretty girl with a story like hers may keep their attention for tonight. But come dawn, they'll pull the manifest to see who was moored there. They'll have the ship, the cargo, your name, my name. Hendec's, for what it's worth. If they connect that name to the body from the coursers' stables, they may get Alethir too."

"They won't get Alethir," said Baran firmly. But the worry had risen to her eyes, which shimmered unsteadily in the fading light.

"Turn us 'round," Odi pleaded. "Get word to the Mage. We need to recover the port manifest, or destroy it. We have no choice. Otherwise we scuttle the ship, make our way east, and lose all we've built here in the city."

Baran shut her eyes tight, as if willing this turn of events to unravel itself. "Do you know where they keep such a thing?"

"No," he said. "But give me the better part of a night on shore, and a couple sovereigns or a few combs of wax iron, and I can find out where it's kept."

"Once you find out, can you get it?"

"No," Odi sighed. "Perhaps I could do it with fifty men, well-armed, who know the streets, and who don't have a healthy interest in coming home."

Baran weighed his answer. "Impossible," she said.

"Then we sail west, as far as cover of night will take us, sink the ship in the shoals, and skirt the whole of the Old Crown on our way back east."

"That way will take weeks," said Baran.

"Months," Odi added, "if the Legions of the Blade are still massed at the Danhorn."

Baran scowled. "You truly care for the other girl, don't you?"

"It may be," Odi said with a shrug. "Or perhaps I just don't fancy the thought of crawling a hundred miles across the Verdant Wastes on my hands and knees in the dead of winter, hiding from the snakes in the field as well as those in the watchtowers."

Baran looked down to the deck, to the hireling crew she had hastily assembled on Odi's hunch. They would tend without question to their duties as long as the money was good—but even that would not be forever.

"We don't have fifty men in the city," she said. "We have ten I'd trust. Sailors, unarmoured. Good in a brawl, maybe."

Odi snorted. "No good." But Baran had made up her mind.

"Give me full sails, gentlemen," she called out to them. "Steady for the gate, and give me the very wind." Their relaxed postures gave way to frenzied activity as heavy movement below began to reflect in a great slow swing of the sails.

"We're running, then?" Odi asked.

"You're going to swim ashore at Mudtown," said Baran sharply. "Come in by the West-gate and do whatever needs doing. You will meet me at the Black Bridge Inn an hour before dawn. You will know by then, backwards and blindfolded, precisely where the manifests are kept. I will plan our escape from the city. If Catrine still lives when your work is done, we will find a place for her, if indeed we can reach her."

"And what of the records? Surely these men can't—"

"That is in the Mage's hands, now," said Baran.

"Who will he send?" Odi asked. But Baran's chilling glance told him all he needed to know.

"You have heard the stories," she said. "I have seen them for myself. I have followed him since the Western Dawn. Since then, his power has only grown. If you swear to me that we are in danger of losing our place in this city, he will see to it by fire and storm, if need be, that our purpose here is not undone."

"I have grown up on those stories," said Odi. "I've long dreamt of bearing witness to them. Only now, now that it's come—I'm rightly afeared of it."

"So am I," said Baran, though her eyes gleamed with an excitement too wild to be tempered by worry.

ELEVEN

THE WOODEN SPOON CLATTERED and scraped noisily against the inside of the pot, disturbing the feeble grip Fen'din had kept on his dreams. He had been dreaming of faraway lands under skies rich and deep as lazuli, and in the haze of his sickness, he did not at first know where he had awoken. The walls of the miners' cottage came into focus slowly—and with them, the memory of the long and difficult road that had led him to the mining camps above Widowvale.

"Is it morning?" he asked groggily.

"It was, once," said a voice. A tall, lanky figure knelt over the fire, spooning some mulled cider into a fat clay mug. Sure enough, a few grey ribbons of something trying hard to be sunlight were streaming in where the cottage windows had been blocked off bricks and clay.

"I didn't mean to wake you," he said. "At least, not until the others get back."

Fen'din sat up and tried to cough the storm out of his chest. "Halgeir, what are you making?"

"An old northern remedy," said the tall man. "They brew this in Tundara. Good for chest, and neck, and nose besides."

"You are too much kind to me," said Fen'din.

"Nonsense," said Halgeir. "If the storm blew out the bridge, as I imagine it did, we'll need help cutting fresh timber and carting it up to the mine. I'd sooner have you well on the trail than in bed by the fire."

"How long have they been gone?" asked Fen'din.

Halgeir blew gently across the top of the mug, and unstoppered another clay pot. "Maybe three hours. They waited out the worst of the storm, which came on almost to highsun. I expect them back anytime. There—add a touch of Grim's blackberry wine, once it's cool enough, to keep the frost off you."

"Be stingy with that," said Fen'din. "There won't be any more of it, once it's gone."

"It's the key to the drink," said Halgeir. "Grim told me himself, once—"

The wind howled as the heavy door was wrenched open. Covered in snow, two men lumbered into the cottage as quickly as they could. It took both of them to pull the door shut against the wind.

"Gentlemen!" Halgeir hastily stoppered the wine and put it back in the shelf.

"Cold as death out there," one of them said, brushing a shower of snow out of his bushy red beard. "Colder than death, up on the mount."

"Good news, though," said the other. "Looks like the bridge held up through the night."

Halgeir sighed with relief. "We owe that to you, Jory," he said.

Jory shook his head. "You have the gods to thank," he replied. "It's beyond my ken to build a bridge that strong. I'm amazed it's still there."

"Has the storm let up?"

"Aye," said Red. "It's no warmer, but the wind is starting to leave us be. I'm starting to rethink staying the winter."

"Rethink it all you like," said Jory. "If it warms up and the trails clear, rethinking might get us somewhere. We can pack up and spend the winter's dotage in Widowvale with the others. Otherwise—nay, we're stuck with our decision now. I'd not chance the climb."

The two men moved to the fire and began unshouldering their packs. Fen'din, embarrassed to be found still in bed, sat up and took his cup from Halgeir. The mixture was spicy, fruity, and a little sour, but the slow heat of it warmed him all the way down to his stomach and all the way up to his clogged nose.

"How's the plague-bearer?" asked Red. "He looks well enough to me."

Fen'din smiled. "Well enough," he agreed. "I am most eager to be in the work again."

"You sure you're well enough?" Halgeir asked.

Fen'din nodded enthusiastically. "Your winters I like not so much, but the mining life, I like it. It's good work and will keep me healthy."

"Surprised you haven't had your fill of it," said Jory, "given the hole we dragged you out of."

"The prison mines are different," said Fen'din. "They are much worse. They destroy the body to work, and they go too deep. They are not ingenious underground like the Danu. They have the rudimentary engineering of men, but the greed of men, too. We go far below, and they work us very hard. It is a cruel and short life. But here, for myself, mining simple veins in shallow rock with simple tools, in fresh air beneath an open sky? When I had mined so much that I could only dream of more mining when I slept, when it was all I could remember or imagine—I thought that when I died, if I was a righteous man, the afterlife would be this kind of mining instead."

Red raised his bushy eyebrows. "That'll teach me to complain," he said.

"My sister served a year in the prison mines," said Jory. "She wasn't so poetical about it. But she was never the same after."

"We are lucky here," said Fen'din. "Even sick, even working through your terrible godless Northern winters, we are lucky men."

"A thought to keep us warm, perhaps," said Red, "if we're to put in a few hours before sunset."

Halgeir nodded and began to layer on his clothing for the outdoors. "Are you sure you're ready to turn right around and go back up the mount?"

Red laughed. "I come from the Dreaming Coast," he said. "North of Kazan-Yeng, this might as well be summer."

"I'm not so eager," Jory admitted.

"You've no excuse," said Red. "If that fairy-girl from the village is out in this weather, a man of your size loses all right to complain."

Halgeir stopped at the mention of the girl. "Aewyn?" he asked. "I thought she rode out with the Havenari."

"She did," said Red. "Soon as she could walk straight. But she's come back."

Halgeir's face darkened. "If I ever again lay eyes on the karach that lamed her," he said, "I'll kill it dead. Mark my words."

"I doubt you'll see him," said Jory. "No sign of him since Celithrand escaped."

"He'll turn up," said Halgeir. "They're territorial. They always come back. Leave a mated pair alive, and they'll keep coming back a thousand years."

"No one's turning up until spring," Jory told him. "Not even a karach. The trails are snowed. The way is shut."

"They're not, though," said Red. "Not in the lowlands. That's what I was saying; I saw Aewyn myself, not two hours ago, from up on the bridge. She must have got back somehow."

Halgeir raised an eyebrow. "They've come all the way home?"

"Some of them have,' said Red. "Couldn't tell how many, through the snow. It was a half-mile below, maybe. Couldn't make much out. But that white winter coat of hers gives her away, doesn't it?"

"Unless somebody's grandmother is out with a scouting party in this cold," said Halgeir. He took the mug from Fen'din, touched his head with tenderness.

"You're on the mend," he said.

"My grandmother could sit a horse to ninety years of age," said Red proudly. "Rode like the wind into her eighties."

"It's good that Aewyn's come home," said Halgeir. "Was Robyn with her?"

Jory shook his head. "None of the riders I recognized. But then, I don't know them so—"

He held his tongue at the sound of someone outside.

The wind had died down. Outside, heavy-booted footfalls crunched in the powdery snow. Fen'din, whose hearing was very fine in spite of his cold, smiled broadly.

"Half a mile indeed," he said. "And I suppose they've all got hearty appetites too. I doubt we've got food enough to—"

The banded door was too heavy to shatter, but it caved in at the jamb and tore off its hinges where the kick landed. Red, closest to the front wall, turned in time to see the door come swinging down like a drawbridge before an arm's length of sharpened steel hit him square at the breastbone and cut clean through his back.

"What?"

Jory backed away as soon as he could see it was not one of the Havenari. He'd fought with a miner's pick more than once, in a pinch, and his hand went to the heavy tool with surprising quickness as Halgeir, the only one of them who owned a real sword, crossed the cottage to reach it. By the time he was there, the figure was moving on Jory, half-swording an immense greatsword that would have been too long to swing freely in the little room. Clad from head to toe in shimmering, red-gilded steel, the intruder brushed Jory's pick aside carelessly, stunned the big man with a swat of the sword-tip, then jerked it back and pumped forward twice, putting two neat holes in his chest that sent him bubbling and bloody to the floor.

Halgeir snapped his sword out of its sheath and charged the intruder, swinging, but the weapon bounced harmlessly across the armour as the figure turned to face him. He froze for a moment too long as the twisted face of a wailing child met him face-to-face, its contorted lips golden, its streaming tears enamelled red as blood. He jerked up to his full height and the thrusting greatsword caught him low enough in the gut that he could keep fighting. But his last stand was short-lived: like the hoof of a galloping horse, the thrusting point of the massive sword slammed in time and time again, placing hole after hole until the hot air of the cottage was filled with the stench of him. Halgeir cried out in pain and frustration as the blood streamed down his long legs; staggered, he took a knee, but kept up his own thrusts with desperate energy.

Across the packed floor of the cottage, Fen'din watched in terror. Never in his short time in Widowvale had they warned him about something like this. He fumbled for a weapon but found none; his breath was already ragged from illness and panic. It was only when both Halgeir's knees were down and his breath came with wet clouds of blood that the figure switched up his grip on the sword, pushing the tall man to the cottage's center, then swinging the long blade wildly at its full reach. It stuck hard in the firewood piled against the front wall as it followed through, but as Halgeir pitched forward onto the floor, his head rolled suddenly away from the rest of him, its face forever locked in a final expression of disbelief.

Outside the little cabin, a line of red-armoured men stood waiting, their faces hidden behind a grotesque menagerie of animal helms. The wind, at least, would have masked the sounds of the slaughter; in the sudden silence of the morning's calm, panther-headed Rasten flinched at every fresh shout and the muffled, ineffectual clank of the defenders' tools against Ashimar's impenetrable second skin.

"Stop it," hissed a voice.

"What?" he whispered.

At his side, Kellan's wolf-helm angled down to him. "You're giving your stomach away."

Rasten set his jaw, glad for the helm that shielded his wet eyes. "I've no stomach left," he said. "Not for this."

The other bloodguards were watching them. Kellan affected a grim curiosity, put himself between them and Rasten.

"We don't get a turn?" he asked the others.

Astagar sighed. Against the front of his antlered helm, his breath was foggy in the winter air.

"It depends," he said. "He's never fought with us, that I can recall. Sometimes he sends us ahead, then comes himself. Other times, he holds us in reserve, and sends for us once he's had his fun."

"He's many things when he hangs back and lets us do the fighting," said another, "but a coward is never one of them. I think sometimes he likes to remind us."

"Oh, he's not afraid," said Kellan. "He's just greedy. Weeks without a good kill, and he leaves us nought but table scraps." He turned away with such fierce disgust, such bloodthirsty arrogance, that his own fear was invisible to them.

"You'll have a feast of wolf's work, thirsty Wolf, when we find that village," said Astagar. The thought did nothing to settle Kellan's stomach.

Inside the cabin, the many scents of home—the stew, the fire, the overripe fruit and the strange Northern medicines—were masked by the smell of blood. One miner alone still lived; his screams were primal, and the string of desperate begging that poured from him was not in a language Ashimar spoke. With casual diffidence, Ashimar let go of his sword, leaving it to hang in the wood where it was stuck, and picked up the grovelling survivor with unreadable calm. He stood the man up against the back wall, twisted his arm out and above his head, and with the flash of a hidden dagger, pinned it to the wall by its sleeve.

"Do you speak the Merchant's Tongue?" he asked.

The miner nodded.

"What is your name?"

"Fen'din," he replied, shocked into the eerie calm of a pinned songbird.

"This hand stays here, Fen'din," Ashimar advised through the glistening mask. "If it moves, we'll put it back with the dagger through it. Do you understand?"

Fen'din, eyes and mouth gaping, nodded absently.

Ashimar moved to the doorway and signalled his men. They had ridden through the night, through the morning, and were in desperate need of rest and shelter by the time he had cleared the miners' cottage for them. After the violence of his entry, the cabin was hardly a welcome home, but Rasten and Kellan, exhausted in mind and spirit as well as in body, were simply too spent to wait in the cold any longer.

One by one, the bloodguards appeared in the doorway—stag, panther, boar, lion, mantis, bear, needle-pierced maiden, grinning skull. Wolf-headed Kellan hauled the girl in by her arms, and the sight of the bodies set her wailing again no matter how he threatened her.

"The cottage is ours," said Ashimar. "We make camp here. Lock down the cottage. Eat what you can find. Change watch every two hours."

Aewyn's wailing gave way to horrified silence as she looked down at the shaggy blond head that lay by the hearth. She raised a fist to her mouth and could say no more.

"Looks like she knew this one," Astagar called. Ashimar looked at the girl, then down to the severed head.

"Good," he said. "We are getting close, then. See that this last fellow stays alive until we are ready to push on. He will help us persuade her."

"We've got persuasions enough of our own," one of the bloodguards protested.

"Torture is unreliable," Ashimar replied. "Pain does strange things to the mind. Compassion, though, can be exploited." With both arms, Ashimar pulled his greatsword free of the wood where it had buried its edge. It was an unwieldy weapon in these close quarters; even slinging it across his back was a difficult and slow ordeal.

"I am going up the hill to look for signs of pursuit," he said. "It may be I catch sight of the village from there, and we can be done with the lot of them. Rest the men; sleep if you can. Wait for my knock." He gestured to Kellan. "Put this one on middle watch."

"As you command."

Kellan frowned as the Weeping Man stepped out into the cold and the bloodguards began ransacking the house. They dragged the bodies one by one out into the snow to save themselves from the smell, but there was nothing to be done about the blood. The girl was far away in her grief—too far to need Kellan's strong grip to keep her still.

"Middle watch," he said. "I don't suppose I should bother sleeping the first two hours."

"Relax," said the mantis-headed bloodguard. "None of us will kill you now until we have the order."

"Aye, and how long will that be?" Kellan could feel the other's sneering smile through the mask, but he resolved to lie down and rethink his options carefully. The storm was lifting. The light would be gone in a few hours. He did not like his chances in the wild—but he doubted he would live to see better ones.

There was only one other thing to be determined. In the moment, half the men were outside sheltering and securing the horses, and the other half had begun raiding the cottage's meagre pantry. Rasten, bless his heart, had found a jug of wine and was making an effort to hide it. With eyes off him for the moment, Kellan approached the prisoner with his arm pinned to the wall. He brought his face in close to the man, let out a sigh that was more of a growl.

"Do you understand the Merchants' Tongue?" he whispered. Wide-eyed, the prisoner nodded feebly.

"Listen to me very carefully," said Kellan. "I will ask you one question, and if you speak a word, to me or anyone else, you will die very painfully. Do you understand?"

The man nodded.

"Do you know the way to the town called Widowvale?"

Fen'din nodded excitedly and raised his free arm to point. Kellan batted it down immediately, fighting his panic. They were close, now. Too close.

"No, you don't," Kellan whispered to the captive. "You've never heard of it. Do you understand?"

The man nodded. Kellan didn't think he understood a damned thing.

"If you speak to anyone," he said, "if you answer any of their questions, I will do terrible unnatural things to you."

The man nodded. He was weeping now, but he kept his silence.

"Good," said Kellan, and sat down to think. The bloodguards whispered among themselves, as they often did, ignoring the two new recruits. Rasten held the girl gently, who had gone still and white and made no move to resist him.

The men ate and drank what there was. Kellan took his fill of stew before approaching the one man he realized, with some regret, he could call a friend.

"Can you sleep?" he asked. Some of the bloodguard, exhausted from the weather and the forced ride, had already begun to unbuckle their armour and lay their cloaks out on the floor.

Rasten shook his head. "This is too much," he said. He looked to the floor beneath his feet, wiped dry but still stained with a bright red that had barely begun to darken. "I'll have no sleep here."

"Wake me in half an hour, then," said Kellan, and laid himself down on the wood.

Rasten leaned in close. "I know what you're thinking," he said.

Kellan shifted uncomfortably, trying to find a way he could lean in his armour that wasn't terribly uncomfortable.

"Best not say it out loud, then," he said. Frustrated, he began at last to unbutton his belt and slip out of the armour's least comfortable pieces. There was no way he would have a moment's rest in it.

"Your chances are better here," said Rasten. "You won't make it far in this."

"Far enough," said Kellan.

"His wrath will give you no rest," said Rasten. "And no quarter, when he finds you. When *we* find you."

"Will you stop me?"

"No," said Rasten, shaking his head. "I don't think so. But I can't help you."

"You can wake me in half an hour. You can do that."

He turned over and shut his eyes, for what little it was worth. Rasten sighed, deep in thought.

"If…if you should make it," he said, "and if you should one day find yourself in Travalaith—"

"I won't," said Kellan. "I'm a fool, but I'm not that big a fool."

"But if you do—"

"I won't see your woman again," said Kellan. "And neither will you, probably." That was just unkind enough to shut him up.

Kellan had taken his full measure of the bloodguards and their Red Captain. He had gauged the climb to the top of the little mountain—Minter's Rock, the locals called it—and counted roughly two hours at most before Ashimar had made the ascent and returned. At that point, if Ashimar could see their destination from the mountainside, Kellan was a dead man; if he could extract the town's location from the sick miner, or from the girl by torturing the miner, Kellan was dead then, too.

He had saved Rasten's life, perhaps, on the deck of the *Providence*; but though the bloodguards were cowed, they had not shared their names, or their stories. He was still an outsider to them. And they waited only for the word of their master to end his life.

Whether the Weeping Man would kill Rasten, too, Kellan didn't know. The two had developed some kind of silent kinship, as impossible as it seemed: Rasten was perhaps the kindest man he had met, and Ashimar certainly the cruellest. Perhaps Rasten might live. Kellan liked to think so.

But Ashimar despised liabilities and dead weight. If he could find his way under his own resources, he would kill Kellan, kill the last miner, and probably kill the girl too. It was a red day already, and about to get redder.

Kellan was tired as a corpse; he needed his great strength more than ever, and was pleased to feel the weight of sleep on him, for whatever short time he could take it. He was on the edge of sleep when the girl found her voice again, and began at last to wail in great loud sobs for the headless man, who had been in the village when Kellan was there, and might have been something of a friend to her. Her cries cut like a knife through the fog of sleep, and had him fully awake again before one of the other bloodguards found some new creative way to silence her. There was no getting back to sleep after that, so he lay still, waiting, gathering his strength.

"That's always the way of it," he said, under his breath, to no one in particular.

The watering hole now called Calvon's Lean was one of the oldest buildings in Travalaith, and a favourite haunt of Odi's even when he wasn't in desperate need of information. Built within a few years of the Siege of Shadow, it was at one time the largest structure in the harbour, an opulent house of decadence built straight out onto the first boardwalks of the restored port.

It was not known, then, that the corruption of Tamnor would linger, and the whole boardwalk itself be given over to rot. By the time the builders discovered their error, it was too late: stones were hastily moved beneath the sagging wood in an effort to save the mansion from its rotting foundations. Now the entire house canted heavily to one side, as if poised to leap into the water; whole wings of its original construction had sloughed off into the sea, leaving only the stony core of the house, listing downward so sharply that a sailor who walked the floorboards was sure he'd drunk his fill before the first barrel was tapped. Most of Calvon's Lean had fallen to ruin; but what remained was a relic of faded opulence whose fixtures and adornments reflected the heady days of joy that followed the end of a terror never before known in the North.

The place was meticulously clean and well-ordered, as always. Odi could not help but admire the spotless common-room as he hoisted himself up onto its crooked floor, but he dared not dawdle too long. Too much of the day had already gone in securing Calvon's bribe. He only hoped it would be enough.

Like a king holding court, Calvon held the highest ground in the room, scrubbing out wooden bowls from a basin of seawater as the sailors came and went. Two great iron cauldrons of pungent stew hung unevenly in the crooked hearths, listing nearly sideways as the flames, too, licked their blackened bellies at an odd angle. At the sound of Odi's footfalls,

Calvon straightened up and turned his head toward the door. A gentle smile blossomed beneath his long black beard.

"Welcome to Calvon's Lean, stranger," he said. "Make my home your own."

"I thought you'd know my heavy step by now," said Odi. Calvon's smile broadened at the sound of his voice.

"Odi!" he said. "You've been away too long. My scraps have been feeding the dogs. They pay even less than you."

"Nonsense," said Odi. "There's no strays in Travalaith. The blackrot kills off whatever your cooking doesn't."

"You sound like a man who wouldn't care for stew," said Calvon.

"I never said that," Odi replied.

With practiced hands, Calvon felt his way around the bar and filled a bowl from the hearth. The sailors at the long benches had grown rowdy in their drinking, and Odi settled into a corner near Calvon's barrels, in the near-blackness at the top of the slanted floor.

"What brings you today?" he asked, handing over the bowl. "I sense it's not the stew."

"Your powers of deduction are sharp as ever," said Odi, sucking the stew straight from the bowl. The rim was still salty from the brine, and added a tang to the meaty broth.

"Mock me if you like," said Calvon. "But I'll do you one better: you've come for information—and you're in a terrible rush. It's information you could find on your own, given time. But time is the one thing you haven't got. So you're praying I've put in the time already. If you're wise, you've spent the better part of the afternoon sorting out how to pay for that time."

Odi grinned. "No mockery intended," he said. "You're a seer, I swear it, the way you figure things out."

Calvon shrugged. "A seer, he says. Trust a native Travalaithi street-weasel to joke at a blind man's expense."

"Not at all," said Odi. "Blind men make the best seers, so all the stories say. The blind are favoured by the Nine Pilgrims, or something."

"D'you want to hear what the harbour children say about my eyes?"

Calvon asked. "It's actually quite a sweet story, bless them."

"I'm afraid you were quite right," said Odi, shaking his head. "I'm in a terrible rush. Perhaps another time."

"Out with it, then," said Calvon. "What do you need?"

"The master registry for the port of Travalaith," said Odi.

Calvon laughed so hard the sailors seated around the Lean set down their mugs and looked his way.

"Come upstairs with me," said Calvon, leaning toward the wall.

The rickety stairs along the side of the taproom canted as much sideways as upwards. Calvon found his way in the blackness with a practiced step as Odi stumbled, creaked, and cursed behind him.

"I can't get you that," Calvon said.

"I just need the current season," said Odi. "They used to keep them in the harbourmaster's library, until—"

"Until they became a military secret," Calvon interjected. "A complete record of fleet movements within and through the Capital region. Do you know what that's worth, now that we're at war?"

"There's an uprising," said Odi. "I'd hardly call it a war."

"That's what any revolutionary would say," said Calvon. "It's in their interest to paint themselves as a popular rebellion. The weak fighting back against the strong, right? It's a heroic story. But they're not so weak in the Outlands. The Empire is breaking apart, if it hasn't already, and our forgotten ghost of an Imperator won't hold it together much longer."

"You think the old man is dead?" Odi asked.

"Don't show so much interest," Calvon warned him. "If he's not dead, he's a recluse, and they're worth about the same. What little kingly mien he had, the Imperial Harper cannot match. Lornock is in a weak position, and needs all the legitimacy it can muster to hold this Empire together. That makes even asking after things like the registry dangerous. It's not a fine and a cuff on the ear anymore to be caught up in smuggling, Odi. It's 'creating an unlawful climate for the Mage to exploit,' that's what they say. If Lornock found out I was abetting a smuggler, it'd be off to Fingrun with me."

"Suppose I wasn't a smuggler anymore," said Odi.

"Word of advice," said Calvon. "*Be* a smuggler. If you're not that, what you are is more likely, not less, to land me in chains."

"You're just an innkeeper," said Odi. "You're no soldier for the Uprising. Have things really gone so bad, so quickly?"

"These days," said Calvon, "they'd jail a gardener for growing a blueberry bush tall enough for Jordac to hide behind. What they'd do to a man who put him onto the movements of the Fleet, I don't want to think."

"I'm not interested in the movements of the Fleet," said Odi—though now that Calvon had said it, he certainly was. "My interest lies in just one little boat—a single line on a single leaf of the Registry—that I'd very much like to disappear."

"You're out of luck, then," said Calvon. "No civil documents are better protected."

"It's a nothing ship," Odi protested. "A small commercial cog of no consequence."

"In Shadowsand," said Calvon, "they have an expression: 'breaking into the palace to steal the bread.' It seems to me that's what you're speaking of. The cheapness of the prize makes the walls no lower."

"Just the same," said Odi, "when your family's starving, you do what you must."

Calvon sighed. "My answer's going to make me rich, isn't it?"

"It might," Odi admitted. "That depends on the quality of your answer."

"At least until it makes me rich and dead. Tell me, Odi—are you a religious man?"

Odi bristled. "Now you're the one asking dangerous questions," said Odi. "Folks here don't talk about such things in public."

"Not anymore," said Calvon. "It used to be different. My parents grew up on the Saltway, but their parents before them were priests."

"Am I about to hear a sermon?" Odi asked.

"You can imagine the crisis of faith," said Calvon. "I'm not even talking about the hundredfaiths. I'm talking just about the Tudrans, the various factions. The Consummates, the Sundrists, the Carnicists, the

Black Skeptics. You name it. When the holy Enemy of your faith is just an idea—a piece of myth—you mostly get along with people. But when he walks into your city and throws down its towers? When he sits there, flesh and blood, and your gods only hide in silence while you do their fighting for them? You can imagine, doctrinal differences became matters of life and death."

Odi sighed. "I can imagine," he said, "but I've no time to talk theology."

"Nobody knew the faiths would go silent," said Calvon. "Nobody thought they'd fight each other in the days after the Siege. Tûr was our beacon of hope against Tamnor. My great-grandparents worked on the first Tudran temples after the Occupation. Built them like fortresses. People wanted a symbol of power, a symbol that the people and the gods were stronger than any evil."

"The Reconstruction temples are behemoths," said Odi. "The Carnicist temple up on Picklefish Lane is big as the centre block of Lornock."

Calvon stifled a laugh. "Picklefish," he chuckled. "The temple up on Temple Street, you mean."

Odi shrugged. "Aye, Temple Street. That's not what they call it anymore. Like you say, public worship just isn't our way after the strife. The whole row is taken by fishmongers, and the temple is deserted."

Calvon's smile gleamed brightly. "Is it?" he asked.

Odi fell silent and thought back to the temple. He had seen it nearly every day since his arrival in the city, towering over Picklefish Lane, its dark gray skin dappled and stained with the droppings of seagulls, its narrow windows boarded and dark. Silent and forgotten behind the bustle of the harbour, it would have dwarfed half the central keeps of the border vasilies, as large as any frontier fortress and twice as sturdy.

"I don't suppose going unnoticed is its only defense," he said.

"Oh no," said Calvon. "Who are the secret-keepers again? The Seventh Legion?"

"The Stormguard," said Odi, turning pale. "The Seventh Legion of the Shield."

"That's them," said Calvon. "I do believe the old temples are well and truly infested with them."

"I thought they were disbanded and took to other work after their magic died off."

"They dwindled in size," said Calvon. "But they're out there. The abandoned temples are all sites of special interest to the powers-that-be."

"They've made inns and such out of them in the Outlands," said Odi. "There's a lovely old Sundrist temple not far from Carmac, being used as a barn for cattle now."

"Those must be very special cows," said Calvon.

"Only the most righteous bovines," laughed Odi. "I've heard tell their milk cures horseblight."

"You'll find no such miracles here," said Calvon. "But in the Carnicists' Harbour Temple, that's where you'll find your Registry. You'll find your death there, to be sure—but the Registry, too, if a dead man still has need of such curiosities."

"Then with that," said Odi, "I must leave you."

Calvon sniffed the air. "You haven't finished your stew."

Odi set the dirty clay bowl down carefully on a shelf at the top of the stairs. "That should tell you the rush I'm in," he said, and hauled up the hood of his cloak.

"Odi…what's going to happen?"

"It's safer that you don't know," said Odi. "You'll be a rich man very soon, my friend. Fool knows, you'll want to live long enough to spend it."

"I can't get involved," Calvon said. "I just like to know."

"Your insight, I'm sure, tells you all you need," said Odi. "My advice to you is to stay here, keep your head down. Close down the information business for a few weeks. Run your alehouse. Polish your counter. That smooth bit—the part you polish when you're trying not to look like you're listening to folk—you just stick to that. You're going to come into some money, sooner or later. When it gets through to you, you'll know the storm has passed."

Calvon nodded sagely. "I've always got a counter to polish," he said. "I can never really tell when I've got it clean."

The sun was well past its zenith when Odi emerged from the lopsided structure, walking with a practiced ease that took all his composure to maintain. He had not expected Calvon to be quite so forthcoming, especially without payment upfront; their visit was longer than he would have liked, but shorter than he would have expected. The long hours between the sunset and his meeting at dawn with Baran, carrying the burden of fresh intelligence, would not be easy for him. She admired him for his connections, he thought, and rightly so. He never failed, even in the Capital, to find the right ally when the time came. But under a sun-dappled, overcast sky that shone at dusk with the colours of all Three Maidens, penned in on all sides by the terrible Shadewall, Odi felt very small and very alone.

For a brief moment, he wondered what he might do, if not this. The island city of Shadowsand, from which so many Calvon's favourite proverbs seemed to come, was still a freehold. Smugglers there, he imagined, were in even higher demand than ordinary merchants. The sound of the open sea had always pleased him. He thought he might be happy there, if he could be happy anywhere.

He found himself in the harbour again. He had not known where he was going, but his feet seemed to lead him to his customary territory. He felt before he saw the increased military presence in the harbour; the purple linings of soldiers' cloaks were nearly hidden as they held the hemmed edges shut against a biting wind. But they were filling the alleys and streets on half-alert, marching in twos and threes, playing at dice and king's table, making their presence known in a quiet way that unsettled him more than a show of force. It was a message, after all, for subtle people: *we know you are here. We are searching for you, even now.*

The first frost had come along the coast, and with it came the great fat codfish that swam inshore for the season. It was always at dawn and just before dusk—not unlike the rebels of the Uprising, it seemed—that they fell hardest into the clutches of the rough-handed men who hunted them down. The codmongers were often the last ships in as night fell, and they still hollered their fresh catch from the boardwalk above the harbour. Following the steady stream of their cries and songs, Odi found himself within sight of the old temple, looming in ponderous silence over the ships at anchor. Its windows were dark and there were no outward signs of life; but its structure, he knew, went deep, and the building now seemed pregnant with possibilities. If the port master's registry were kept there, what else might lurk behind those walls?

He watched the building in perfect, practiced stillness for as long as he dared, as if man and temple were silently sizing each other up. The cries of the fishmongers were echoed only by the circling seagulls, waiting eagerly for the merchants to abandon their bloody stands and stalls for the night. In the gloom of twilight, the Tudran temple seemed thoroughly dead, and soon the wheeling birds were the only sign of life on the little promontory.

The god of the karach had been a bird-god, he remembered. The birds, Old Garrh had told him once, were his messengers. He chuckled at that, squinting at the distant rooftop spattered with bird-droppings. It was small recompense, maybe, for the Clearances, but he knew if his old smuggling partner Garrh had lived to see it, the thought would have pleased him.

"The place is marked, isn't it? Marked with bird shit," he said, chuckling softly. "Old friend, you've been trying to show me all along, haven't you?"

There was, of course, no answer but the wind and the cry of the gulls.

In the long hours of his childhood summers, hiding from his father beneath the floorboards of an expensive manor house, Kellan had watched the stillness and suddenness of the big wolf spiders as they preyed upon lesser insects. Their patience and silence were the art his father lacked: they caught their prey with ease nearly every day, while the old man's prey slipped away from him again and again. Now, Kellan stood seven feet—then six and a half—then six feet—behind the lone bloodguard who sat awake at the window. His every human instinct urged him to lunge the last few feet, like his father would have done in a rage, and overcome his prey with sheer and sudden ferocity. He was a big man too, like his father was, and ferocity had served him well against smaller and weaker men.

But Kellan had been there, too, the day his father's ferocity had failed him, and he had learned that lesson well. So instead, he waited with a spider's patience for the sudden howls of the wind and the cracking of the roof-beams in the cold, and inched his bare feet forward as the rafters creaked.

Five feet to go, now.

As the sun had gone, even he had succumbed to the exhaustion that took the other men for a few short minutes. He had dreamt so deeply of the manor and the spiders and his father that the loamy scent of dirt beneath the wooden floor, the profound earthy silence of both predator and prey, was still fresh in his mind. He understood now that it was not Ashimar's brutality, but rather his cruelty, that shook him to his bones. The spiders, in their own way, had been savage and brutal killers, but there was no touch of cruelty in them. He took that lesson to heart as he crept forward, eager to be done with his prey, but terrified—more terrified now than he ever was in his youth—of the cruel man who would come home at any moment and teach him what brutality truly was.

Four feet, now. Half of him was as silent and full of grace as a sleek spider bearing down on its unsuspecting prey. Half of him was as silent and full of grace as a frightened little boy.

It helped, somewhat, that the bloodguard were unfeeling men without songs, without stories. If anything, they were even more callous than their master, whose occasional moments of furious rage set him apart from the men that might have been called emotionless. Quiet as ghosts around him, revealing nothing of themselves, they had first treated Kellan as a human being—a troublesome one, an outsider to be bullied, but a human being just the same. There was no such pretense now. He was a loose end, of no more consequence than a goat fit for slaughter. His chances were not good, he knew. But if nothing else, he would leave them only the bitter and toughened meat of an animal that had to be run down a long time.

The men had dropped off to sleep, overwhelmed by the food and warmth of the miners' hut. The evening was still and dark, and with winter coming on there would be plenty more darkness to come. Even the dark-skinned Rahastan miner and the white-haired girl nodded in the half-sleep of exhaustion, made drowsy at last by too much panic. The sentry was the only one awake, armed for battle but with his helm at his feet, and the full attention of his vigil was directed outward, not inward, as he watched the single navigable approach to the house and awaited Ashimar's return.

Three feet to go. He raised his hands and leaned in. The sentry's chair would scrape the wood if he were anything less than perfectly precise.

There would be no better chance than this—and no second chance after it.

Kellan held his breath.

His long fingers spread open like spiders' legs.

Two feet.

He waited for the howl of the wind.

The sentry began to turn—

With sudden swiftness, Kellan swung the ridge of his hand hard around the front of the sentry's throat and threw his free hand over the bloodguard's mouth and jaw. Clamping him by the head and neck, Kellan tightened his stomach with breathless effort as he hoisted the sentry outward and up from his chair. He jerked him aside silently, hoping for a clean and instant kill, but could not find the proper angle at which to work. Again and again he jerked the smaller man's head round as hard as he could, as he had heard it done in the boasting of many braver men. But although he had the strength for it, the finesse eluded him in the sloppy and desperate confines of the struggle. Caught breathless, unable to scream in pain, the sentry bit hard into Kellan's hand, hoping to pull the needed shout of alarm from his attacker, or even to take a few fingers for his trouble. Hot blood streamed from the fleshy hollow between Kellan's thumb and forefinger as the man's teeth sank deep. But Kellan's sinful hands had been the target of cruelties for most of his life; they felt little if any pain, now, and he continued his lethal work. The neck gave way not with a single twist of deadly precision, as the stories boasted, but with a series of repeated wrenching movements that wore down the poor man's ability to fight back. The damage began to show in the shuddering jerks of his arms and legs, in the sudden foul stench as the spasming body unburdened itself for the last time.

Kellan set the body back on its chair when he was done. Perhaps it would buy him a few precious minutes, if a half-asleep bloodguard chanced to look up. Or perhaps the posture added a little much-needed dignity to the end of a man who had died a most undignified death. Although he had grown to hate it, Kellan inched back to his place on the floor and retrieved his snarling wolf-helm. If the winds picked up again, having something to cover his head would matter.

There was no telling when Ashimar would return, but it could not be long. Now that Kellan's choice was made, now that the sentry was filling the little house again with the renewed stink of death, its rough-hewn walls felt more menacing than ever. Kellan slipped out with his armour and boots bundled in his hands, tramping into the snow in his bare feet, more eager to be out in the wicked cold than to spend another moment in the cabin that would surely be his death if he stayed.

"Put on your boots, at least," said a voice. "It's bad form to draw steel on a man with no boots on."

For a moment, even steadfast Kellan's blood turned cold in his veins. But the voice was not Ashimar's hollow hiss—it was the deep, steady whisper of a man whose own determination frightened him. He turned in the snow to find Rasten staring up at him, sword and axe in hand. His heart sank within him as he reached down with seeming nonchalance and pulled on the first of his boots.

"I knew the others would stop me, if I'd been seen," he said. "Never imagined you would."

Rasten circled to stand astride the little path that led up to the trail. "I don't mean to stop you," he said.

Kellan raised his eyebrows at the smaller man's weapons as he pulled on his other boot, brushing the snow from his freezing toes.

"No? I suppose you're offering me a good shave before I make a run for civilized lands."

"It's not what you think," said Rasten, careful to keep his voice down even in the wind. "I have a terrible imposition to ask of you."

"Dumb shit," Kellan spat. "You don't draw weapons to beg."

Rasten clears his throat. "I do when you'd surely refuse."

Kellan drew his own sword, testing its balance. The bloodguards' swords were finer weapons than he was used to. In his big hands, the weapon felt nearly weightless.

"Let me explain something to you, friend Rasten. I know what fate awaits me when Ashimar returns. The little Rahastan bound up inside knows the way to the village. Ashimar will find that out soon enough, if he hasn't already seen it from atop that rock, and he'll crack the poor man's resolve like a fresh egg. You know what'll become of me, soon as he's got no need of me. He doesn't like complications, and he especially doesn't like outsiders. The minute he can get what he needs from that miner, I'm done for. Only I mean not to be here for my execution."

"That's fine," said Rasten. "I'm not here to stop you."

"Then why are you spoiling for a fight?"

Ras jerked his head toward the cabin. "You speak the truth. He'll find his way, soon, and when he does he'll kill whoever he doesn't need. If you're going…you're taking the girl with you."

"Out of the question," Kellan said.

"You said it yourself," Ras pressed. "He doesn't like complications. You think a kidnapped Havenar isn't a complication?"

"Bringing her along was *your* idea," Kellan reminded him.

"She's an innocent," said Rasten. "We both took her. We're both responsible for her, now. If Ashimar has no use for you, he has no use for her. He'll kill her as readily as he kills you, and I daresay he'll have half the trouble. I can take my chances with the bloodguards. She can't. If you're leaving, you're taking her with you…or you're not leaving at all."

Kellan cast his eyes around the dark woods, suddenly aware of how long they had spoken.

"I won't take her," he insisted. "I've no reason to, and every reason not to."

Rasten tapped his weapons together with a metallic clink. Kellan winced at the noise.

"You will," Rasten said. "Or you'll never make it out of this glade before the whole pack of them are on you."

"The only way out is through you," Kellan said.

Rasten nodded, resolute.

"That's a foolish mistake," said Kellan. "You're a fool to pen me in. I hadn't wished to hurt you, boy, but I will. This is the second time you've drawn steel on me, but there won't be a third. You haven't got the mettle for this fight you're spoiling for so badly."

"I just want the girl to be safe," said Rasten. "Her life is bound to yours. If she escapes, you escape. If not…"

"I told you," said Kellan, "she's not coming with me. That's the end of it."

Rasten sighed, his steamy breath pooling in the winter air. "Then steel will be the end of it."

It was more desperation than impatience that fuelled Kellan's anger. They were close enough, for they had been near-whispering, for Kellan to snap out the tip of his sword, take a nip out of Rasten's scruffy chin, and make clear the point that words seemed not to capture. Quick for his size, he flicked out the weapon, only to be met with a sharp clang as Rasten's axe swung up and batted it away. He thrust in twice more, and twice Rasten's weapons conspired to throw his sword-point wildly off to the side. His smile gone, his face intense, Rasten spun both weapons in his hands in a flourish that, to a practical man like Kellan, seemed like a foppish display. But two more failed attacks brought him nothing more than the ring of steel. Rasten thrust back in, and to Kellan's surprise he was good with a blade—and better with two. His barrel chest and thick forearms swung the weapons with ease and swiftness; even one-handed, the axe came in with such hunger in its attack that Kellan had to parry it hard. His arms buzzed from the force of the blow, and the trees echoed the ring of its bearded blade.

"You're good," Kellan said, "for a palace dancer."

"I don't want to hurt you," said Rasten. "I don't want *them* to hurt you. Take her with you. That's all I ask."

Kellan came on in anger this time, swinging his weapon with such ferocity that even Rasten's mighty arms could not withstand him. Feeling the shift, Rasten moved lightly and freely with the blows, spinning his weapons, dancing nimbly. Kellan had an immense reserve of ferocity in him, waiting—but the faster and harder he struck, the louder and more frequently the deflections rang out. If the sleeping men had not heard the sounds of battle inside, certainly Ashimar would have in the open air.

"You're no match for me," Kellan barked, "but I haven't got time to show it." He ducked left to make for the trail, but Rasten cut him off.

"No," Rasten agreed, "you haven't."

Their swords met as Kellan tried to cross to the right, but was again fenced in. He chanced a couple of blows, but they fell without conviction as the axe whirled in and he tried not to strike it too hard.

"You can't win," Kellan said.

"I don't have to," Rasten countered. He was breathing heavy, now, as the exertions of his acrobatic style took their toll. Kellan, lumbering on with brutal efficiency, suspected he could keep this up for an hour. But it was an hour he did not have.

"You're going to wake them," the big man warned, backing away for a moment as he considered his options.

"I'll tell them I caught you escaping," said Rasten.

"You'd betray me so cheaply?"

"Take the girl," said Rasten. "Take her as far as the first Imperial outpost. Drop her there and go where you like." He struck his weapons together with another clang. "Or share her fate here."

"If I could fight you full force," Kellan warned, "you'd be dead before they got to me."

Rasten spun his weapons again. "Maybe," he agreed. "But they *would* get to you."

Kellan moved to strike again, but his sword-point wavered ineffectually.

"You're a practical man," said Rasten. "Do you want to win? Or do you want to live?"

Kellan stepped back, not yet ready to sheath his weapon.

"Choosing my own survival doesn't mean I lost."

"Of course not," said Rasten. "Take her. Go quickly. Our fight ends in a draw."

"Fights don't end in draws," Kellan said. "That's stupid."

Rasten's insufferable smile was back. "I think it's poetic," he said. "Two men, equally matched, not so different from each other in the end…"

"Different enough," said Kellan. "I'm not the sort of man who spends his days on the road pining for some soft city lover he'll never see again."

If Rasten was rattled, he did not show it. "And I'm not the kind who would throw an armoured comrade into the sea to drown."

"I'm sorry I saved your life."

"I've thought it through," said Rasten. "We don't know how far they would have gone. I think it's an initiation—"

"Enough," said Kellan, as loud as he dared. "I'll swallow your shit, but I'm not about to call it pork pie. Bring her to me, and stop talking."

"You get her," Rasten said, defeating Kellan's last chance to make a run for it. Cursing under his breath, he trudged back to the cabin.

Even through fifty feet of howling wind and thickly insulated walls, he was amazed that the exhausted bloodguards had slept soundly through the commotion outside. The girl was bound at the wrists and legs, and also tied to a heavy barrel. Half-awake, too tired herself to react with much fear, she flinched away as he cut the securing ropes and hoisted her over his shoulder. The smell of death had spread through the hut again, and would wake at least one of them before much longer.

Rasten seemed pleased when Kellan emerged from the hut with the little prisoner slung over a shoulder.

"She gets none of my food," Kellan warned. "She lives or dies by the Fool's grace."

"Fine," said Rasten. "But I want your vow that you won't hurt her."

Kellan scoffed. "My word means nothing. I'll kill her, probably, soon as I'm rid of you."

"I'll let the Havenari know she's in your capable hands," said Rasten. "I'll tell Lord Ashimar too. If anything happens to her, they'll make your survival so miserable that you'll wish they'd put you down here and now."

"Too much talk," said Kellan. "I'm going."

"Keep her safe," said Rasten. "I'll hold them off your trail as long as I can."

"Am I supposed to thank you?" asked Kellan. "You've betrayed me, little man, and I won't ever forget it." He moved to walk away, desperate to be gone—but a final thought entered his mind.

"If I see your woman," he added, his voice deadly serious, "I'll see she doesn't ever forget it either."

Rasten's glare turned suddenly cold. "If I raise the alarm now," he said, "they'll kill you without question. Don't make me."

Kellan shrugged and adjusted the girl's weight on his shoulder. "You won't," he said. "I've got a hostage now. If I so much as see the hem of a red cloak behind me, yours or the Scourge's, she dies. Whatever you're doing to keep them off my trail, you'd better pray for her sake that it works."

"Go," Rasten said. "If Ashimar finds you like this, we're all dead."

With a curse unfit for even the winter wind, Kellan made for the trail, shoving past Rasten's stocky frame as he went. He looked once to the where the horses were tied, heavily blanketed against the cold; but they were a trap, and he did not touch them. He expected to pass Ashimar along the single trail as he went, and a horse would have given him away immediately. Instead, he walked the edge of the ditch that lined the trail, and within ten minutes of his departure the girl over his shoulder began to shiver and panic. Taking her feelings into account, weighing them against his own hunch, Kellan slipped off the trail into the deep snow and brambles, cupping his big hand over the girl's mouth as a solitary figure in heavy armour passed by them overhead, walking unevenly. It had taken longer than Kellan had expected for the Weeping Man to return; indeed, that was the only reason he still drew breath. As soon as the figure had passed from earshot, Kellan lifted his burden and made his way up the hilly trail—not down the way they had come, as he was sure they would suspect. Where the wild slope was gentle and the thicketed bushes tamest, he slipped away from the trail altogether and began his descent into an unknown valley. He would go by the stars, as he had once been taught—and though he cursed his burden and seethed with old anger over carrying the girl who had sunk an arrow in his chest, he was glad now for the protection of a hostage against whichever of the hunting parties might find him first.

In the little hut atop the ridge, packed to capacity with vicious bloodguards, Rasten thought of home as he pulled his red cloak tighter around himself and feigned sleep as best he could. He had nearly stumbled over one of the sleeping men on his return, so raw were his nerves. But beneath the jitters and panic of what he had done, and the knowledge of the terrible consequences that would come to the group for letting the two escape, he felt a quiet stillness. Whatever turn his suffering was to take when Ashimar returned, he had made his peace with himself, and that gave him strength. When the Weeping Man arrived only a few minutes later, monstrous in his rage when he saw the body left behind, Rasten was woken by shouted commands from a sleep that had come on easily for the first time in days.

He was dreaming of his brother again when Ashimar's fury woke him. Again they stood back to back on a hill, fighting all who opposed them—only this time, for perhaps the first time in Rasten's memory, the festering wound that had taken Jalen Varhame's life was gone from his shoulder, and he stood straight and tall as he had in his youth.

"Find him! Where did he go?!" Ashimar bellowed, smashing the sentry's chair against the front wall of the cabin in a scatter of splinters. Half-groggily, coming out of sleep, Rasten sighed and muttered something that made little sense to anyone:

"He's not gone," Rasten mumbled, half-asleep, closing his fingers around Jalen's axe. "Not really."

TWELVE

THE QUEEN BEE WAS CALLED ITHURIEL, after the fairest of the aeril princesses in the Age of Sun. Beloved by the sun, by the aerils, and by all the North, Ithuriel the Most Fair ruled over the greatest of the Four Cities, centuries before the coming of the Vosi people first gave it the name Travost—and millennia, perhaps, before it was renamed Travalaith in honour of its saviour Valithar. Many and secret were the ancient legends of the aerils, and most of their stories were kept from humankind—but even their secretive and hard-hearted lords could not bear to keep the legends of Ithuriel the Most Fair to themselves.

Alec Mercy had grown up a lover of stories. Before his service in the Grand Army, while still a child at his grandfather's knee, the stories of Ithuriel were told to him. She governed the aerils and the Vosi in the First Days with such bearing and charm that her father, the nominal King, was nearly forgotten behind her majesty. A magnificent golden crown, Vervuşil the Starmantle, was made for her by the ancients, though she refused to be coronated. By the reckoning of the Hanes, when the time of her Merging came and she passed into the sea, it rained for a year and a day as the skies mourned her. It was perhaps some small justice to the Queen who Never Was that Alec Mercy had bestowed the name, with some reverence, upon the eldest of his hive-queens, and on all those buzzing daughters who came after her.

Alec came to her court in the north field like a timid bride, veiled and perfumed. He would not smoke the bees to quell them, especially not in winter, for they would gorge themselves, fearing a hive-fire, and there was little enough honey to last the season. But a touch of mollhive dabbed on his wrists, and over the part of the veil that caught his breath, would still them without petrifying them. Bees could smell each other's fear, his grandfather said, like dogs. There was no doubt they could smell his if he did not perfume it away.

He dared not dawdle, but moved as gently as he could to the great framed house he had built for his largest hive. The bees detested small-talk, of course, but it was proper to sing them down before he came to the business at hand. Alec Mercy had a fine singing-voice, both strong and gentle, when he chose to unlock it. For Ithuriel and her court, he did so with very great reverence:

Ye damsels of dusk, nor waly nor wail,
But settle, o settle ye, lie-a-lor-ee,
And bear me no tusk, but attend to my tale,
O settle, o settle, and shrive you poor me.

It was a simple verse, but old beyond reckoning, passed down by grandfathers long years past, and by their grandmothers before them. It centered him and calmed him, and though he came to them quickly it was without any of the panic and urgency with which he had ransacked his house and made up his pack only a few minutes before. He was in Ithuriel's court now, and felt safe there. If death itself was riding for him, as Tsúla had warned, it would not intrude upon him until he had made his peace.

He knocked three times at the wall of her home and waited.

"I've come to say goodbye," whispered Alec, when the bees were calm. Clustered tight for the winter, basking in one another's warmth, he seemed to have them all in one place, which was best. He cleared his throat.

"I know this is not the news you had hoped for over the winter," he said. "Robyn could not have wintered here, in the end. It would not have been safe for Aewyn to stay. But—I don't suppose it matters, now. They lie at the heart of the matter. It seems, Your Majesty, that the wars of men have come home to us at last. The stranger who came to us in the fall—Celithrand, as I told you—is hunted by the Imperator. His Scourge, Ashimar, is coming here, and he does not mean us well. He has taken Aewyn from us—from the Havenari—and Bram is sore wounded at his hand. Or…or he was, some days ago. I know not if he still lives. I know not… if Robyn still lives."

He paused to let the bees listen, and to consider his next words carefully. The bees loved Robyn, and they loved Bram still more. Tradition held that when the news was bad, especially, there was a tricky art to telling the bees without currying their disfavour.

"We've heard of his bloodguards razing whole villages," said Alec. "He has put everyone to the sword—the old, the young. Our women—excepting Robyn, you understand—are not fighters, not like yours. We have no stings to protect our home. So it is best, for now, that we leave. Tsúla knows the way. We have supplies enough for a time, though there are too many to survive the whole winter, I fear. Too many mouths to feed without our crops and our fields. Ithuriel, your Majesty…I am afraid. I don't know what will become of us. I don't know if Ashimar will give chase. I can't say when, or if, we will return. The others are already on their way. I thought it best not to alarm you…until the last. It is my hope they will not think to harm you. The affairs of men, I think, are beneath those of your noble kind. But the morning dawns uncertain for me, so…I thank you for the joy you have brought me, for your honey, and the mead we brewed together, and for the new life you have shared with me in Widowvale."

He looked to the tree line. The sun was rising.

"I suppose you'll all be *my* widows, if I'm not away before the sun," he said. "May Tûr and the Ten bring you flowers and fat winters. May your children be plentiful, and your honey sweet. May fire and famine never trouble you; may you rule always in wisdom, and in peace. Bless me, ladies, and pray for me before the gods when you meet them in the fields. That's all, bees. Farewell."

He walked gently and slowly away from the bees—then strode with urgent purpose across the field—then flat-out ran the distance from the field's edge to the heavy brush that fringed the escarpment north of town. In the cold blue light of pre-dawn, in motionless silence, Tsúla stood waiting for him. His horse, Rascal, was nowhere to be seen. Bram's big late-gelded roan, Jumper, jerked and tugged at the reins in Tsúla's hand.

"Are you done?" Tsúla asked.

"It's done," said Alec. "The bees have been told."

"Good. We've got a hard climb to catch up with the others. Climb on."

Alec looked at the steep escarpment with some surprise. "You sure?"

"Go ahead," said Tsúla. "He loves the slopes." Alec mounted up and Tsúla gave the reins a quick tug, indicating overall direction of travel, before handing them up to Alec.

"We won't keep the others waiting," Alec said. It was a hopeful statement, almost a question.

"They're on the Serpent Trail, and having an awful time of it," said Tsúla. "Orin doesn't walk so well, anymore. And Darmod's sheep are ungovernable, as you'd expect."

"Just the same," said Alec, "if we're out more than a week, we'll be glad he's brought what few he could."

Tsúla knew the way straight up the escarpment, and led Jumper with a steady hand. The horse seemed not to mind the slope, though

Alec was dizzy enough on the ascent without being seated atop a long-legged horse. A few feet above the frozen earth, the slope seemed even more treacherous, and his white-knuckled hands choked tightly on the reins.

"You're making him nervous," said Tsúla. "Just relax."

"It must seem awfully strange to you," said Alec. "Telling the bees."

"Not so strange," said Tsúla. "In Ulitsa, in Estelonne, it was our ancestors we speak to. We bury our dead, too, and it's considered respectful to speak at their graves. Very young, our children learn the stories of their many ancestors, and when you have bad news, you speak to the ancestor who in life was most able to help."

"Not so strange, then," said Alec, though he could not relax his grip on the reins.

"My grandmother, my mother's mother," said Tsúla, "had a brother who was a marbler, a great carver of stone. He was renowned for the skill of his hands. He was in demand from one side of the mountains to the other. Always he spent his money, but always he went where the work was. He loved many women, though I learned this later, and somehow when he moved on, they grieved him not. If your bees are females, as tradition holds here they are, he is the ancestor I would consult. Great-uncle Údai. He was safe on the roads, and always had the right word for leaving women behind."

Alec nodded. "You don't talk of your family much, Tsúla."

Tsúla rubbed at his wrists thoughtfully. "Not so much, I don't. My parents—to *their* spirits, I have nothing to say. But two generations before them, my family were wise."

"And you make your family wise once more," said Alec.

Tsúla smiled politely, but there was a quiet sadness in him so out of place that Alec could not bear the silence, and strained hard to hear the movements of the village. The townsfolk of Widowvale were still too distant to hear, but between his ear and Darmod Pick's troublesome ewes lay a mile or more of deep forest teeming with life. Owls and those insects too hardy to sleep through the winter filled the trees with a delicate chorus, and the sharp rustle of woodland rodents fleeing as the two men drew too close reassured him that Ashimar's men, if they were anywhere in the woods, were not waiting ahead.

They reached the top of the escarpment in only a few minutes, and Jumper was glad to be back on level ground and made no secret of it in the spring of his trot. Alec's horsemanship was a skill long neglected, but his instincts were still there. After the unseasonal storm that had passed, the woods seemed warmer and more pleasant than the unforgiving slope had been, and the wind had died down and did not bite so terribly. A half-mile in, they caught up with the others: shivering from the cold, bundled in cloaks and blankets, they had made as good time as they could. An ox hauled a heavy cart with the youngest children and some of the supplies; they were still and silent, and seemed to understand the seriousness of the trip if not the cause.

Darmod had brought his thirteen strongest ewes, who followed the crude lantern hanging from his crook obligingly. A thick coat of snow had knit itself onto their puffed coats, and their wool kept in their heat so well that the snow did not melt. They looked twice their size under their mantles of white, beasts so immense that even Jumper started at them as he returned to the flock. Where one ewe seemed to break away from the others, Aeric the Miller's lame talbot-hound, Banning, was still quick enough to get in front of her and yap her back into line. Ahead of them, under a battered, snow-covered traveler's hat, Aeric held his wife's hand as they strolled beside the ox, as if they were a young couple in love who knew not what it was to be hunted. Here and there, he would point to the songbirds who went quiet and still as the train of villagers approached; as one of the men gone to mining, he was used to the cold and hardship of lucrative winters, and seemed not to notice the surrounding cold at all.

Behind them, clustered among the able-bodied miners, Marin the Reeve and his wife trudged on with careworn faces, so intent on their steps that they failed to notice Tsúla and Alec returning until the two were nearly upon them.

"Glad you could join us," said Marin. His mocking tone hid the relief that was clear in his eyes.

"It's done," said Alec. "The bees have been told."

"You don't look too stung. I presume they took it well. We could use a bit of good luck."

"If we're gone too long," said Alec, "they'll have to make do over the winter without my beet sugar. It's unfair to the bees. They are too small to be wrapped up in the mad wars of men."

"So too, I thought, were we," the Reeve's wife chimed in. Alec nodded, but his smile was weak.

"As did I."

Marin studied his friend's careworn face. "She'll be all right," he said.

"Eleven wounds, I hope so," said Alec.

"Will you?"

The beekeeper nodded. "I know who Robyn is. I know what she must do. I know what that might mean, one day. I just… I thought there was hope out here, Marin. Hope for a new life. Selfish hope, that a better life awaited me."

Marin looked skyward. "Looks like more snow," he said. "A cold day, a colder night, and a blustery storm to boot. All bad news, if it's comfort you seek—but good news, if a clean escape is what you're after."

"A miserable day and a night of suffering," said Alec. "We haven't enough to keep everyone dry. We'll look after the children and the old, and it'll go hard for the women and men."

"That snow will fill our tracks, fast as anyone can find them," said Marin. "I'll take hope over comfort any day." He shuddered suddenly as they skirted a deep ravine, feeling an altogether different chill in his bones that would not leave him be. His wife saw it, clutched his hand tightly, and whispered softly to him. But there was some nightmare in him that gripped his heart so fiercely it almost sent him flying back to the village, Ashimar or no.

Ahead of them, old Orin stumbled on his cane, and could fare no farther on his own legs. They called a halt, and the whole village's forced march came to an end as they brought him to the cart and laid him up where the smallest children had been. The twins were made to walk, which they did with some protest, and Rinnie was handed up to his brother Arran, whose shoulders were no less broad than the ox at the yoke. He hoisted the boy with a field-calloused hand under his rump and soothed his back with the other.

"I want to go home," said the boy.

"I think it's an adventure," said Arran. "Did you know most men who work the land are born, and live, and die, all within twenty miles of their door? Their whole lives, Rin, without ever crossing a river or cresting a mountain."

"I've never left the village," said the boy.

"Nor I," said Arran, who did not like the prospect of adventure after all. "But Father walked a thousand miles, or ten thousand, all over the North. Clear from Tundara to the Ban, and the Ban to the green fields of Carmac. And from there to the Iron City, the black jewel of all the Empire, where he met Mother, and west to our very door." He walked with the boy away from the cart, to the edge of the trail that skirted a deep ravine. The hill that rose on the far side did not conceal the rocky outcroppings of a whole different size and shape and bedrock than the ones near the village.

Arran held his brother high to see them, peering over the green hill to their jagged edges on the horizon. "Those rocks are to mountains," he said, "as the little house spiders are to the great woodcobs that spin their webs for squirrels and owls alike. I pray you'll cross a real mountain someday. They're as tall as giants, as tall as the sky, and so wide you could run yourself to death before you ever got 'round one."

"I'm a fast runner," said Rinnie, thoroughly distracted from his misery as the village trudged on through the cold. "Ask Ali. I'm the fastest runner in all of Haveïl. Ask anyone. Nobody's faster than me."

Arran ruffled his brother's hair as Grim had once done, and kept up his pace. Distantly, the scream of a pig—one of the Oltman pigs—cut the air with a terrible sound that shook the horses where they stood.

"Gods be praised," Arran murmured, in imitation of his mother. "I hope you're right."

In the chill of the morning, Rasten shivered and cinched the leather straps on his panther-headed helm even tighter. He could not drown out the sound of the pig at slaughter, but it was better somehow with his ears covered. With the departure of Kellan and the girl, he had made his peace and found a place within himself where the bloodthirst of his monstrous companions could not reach him.

"No druid to be found," said the bear-headed bloodguard. "No Celithrand. No village. No Kellan. No girl. But we've got fresh pork belly to break our fast, and that's something."

The others nodded with amusement, though laughter was not their way. Only Ashimar was silent, standing with quiet fury before the moot-hall, pondering his next move. For once, the twisted lips of the weeping child betrayed his own frustration.

With the lazy wave of his gauntleted hand, Ashimar motioned for their last remaining prisoner. Rasten might have brought him over, but waited until one of the others took him. At the Red Captain's side, the Rahastan needed no prompting to sink to his knees.

"Please, Sir," he begged, though he knew not for what. "Please, Sir, please..."

"I am disappointed with your failure, Fen'din," said Ashimar.

"I have not failed, Sir, please," said Fen'din. "You asked for the village. You asked me for Widowvale. This I have given you. This is she. This is my home."

He held Fen'din's chin in his hand, deep in malevolent thought as the mantis-headed bloodguard returned to his side.

"Report," said Ashimar.

"The houses are barren," said the bloodguard. "Little enough left in the larders. No fires in the hearths, but the houses are warm. They're gone, but they've not been gone long."

"Are there any tracks?"

"No, milord, but the weather would make it deadly country for any who fare off-road. There's a narrow trail going north, and a second trail southeast that links with the Iron Road. They've gone one of those ways, or the other, unless they passed us in fairy-cloaks coming down the mountain."

"They can't have gone far," said one of the others. "It's an entire village. How quick can they be?"

Ashimar turned and glared at him until he buckled in silent embarrassment.

"Any sign of Kellan or his prisoner?"

"No sign," the mantis-headed bloodguard confirmed. "No telling which way he's gone."

"Could a strong man alone survive in open country?"

"For a while, milord, unless the wind picks up. But not easily. If he means to live, he's headed north, or east as well. West is nothing but snowed-out trails and death. South he could make for Orrath, but there's a lot of open country. No shelter to speak of, nor help to be had except our own garrisons."

Ashimar nodded cryptically, pacing several steps around the moot-hall. He motioned to Rasten.

"Come," he said. "The rest of you…burn this down." He gestured to the towering moot-hall with some distaste. "Perhaps the smoke will lure back someone sentimental."

The men set about kindling a fire with no delay: the thick padding beneath their heavy armour was enough to keep them safely warm, but it was not quite enough for comfort. The moot-hall was mostly timbered and would go up easily once the campfire was strong enough.

"What about him?" Astagar asked, indicating Fen'din. "He led us here. Are we done with him?"

"Wait," said Ashimar. "Do not hurt him." He moved away from the others toward Rasten, whose approving nod could be seen behind the panther's head even if his smile could not.

"You need something, lord?" asked Rasten. He had a friendly remark about the value of mercy, but felt it was better left unshared.

"Where has your friend gone?" Ashimar asked. "Where has he taken my prisoner?"

"On my honour, I don't know," said Rasten. "He spoke of no destination."

"So you did speak," said Ashimar. Rasten's blood ran suddenly cold.

"Milord, I—"

"I thought as much. He was with you, the night on the ship when you spoke of…Illyria."

"I…I don't know how to answer."

"He was there."

"I was… I seem to recall being told to forget that name."

Ashimar leaned in. The rising sun played red across the tears streaming down his mask.

"Did you speak of her? In the many days since?"

"I… no, milord."

"That is fear talking. Calm yourself and think. Are you certain?"

"Not… not that I can recall."

Ashimar nodded. "You are a fool," he said. "You risk her very life by betraying her thus."

Rasten was caught-off guard by the Red Captain's interest. He tried to form a reply, but Ashimar was already done with him. Whatever conversation they might have had was cut off when he returned to his men.

"Cut him loose," Ashimar ordered. Surprised, the bloodguard hesitated a moment before unbinding the prisoner's hands. Shivering, he inched closer to the fire they were building, but kept his eyes on Ashimar.

"You know the girl," said Ashimar.

"Y-yes," said Fen'din. "A little. Aewyn is her name."

"The man who took her from me is Kellan Fyldron. You know him as well."

"Y-yes."

"You can describe them both. You would know them at a hundred paces."

"I would know them at a mile, Sir, if it means my life."

Ashimar paid the comment no heed. "We will clothe you and provision you. If you do as you are told, this is where we part ways forever."

Rasten had not recognized how devoid of hope the Rahastan was until a little mote of it crept back into his dark eyes.

"What must I do, Sir? Please."

"We are riding for Wescairn," said Ashimar. "You are not. You are riding up the Serpent Trail, on one of our very few horses. What is the closest major town by that way?"

"A-Aslea," stammered Fen'din.

"Good. You know the trail and the towns. Spread word from here to the coast. Settle in Seton when you reach it. Tell all who will listen—the Havenari, Grand Army troops, the local Reeve, *everyone*—that there is a price on Kellan Fyldron's head. Dead or living, if there is enough of him left to identify. By decree of the Imperial Scourge."

"I swear I'll do it," said Fen'din, who was never far from begging now.

"To the man who brings me the head of Kellan Fyldron, attached or no, his reward shall be twenty gold sovereigns in gold…"

Rasten almost gasped. Twenty sovereigns for a common soldier? It was the highest bounty he had ever heard of. It was equal, nearly, to Celithrand's.

"…immediately upon delivery, and within one year the demesne, in chief to the Vasil of Haukmere, of Egestor, and a thousand acres adjoining it." Ashimar finished.

"Sir, it's too much," said Fen'din. "I don't understand the words."

"It is a grant of my land," said Ashimar. "Egestor is a fortress on the coast. It is a smaller freehold. The Vasil of Haukmere answers to the Imperator, and the lord of Egestor answers to him."

The bloodguards were stunned.

"I don't suppose it's an instant lordship for us if we catch him ourselves," said one.

"I knew I should have put a knife in him the first night," said another.

"There was no money in it back then," said a third.

"I want every bounty hunter, every assassin, every sellsword to know his face," said Ashimar. "I want the name Kellan Fyldron on every wall of every inn and hostel from here to the Ban. Do you understand?"

Fen'din nodded.

"Good," said Ashimar. "Astagar, go east immediately. Take the message to the first post and dispatch all riders to the surrounding farms. The rest of you, do a wider sweep of the houses. Get our prisoner provisioned, and give him something warm to wear for the road. Spread the word, as far as you can. I will send a man on to Seton after you in a white month's time. If he finds you there and he is satisfied with the spread of the bounty, you will be rewarded with gold. If not, with steel."

"And Celithrand, milord?" one of the bloodguards asked. The Weeping Man only shrugged.

"He has been gone for weeks," said Ashimar. "Kellan has been gone for an hour, perhaps two. Celithrand can move unseen in the woods. Our deserter travels in full armour with little in his pack, and a young hostage in tow. We serve the Imperator—not his trueblacked lackeys. There is a point at which we must admit Olferth has sent us on a fool's errand, and make of that what we may."

Rasten hesitated, nearly thought better of it, but raised a big hand timidly. "If catching Celithrand is a fool's errand, then the girl can be of no more use to us. We've found her village already, such as it is. We may as well let her go."

"If it flatters your weak heart," said Ashimar, "we may well do, once we learn how much she has heard of secret matters you should not have discussed. If you had killed your friend for me, as well you should have, she might be free even now."

Rasten inhaled deeply, meant to say something more, but Ashimar advanced two quick steps toward him and his words caught in his throat.

"That breath is a a privilege by my hand," the Red Captain told him. "Do not give me cause to revoke it. You have expended your goodwill with me, and spent it rashly. Tell me, is your loyalty to Travalaith absolute?"

"Absolute," Rasten confirmed.

"Then we are of different minds on how best to serve." Ashimar waved the other bloodguards off to their various duties. His other hand rested menacingly on the scourge at his hip.

"Until I release you," he finished, "your loyalty is to me."

Rasten cleared his throat. "I must advise, my lord," he said, "that we return to the capital. The heavy fighting in the East means the enemy will soon have cause to try his luck in the West. We are an elite force, meant for better than hunting down deserters. The Imperator needs us."

Ashimar was unreadable behind the glistening mask. After an uneasy moment, he simply walked away. The bonfire was going handsomely, now; the bloodguards had made hasty torches out of branches, straw, and manure, and had set themselves to lighting up the moot-hall in a dozen different places. The hall was certainly not clad from groundstone to gable in precious metals, but a few ornaments dotted the wood here and there. These they pried from their fittings with quiet satisfaction as the wood went up, and threw into a sack to be divided and bartered for at their leisure.

As the flames rose and licked their way across the timbers, the Weeping Man stood before the door and watched in silence as the smoke poured over and past him in the crisp northerly breeze. The air burned hot and cold around him, and he stretched out his arms to take in the destruction in grave and inscrutable silence.

Like a chicken awkwardly trying to fly, the sun never really soared across the northern sky in winter. In the godless cold of Teurmaunt's last days, with the solstice looming ahead, it could not reach the ceiling of the cruel blue sky. As Kellan ran, then walked, then plodded, then trudged through the heavy drifts left behind by the storm, the sun rose feebly, hung in the air a while as if trying to climb higher, then slipped away beneath the trees, giving up the futile struggle well before its time. It was a piss-poor time to cut a path across open country, of course, which naturally meant that Kellan had no other choice.

For a while it looked as if the clouds would follow him and bless him with another bountiful squall—something to hide his tall, dark silhouette from the hills behind, and if the gods were feeling generous, to fill in his tracks. But no, the storm had bent off to the north, blanketing the deepest parts of the wood and leaving Kellan mercilessly exposed. Frustrated by the weather, by the climate, by his perilous circumstance, by the dead weight of his silent burden, Kellan knew as the sun came down that he was a fine enough soldier, but a poor outrider ill-suited for survival in open country.

Not long after he had made his escape, the little hostage had tried to make a break for it, and he'd had to club her back into silence. He hadn't meant to knock her out again, and didn't think he struck her that hard. But she pitched down into the snow, not like a man stunned but like a doll of wet straw, and though he tried throughout the day, no further shouting or abuse would wake her. In the stories he'd read as a young man, knights were always knocking each other on the head: the swoon lasted just long enough to tie them up, or to escape the castle, and then the villains would rise without harm and plot their revenge. But the girl was pale and her breathing shallow, and as the day wore on and she barely stirred, it began to excite even Kellan's pity. Every few minutes, even knowing he was being hunted, Kellan stopped to see to her breathing and make sure she was no colder than before.

This was not how such things went in the stories, though Kellan had no illusions that the world was ever so pleasant and well-ordered as a good saga.

His arms were strong and the girl was light, and so she did not slow him much. But he did sweat under the increased exertion, and in the light of day he felt the slick sweat turning to dew inside the plates of his armour and around the muzzle of his wolf's helm. By night, he knew, when worse came of the cold, it would play havoc on the joints of the armour and be mercilessly cold to walk in. His feet were frozen through to numbness, and that worried him. The pain of the cold he could stand; if it was mere pain, he could bear it. But the North had a thousand ways of unmaking a man, and frost was not among the hundred kindest.

"Mighty Dagan," he muttered on parched, chapped lips when he was sure he was too far from civilized folk to be heard. "Lord of the Ashen Meadow. King of the Dead, and Dread Consort of Time…O tallest and handsomest of the northern gods. Long have I served you. I have fed your wolves by land and by sea. I have killed birds, and spiders, and rats, and game beasts, and no shortage of men besides. You know me by the strength of my arms, and by my bad luck, most likely. Well, I've come to the thick of it. I'm lost and I'm cold—so cold that the Evermead seems a pleasant summer field by comparison. But I don't want to lie me down just yet. I've got more to do, O sad and beautiful God of Death. I've killed many in life, and we both know my days of it needn't be over. Let go your grip on me, and make no claim. Let me live, at least, until the men who hunt me put me at bay. I swear if you see me through this cold, I'll put as many as I can to the sword before they get me. Let me live my days beyond, and we both know there will be more dead to come—all for your glory, of course."

He walked and waited, waited and walked. He wondered why others didn't feel this stupid talking to the gods.

"Wise Tûr, hear me," he said at last. "O great god of the Tudrans and the Sundrists, god above all other gods, Tûr the Silent, Tûr who does not answer prayers—make a humble exception, this one time, for mine. Mysterious in your, uh, mysteries. Lead me to your will, if it be gentle. Show to me the cabin or the shelter you mean me to find. Let me blame my good luck on you, as so many in the cities do."

He trudged on, as expected, without an answer.

"Great Kedwyn," he began again. "Marshal of Keddensday and the Fairy Hunts. Lord of Chaos, god of madness, and secrets, and riddles, and hidden things. Mighty Fool, Trickster who wove the Chain of Night from all the true magic left in the world, and bound Tamnor himself in it. I've left a right shitstorm in my wake. Get me through this, and you're like to see more of it, I swear."

As the light began to die, a cruel wind picked up again, but there was no blessing of snow to go with it.

"O mighty Gurka—or whatever your name is. Bird God of the

Karach of Adân, who yet roam beyond the reach of this godawful Empire. You don't know me, and I don't know you. But as you're the only god who never did me a lick of wrong, I've more cause to love you than any. Call off your feathered wolves, my lord. Send your eagles and ravens home, and I'll give you… whatever it is you lot like sacrificed. Birds? Beasts? Men? It makes little difference to me."

"Sweet Myrine, the Ever-Merciful, Queen of Spring, Goddess of the Loving Hunt, Consort of Kedwyn, that prick who had his chance already, and gave me nothing. Long have I been most faithful of all to you, loving Goddess. Long have I pined for the men of my first quire, now dead under Draden for the sake of an ugly lust you gave to them. Long have I wandered lost, forlorn by love. By your grace, you who cherish all wild hearts without shame, I might find myself in a love-story yet. See me through the storm, and I'll try."

"Grandmother Sarúitsa, you spiteful hag. Love-goddess of Estelonne—marriage-goddess, rather, I should say—you've no kind words for me, and I've none for you. You'll get no love from me, after all the young men your temple whores have strung up by the wrists for loving backwards. But I'm in a hard way, you miserable old harridan. Put me indoors with a warm fire and all ten toes, and I *might* come 'round to some forgiveness. Hang me out to rot like a chick-apple, though, and Tamnor himself take you."

His stride had faltered some; he was dizzy in the cold and weak from thirst. He knew enough not to eat the snow frozen, not as the cold was setting in. Was it better to die of thirst or cold? He wasn't sure. Half-delirious, he wracked his brain for any of the more obscure gods he might try. The gods of his own kind seemed not to care—it was why, in the end, he might have preferred the Tudran way if the Siege hadn't broken all the faiths of the North some decades past. There was no help coming; the gods gave no answer anymore. Tûr, at least, promised none.

The sun was out of sight and the wind was starting to pick up again when Kellan felt the snare bite into his leg. The steel greave over his shin prevented the little spikes from digging in, but the wire caught him hard, and broke his stride. The white-haired girl came tumbling off his shoulder and pitched forward into the snow, though he strained his shoulder trying to catch her. She moaned softly, finally stirred by the chill of the snow.

Kellan grunted with impatience as he knelt and tried to take the snare off. It was the work of a good trapper; meant for foxes or hares, maybe, it had slipped tight around his calf and buried its barbs deep in the leather of his boot where the greaves did not protect. He'd been given no dagger or arming knife with his bloodguard's armour, but had been wise enough to take the table knife from the little cabin before he made his escape. As he reached for his pack, he met the girl's eyes. They were bright, green, and terrified.

Kellan rolled his own eyes in frustration. "Don't run," he croaked hoarsely. Indeed, she stood as if to try, but swooned and dropped to a knee almost immediately. Even that seemed a high perch for her, and she swerved as if a strong breeze might put her face-down again.

"Don't you dare run," he said again, and reached a big hand toward his pack. But she was still quick, if unsteady on her feet, and she jerked an arm out and seized it, pulling it away. Kellan gripped the trailing strap and wrenched it back. The string loosened and the little knife tumbled out of the pack and into the snow. Kellan watched it in sour disbelief as the girl plucked it out of the snow and held it menacingly, though she winced at the cold touch of it. She was armed now, and he had only his sword, if he could get to it in time. She was free, and he was chained. Kellan felt the fight was suddenly a dangerously even one.

"I can't find my feet," she said, circling him awkwardly on two knees and a hand. "What...what did you do to me?"

"I punched you," said Kellan. "That's what you've got coming when you try to kill a man, and can't finish the job."

"I could finish the job now," she warned, but took care not to get within reach of him. She held out the little table-knife menacingly.

"I've had bigger knives than that put through me before," said Kellan, "and by tougher folk than you. You think about that long and hard, and if you still mean to kill me, take one more step toward me, and we'll see how you fare." Her green eyes were full of anger, but there ws no cruelty in them. Kellan had seen enough cruelty in his lifetime—no, even in the last day—to know it on sight.

"Don't trouble yourself," she said. "I'm not interested." She wound up her arm—

"No—" Kellan started, but she threw the knife far into the open field. She showed him her empty hands as a gesture of peace, though not one of trust.

"You fool!" spat Kellan. "I need that knife for the snare! We could die out here, you know."

She shivered at that, as if noticing the winter wind for the first time.

"Where are we?"

Kellan shrugged. "Open meadow. Somewhere north of the Iron Road, somewhere east of that tanglewood you call home. Thankfully, a snare like this means we're probably not far from those who set it."

She raised a skinny arm. "Behind those trees, down the hill. Where the wind doesn't hit so hard."

Kellan looked at her. "You know this land?"

"I know where you'd dig a well and a latrine. I know where you'd pen your sheep, if you didn't want the sight of them to carry to men, or the smell to wolves."

"Fair enough, then," said Kellan, and wrapped the snare wire tightly around his gloved hand. With a few hard, uncomfortable tugs, he broke the little trap and set about untangling it once the other end of the wire was free. The girl tested her feet again, but she was still staggering unsteadily, like a deer taking its first steps, and could not have made it far or fast on her own.

"Lucky it was a snare for rabbit or somesuch," he said, finally tearing himself free. "If there's wolves in these hills, we're lucky it wasn't sized for them." The girl laughed at that so sharply that Kellan met her eyes in confusion.

"Your helmet," she said. Over the past hours, he'd forgotten he was wearing it.

"Can't hold a wolf," he conceded. He might have smiled himself if he weren't so hungry, and thirsty, and tired, and sick of the whole business of hostage-taking.

"Have you got a name?"

"Aewyn," she said. "What's yours?"

"Never you mind," he said, and hauled her to her feet. Even dragging her a few dozen feet to the discarded knife was an effort.

"I can't stand," she said. "Really."

"Of course you can't," said Kellan. "Just my luck you can't." He moved to reach around her body—but now that she was conscious, she recoiled from his touch in a way that saddened him.

"Don't trouble yourself," he repeated back to her. "I'm not interested either."

Against her protests, he threw her over his shoulder and started marching. The field was a wide one, but he had made it nearly all the way across before her questions began in earnest.

"Your first time taking a hostage?" she asked him. He sneered, but ultimately nodded.

"First time," he said. "Hopefully the last."

"I don't understand it," said Aewyn.

"It's not hard," said Kellan. "I'm leaving, and headed somewhere safe. If someone tries to get in my way, I hurt you or kill you. That's how a hostage works."

"It makes no sense," Aewyn protested. "The Havenari will come after me, but only because you took me. And your friends in red—"

"They're not my friends."

"Do you suppose they'll hesitate to cut you down because they value my life?"

For that, Kellan had no answer.

"You're naïve to think so," said Aewyn.

"I'm anything but," snapped Kellan. "And unless you want to be left in this pasture for Ashimar to find, you should quit making so good a case to be left behind."

He felt her shiver suddenly at the name. "I expected him to be taller," she quipped.

"Most do, I imagine," said Kellan. "He casts a long shadow."

"C-can you walk any faster?"

"A little."

They crossed the open meadow unharried, though Kellan was careful to watch for more snares as they came to the far side. The tracks of rabbits and maybe of hungry foxes dimpled the snow at the meadow's edge, and high above them in the bare trees, squirrels slumbered in fat, round watchtower nests laid bare by winter. With the snowstorm past, warmer air had come again to the lowlands, and brought with it a thin fog that collected in the valley and made the snow sticky and wet where they descended from the high flat earth.

True to her best guess, they found an old square stone well in the narrow dell, covered and boarded against the weather. It was unroofed, serviced only by an arm and pulley, but bucket and rope had both been taken indoors. Kellan unbolted the wooden cover and peered into the well, but could not tell in the dark whether it was quick or frozen.

"Well maintained," he said at last. "Someone lives out here, at least."

The path to the well was trod frequently enough—or it had been, upon a time—that it was not hard to find beneath the snow. It led in short order to a low cluster of wattled buildings—a cottage of a single room, a low wooden barn, and a building for crops and silage.

Approaching the door of the cottage, Kellan unfastened his helm and took it off. The moisture in his hair froze almost at once in the wind, and the sudden cold air revived him a moment from his exhaustion, though it might do more harm than good in time.

His hand was on his sword before he knocked. The little farm was well off the road, hidden so as not to be seen, but there were bandits enough who ran the Iron Road that a wary farmer might come armed to the door. When the door opened, he moved back into the shadows. The man within bore no light, and seemed to need none.

"Providence to you," said a voice grown soft and wooden with age. It was a civil greeting among strangers, wishing them what they deserved.

"Providence," said Kellan. "We mean you no harm, old man. We've no grudge with you. But a mighty grudge against the weather. Me and the little one, we'd be obliged—"

"Come in," said the old man, stepping back. "Come in and shelter. Make your case while you're in, so I don't stand with the door open."

"You're trusting," said Kellan, not with admiration.

"I'm trusting," said the old man, "but I'm not weak. You'll be wanting food, I expect."

At the thought of it, Kellan's stomach burned hollow.

"We haven't eaten in days," Aewyn blurted out. Both men looked at her as she entered, stumbled, fell nearly to the floor. Kellan caught her more gently than he might have without an audience.

"You heard her," he said. "She's wasting away. I'll ask nothing of you, but food for—for my daughter, if you've any to spare. Anything." Though he was dizzy from hunger and thirst himself, Kellan thought a little compassion might disguise him.

"Nonsense," said the old man. "You'll have what I've got, though there's not much in the house, and I'd sooner venture out to the stores in the light of day. Haven't eaten in days, eh? Where did you say you rode from?"

"Didn't," Kellan said tersely. Then, after a pause, "Up by Seton way. Our farm burned down. Lost my wife, my childer. This one's all I got left."

"That's kingly armour for a farmer," said the old man, not quite innocently. Kellan fixed him with the eyes one predator reserved for another.

"I've got a fine sword for a farmer, too," he warned. "See, I used to be Imperial. Deserter. I'm not proud of it."

"You don't say," said the old man. "Me, too. You're in safe company, at least until those riders come back. Will you have some fire?"

It took Kellan a moment to realize they stood in darkness. The fire had been put right to sleep, yet there was still a comfortable warmth in the house after so long a trek. He set his helm down and shook his snowy pack off his shoulder.

"I will, thank you," he said. He lifted Aewyn, still weak, to the single straw bed in the little house. She stirred but was already half-asleep with exhaustion, even though Kellan had done most of the trudging. He laid a pillow gently under her head, keeping up the appearance of caring, but she seemed to mistake him for sincere, and clutched his big hand briefly as he lowered her down.

"Have you got a name, stranger?"

"I do," said Kellan.

"Well?"

Kellan's eyes darted around the room until they settled on the wolf's-head helm he had set down by the door.

"Wulf," he blurted out.

The old man chuckled and knelt low by the fireplace. "I should have guessed," he said. There was fuel enough, but he'd let the flames go right out, until only a few faintly glowing embers remained. Kellan, having grown up in a home where the fires had never fully gone out, had never been much good rekindling a fire from them. But the old man knelt and nursed the flame with a little breath and an easy patience until a stubborn flame fought its way back onto the surface of the firewood and began to thrive.

"You're a brave man," said Kellan, "letting the fire die so low this far from anyone. You have neighbours? Other homesteads?"

"None it would please you to walk to tonight," said the old man.

"You're not short for wood," Kellan noted, "though I'll cut you some in the morning."

"I've wood enough," said the old man.

Kellan shrugged and began to unbuckle his armour. The rush of cold air on his wet joints made him shiver as he moved closer to the guttering fire.

"Well, you're not afraid of the dark, I'll give you that."

"It's the light I fear more," said the old man. "It's an ill night, tonight. I've had a rider to my door already. Followed the smoke straight to me."

Kellan shuddered. He did not need to ask what sort of rider. The orange glow of the new fire illuminated the near side of the old man's face: he was Oldborn, clearly, descended from those aerils who had sought new homes and families among the Vosi in ancient times. His half-blooded heritage was clear in the shimmering skin and glimmering golden eyes—but clear, too, in those eyes was the wary recognition of a homesteader who had been told to expect a traveler, and perhaps to report him.

Kellan stared him down a long moment. Half-unbuckled, with his mail draped over his arms, his armour would be more a hindrance than a help if he struck now. He feigned disinterest the only way he knew how, looking away in mock boredom even though his voice gave him away.

"They likely to come back?" he asked.

"If they can find their way," said the old man. He looked to the fire.

"Yeah, kill it," Kellan agreed reluctantly. "Blankets will make do, if you have one."

"You ought not to travel with that helmet," said the old man. "Not while the First Legion is hot on you." He covered the fire again, but poured some water or weak wine into a large clay mug and lay it among the burning coals for his guest.

"The First Legion?" Kellan asked.

"The Bloodguard," said the old man. "I know them when I see them. As I said, I'm a deserter, too. I served the Travalaithi Empire, once. But I left in the dead of night without looking back. So don't worry; I shan't turn you in."

Kellan let the air out of his lungs. He hadn't realized he was holding his breath.

"What's your name?" he asked. "Are you long gone to green, old man?"

"Mivaldar," said the old man.

"Never heard it before. Viluri? What's it mean?"

"Pilgrim," said Mivaldar. "*Mith*, within. *Val*, home. *Alda*, away. 'Inner traveler,' it means."

"Wulf means 'wolf,'" said Kellan, without a hint of irony.

Mivaldar stooped to pick the cup out of the coals with hands callused from farm work. It was warm enough, at least.

"If I recall correctly," he said, "Kellan's an old name too."

Kellan cursed under his breath. "So you *have* heard. They've already been to your door, then. I didn't expect they'd beat me to every farmhouse between here and the Iron City." He took the mug and drained it at a single pull. It was wine after all, and brought the heat back to him quickly.

"Kellan's an Orrathi name, isn't it? Far enough back."

"I suppose so," said Kellan. "Wouldn't know."

"It means 'slender and fair,' doesn't it?"

The big dark-haired man nodded. "My father had a fierce sense of humour."

Mivaldar took a seat on the single bed on what seemed suddenly to be thin, fragile legs. He was older, up close in the darkness, than Kellan had taken him to be.

"It's a perfectly good name, I think."

"Not anymore," said Kellan. "Not if a hermit farmer ten miles from the nearest dirt road has already heard it within a day of my leaving."

"It was many things that gave you away," said Mivaldar. "It was foolish of you to keep that helm. It was foolish of you to think you'd fare more swiftly than the Red Legion in darkness, on foot, over open country with a heavy load. They're riding the Iron Road, changing horses at every post. Whatever you've done, friend, I won't be lighting a proper fire for a day or two, especially not now that you've been here."

"I won't trouble you long," said Kellan. "I mean only to get my bearings, warm my bones, and be on my way."

"That girl needs rest," Mivaldar warned. "Proper rest, a good night of it. You rescued her from the Bloodguard?"

"Not really."

Mivaldar brushed back the straight white hair from Aewyn's forehead. Her temple was bruised where she'd been struck hard.

"Well, you're staying the night," said Mivaldar. "She's had a hard knock; she'll need the rest. Get moving at dawn. Cross open country at dawn and dusk. Let the trees cover you by day. And may Ataur of the Forests keep and protect you both."

"Ataur," Kellan muttered. "Knew I forgot one of the big ones. Should have prayed to him from the beginning."

Aewyn shifted uncomfortably in her half-sleep, and the two men lowered their voices.

"How far is it to Wescairn by the Iron Road?" asked Kellan.

"Far enough," said Mivaldar. "The soldiers there won't trouble you. They might ride out twenty miles or so. Beyond that, you're past their reach."

Kellan set down his mug. "That's where I'm heading."

Mivaldar shook his head as if it were a mad idea, which it very nearly was. "Don't wear that helm again," he warned. "I'd leave your whole amour, if I can help it. I've got furs that would serve you better."

"The armour I can leave," said Kellan. "But the helm is my wagon-chit out of here. Out of Haukmere, which I can't cross on my own with the Red Captain after me."

"You have a buyer?"

Kellan nodded.

"Wulf's as good a name as any," said the old man. "But grow your hair out. Grow it long, and have done with the beard. You've got the complexion for it, fair one. I can change out that billowing scarlet cloak for something that won't give you away at a half-mile in good light. There's not much you can do about your height, though."

"The rider," said Kellan. "He gave you a description?"

"He did."

"Did he mention my scars?"

Mivaldar shook his head. "What scars?"

Kellan unbuttoned the damp gambeson beneath his armour and lifted his tunic. "People forget faces when they remember scars," he said.

Mivaldar winced in spite of himself when he saw the state of Kellan's chest and stomach. After hard weeks on the road, untended by the cellwives of Travalaith, the deep gashes had healed into jagged and unsightly stripes of scarred flesh, white and hairless across his swarthy chest.

"You're not wrong," Mivaldar said, somewhat sympathetically. "Let them show if you end up somewhere warm."

"Warmth," Kellan sighed. "I remember warmth." He allowed himself the luxury of a smile as he slumped down against the hard clay bricks of the hearth. They were wreathed in soot, and soon so was he, but there was still a pleasing heat within them. He felt the exhaustion hit him at last, and might have drifted off if a sudden panic had not jolted him back awake.

"Why are you helping us?" he asked, suddenly wary. "How can I be sure you won't stab me in my sleep?"

Mivaldar smiled dismissively. "My red days are far behind me," he said. "I've seen enough of blood." There was a heaviness to the way he said it that put Kellan at ease.

"Just the same," Kellan said. "Losing the nerve for killing, that's one thing. But taking in a stranger, feeding him, giving him his bearings, clothing him when you've got precious little yourself—"

"I've got plenty," said Mivaldar. "And I haven't fed you."

"If you've got plenty," Kellan insisted, "then you'll feed us in the morning." The two men laughed quietly.

"Thank you," Kellan muttered. The words came out of his mouth like the dagger from his boot—quietly, unexpectedly, and on only the rarest and most desperate of occasions.

"We are in this war together, friend," said the old man. "Every one of us. Legionaries, deserters—even insurgents. Perhaps the young have forgotten it. But we weary few who shook our spears in the Siege shall always remember."

Even in his exhaustion, Kellan had a dozen questions for Mivaldar. But now that he could feel the burning pain returning just in time to his frozen toes, now that he lay warming himself against the hearth-stones, a heavy weight seemed to come over him. What words he said in his delirium he would not remember in the light of day. He knew only that he was falling, and in his fall he saw glimpses of Aewyn, and Castor Stannon, and the weeping helm of Ashimar, and strange shadows in the woods that lingered cold on the edge of his rattled mind. He wondered, at the end, whether he might have a pleasant dream to look forward to, now that he was free of Ashimar. But the sleep that came was swift and deep, and he passed easily, too easily, into the dreamless dark of the world beyond waking.

Thirteen

O DO YOU LIE WITH MEN—with human men?"

"Excuse me?"

Odi sniffed his nose clear in the rank odour of the lower chamber and tried to forget where he was standing.

"I'd heard tell the aerils have it as you please with lovers fast as you can bed them," he said. "What's the poem say it goes: 'as fair and innumerable as the stars,' isn't it?"

Baran's white cheeks blushed red but she did not smile. "It fascinates me," she said, "and it always has, just how much of your kind's lives are devoted to wiving and swiving."

Odi shrugged. "D'you ever have children?" he asked. Baran shook her head.

"Two," said Odi. "Edie and Hickory. They'd be eight and six, now. You're like to remember what you had for breakfast eight years past. But for a man, a human, eight years is a lifetime ago…"

"Hold," whispered Baran, and Odi shut his mouth. They pressed themselves hard against the side of the pipe, crowding back into the darkness as one of the tower stoolmen emptied a chamber pot into the flowing water of the ingenious drainage system. A few feet above them lay the Black Forges, the sprawling former smithy beneath Cîr-Valithar itself, wrought by the Second Craftsman's terrible hands and since repurposed as the opulent Imperial Baths for the benefit of those rich in wealth and poor in taste.

Odi held his breath until the water had washed away the offending stench, but his stomach did not settle. One wrong misstep under the narrow opening, and they risked being discovered in the most unpleasant of ways. Baran held her breath substantially longer, until the footsteps above them had faded and the lower room of the Imperial baths had resumed its weighty silence.

"They're fostered to my uncle's *meslekûl*," Odi whispered. "His son-in-trade. Smithy work. Imagine my little girl, shoulders like a stallion's, pounding steel to make axe heads."

Baran's eyes were impassive. "For the Uprising?" she prompted him coldly.

Odi looked away defensively. "For them that pay," he said. "Such are the times."

They waited in silence after that, as long as was bearable. But Odi was a keen student of faces, even the faces of aerils, and he could see in the darkness the great worry that lay hidden beneath her high cheekbones and tightly drawn lips, shining through only at the eyes.

"We'll be all right," he said. "I'm his best harbour rat, or he wouldn't have sent me. If the alarm sounds, I've bolt-holes enough for the both of us—clean, safe ones."

"We are not the ones I fear for," she whispered. "He has chosen to come himself—not to send another, not even one of his apprentices, but to come himself. I cannot fathom why. He doesn't take chances like this,

Odi, and he ought not to take any chances now. If he dies, we are all lost. All of us, and generations after us."

"You love him," said Odi. Her eyes wide, she was lost for a reply. He regretted his words at once, and stared at his feet in sheepish deference.

"I only meant—" he began. "Not for, y'know, wiving and swiving, as you say. Though I've an answer for that too. I just mean… you'd follow him to the end."

"That's not remarkable," said Baran. "There are many whose loyalty to the Mage is unquestionable. You included, unless my judgment fails me."

"I know whose side I'm on, no doubt," he said. "But it's a little different. The life of an aeril—that's a momentous thing. More so now that your kind have gone into the sea, mostly. The life of a man, well…I've been fighting long enough to know how little that's worth. To any but the man himself, at least."

"You do yourself a disservice," she said, but he waved away her concern.

"*Att, att, att,*" he said dismissively. "That's why we humans have dirty minds, if you want to know. Only in this world a short time. Maybe kings and the well-fed, at the best of times, live seventy or eighty years, unless disease or revolt fells them. But low people live a short time and have low humour to match. I don't just mean *poor* people, mind you. Poets are poor, and they think on very high-minded things. But a poor poet can live to be an *old* poor poet. A poor soldier, a poor spy… we're not long for the world, lass. We're dead in a moment, and our footprints are washed away soon after. If human minds turn too easy to procreation, I'll warrant you that's why."

Baran let the hint of a smile escape her lips, in spite of herself. "You're a nervous talker."

"Poor habit for a spy," Odi admitted. "I'm restless, is all. If we're breaking into the records, the best time is an hour ago. The second-best time is now."

"We wait for the Mage's signal," said Baran. "When the way is clear, he will send for me. When he does, you must stay in the passage, tend our disguises, and keep it clear for us. When the alarm comes, this will be our only way out."

Odi shuffled his feet nervously on the dry edge of the tunnel floor. "Someday you'll have to tell me how the Mage won a highborn aeril's neverending loyalty."

Baran pressed her cheek to the stone wall, listening hard. "It's a dull tale, and a private one," she whispered.

Odi nodded pensively, lowering his own voice as they prepared to move. "I only meant it," he said, "as the veiled hope that you survive, and come back to us with more stories to tell."

Baran lay motionless against the wall for a long moment before her eyes narrowed in concentration: she had heard something, evidently, that Odi had not.

"It's time," she said. "I must leave you."

"Watch yourself," warned Odi. "The former Stormguard are still top of the top. They don't play gently. And our informant swears they have a few war-karach penned up in there, too."

"They'll all be dead before I get to tunnel's end," said Baran. "As I said, he's not one to take chances."

The white moon, the Mother of Sorcery, had turned her bashful face almost entirely away; the thinnest sliver of her cheek shone directly over the old Carnicist temple overlooking the Travalaithi harbour. Lower in the sky, the red moon shone fat and full, and bathed the stone parapet in its warmer light—not a true red like the skin of an apple, but a warm, bloodied gold, like the inside of the Imperial treasury by rushlight. In the fullness of its bloom, the red moon was enough to read by, and a fine companion for a solitary Stormguard, his pipe, and his pensive thoughts.

Devlyn's grandparents had been raised as Carnicists, once. Like so many, they lost their faith during the Occupation and never found it again. Even so, it brought him comfort to feel the realness of the stone, to walk the rampart of the old temple in the small hours of the night, and to stand in the protective shadow of Tûr the Vigilant. On the summer side of the temple, the immense copper statue of Tûr stared ever southward to the Spire with his sword half-drawn; imagined in the likeness of a beardless Vosi warrior, his gaze was somehow soft but stern at the same time. He had been carved both to comfort the people and to cry defiance to the dark god that had come down among them. He was a hope, a prediction, that the forces of good might one day come incarnate into the world just as the forces of evil had done. Carnicists were plain-speaking, literal folk, and in the early days after Tamnor came to them in his terrible living body, they were easily the most numerous of the Tudran sects in the Iron City. It was comforting to the people to think that Tûr, too, could take the body of a living man and defend them in plain, literal terms. It did not sit well among the common folk that Tamnor could roam where he pleased, killing and corrupting at leisure, while Tûr the Silent would not so much as answer a mother's prayer for her stillborn child.

Devlyn wanted to believe, but belief was harder than it used to be. He had joined the Stormguard because he had heard wondrous tales of their magic in the early days of the Annexation. He had indeed studied the mysteries and moon-lore with them, as was the tradition; but there had been no magic to speak of, to his perpetual disappointment. It irritated him now, to no end, that there was a Mages' Uprising in the East, and that the enemy were said to wield the forces of making and unmaking in a way that was now lost to him.

As he took in his pipe on the temple's fortresslike rampart, he imagined lighting it with the forces of the elements, not with a rush light that burned low in its holder and stank of mutton fat. He wondered at the ways he might bend the world to his liking, if only he had the power. He thought of the other Stormguard—some kind, some cruel—and which ones he would reward, and which ones he would punish. Mostly he thought of his parents, who had raised him poor and whose life he had meant to restore to wealth with his magic. Pushing forty, now, it troubled him that he had not already done so.

It was with these thoughts in mind that he happened upon the mysterious jewel. As he came down from the rampart to the roof-gate with his pipe exhausted and his rush light burning low, it caught the reflection of the flame and glimmered softly where it lay among the bird-droppings that sometimes collected on the roof. He cleaned it off, almost reverently, and scrutinized his face in its many facets. It was a red gem, like a ruby or a garnet, exquisitely cut and easily too large to set in a finger-ring or bracelet. In his rude hands it seemed a kingly treasure, better fit for a crown or sceptre, and Devlyn had never before seen its like.

"Hullo, there," he breathed, turning the gem over in the moonlight. It sparkled in his hand as if he had caught a fallen star.

A weak-willed soldier might have pocketed the jewel and said no more of it, but the Stormguard, at least, were men of supreme loyalty: he would have to tell the others and hope that a finder's fee would give him the largest share of its worth. With grudging resentment, Devlyn pocketed the stone and returned to the Temple through a hidden roof-gate, hoping he could get down to Captain Stohn's desk before the others realized he was gone.

"Dev," snarled a deep, familiar voice. "Smoke."

"Is that right?" muttered a second voice in a lilting Orrathi accent. "You can come down, Devlyn."

Devlyn shut his eyes in frustration and lowered himself onto the high catwalk that overlooked the records room. Below him, the Stormguards waited in the near-darkness, playing cards and four-tower over low-burning rush lights. Their orange faces were all that could be seen, for the dark-coated karach usually kept to the shadows. And here, the karach-master himself, Keenan Latkey, was making the rounds of the upper levels.

"Hullo, Keenan," he muttered, not making eye contact. Behind the karach-master, led by a chain, one of the massive beasts teetered on the flimsy catwalk, barely balancing its enormous weight.

"Smoke," it growled again. "Pipe smoke. I smell it. Brimstone, too."

"Have you been on the roof again, Dev?" Keenan asked with disapproval.

"I have," said Devlyn. "You can't expect a man to stand six hours without his pipe—"

"Were you seen?" Keenan probed.

"Seen—of course not," said Devlyn. "The ramparts are too high. No one from the ground can see what goes on up here."

"The roof is to be sealed at all times," Keenan ordered. "You know that."

"The doors are sealed, too," Devlyn protested. "The windows are sealed. The chimneys are barred. The only way in or out is through that reeking sewer that runs all the way to the Spire. It's ten minutes down, and ten minutes back, and I've no mind to spend my leisure in the dark with plague-ridden rats grown fat on the Imperator's shit."

"Mind your tongue, soldier," Keenan warned.

"We're of equal rank," Devlyn sneered. "I take my orders from the Captain, not from you."

Keenan rolled his eyes. "Pock, teach him some etiquette."

Keenan moved aside and let go of the chain, and that was all the warning Dev had. He'd taken a single step back when the karach was on him, seizing him by the arm with a grip that closed cleanly around his bicep. It pushed him slowly but with unstoppable firmness against the outer wall of the temple, squeezing the air from him as it pressed him gradually harder against the stone. It was a gesture of dominance, a show of force executed so gradually: *I need no momentum. I need no surprise. My strength is enough.*

"No talk back," growled Pock, and a panicked Devlyn nodded.

"W-with respect," Devlyn stammered, his position and his spine softening, "the situation is impossible. We cannot over-emphasize security at the expense of vigilance. If I can't go on the roof, and we can't open anything at ground level, you have to let us smoke in the records room."

"That won't happen," Keenan said.

"Fresh air keeps me awake," said Devlyn. "A good smoke keeps me awake, too. Half the men down there are dozing. It's not much good for—"

"What is this?" Keenan asked. He bent to the catwalk to retrieve the red gem. It must have been knocked from Devlyn's grasp.

"I found that," Devlyn said. "On the roof. It's mine. I mean, I'm taking it to the Captain."

"Pretty thing," Keenan said, turning it over. "Wouldn't you say, Pock?"

"It light," Pock agreed. "It shine."

"I found it," Devlyn insisted. A heavy gloom passed over his face, and sudden anger burned in his eyes.

"I want it," said Pock. But Keenan retrieved the beast's chain and gave it a sharp tug that lowered the karach's head and flattened its ears into submission.

"You should have taken it to the Captain," said Keenan. "Now I'll have to do it myself."

Keenan's massive bodyguard should not have taken its eyes off Devlyn. But it was so transfixed with the stone that it loosened its grip; and with a sudden jerk, Devlyn tore himself free and grabbed the karach-master's wrist.

"It's *mine*," he barked. "*I* found it!" He pulled sharply on Keenan's wrist, but the karach-master did not let go, pivoting instead to give Devlyn a hard shove in the chest that nearly sent him over.

"Get off me!" he shouted. The men below were beginning to look up at the commotion on the narrow catwalk. The karach swung its head, confused, as its terrible yellow eyes darted between the two men in confusion.

"Put him down," Keenan ordered, pointing to his rival. But Pock's eyes, too, locked on the stone, and the karach swung out a meaty hand to take it.

"Give to me," Pock begged. But when Keenan's hand would not open, it put its clawed hand overtop of the man's fist and began to squeeze.

"Dumb animal," Keenan snapped, jerking hard as he could at the chain, digging the iron collar deep into Pock's training-scars. "You dumb, filthy—"

Keenan's curse faded to a scream as Pock crushed his fist into a bag of bone shards, popping his little human knuckles like nutshells before peeling the sinewy mass away from the gemstone. With its prize attained, the karach threw its former master away with distaste, staring into the gem with fascination until it felt a blade bite in through its ribs. Still wheezing, still staggering under his own weight, Devlyn had plunged his dagger in toward the beast's heart, hoping it was long enough to reach. The karach turned, furious, and snuffed out the flame of Devlyn's life with one dismissive backhand that caved in his skull. The sudden, jerking shift of its four-hundred-pound weight, coupled with the crumpling weight of Devlyn's lifeless body, finally pulled the catwalk from its riveted moorings and sent all three bodies spinning down into the records room. Devlyn's corpse fell straight into a game of four-tower, shattering the table and throwing clay tokens in every direction; the karach's chain snagged on the broken catwalk as it fell, and its weight was enough to snap its neck and leave it swinging on its chain like a chandelier. Keenan came down lightest, surviving the fall, but was lost to the shock and delirium of his maimed hand. Among the three of them, the glistening gem skipped across the record room floor and rattled to a stop within sight of the guards who were now at full alarm, swords drawn, at a loss for the grisly spectacle before them.

"Watchers alive!" one cursed. "What just happened?"

"Are you all right?" called another, standing up so sharply that his chair toppled back over the fragments of his shattered desk.

One of the younger Stormguards bent low in the scattered game-pieces to pluck a solitary gem from the wreckage.

"Hey, what's this?" he asked, holding it up.

"Where'd you find that?" asked one.

"It fell with them," said the younger man. "I think it's a ruby."

"A garnet, I think," said Captain Stohn, who had just arrived to find his records room nearly in shambles. "It's too dark to be a ruby. And I heard a treasure-coach was hit east of Carmac, and only the garnets taken." Transfixed by the glittering gem, he ignored the wounded men shuddering on the floor of the records room and moved toward the object of his interest.

"It looks like a ruby to me," said one young man.

"Could be a red diamond," said another.

"We shall see," said Captain Stohn. "Give it here." But the young man's eyes were a mask of hateful defiance.

"Kee-nan!" a voice thundered. In the darkness surrounding the carnage, the orange firelight glimmered green as it reflected back from three strange pairs of eyes.

The men froze in terror as the hulking shapes of three karach, each of them larger and more scarred than young Pock, came into the light toward their fallen master, long muzzles twitching at the smell of his blood—then paused.

"What is it?" one asked.

"Red rock," said the next.

"Rock shine," said the third. "I want it."

Captain Stohn's arming sword came alive in his hand as he eyed the defiant, mutinous young soldier with the stone. They watched each other's eyes with a hateful hunger, and broke concentration only when the room began to darken. The largest karach was circling the room as the others closed in, snuffing the ensconced torches with the leathery palm of its clawed hand. With each torch snuffed, the room fell a little darker, and the karachs' eyes shone a bright green, like cats' eyes, in the glare of the small rush lights that remained.

"Give to me now," one of the karach growled. Captain Stohn tightened his grip on his sword. Every instinct told him that he should back down, and he had not become a captain by caring overmuch about pride or ego.

"Come and take it," he said in a voice very much like his own.

And they did.

The ears of a karach were keen, and might have pricked up at the soft creak of the well-oiled roof-gate. They certainly would have detected the lone set of footfalls on the wooden planks that remained of the catwalk, not far from where a broad section of the structure came down. Their keen noses would have told them that the small, black-robed man who came in from the roof had picked up a dozen strange scents from the swamp north of the city, almost as if masking his own particular scent from them. Where his broad black hood shadowed his face from ordinary men and women, their green-glinting eyes and their uncanny night vision would have pierced through the darkness to his narrow, serious gaze, his taut mouth, and the impatient darting glances of a furtive scavenger, a jackal among men who did not have much time before the sabercats returned.

All this the karach would have seen, if they had survived. But all four of them now lay dead or dying in the center of the bloody records room, having fought past all exhaustion, past all hope of survival. With practiced eyes and careful steps, Jordac paced the catwalk, scrutinizing the bloody floor of the records room below as the ruby streaks of blood began to dry brown against the wooden boards. The changing colour of the blood, and the exquisite patterns where it fell and sprayed, told a story in time—a brutal and tragic drama. The two dozen men and four karach below him had been the players.

As the mage came down from the catwalk on loose and rattling stairs, he placed two fingers against his lips and drew a slow, deliberate line from his mouth to the stones of the outer wall. The rock was cold, but he felt its surface for some inner quickness his living eyes could not see. He found the energy of the place already awaiting him, already quickened to his will. He felt the bones and sinews of the ancient temple, felt the consecration and faith, the hope, and finally the cynicism and despair that had shuttered it to the outside world and turned it into the lifeless Imperial vault it had become. He felt, too, the half-dozen rats in the rafters, and the hundreds in the sewers; he felt the old and patient sadness of the aeril woman awaiting him in the tunnel beneath the old temple chancel.

In a soft voice, wary of echoes and survivors, he whispered: "It's clear. Come up."

At the centre of the old temple stood a copper statue of Tûr the Purefactor, the equal in size and splendour of Tûr the Vigilant on the south wall. Protected from the elements and maintained for several years by the worshippers, its ruddy, shimmering skin had not yet tarnished to the pockmarked green of the statue outside. Its lordly features—all modeled after a man of Vosi stock, of course—were still crisp, stern, and readable. Below the statue, in a great stone basin, a narrow spiral stair now stood where the drain of the purification fountain had once been. Widened to a passage by the Stormguard during the Annexation, it marked the end of the temple as a holy place and the beginning of its use as a fortified repository of Imperial secrets.

With a tapered candle held behind her and a long knife in her outstretched hand, Baran ascended from the tunnel beneath the temple and crossed the long aisle of worship to the records room. She was clad in the coarse brown robes of a Carnicist penitent: though they were mostly extinct now, she had heard that underground Tudrans still sometimes hassled the guards at the old temples. If she were cornered, she would be more convincing as an eccentric penitent than one of the all-male Stormguard.

She found Jordac, silent and black-robed, at the centre of a swarmed circle of bodies, kneeling over the broad-shouldered carcass of one of the karach war-dogs. With a crooked tool and gentle hands, he was working at prying open the chained collar bolted around the creature's neck. Even in death, its last laboured breaths rolled on in its mutilated chest, wet and desperate. It alarmed her when it reached up toward the mage with a massive arm; but it had come to such weakness that Jordac seized the arm and pushed it away dismissively.

"Enough," he said to it. "Enough. No more fighting, hush. The *mănuk* have already left their nest, great one. *Mrkurr ruh rŏthrr Thrvirr. Ĭvurrgh ban thirrĭ hărn.*" At these words, the karach seemed to cease its struggles and placed its hands gently over the mage's. With a satisfying clank, the bolt sprang loose from the chain beneath his hands and the karach's collar fell to the bloody floor before it died.

Baran counted the bodies strewn around it. "There were more men here than I anticipated. More than Odi predicted."

"As I expected," said Jordac. "Reinforcements were stationed below, or close by. I cannot imagine they sent everyone, either. You should make yourself hidden, and find what you must find."

"And you?" she asked. "What will you do?"

"I will free the dead," he said, "and then see what is worth taking." He knelt before the second karach, plucking something out of its dead hand that sparkled invitingly.

"What is that?" Baran asked. Jordac tossed it to her casually; she caught it even in the dimness of the temple.

"Fuel for the fire," he said.

She opened her hands to find them stained black and sooty. A jagged lump of jet-black coal lay crumbling in her hands, and she passed it from hand to hand and back again, mesmerised by its craggy texture and the way its ashen surface flaked under pressure from her thumb. Beneath the surface ash she could make out subtle bands of glimmering reddish-brown where a waxy resin of some kind permeated the coal. It smelled faintly, now that she held it close, of brimstone.

She clutched it in both hands and looked entreatingly to Jordac.

"Can I keep this?" she asked in earnest. He frowned so sharply she feared he might try to take it back.

"Keep it out of sight," he said, "and don't stare at it overmuch. It's still suffused, I think."

She jealously slipped it into the sleeve-pocket of her penitent's robes and said no more of it. "I'll find that manifest," she said, and hid from him so that he might soon forget the coal.

Jordac took note of her hurried steps, then finished unbolting the chains from the karachs' necks. When that was done, he crept from body to body, brushing and cleaning the soot from the hands of the men who had been lucky enough to hold the stone themselves before the end.

As her mind returned to the task at hand, Baran slipped a pinch of sea salt under her tongue, and reached beneath her coarse robes to the true jewel she wore around her neck. She felt there the low pulse of an energy she had been trusted with, an energy that had ebbed and flowed within the world, once, but fell ever farther away from it now, like a sea drawn back by two sister moons in rare agreement.

She was a slow study, perhaps, but under Jordac's tutelage there was a truth to her magic that had largely gone from the occult traditions of the world. In her long travels she had studied with the mystics of Khihana, with fellow refugees from the Floating City, with the Lost Woodsmen of Daer Móran. She had filled her head with elemental symbols, strange alchemies, mnemonic finger-shapes, crystals and charms, monotonous chants; all the gadgetry and gimmickry that a world of Weavecrafters might cling to as their power over the world spilled away. The Age of Sun was gone, and with it were gone the days of unbridled eldritch magic—especially magic without cost. But the Mage himself seemed wise beyond all ken to her; and when he called upon the Weave, it simply answered him. With Jordac, there was never (or she had not seen) any waggling of fingers or babbling in forgotten tongues of spirits or demons. He was simply a fount of power unto himself, and now, in his otherworldly shadow, so was she.

The feeling of salt, of the sea, did not come as quickly to her face and fingertips as it might have come to his. But as the hard stony taste of the sea faded on her tongue and passed into her, she felt with new senses the crispness of the salty air that blew in from the water, girding the old temple and blasting away at the statues, the carvings, the bricks themselves with frigid air whose salt over time had caked the grey stone almost white on the sides of the temple where the wind was wont to blow.

Within the stuffy confines of the secret Imperial archive, the salt did not really penetrate. If the Records Room shared any air with the winds outside, she did not feel it. But the acrid salt collected by degrees in the porous animal skin of the Imperial parchment, which was meticulously selected and scraped to take on ink. Among the towering walls of nooks and shelves stuffed with rolls, scrolls, and codices, there were probably records not just from across the city, but from across the whole Travalaithi Empire, dating back at least to the Annexation. Most were written, rolled, and sealed in keeps and counting-houses far from the sea, and even those documents sent down from Lornock were brought from a half-mile or so inland—perhaps even through the sewers that had once served as the cisterns, ducts, and drains servicing Tamnor's black forges during the Occupation.

Only the harbourmaster's records, kept for days in the heavily guarded compound overlooking the pier, were thick with the essence of the sea: The so-called Stormguard, in a moment of sweet irony, could have defended the records against any assault, but could not guard them against the storms. To Baran, lost in a reverie of brine and seamist, the last ten years of harbourmasters' records nearly shone within their sheltered, curtained, weatherproof nook, in a low shelf beneath an otherwise dull stack of magistrates' pronouncements and land conveyances.

With the smell of death rising around her, everything felt slow. She calmed her racing heart with steady breathing and whispered chants—not all of the mystics' teachings had been phony or without value—but she felt acutely the encroaching pressure and peril of how long every step of the search took. While she concentrated slowly, moved slowly, Jordac was a flurry of motion: despite his greater power, he was forced to search the old-fashioned way, ransacking the central shelves almost at random, hauling down heavy tomes for long enough to gauge their worth against their weight and the risk of smuggling them out. So far, he had seized only a handful of maps and bound books, and was careful to place the others gently back on the shelves so that those he handled would not arouse suspicion.

The parchment used for harbour records was not of the same quality as that used for the archival records. It was unlikely that they would be consulted twenty or even ten years hence, and so the low-grade charts and scrolls could be sorted almost by touch as they decayed. The recent rolls, the ones that would have plainly told any reader exactly which ship Madge had been fleeing to, were marked for ready consultation.

"I've found them!" she called.

"Keep your voice down," said Jordac, from somewhere. "Take the whole year, if it's complete."

She rejoined him in the shelves nearest the center of the immense records hall. A cloud had passed over the red moon, darkening the center room where most of the rush lights had burned themselves out. His treasures from the theft, a loosely tied bundle of records and small codices, lay on one of the few intact tables, but still he pawed at the shelves, troubled.

"There's nothing here on the Spire," he said. "No records of the Imperial Family. None of the girl."

"They've worked for years to keep her a secret," said Baran. "It doesn't surprise me they'd keep no records."

"The genealogies are numbered in sequence," said the Mage. "They've kept records. But someone has taken them, and I can say no more for certain. Perhaps if Catrine can reel in her mark, who seems to know the girl personally, the truth will out. But the Spire and that girl are surrounded by secrets beyond even my powers of discovery. I would find them out, if I could."

"And what *did* you find?"

He looked back to table, and it seemed to console him. "Mining records. Payment ledgers for the soldiers staffing the mine at Orrath."

"Orrath?" said Baran. "I thought your designs were on—"

"Quiet," Jordac entreated again. "The records from Fingrun are here, but they match the ones I have already secured. Madge has seen to that for us. This theft will be discovered, and soon. If Orrath is under threat, they will reinforce it with a garrison from the other mines, and make our lives easier elsewhere. This one we must take—and be seen taking it."

Distantly, a heavy key turned in an iron-banded door. They were out of time.

"Quickly, now," he urged.

They hurried back to the dried-out immersion pool at the feet of Tûr the Purefactor. Risking no light of his own, Jordac let Baran and her keen aeril eyes lead him down into the darkness just as a voice filled the hall above them.

"Captain?" someone called, loudly. "Did you sort out those rowdies?"

The silence that followed filled them with as much dread as any alarm. Baran's knife was at the ready, but the guard was slow in coming. If there were others left alive somewhere in the massive temple, he might have gone to bring them--or perhaps just to raise the city's alarms, which would make any kind of escape difficult for hours or days, now.

In the darkness, Jordac felt for the blocky outline of an ornate wooden box. Made up to look like the commodes at use in Lornock and the Spire, it might draw attention, but certainly not curiosity. He unhinged the lid and began filing the records into it.

"We need to move," whispered Baran, fidgeting nervously with the gem around her neck. But Jordac was already loading the heavy box onto his back, hunched low under its weight as his posture began to change. It took him several steps to fall back into the gait he had adopted for skulking about the capital, but the disguise was second nature to him now. Baran moved along the passageway, feeling self-conscious of her elegant steps and exposed before any who might chance to look her way.

She tried not to think of what they trudged through as they hurried down the passage. The tunnel was cold and damp, and although the rats were used to visitors, something about the urgency and darkness of their flight set them scurrying and chittering in the darkness, as if the tunnel itself were alive. The darkness here was near-total, but the aerils, it was said, once came out of the sea, and their eyes were still suited to its depths. Leading the way through the darkness, Baran cringed at whole clusters and sheets of rats that leered at them from the wall, like living tapestries of fur and disease.

A dim light that pulsed in the heart of her jewelled pendant, too faint to be seen in any but the purest darkness, was picked up and reflected in jittering walls of five hundred glassy black eyes. She wondered if their retreat was harder for her, as she could see and count the little grey faces scurrying around them, locked in an internal battle between their fear and their hunger. She wondered if it was harder for Jordac, who could see nothing but fumbled his way behind her in the darkness, never knowing how close he came to them, or how numerous they were around his boots and the edge of his cloak.

Distantly at their backs, a man screamed in horror, and the ghastly echo of his cry was enough to complete the experience and set even Baran into a panic. She felt her heart drop cold inside her chest, and shivered so hard she nearly stumbled; but even so, in this most frightful of circumstances, she tried to dwell on what it must be like for the stormguard who came upon that grisly scene unprepared. However great her fear was in that moment, it brought her some relief to know that his was certainly all the greater. Reaching into the pocket of her sleeve, she had thought to hold the little lump of coal for comfort as she ran. Now, though, it felt cold and utterly meaningless, and she felt all the more foolish for coveting it. With equal parts embarrassment and disgust, she wanted nothing more than to let it drop away into the darkness of the tunnel and be forgotten.

"Do we still need this coal?" she asked.

"I have no plans for it," whispered Jordac. "Let it go, if you can."

She let it fall silently into the muck that lined the tunnel floor. "How long will it be…resonant?" she asked him.

"The lessons are for another day," he said. "Follow me now in silence."

Nothing Odi had said, nothing Jordac had gleaned himself, told them how long it would take reinforcements to arrive, nor whence they would come. The tunnel was the most dangerous part of their escape, at least until they connected with the main duct that carried water and sewage down to the sea. A few enemies ahead, and a few more behind, and they would have a hard time of it. But they reached the junction in time, and met there with Odi, and as they headed up toward the bowels of the Black Forges, Baran shed her penitent's robe and recovered her dry shoes from where they had been left.

The three came up below the Forges through an empty cistern and found themselves in the lavish chambers below the Imperial baths. Every hideous surface here had been beautified, and only the Magistrates and their wives (and mistresses) came to enjoy the waters at their ease. Dishevelled and damp in a fine gown that had until now been hidden, and soon reeking of too much delicate perfume, all the better to cover the smell of the lower ducts, Baran's disguise was somewhere between a courtier and a courtesan. But the state of her hair and her powders would not matter: at her full height and moving with splendid grace, she seemed the picture of Ithuriel herself next to the crooked, hunching shape of a tower stoolman.

"Off with ye," Jordac muttered under his breath. "I goes out another way, I does."

She took a deep breath, calming herself. "When will we meet again?"

Jordac shook his head. "Not before your assault on the Mine," he said.

"But I thought we would plan the attack togeth—"

Jordac thrust a bundle of papers into her hands. "Here is what you need," he said. "I have every faith in you. But you must go now. Odi, have you secured a ship?"

"Not cheaply," he said. "The corsairs of Adân can be real pirates. But a man called Hormer will take us where we're headed. Catrine is their lookout, for now. And thank you for giving me leave to go and get her."

"How many fighters?"

"Fifty-one warm bodies," said Odi. "Including myself. That's every last man and woman. That's the forgers, the informants. It includes the other Widows, now that their cover is lost."

"That's not many," said Jordac. "Not what I'd asked for."

"It's what there is," Odi said, shrugging. "It's the truth. And the truth is awfully sorry to disobey you."

"It's what we have, then," echoed Jordac. "It should be enough for a surprise attack on an undermanned mine. When they find I've taken every last document on Orrath, they'll send the bulk of their defenses south. Are you seaworthy? Immediately?"

Odi nodded. "Ready to pull everyone out on your go."

"Go," ordered Jordac. "Both of you, meet me at the Last Call in Carmac when this is over."

Odi and Baran split from him before they could be seen talking, and headed up toward the baths. In the last hours before dawn there were few who came down below the Spire—only the stewards and grimy little attendants like Jordac making the lower levels ready for the day to come. They slipped up the hard steps of marble-clad iron without incident; they floated, silent as twin swans, across the tiled floor of the entrance hall. Beyond the heavy banded doors and the Inner Wall, the Cerulean Guard were hard at work on their drills in the blue light of the morning. She raised her head haughtily as she passed, though every instinct told her otherwise. These ones had heard no alarm yet, but it might be mere minutes—mere seconds—before the cries were raised in the harbour, and the great bells rung. There was no outrunning the bells after that. With her own nerves buzzing and her heart in her throat, Baran passed by the Cerulean Guard in silence and began to hurry. *It will all be like this, now*, she thought. The city would have to be emptied, the spies rehomed—and Madge, unfortunately, left to her fate. It was a hard loss, to be sure, but for all they had gleaned from the operation, the price was more than fair. She had spoken to the Widows always as if they had been soldiers, and now, in the end, there was some truth to it.

She remembered, just after the Annexation, when Jordac was much younger and she a little bit so, the exhausting process of recruiting from the border towns. Resources had been scant, and Jordac was then a pauper, having not yet come into his wealth. They had taken rebels from isolated farming and fishing communities, and once at Rackham the Grand Army had already conscripted the fighting men and put the karach who dwelt there to the chain or the sword. Fifteen women and four sickly men were all they could convince, and Baran had been baffled at first by the Mage's satisfaction.

"They'll serve, for now," Jordac had said.

"They're not soldiers," Baran had replied. "Not a one of them. They're not fighting men."

As she passed the Lornock Citadel and dashed down the iron-hedged steps of the Tower Stair, his words rang clearly in her mind.

"Not yet," he had said. "But they're a family. If they're as weak as you say, one of them will die, in time—surely. And they'll all be soldiers after that."

FOURTEEN

THE WIND WAS COLD along the edge of Haveïl, where the naked, gale-shivering birch trees and indifferent pines gave way to low-lying brush and broom. With cautious steps over uneven ground, Aewyn and Kellan kept the tree line at their backs and made their way along the edge of the forest to where it stretched as far into the lowland vasily of Haukmere as it dared. It was easy for them to forget how young the winter was along that high windswept tree line, where the biting chill of the air was at its sharpest. But below them where the salt marshes rolled out under a blanket of heavy fog and a weak dusting of wet snow, the air was warmer and wetter, and permeated with the unhealthy reek of the hardy bogflowers that clung to life in the brackish water.

The lowlands of Haukmere were muddy and pockmarked by stagnant tidal pools stirred only on those rare occasions when both moons were in full agreement. It was poor country for travel, and the most reliable roads were lifted above the marshes on a series of raised dikes that surrounded and fed into the regional fort town of Wescairn. The fog that rolled over the trade and farm roads spilled into the deep marshy pockets and covered the swamp completely; the veiny ridges of gravel and packed earth surrounding Wescairn were only half-lost in fog, and seemed to them like a mile-wide spiderweb half-suspended in clouds.

Rising above the cobweb of roads and floodbanks, solitary and imperious in its vigil, the fearsome keep of Wescairn was perched atop a massive craggy hill of stone left half-buried in the swamp by unseen forces long ago. Surrounding its base, shrouded in mist, the town proper lay clustered at the feet of the towering keep, clinging to the stone above the floodline where homes and permanent town buildings could be safely built. As the orange light of an angry dawn intensified and began to cut through the fog, Kellan could make out the busy dark specks of horses, townsfolk, and travelers milling about in the mist outside the walls of the high keep.

"Busy town," he remarked through gritted teeth. He brushed the line of his jaw nervously. He felt naked and exposed up here on the right, and not just because he had shaven off his distinctive beard and left his face exposed to the bitter air.

"Those aren't farm horses," Aewyn whispered, her voice lowering even though the nearest of them was still a long way off.

"No," Kellan sighed. "No, they're not farm horses."

"We can wait," said Aewyn. "We can go back to the trees, get a fire going, wait out the day. Make our way to the keep when night falls, when the soldiers are in their beds."

"You've never been hunted before, have you?"

Aewyn shook her head. "And won't be again, if I can make my way back to the Havenari."

"The way forward's through those gates," said Kellan. "And we've no special protection until we do."

"Special protection?" Aewyn echoed. Kellan had started down the hill, and she followed him only with skepticism.

"Guilt makes men do things you wouldn't expect," said Kellan. "There's not much I trust in the world. But a man gets to feeling a pain inside that won't go away—and guilt's the worst of them all—he'll do anything he can to think himself rid of it for a while."

"You're very philosophical for a thug," Aewyn observed.

The two of them came down the slope and laid their feet at last on one of the farm roads circling the fort town. It was easy going from there; even the paths that from above were hidden in fog were less obscure now that they were standing on the road and could see the next fifty or sixty feet ahead of them.

"How do you want to play this?" Aewyn asked. Kellan looked at her with surprise.

"Play this?" he asked.

"They're going to stop us," said Aewyn. "We're exactly who they're looking for, less one beard. And it doesn't matter whether you've stuffed that helm in a sack or not. They'll know a bloodguard's armour when they see it."

"Then they'll know better than to stop me," said Kellan. "If they don't, they'll learn."

Aewyn looked at him incredulously. "You've never been hunted before either," she said.

Kellan drew his mouth tight. "Not like this, I haven't."

"I'm your prisoner, aren't I?" said Aewyn. "We could use that. You caught up with me, and you're delivering me to the lord. You outrank the regular troops. If they don't fear you, they'll fear Ashimar's name. If they're out looking for me, you're the one who's found me."

"That's weak," Kellan said, frowning. "It's risky."

"Maybe," said Aewyn. But she had passed him, now, moving down the road as quickly as she dared, and it took him long strides to keep pace with her. He noticed she favoured one leg slightly as she hustled down the road. Perhaps she had had a hard time of it, too.

Their passage was not unnoticed, and Kellan cut a striking figure at the best of times, but none of the town guard moved to check the pair's passage until they had come through the townhouses, past the stables, to the very outer gates of Wescairn. Here, the soldiers approached with the vigilance of trained sentries. Kellan cleared his throat and tried to affect an air of command. He was taller than the gate sentries, and hoped that would be enough: there wasn't much else going for him. He waited patiently for the lead gatekeeper to open his mouth to speak—then interrupted him.

"I've come in from Widowvale," said Kellan, with all the authority he could muster.

The gatekeeper, an immaculately groomed man, looked him up and down. "Rolled all the way here, did you?"

Kellan sneered and brushed down his armour. "Funny. I've brought a prisoner for your lord." He shoved Aewyn forward roughly.

The gatekeper looked at her. She scowled back.

"Lord Stannon doesn't handle such things personally," he said. "Not anymore."

Kellan kept his face hard. "Lord Ashimar says he does."

The gatekeeper weighed the words, nodded at them. His eyes narrowed suspiciously.

"This the girl?"

"It is," said Kellan.

The gatekeeper leaned back to the men flanking him. "Check her hair."

It was only then that Kellan understood how well-manned the gatehouse really was. The two men who seized Aewyn by the shoulders were hardly the only ones the gatekeeper could have called on; they were merely the closest, and the keenest to handle a prisoner roughly. Kellan's jaw tightened with an anger he did not understand as they jerked back her head and tore a few white hairs from it.

"Careful with my reward," he warned. "She's worth a lot."

"You'll forgive us," said the gatekeeper. "We know what she's worth. Girls her size aren't hard to find. We expect more than a few ruffians will try to bring us a few outlanders and pass them off."

"It's her," called one of the others. "Bone-white to the root."

Aewyn shuddered in their grasp.

That seemed to satisfy the gatekeeper. "Did you get a look at the other one? He's the one that would have made your fortune."

Kellan feigned sour regret. "Almost had them both for you. He was as close as you to me. Just couldn't get my hands around him."

"Sorry to hear it," said the gatekeeper. "Is Lord Ashimar far behind you?"

"Not so far as I'd like," Kellan said with sincerity. "He'll be here ere long, I've no doubt. But every day I'm free of his presence is a day I can breathe freely." He almost smiled, but caught himself: Ashimar's bloodguards weren't the smiling kind.

"You'll get on very well with Lord Stannon," said the gatekeeper, though his suspicions were slow to fade. "He's no lover of the Scourge, either."

Aewyn turned pale suddenly at Kellan's side.

"Wait," she breathed. "Lord—"

"Quiet, you," Kellan snapped. He had her trained, now: a quick jerk of his hand and she flinched as if she were going to be struck. It was a good sell.

"Take her," said the gatekeeper. "Get irons on her, and clean this one up."

The guards took hold of her and began to drag her away. Kellan started after her instinctively.

"Not so fast," said Kellan. "She's mine."

"You'll get your credit," the gatekeeper assured him. "Lord Stannon's become…more cautious since last winter. Suffers no prisoner in his presence who's not chained. Won't be long. There's some stew and salt pork in the gatehouse, if you're hungry."

It pained Kellan to watch them take her away, but he dared not protest overmuch. He wondered if he would be harder to identify without her than with her. His mind drifted to his sword, but there were too many men here and in the surrounding streets to get far.

"Get our friend fed and watered," the gatekeeper said to another of the guards. "And clean him up, if you can."

"Come on, then," said the guard. "Hard luck about that Kellan fellow. But I suppose a lordship's not for everyone."

"Bind her tight," the gatekeeper instructed. "I'm off to announce them. What's your name, little runaway?"

Aewyn twisted round in their grasp. Her face was a mask of defiance fading quickly to confusion.

"Aewyn," she said.

"Right," said the gatekeeper. "And your friend, there? Did you get the name of the man who caught you?"

Aewyn was no liar—at least, not a good one. He had never given her his name, which she knew now must be Kellan; and she half-wanted to spoil his deception by blurting it out. But she feared Ashimar more than she feared him, and did not know how things would go for her if she exposed him. She hesitated a moment, but in her panic, the name that rose to her lips was the first man's name she could think of.

"G-Grim—" she stammered.

"Wulf," Kellan called hastily, in the same moment, upon hearing Aewyn's hesitation.

The gatekeeper froze. He turned back to the tall bloodguard. Whether he pierced the ruse or not, it was clear he did not like being made a fool of.

"Wait," said the gatekeeper. Kellan's grip tightened on the hilt of his sword, though it likely would have been the end of him.

Perhaps the wandering spirit of Haveïl's best liar had not wandered far from the wood. Perhaps it had come running, upon hearing Aewyn call its name. But in a moment of terror, Kellan caught his breath and blurted out the only solution that came to mind.

"Grimwulf," he said with feigned calm. "It's Grimwulf. Of Adân. My friends—my fellows in His Imperial Majesty's, especially—can just call me Wulf."

He shot a sincerely furious glare at Aewyn. "My prisoners, generally speaking, do not share that high honour."

"Her impudence will be corrected," assured the gatekeeper. "Take some rest and break your fast with the men. I will announce you as

Grimwulf, then, though Lord Stannon may call you what he pleases."

"I don't suppose it matters," Kellan breathed, "so long as my wife calls me a rich man when he's done with me."

For all his anxious urge to be reunited with Aewyn, if only to keep her from slipping away and giving him up, Kellan suffered himself to be led to a warm meal, if not a hot one, and to warm ale if not to cold. The guards of the keep were not quite friendly, but made ready conversation and asked him especially about the prisoner Kellan's escape: they were keenest above all to hear of Kellan's direction of travel, whether the pack he had carried was light or heavy, whether he had been sore wounded in his escape from the Red Captain, or from "Grimwulf" himself.

Over time, answering them with tales of his own adventures, Kellan became so used to speaking of himself at arm's length that he grew accustomed his to new name, and the lies flowed freely from him as he described his boastful journey inland to Haukmere. The story would not have to hold up for long. At last the heavy door on the inner wall of the gatehouse was thrown open, and the gatekeeper returned.

"Grimwulf," he called. "The lord is ready for you."

The two men climbed together up a flight of wide stone steps and crossed a small grassy yard to the keep itself. The only point of entry was a door high above them, reached by mounting a narrow wooden staircase that could be thrown down in the event of a siege. Within the keep, it was as unreasonably warm as Kellan remembered it: Castor Stannon was a small man, not of hardy stock, and saw fit to keep a fire going in every room when he could.

At the end of the hall, the guards from the gate were waiting for him with Aewyn pushed down to her knees, though she seemed no worse off than when he had left her. She was pale and trembling as the two men approached—and Kellan suddenly understood why.

"Don't you say a word," warned Kellan. "Not one, until you're spoken to. Play your pieces right, and you may yet get out of this alive."

She gave a meek nod and Kellan looked to the gatekeeper expectantly.

"Grimwulf of Adân, milord," called the gatekeeper. "Travelling a prisoner." He threw open the great double doors with a mighty shove, and led the way into the counting-house.

The room was hot as a Rahastan summer, and a large fire burned furiously in a hearth on the far side of a long table. The shadows it threw up were haggard and strange when thrown against the three dozen frightful great-helms that looked down from the high walls. Never one to trust a stranger, Castor Stannon had cleared the plush chequered counting-table of its coins and hidden them away before his guests arrived. He stood with his back to the fire, and only as he made his way around the great table did the flickering light find itself to his face. Unlike the fighting men, Castor Stannon was slightly built and delicate-boned, and took to wearing such fineries in the safety of his keep as would have been ill-thought for travel. His softly handsome face was dominated now by a black leather eyepatch with a small silver coin stitched in its centre. Aewyn recoiled at the sight, and would have fallen trembling off of her feet if the gatekeeper had not caught her roughly from behind.

"Providence to you, milord," said Kellan with a nervous glance at the gatekeeper. Castor's single eye, ice-blue and filled with a piercing intelligence, widened with shock upon seeing him.

"Ke...Kedwyn's bones, it's you—Grimwulf!" he cried at the last moment, though the name stumbled off his tongue awkwardly. "Yes, I have been expecting you. And with a prisoner no less! Very impressive, old friend."

He fixed his cold gaze on the gatekeeper. "Thank you. You may leave us."

"Milord," began the gatekeeper.

"No fussing," said Castor. "Go, man, go. Fool knows I'll be safe enough here with the man who caught her in the first place."

The gatekeeper reluctantly stepped out of the room, and Kellan was only too quick to swing the doors shut behind him.

"Hullo, Castor," he said.

Castor crossed the floor to him quickly, seizing his broad arms in disbelief.

"It's you," he breathed, not unhappily. "You...Grimwulf, is it?"

Kellan nodded his shaggy head. "I suppose you've heard the news about Kellan Fyldron," he said. He thought he saw a glimmer of relief, of joy even, in Castor's good eye as they met.

"For months I heard nothing at all," said Castor, "No news until yesterday. I sent you eastward with your report to take your reward from the Magistrates personally. Months went by. Not a letter from you—and I know you can write as well as any tower scribe." He turned toward the fire, pacing. "I presumed you got your reward, and were off making the most of it."

"Aye, I got it," said Kellan, burning with resentment. "Every lash of it."

"A day and a night ago, a rider in red comes to my door," said Castor, looking back. "He tells me that Kellan Fyldron, my lowly messenger, the foot soldier garrisoned here just last summer, had become the most wanted man in the Empire. I had a mind to hunt you down myself for that price."

Kellan shook his head. "I'm nowhere near that important."

"Oh, but you are," said Castor. "You…don't know, do you? You haven't heard."

"Heard what?"

"The price on your head."

"I never asked," said Kellan laconically. "I'm greedy, but I'm not *that* greedy. My head's not for sale, not for any price."

Castor smiled in spite of Kellan's plight. "Not even for lordship of Egestor?"

Kellan froze, stunned. "No. No, that's impossible."

"I was told by the bloodguard himself. Believe me. Ashimar has promised Egestor and a thousand acres to the man who brings him your head."

"That's absurd!" cried Kellan, a little too loudly.

"Keep your voice down," Castor urged.

"That's Kelmor land," said Kellan. "Ashimar renounced his claim to their line on taking the Scourge. It's not his to give, is it?"

Castor sat back down at the counting-table. "Try to tell him that," he said.

Kellan leaned in and lowered his voice. "Listen," he said. "This makes no sense. I don't mean that in the way that I'm shocked, oh my stars, isn't it just mad. I mean that it really makes no sense. It doesn't add up. It's...Castor, it's more than the bounty on Celithrand."

"Far more," said Castor, brushing his eyebrow absently. "I do remember."

"He was guilty of treason," said Kellan. "Treason. He was the closest rival claimant to the whole Empire, and he had designs to seize it for himself, if that's what you believe. But me? What's my thousand-acre crime? I threw one man into the sea, was that it? I embarrassed Ashimar when I got his men lost in the wood. What unforgivable crime have I taken a hand in to earn such a kingly bounty as this?"

"I have no idea," said Castor. "Maybe nothing. Maybe Ashimar's just raving mad, as many have long said. Maybe you heard some terrible secret on your travels, some squirrely pet-name a mistress calls him that he means not to get out. Or he had a castle to spare, and just wants the whole Travalaithi Empire to know what an example he makes of traitors like you."

Kellan turned his gaze toward Aewyn. She had backed herself against the wall of the counting-house and was trembling with fright.

"Aye, traitors like me," he breathed. "Any mention of her?"

Castor came closer, looked into her eyes. There was something familiar about her.

"The rider said you might be travelling with her," he said. "Said she was one of the Havenari, though she's a bit young for it, I'd say. No mention of a price on her head."

Kellan relaxed visibly, though Aewyn did not.

"She doesn't seem to like me," Castor said with a cold smile.

Kellan laughed. "Probably never seen a man with one eye before. I told you once, Stannon, you'd have a long road, learning how to be so ugly."

Castor's smile, with the patch, was more rakish than hideous. "I've had no time for lessons at it," he teased, "with my Master away in the capital. Have you got a name, young woman?"

Aewyn, trembling, shook her head.

"Answer him," Kellan barked.

"Aewyn," she spat suddenly.

Castor ran a thumb across his lip. "Aewyn," he said. "Yes… that's it. You found her in the village?"

"Aye," Kellan lied. "No price on her?"

"No," said Castor again, eyeing her suspiciously. "Should there be? Or—you *were* Celithrand's friend, weren't you, Aewyn? You told me so. Do you remember?"

He leaned in close. Aewyn, tears in her eyes, shook her head.

"It's what you said to me," said Castor. "The day I came to your little village."

"Truly, you have a freakish memory," Kellan said. "But she's his friend, aye. Ashimar had a mind to do some real cruelties on her, unless she led him straight to Celithrand. And you know that's not going to happen now."

"Oh, Kellan," Castor said, smiling.

"Grimwulf," the taller man protested. "Please."

Castor sucked in his breath, realizing his error. "Sorry. I had no idea you were given over to suicidal acts of kindness."

Kellan looked awkwardly to Aewyn, who was on the edge of losing her composure.

"This one hasn't killed me yet," he insisted. "And neither will Ashimar, if I can help it. Kingly bounty or no."

Castor nodded. "You can't stay here," he said.

"I know," echoed Kellan. But Castor took him by the shoulders and turned him around, catching his gaze.

"No," he said. "What I mean is…he'll be coming back. You can't be here when he does. We both know Celithrand's across the sea now, if he has any sense. Far past his reach. Soon as the Scourge is done his search, he'll be headed back to the capital. Certainly empty-handed. Probably in very poor cheer. We're his first stop on the way, and you've got to be gone by then."

"You're sure about the reward?" Kellan asked again.

"Deadly sure," said Castor. He stood back from them, paced around the table, reached for a decanter. "Sit. Drink."

Kellan sat. "We were damned lucky to make it this far with a price like that on my head. Every soldier in the Grand Army will be looking out for me."

Castor poured out two goblets of cheap wine. The first went to Kellan; the second, surprisingly, he offered to Aewyn. She nearly reached for it, but looked away and could not meet his one-eyed gaze.

"Suit yourself," he said. "Have you any idea whither you're going?"

Kellan shook his head. "North, maybe. The coast. But they'll be watching too. I think we'll have a hard time of it."

Castor tasted the wine that was meant for Aewyn. It clearly did not please him.

"I am the Censor of Haukmere and a lord of the Travalaithi Empire," said Castor. "And both of them in a wartime age, you'll note, that's rather unkind to traitors. What you are asking me to do—"

"I asked for nothing," Kellan insisted. "I shouldn't have come, after all."

"I never said that," Castor shot back, genuinely offended. "You're a dead man unless I help you."

"You haven't turned me in yet," said Kellan. "There must be a reason."

Castor turned away again, resumed pacing.

"Egestor's a modest keep," he said, with feigned indifference. "It's on a coast plagued by smugglers and pirates. Not so much to my liking. Don't misunderstand me: a lordship is still a prize to be had, as rewards go."

"A better reward than forty lashes," Kellan said.

"How fortunate you are," said Castor, "to have put your life in the hands of the one man in a hundred miles with a superior lordship already."

"I could kneel, if that would help my case."

Castor's smile was fleeting as he turned his wits to their escape.

"You have your red armour," he said, not unappreciatively. "And Aewyn, here…you are truly one of the Havenari, now?"

"I…I…yes," she stammered.

"And have you some badge of office? Some kind of uniform?"

"There is an emblem," she said. "Gold oak leaf entire over green. But I have no banner."

"A sorry lot," Castor sighed, "but you'll serve just the same. There are corsairs all along the northern coast—pirates out of Adân, harrying the civilized coastal towns. They're a serious problem, you can imagine, for an empire at war. With a hard winter coming, they'll put ashore and settle. Maybe raid some of the surrounding villages."

"Aslea will be hard hit this year," said Aewyn suddenly. "The town supports the nearby prison camps at Fingrun, and it's been a year of plenty for them. We were headed there to ensure that those who settle for winter have the food and supplies they need—and if not, to trade for goods rather than raid for them."

Castor considered her words carefully. "It is good that the Havenari has given these concerns some thought."

"We have had little choice," said Aewyn, with a sharp gaze, "since the vasil and lesser lords of Haukmere refuse to send them aid."

"Soldiers must eat," Castor snapped sharply. "And away from the front, it's *taxes* that feed them. It's been a lean tax year for the western garrisons. I suppose I don't need to tell you why." The look of hollow shock on her face was gratifying: the world was more complex than she knew.

"Still, it is time Wescairn sent some support to the coast," the censor went on. "A small detachment, of course. Seven or eight men. Tell me, girl, where is your brave company?"

Looking for me, most likely. "I don't know," said Aewyn. "They were snowed in at the Sunderhouse last I saw them."

"And likely delayed in the storms, I'll wager," said Castor. "Very well. I think you ought to travel with my men. Pass on word that the Havenari are coming, they've been delayed, and by the grace of the Imperator, I have sent seven or eight men in their place to protect the town."

"I suppose that makes me the eighth," said Kellan.

"You're not one of them," said Castor. "It would arouse too much suspicion to introduce you as a regular. Remain as you are, as part of an elite force known to have split up in the region: Grimwulf, bloodguard to the Imperial Scourge. I think it suits you."

"That's a rather gory set of titles, when you lay them all end-to-end," Kellan said.

"Precisely," Castor said with a smile. "None of them will dare question you. Not with the fear I put into them. They will be your escort to the coast. I know not what dealings the townsfolk have with the corsairs. Relations have been good in the past. Regardless, for the right coin, they'll take you on, you'll disappear. And if you mean to go your separate ways…this one can wait at Aslea for the Havenari to claim her."

Kellan turned it over in his mind. "It's the least worst choice I have," he said. "How about it, Aewyn? Will you suffer to be my captive a few more days?"

Aewyn smiled at him, somewhat cheekily—the first time she had smiled at him, ever. Perhaps the prospect of being reunited with her companions gave her new hope.

"If it weren't my best option, I'd be gone by now," she said. "You're a fool if you think I couldn't have slipped away by now—once or twice, at least."

Castor's laugh was high and sharp. He hadn't laughed in a while, either.

"Once or twice," Kellan repeated skeptically. "Why didn't you? I've done you no kindness."

"You're a sinking ship in stormy seas," said Aewyn. "I'm unhappy on board, and eager to be off you, but not so eager as to swim for it."

Kellan nodded. "The corsairs, I think, will like you."

"They like anyone who can pay," said Castor. "I'll make the arrangements. You leave at dawn."

Kellan fished for his words carefully. "I…thank you. I wish I could tell you the whole story."

"Perhaps when you return."

Kellan smiled at the mouth, but there was a sudden pain hidden in the darkness of his eyes.

"All right, then. When I return."

As lord, soldier, and prisoner, at least in name, the three were separated by protocols that could not safely be circumvented without exposing their conspiracy. Aewyn was escorted to a cell, though the food and drink that was brought for her was no prisoner's fare, but a courtier's service—the finest, perhaps, she had ever had the fortune to eat. Grimwulf—for that had to become his name, now—dined with the soldiers, weathering one insufferable joke after another, fending off inquiries as to who Kellan Fyldron really was and how he had managed to escape.

Castor Stannon dined with his wife, who was pleasant enough. She kept her own quarters and tended garden in a well-lit set of chambers on the inner courtyard. They talked some about the winter mists and the changing of the season, and in the circle of rush lights that adorned her parlour, he set ink to paper, wax to flame, and drew up the order that would dispatch some of the fighting men he had garrisoned at Wescairn. Everything had to be done right, or it would be all for nothing—less than nothing, he reminded himself. It turned his stomach to think what Ashimar would do if he rode back to Wescairn and found the Imperial censor abetting a fugitive worth such a kingly bounty.

On another night, when he had finished the order, he might have called for a page or scribe to turn out a second copy for the Reeve at Aslea. But restlessly awake, lulled into an uneasy peace by his wife's unending litany of garden-stories and cat-stories, he patiently drew up a second copy of the writ, word for word, looping the stems of the letters and nursing a glass of Rahastan blueberry wine until the light in the little room was nearly gone—too far gone, to be sure, for a man trying to write elegantly with the sight of one eye. By the end of the second copy of the dispatch, his meticulously elegant penmanship had run to a sloppy and ink-spattered scrawl. They would have to be sent out by morning; even if he had been so fussy as to redraft it for his own pride, there was no time for it now.

As he ascended the long stair to the upper gallery and his extravagant bedchamber, Castor weighed the two sealed scrolls in his delicate hands, silently debating whether he would send the fairer copy to the Vasil of Haukmere and the fouler copy to the Marshal of the Third Legion, or let the reverse reflect his true affection for the noble Marshal Blaine and the indolent Lord Kelmor. More than likely, the Marshal would read every word of the dispatch twice over, and keep it at his side in the command tent while repositioning his forces. More than likely, Lord Kelmor, who fancied himself fierce only by dint of being vaguely related to Ashimar, would leave the scroll unread for weeks, perhaps burning it by mistake with the tracts and pamphlets deemed too seditious to Travalaith to be spared the fire.

An otherwise faithless man, Castor navigated the stairs and the gallery on faith. His feet found the familiar flagstones and he ducked with skill the iron sconces where expensive torches would have burned only for the most formal of receptions in the hall below. His hearth-fire would be roaring when he reached his bedchamber, and that would be enough.

The warm light that streamed up from below found no foothold on the edges of the dark grey stone, nor upon the towering silhouette that stood waiting by his chamber door. But the figure held at his chest a leering, snarling wolf's head, and there along the edges of the richly enamelled red metal, the light from below glinted and shone, limning the exquisite mask with a fiery glow, as if the wolf itself had caught fire some time ago. Castor was nearly upon it before he started backward in shock. But the figure said nothing, only waited.

"That's a frightening piece," he said, recovering his composure quickly.

"It's yours," said Kellan's voice in the darkness. "For your collection."

"I couldn't," said Castor. "It's Imperial property."

"It's my property now," said Kellan, "and I'm giving it to you."

He pushed the masked helmet forward, but with scrolls in hand,

Castor could not accept it.

"Bring it in," the censor ordered.

The bedchamber, like most of the upper rooms, was uncomfortably hot. The upper keep was timber-floored, and upper-storey fireplaces were a sometimes dangerous rarity, but the fireplace here was surrounded by a massive hearthstone, supported and buttressed from below, that not only caught stray sparks launched far from the flames, but held the heat of the blazing fire with a quiet intensity. It was perhaps why the lord of Wescairn had chosen a smaller, simpler bedchamber than many of the others, which in its crampedness was even warmer than the counting-house below. Castor was many years accustomed to it, and shed his supple leather turnshoes to walk barefoot across the hot stone with comfort and relief. In the darkness of the room's edge, savouring the cool of the outer stone wall, Kellan circled the hearth and laid the wolf helm on a low oaken hutch.

"You must have seen my collection," said Castor.

"I've seen them. In the gallery."

Castor unfastened his doublet and crossed back to the helm in spite of himself, studying the artistry.

"I had already agreed to help you," said Castor, without looking up.

"You had," Kellan agreed. "Without complaint, without a moment's pause. Without reservation."

Castor looked the wolf-helm in the eyes, mimicked its snarling face. "Not without reservation," he said.

"I know what it means to you," said Kellan. "The Empire, your post, your place in this world of rank stripes and bruised knees."

"You've had a hard time of it," said Castor, dismissively.

Kellan shrugged. "I suppose I have."

"I haven't," said Castor. "I've had a gentle life—till last year, when I got a taste of how men like you live." He turned at last to face Kellan, and the silver piece stitched over his missing eye glinted in the firelight.

"You'll forgive me," he said, "if I'm not eager to repeat it."

"Begging your pardon, but you are," said Kellan. "There's a thousand acres on my head, Stannon. A landed lordship. If Ashimar finds out you gave us passage, took us in..."

"I've never known you to be afraid of a man like that," said Castor. With a shrug of his eyebrows, Kellan bent down and pulled his tunic over his shoulders.

"You tell me if I shouldn't be," he said.

In the firelight, Kellan's corded muscles shone a deep orange, but they were cris-crossed, nearly spiderwebbed, with bright raised scars that shone almost yellow-white against the tanned skin.

"Gods give answer," Castor breathed.

"Come," said Kellan. "You've traded words with Ashimar enough times. If you really mean to stand between him and me, it's time you truly met the man."

He took Castor's pale hand and pressed it to the jagged rippling scars.

"How?" asked the censor.

"The Imperator's Scourge," said Kellan. "I thought that was a figure of speech too. Apparently not. He carries it like a badge of office. He's knotted the Keys of Valithar into its tails. They bite hard and feast hungry."

"How old are these wounds?" asked Castor, ever inquisitive.

"I don't even know what day it is."

"Twenty-second of Teurmaunt, if it's past midnight."

"It's not."

"Twenty-first, then."

Kellan moved away, into the darkness.

"A month to the day," he said. "A white month, not even a red month."

"So soon," said Castor. "Fewer than sixty days since you left."

"Less than sixty days since you sent me to the slaughterhouse," said Kellan.

Castor sat close to the fire. "I thought you would be richly rewarded."

"Aye," said Kellan. "I'll carry this reward the rest of my days."

"I am so sorry, my friend."

Reluctantly, Kellan moved into the firelight, studying his own scars for the first time.

"Does it matter?" he asked. It was as vulnerable a question as he was ever likely to ask.

Castor looked up, one blue eye gleaming. "Why are you asking me?"

Kellan set his jaw hard. "You know why."

"It might have, once," said Castor. "But now? Just sit to the right of me."

Kellan did as he was bid, wholly eclipsed in the shadow of Castor's blind eye.

"Better?"

"No," said Castor. "Now we're both broken men."

"Tamnor take your 'broken men' shit," snapped Kellan. "I'm more whole than I've any right to be after the days I've seen. So are you. We both should have died in Widowvale, if…"

Kellan trailed off before he exposed Aewyn's role in Castor's maiming. He understood now that he was protecting her—but could not yet fathom why.

"I wish I had been there," said Castor. Kellan laughed.

"Forgive me," he said. "The thought of you grappling Ashimar for my sake…"

"As you were there for me, I mean." Castor clarified. "You don't need another man to fight your battles for you."

"Don't I?"

Castor brushed the scars on his shoulders again. "Come sit on my good side."

Kellan's weary limbs ached as he stood, then sat. "Fussy man. You could quench the fire, if the sight of it bothers you."

"I'll get cold," Castor protested.

"You won't," promised Kellan.

Castor tilted his head, listening to the snap and crack of the flames.

"You're not leaving," Castor observed.

"I am leaving," said Kellan. "At first light, and not an hour past. There's no flaying worse than that."

"But…not right away."

Kellan brushed a lock of black hair back from the censor's good eye. "No, gentle boy," he said. "Not right away."

Aewyn slept easiest in open air, under the moon-gilded canopy of old trees, leaves shining under Luna's white grace like hammered silver foil. Failing that, a cloudy sky would serve; and if no open sky could be found, a roof of thatched straw like the one she was raised under would bring her some comfort. The dank stone dungeon of Wescairn's central keep, though, seemed a thousand miles away from Haveïl, even though the mist had cleared and Aewyn could see the forest's edge from her barred window. The cell was miserable, in spite of everything Castor Stannon had done to make it comfortable—but there was a different sort of comfort, perhaps, in that misery.

Outside under just one moon, it was a dull red night, unbrightened by Luna's hidden face, and the tall grasses glimmered dully in the fens like yellow bones. Pressed up against the iron bars so closely that the touch of the metal pained her hands, she could see the flickering light in the upper window of Castor's keep wink out as the whole town fell into a restless nocturnal peace. Her voice, when she spoke, was dry from disuse.

"Someday I'll tell you all about this," whispered Aewyn. "About my abduction—and about each new abduction, which is a welcome rescue from the last. I hope you're under a sky of your choosing, my friend, but a ceiling of stone suits my mood. If Lord Stannon knew what I've done, if he knew my place in this war, he wouldn't be helping me. I made to kill these men, both of them, only months ago. Now I wonder how war has changed us all."

She watched the trees for the green glint of her old friend's eyes, though she did not expect to see them.

"When did I become a killer, Poe?" she asked the night air. "When did you? I can't imagine we should all have been friends—you, me, Celithrand, Grimwulf, Castor—in a different world. But I think you were always right about the Iron City. Some evil comes out from it that I cannot name, whose shape I cannot see. But perhaps it does not ride in the hearts of men after all. How can those who kill with one hand be so gentle with the other? Is being a gentle-handed killer the best any of us can hope for, now? I imagine if you were here, you'd have a wise old story to put me at ease. Perhaps, when next we meet, I'll have a good story for you too."

She was silent after these words for a long time, hanging on the edge of sleep, jolted from her reverie as her nodding face slumped against the bars of the window. The sleep that took her in the end was not quite the sleep of a free woman, nor the hard, heavy sleep of a true prisoner. Behind the heavy, iron-banded cell door that might not even have been locked, she lingered on the edge of waking as the faintest of stars glimmered along the high horizon to the west.

In the blue hour of the morning, the mists returned again, rolling over the fens and pooling in the lowlands beneath the jagged roads. The sky lightened feebly for a while; then, when the cold orb of the winter crested the eastern highlands and cut effortlessly through the fog, the mystery of the lowlands seemed to burn away, and the houses of Haukmere's lowly inhabitants, from the hovels of its mosquitoes to the palatial nests of its slithering marsh adders, came starkly into the sunlight.

Although she had never come to Wescairn, Aewyn knew the landscape, or this sort of landscape, with a long and easy familiarity: the restless breaths of the land itself, the steady inhalations of the tides and the exhalations of its bogflowers opening to the wind, were known to her and brought her comfort even in the uncertainty of a morning spent halfway between protection and captivity. As she brought herself out of the half-sleep that calmed her and gave her focus, the first of the dungeon's doors creaked open outside, then the second. She steeled herself for another turn in the tight iron manacles that burned her wrists and left her dizzy with pain, but it was not Castor's usual jailers who came to retrieve her.

"Hope you're awake," said a familiar, deep voice. "It's time to look presentable."

"Grimwulf," she groaned, rubbing her tired eyes. It was better, safer, that she called him that.

"It's time we were gone," he said. "Past time, if you like. Get your boots on, little snowdrop."

She had mostly kept her riding-clothes together, and pulled on her boots and green jerkin with a mixture of confusion and resentment. *I'm not little, anymore*, she thought. *You're just uncommonly big.* But she did as she was told and made ready for leaving as if commanded by her First Spear. Something in her captor had changed a little, and with the weight of his cutting resentment finally off of her, it might be easier going. If she had to make a run for it, and escape him at speed, the time would be when they reached the wilderness. If she had to break from him by guile, the time would be in the towns, where he could not reclaim her without drawing too much attention to himself.

"Where are Stannon's guards?" she asked.

"Most already know you for a prisoner, I'll wager," said Grimwulf. "Or know me for the wanted man I used to be. Try not to look so bedraggled. You're to pass for my partner, if we can swing it." She was on her feet then, eyeing him curiously.

"Where are we going?"

"Stables. Hope you can ride."

Aewyn had been right, of course: the heavy black destriers were no farm-horses. Seeing them close up, they were not only bred for war, but for a very particular kind of war. Sixteen hands tall and thickly muscled, the powerful stallions were bred for sustained battles and highly defensive cavalry fighting. They were altogether too costly for the regular cavalry of the Grand Army to breed and keep, and their provision to the soldiers at Wescairn, who favoured fast-moving light coursers, was an unpleasant sign that the war had come home. They were magnificent creatures, silky-maned and expertly trained, and Aewyn might once have taken in their sleek beauty with naïve delight. But she was no more a child, and her excitement was tempered with the sobering knowledge that their presence in the region meant the Grand Army expected there would soon be serious blood, if there hadn't been already.

"They're a few hands big for you," Grimwulf warned.

"I can ride," said Aewyn, though she had to cinch up the stirrups as high as she could. To the big man at her side, the heavy destrier was supremely comfortable. Aewyn mounted from the right side, as she was most able, though her weak leg pained her as she swung it into position.

Grimwulf reached over a broad hand to steady her as she settled into the saddle: stretching wide, his broad shirt opened at the chest, for he had dressed in haste, and she could see the mark of her little arrow still, nestled in the hair of his chest within a bed of unhappy scars. For only a moment, her mind drifted back to a cold day on a frosty meadow, surrounded by the smaller, gentler horses of the Havenari, and by smaller, gentler men besides. Not long after she had broken her leg, Bram had begun teaching her to dance to aid in her recovery, frustrating her at first with the elegant court steps and graceful turns of a high old nobility that had mostly passed from the Empire. They had danced like that for weeks, until the strength came back to her leg and there was no more time for such frivolities.

"War makes dog-eared storybooks of us all," he had said, though she did not understand what he meant then. She understood now.

Beneath her, the muscled horse twisted and bucked, testing her, and she tightened her knees and gently took control of it, though she was half the weight of its usual rider. With a whole but fragile confidence, she guided the stallion to Grimwulf's flank and followed him to the gatehouse, where six of the Grand Army's heavy troops sat waiting.

"Providence, lady," said one of the men. His voice was higher than she expected, and his face leaner. "And to you, Your Dread."

Grimwulf grunted and nodded.

"I trust the steeds are to your liking? The stallions can be a bit much."

Aewyn smiled, genuinely, for the first time in a long while. "He's beautiful," she said.

The young man smiled at her. "If you fall, just roll away if you can. Most horses don't care to have you underfoot, but this fellow's trained to trample you if he thinks you're a felled enemy."

Grimwulf jerked at the reins as his horse pulled away from him, gave it a taste of his strength and let it know there was plenty more on reserve. "It's a lot of horse for an Outlander to feed," he said. "I don't suppose it's Stannon's silver they're eating?"

"Marshal Blaine's silver," said the soldier. "His gold, if you want to know the whole of it. These stallions are as expensive to keep as their weight in wives, no doubt about it. But until the Master General returns from the front, Blaine's word is law. He wants forest patrols riding top fighting mounts after what happened to the last lot."

"I don't suppose I should ask."

"Twenty men cut down on the trails," said the soldier. "The whole company lost, men and horses both. The sumpter horse came back mad and had to be put down. Lord Kelmor says it's the Mage's doing. The horses that survived the fields of fire at the Danhorn were much the same. But the Marshal's taking no chances."

Aewyn's stallion bucked restlessly as he felt her shudder with fear. Grimwulf cursed under his breath so softly only she could hear. "I suppose the Mage will be looking to burn us alive, as well."

The soldier looked back to his comrades. "Begging your pardon, Your Dread, but we consider it less likely now that you're here. A few patrols here and there, if the insurgents think they can take us on, they will, Mage or no Mage. But he won't be so quick to provoke the Red Captain if he doesn't have to. Your master's wrath is the stuff of legend out here."

"I've heard stories," said Grimwulf.

On a cold, sunny mid-morning, eight riders set out from the gates of Wescairn with nine horses—eight black stallions leading a dappled palfrey as a pack-horse. Waried and wizened by the disturbing rumours that had begun to circulate on the edge of Haveïl, they kept to the main roads and avoided the cover of the trees. Aewyn wore the deep hood of her traveling-cloak drawn up over her head, and kept her distinctive white hair bound far back beneath it. Grimwulf wore his red armour uneasily, not beneath the cloak of a bloodguard, but beneath the fine black riding-cloak Castor Stannon had given him. It was fringed and fully lined with rich black sable, and felt utterly out of place in a military company, but it kept him warm almost to hot and concealed the armour at a distance.

Aewyn watched them with a Havenar's eyes, the eyes of an outrider who knew the nuances of formation riding. She watched the way the soldiers distanced themselves from him, wary of the Red Legion's reputation if not quite trembling at it. With no small measure of pride, she rode boldly close to him at the front of their formation, representing her order even in captivity. Here in the outlands among the small frontier towns, she considered the Havenari an equal or higher authority than the Grand Army, easily worthy of riding athwart the Bloodguard.

They rode in uneasy silence for much of the morning, and that suited Aewyn well enough. An hour or more into their ride, crossing above a brackish lowland marsh, Aewyn caught sight of another red-armoured Bloodguard riding south, perhaps back toward Wescairn. A wide bog of salty water separated them, and at that distance Grimwulf's disguise was never really tested. He bent low in the saddle as they rode, and kept his unhelmed head at the height of the other men's.

"It was wise of you to leave the helmet," Aewyn told him.

Grimwulf sighed as she broke their pleasant silence. "Aye," he said.

"You…don't want them to find me," she said.

"I don't want to be *found*," Grimwulf corrected. "You've got nothing to do with it."

"Why are you helping me?" she asked him. "After all that's happened."

He turned in the saddle, eyes narrowed in skepticism. "Helping you? Is that what you call this? I must have knocked you on the head harder than I thought."

"You could have turned me over to… to Lord Stannon. You could have told him what I did to him."

The big man thought it over. "Aye. I could've done."

"But you didn't."

Grimwulf shrugged. "Castor would've killed you. He would've had every right. And killing doesn't much suit him. It's not good for men like him."

"He'd be furious if he found out."

Grimwulf shrugged. "Men always think they'll be happier knowing the truth. He'd pay good coin to know who took his eye—I imagine becase he thinks that finding that out would somehow improve his lot. Whether he killed you or not, I don't suppose it'd better him one bit."

"I…I'm sorry this all happened," she said. "I'm sorry about his eye."

"Ah," said Grimwulf. "You're sorry. Yes. That'll grow it right back."

Aewyn drew her mouth tight and balled her fists on the reins. "I'm sorry," she repeated, hardening her tone, "but he was going to kill my friend. So were you, if you recall. An aeril who never meant you ill, never did any wrong to you or yours. He was innocent."

Grimwulf snorted. "Innocent?"

"Innocent of treason, at least," Aewyn said sharply. "Castor knew it. You probably did, too."

"I know what I'm told to know," Grimwulf snapped. "That's how I stay alive."

"I know right from wrong, when I can," said Aewyn. "Whether it's kept me alive, I don't know. But you're worse for wear than I am."

Grimwulf was ready to respond with something shouted, but paused to consider the regular soldiers all around him. "You put these scars on me too," he said, "when you cut that old man free. Not to mention the maker's mark on top of all Ashimar's handiwork, the little scar you put here yourself." Covering the side of his neck he did not want exposed, he jerked his collar open and showed her the little yeoman's-nipple scar she had left in his chest.

"You're still angry," she said.

"Yes!" he barked, so sharply that the other soldiers turned their heads toward him. He waved them off, and rode in closer to her.

"One would think that fairly obvious," he said, measuring his words through clenched teeth.

Aewyn inhaled deeply. "Then tell me again, why are you helping me?" she repeated.

Grimwulf threw up his hands and let the uneasy silence rebuild itself. He had no more words for her after that, and it was clear that his mind was elsewhere. It served him well enough merely to ride, and to drink from a skin of fine wine he had brought from Wescairn, and to look back over his shoulder from time to time in sullen silence. If he was afraid of pursuit, he wore his fear well; if it was something else troubling him, it was a burden he had carried for a long time.

They rode until nightfall, and stopped mainly to water the horses and to decide whether to press on or make camp. Aewyn's weak leg pained her after so long in the saddle, though after days of forced marching—and being dizzily carried—she dared not complain. The others, Grimwulf included, were seasoned riders and fresh from a long rest, and their horses were of uncommonly fine stock and stamina, bred for endurance rides under heavy barding. It was decided that after an hour to stretch their legs, rest the horses, and take some coarse rations, they would press on through the night, make the coast by dawn, and sleep away the morning if an Adâni ship could not be found. In the restless quiet of their leisure, the men had begun swapping rumours and stories of the road. Many spoke of the front, of the movements of the Mage; some lamented the loss of their brethren at the Danhorn, and regretted that there were no songs to be sung in their honour yet. Most, though, were preoccupied by the disappearance of an entire quire of men in the woods to the west. Aewyn shuddered as she heard their rumours, surer than most what might have happened there. No songs would be written for those men, she knew, who were far from the field of glory when they left the world in silence.

"I would hear a song," she said, "once we have rested. If you know any."

A few of the soldiers nodded. "Our pardon, lady," said one. "These are hard matters for a woman's ears."

"They're a hard matter for anyone's ears, I should think," said Aewyn. "It's not women, after all, who were swallowed up in that darkness."

Grimwulf laughed once and sharply and that. "Sing her a song, if you've got one," he barked. "Something with spirit."

"All we know are soldier's songs," said another. "Most are unfit for a lady's company. I could manage a bit of 'The Ghosts of Draden,' if pressed…"

"Not that one," Grimwulf snapped. "Anything else."

"Have you got a song, Your Dread?"

Grimwulf bit his lip in thought. "Aye," he said. "I just might do." Then, in a crude and roadworn baritone voice, with no great reverence or love of the song, he bellowed a familiar refrain with exaggerated, facetious fervor, and soon the rest were singing too:

> *From Creslyn's edge the song descends*
> *Like thunder from a silent sky:*
> *"To Ban! To Ban! To Vostarban!*
> *The valley where three waters ran*
> *Is red with those who will not die!*
>
> *Where lord and thane were shoulder-friends,*
> *Where crystal tears adorned the eye*
> *Of every man at Vostarban*
> *Who clove unto his countryman*
> *In walls of iron beneath the sky.*
>
> *There ran a river red as blood,*
> *There ran a river blue as sky,*
> *There too a river violet ran,*
> *At Ban! At Ban! At Vostarban,*
> *The ground of those who will not die!*
>
> *The Watch that rode upon the flood,*
> *The heroes who, at Outlands' end,*
> *Bore Vostar's blood and Vostar's clan*
> *Within their breasts at Vostarban,*
> *With valour still that land defend.*

The Season Of The Cerulyn

The Maidens Three upon its banks
Attend the war-spent where they lie,
Ensure the men who lie unmanned
Reclaim unto their bloody hand
The fallen sword before they die.

To bloody lips no word of thanks
Is born, but this courageous cry:
"To Ban! To Ban! To Vostarban!
The valley where three waters ran
Is red with those will not die!

"Whatever blood has here been shed,
Whatever ground may bear its stains,
Our honour and our fatherland
Shall not pass out of Vostar's hand
While any drop of blood remains.

"When I am lain among the dead,
The ramparts of our flesh raised high
By comrades whom, at Vostarban
No foreign host e'er overran,
Nor death could e'er compel to die,

"Will not, before Silvalis ends
And moons fall dark, in deed or word
Give way in times of peace or war,
Surrender to the wicked, nor
Betray us to the foreign sword!"

From Creslyn's edge the song descends
Like lightning from a darkened sky:
"To Ban! To Ban! To Vostarban!
The valley where three waters ran
Is red with those who will not die!"

With each line and each verse, the soldiers' zeal and intensity waxed, and soon they were each singing to outdo the others, and those who had quitted their armour shook their mail-coats and thumped their breastplates in almost pious ferocity. About halfway through, grinning like the hound who had set the whole pack barking, Grimwulf slipped away from them, back to the horses, and found Aewyn waiting there.

"There, I gave you your song," he said, jerking his head toward the men. "You're not singing it."

"It's an ugly song," she said.

He laughed. "Aye."

"And the company of horses always suited me better." She looked up with affection, but also with a rider's caution, at the heavy war horses. In the winter cold, a day's ride had done little to tire them, and they were still unpredictable when riled.

Grimwulf jerked his chin toward the tree line. "That right there," he said, "that rollicking chorus, was just the sort of moment a captive could have slipped away."

She was still studying the horses. "I suppose so," she said without turning back.

Grimwulf busied himself with his horse's tack. As the men brought their song to a roaring climax, he moved as if to speak twice before unburdening his tongue.

"The old aeril," he said. "The man I moved to hang. Was he truly Celithrand of the Owl?"

"He was simply Celithrand," said Aewyn. "Of what bird, or what family, I cannot say."

"It's what the four heroes were called," said Grimwulf. "The Company of the Owl. It was Valithar's charge, in the beginning, and now it's Travalaith's. He was not the sort of man I expected."

"And what did you expect?"

Grimwulf shrugged. "A fight, for one. They say he trained Jordac in the ways of magic. The centuries have not been kind to sorcerers and conjurers. Illusionists and charlatans I've seen in droves, but true mages are nearly gone from the world. Your old friend was born in a different time. The way Jordac burned up the Danhorn—if Celithrand was his better, there'd be nothing left of us. Not Castor, nor me, nor probably you."

"Perhaps destruction is a poor measure of who's *better*," said Aewyn. Grimwulf raised his eyebrows and nodded thoughtfully.

"Even so," said Grimwulf. "He was vulnerable, that man. He let us string him up like a haddock for smoking. I've heard tales of druid magic before. I fully expected to see some."

"He managed to escape you," said Aewyn. "An old man, centuries old maybe, and your noose was tight around his neck. You had him at the end of a rope, and now the whole Grand Army can't put their hands on him. Ashimar can't find him. You can't find him, either."

"You sound rather happy about it," said Grimwulf. "I suppose you've a right to be."

Aewyn narrowed her eyes in thought. "That's why I was taken," she said. "Wasn't it? But *I* certainly can't find him, though I'd like nothing more than to see his face again. And all this trouble we've been through—both of us—is because, from a noose you straitened yourself, he's vanished into mist and thrown his enemies into total disarray. Is that not magic enough?"

Grimwulf leaned in close and lowered his voice as the men began wandering back to the horses, their song ended for now.

"I could stand a touch of that same magic myself right now," he reminded her. "And so could you."

She put her little hand on his wrist, which surprised her as much as it did him.

"The corsairs of Adân take on sailors from every port in the Northlands," she said. "They will not cross the Miumuranai, not with their coastal skiffs and their landing boats. But anywhere else you want to go, they'll take you. Rahasta? Shadowsand, maybe? If Ashimar doesn't catch you by the time you have the salt of the sea in your hair, he's never going to. You'll be a thousand miles away before you know it."

Grimwulf turned away from her, and cast one final look back in the direction of Wescairn, as if to ensure they had not been followed.

"Aye," he said thoughtfully. "A thousand miles."

The last leg of their journey, by night, was an easy ride. The low country air was cold enough to keep the well-muscled horses at ease, even when trotting at speed. The other soldiers had thought to ride clear to the sea, to wet their boots in the high tide and ride along the coast until they spotted the sharp-edged, Aleris-rigged sails of the Adâni corsairs who had come ashore to winter. With Aewyn first in tow, then among their vanguard, then at last riding ahead of them as a scout, a ten-mile detour to the coast was hardly necessary. They rode on through the latest hours of the night, when the colour-shedding winter-white court owls were out in force against a black and cloudless night sky.

The red moon, still nearly full and alone in the sky, lit them with an eerie gold as Aewyn followed their flights in the dark with keen eyes. The owls had learned, she knew, to follow the Adâni hunters and trappers who were wise in the way of ground creatures, and to steal hares or other small game from the snares before the foragers did. Through the owls, she found the snares; through the snares, she found the tracks, and through the tracks, it would not be far to find the corsairs.

"These prints are fresh," said Aewyn. "We're an hour out, or less, from wherever they make camp. Start looking and smelling for fire and smoke."

Grimwulf frowned. "Anytime I think I'm about to be lucky, I keep my hand on my weapon. There's an ill wind to this."

"I've seen it before," said Aewyn. "The Havenari—"
"You haven't been with them even a full winter yet," said Grimwulf. Under his breath, he whispered: "You weren't with them when you shot me, or your Captain would've skinned you alive for it. Just keep your eyes open and your mouth shut. We're close to freedom—a hair's breadth. If anything bad's likely to befall us, it's likely to be now."

The tracks were not hard to follow. They had come west and north to firmer ground, where the corsairs were more likely to land, and the snow told the story of more men than Aewyn had expected, coming farther inland than she expected. Their trail of walking, eating, and idle branch-swinging was not hard to follow; but still Aewyn moved ever slower, sometimes barely walking her horse at all before dismounting and feeling her way through the crushed plants.

"The cerulyns," she said at last.

Grimwulf narrowed his eyes. "What of them?"

"They're native plants here. They always have been. I've seen them, and you can't miss them when you do. Only—I'm looking at leaves and stems here."

"That's what that is? They breed them a lot bigger in the capital. Fuller blossoms, very rich in blue."

"These are blue enough," said Aewyn, "or they would be, if they'd left any. What an odd thing for them to wipe out."

"Odd and forbidden," said Grimwulf. "It's a crime to pluck cerulyns. Any of the Three Maidens, really, without a grant of right from Lornock."

"These weren't plucked," said Aewyn, kneeling. "They were cut."

Grimwulf leaned in close. "D'you much care who gets you safely home?"

Aewyn shrugged. "Not much," she said, "so long as I get there."

"Then don't speak to the others," he said. "Wait for my signal. You think you can slip away without anyone noticing?"

"I have done," Aewyn said with confidence, "a half-dozen times so far on this trip already. Unless you've been months on the trail—and these men haven't—a woman does not relieve herself in the company of men."

Grimwulf nodded, smirking. "I suppose she doesn't. Just be ready."

"You think something's wrong?"

"Not for us," said Grimwulf, "unless the people who cut these blossoms find us traveling with this lot. Which way are these tracks taking us?"

"Northwest," she said.

"Take us northeast, then," he urged. "We'll be rid of them soon."

Grimwulf rode back into formation, leaving Aewyn alone to study the tracks. Really, she was scouting for ambushes now, and turning some hard decisions over in her mind. Could Grimwulf be trusted? She knew that he could not. And yet, there was something in him that she understood. The world beyond Haveïl was full of men like him, she imagined—and it was a world that forged men like him from even the gentlest children. This land was a hard place, and she was determined to be free of it as quickly as possible. So too, she knew, was he—and that made him trustworthy, even where his ill character did not. As long as they shared an interest, she knew he would be true to it, if not to her.

And so, when the moment came, she went away with him. She did not stay to hear what sort of distraction he had concocted, but slipped away in silence, as was her natural talent, the moment he signalled her with a quiet nod. Cutting east as he directed, she was moving a long time before she heard the unmistakable sound of him on horseback, headed in the same direction. It was just one man, a tall one, and he would have passed right by her in a moment without seeing her, if she had not reached out to alert him.

"So what's going on?" she asked him.

"Insurrectionists," said Grimwulf. "Only they'd make a point of cutting every single one of the Maidens they come across in these lands. If they catch us riding with the Grand Army, we're dead. If our escorts realize they're taking us to Jordac's people, we're also dead."

He threw off his cloak, baring his shoulders to the cold, and she realized he was discarding as much as he could of his bloodguard's uniform. Piece by piece, his arms and armour fell away from him; she shivered just watching him strip it away.

"You'll be wanting that in a fight," she warned as he threw the last of it into the snow.

"I won't be wanting the fight itself," said Grimwulf. "And if I'm in Imperial rags, I'm likely to get one."

"You're so sure," she said.

"Mark my words," he replied. "The Mage's Uprising has come now to these woods, too—or those who keep faith with him, at least. They've come inland, and they're close. Not a mile hence."

Aewyn let her reply die on her tongue. The woods were thinner here than in the heart of Haveïl, but the winter birds were much the same. The owls still soared and swooped in silence, pinpointing where the camps had been set up ahead of them; but the forest was silent as death around them. She could feel their eyes on her, somehow. The horses were no help at all; in the wild, the perpetual fear of a gently trained horse could be a rider's friend, but these mounts were bred and raised to be fearless. Perhaps they had seen war, and the death of their own kin. Compared to that, the men lurking behind trees and over ridges were no concern to warn their riders about.

"You may as well come out," Aewyn called, suddenly. Grimwulf cursed and reached for his sword, until he realized where he'd been given it. Better to leave the weapon of a bloodguard sheathed until there was no choice.

They came from all directions at once, seven scouts, all in heavier armour than Grimwulf would have expected. They wore no uniform, and their cloaks were patchwork garments without sigil or crest, but there was no mistaking what sort of men—and women—they were. A few brandished Selikhan sabers, and all of them had a hard bludgeon at their belt—maces and war-hammers, mostly. They were ready to face armoured warriors—elite warriors.

"Providence to you, friends." He immediately regretted the greeting as the name of Ashimar's warship, the *Providence*, crossed his mind.

"Fool's blessing, we hope not," said one of the scouts. "What's your business, travellers?"

"Seeking passage," said Grimwulf.

"Any particular direction?"

Grimwulf shrugged his broad shoulders. "West," he said. "Or east, maybe. Or straight up to the red moon herself, if need be—but out of Imperial lands, if you want to know, by any road there is."

"Those are fine horses," said one of the scouts. "Garrison horses, it looks like."

"They are," said Grimwulf. "And there's a garrison that will soon be missing them. Part of the reason our travel is urgent, if you understand me. They're yours, if you want them."

"And who's the girl?" one of the scouts asked.

"I am Aewyn of the Havenari," she replied. "I serve under Robyn, who carries First Spear for the Havenari north of the Iron Road."

The scouts murmured among themselves as Grimwulf cursed her inability to lie. One, a dark-skinned woman with a Selikhan sabre as long as her leg, gestured for them to dismount.

"We're going to search you," she said.

"You're going to find some weapons," Grimwulf warned. "Doesn't mean I've any desire to use them, but be advised, you'll find them just the same." He looked cautiously at the young man selected to pat him down. Aewyn raised her arms and stepped well back from the stallion, wary of its temperament.

The woman found Aewyn's little black knife first, a razor-sharp whittling knife cut or shaped from obsidian. She held it in her hand until she uncovered the green of Aewyn's jerkin and the crest that marked her as one of the Havenari of Haveïl. Without apology, but without delay, she handed the little knife back.

"It seems they're Havenari after all," said the woman.

"Havenari are Imperial Army," one of the others called.

"Hardly," said Aewyn. "We're not numbered among the Legions, and we keep to ourselves out here. We're charged to keep the Protectorate safe, that's all. For the Imperator and the good of the Empire, if that's who you believe holds the land. For the people and their own good, if not."

"Do you know who we are?" one of the scouts asked.

Grimwulf nodded. "You're the folk who want to put out to sea again before the Grand Army catches up with us. And that suits us just fine."

The scouts threw one another a series of concerned looks.

"*Traualat'tio gwan'wiðyu?*" asked one.

Another gestured hurriedly to Grimwulf. "*Nan'ikh*," he breathed. "*Sivan, ott amest wiðo.*" The tall man exchanged nervous glances with Aewyn but deigned not to press his luck.

"*Sormyo â Odi ne?*" asked the tall man, eyes narrowing cautiously.

"*Sormyo ae Baran,*" the dark-skinned woman corrected him. He paused, then shrugged his shoulders deferentially.

"We would like you to accompany us to our ship," he said, smiling.

Grimwulf nodded. "We can pay for passage," he said. "Not much, but a little. I've a stout back, and the girl's a good climber. If you're bound for Aslea, we can make our passage worth—"

"We are not going to Aslea," said the tall man. "We sail only for the cliffs at Fingrun."

The woman shot him a deadly look and clicked her tongue at him before jerking her head back to the two strangers. In a moment her smile had blossomed as bright and wide as his.

"And now, that you come we must insist," she said.

FIFTEEN

28 Teurmaunt ☾3413

My most deare Lysandra,

The Moons shal each in their half meet to-night or to-morrow, one coming and one going. It is an auspic aspish most lucky time for lovers, and so may it be for us. The scholers deem that if they be each half moons upon my face so shal they be upon youres also, what ever the miles be-tween us two. It is by-neath the same moons that I remember myself unto you and the baby with loving thoughts in plenty.

By day your love has only maad me

the stronger. You give to me a distant star fixed above my home the which to find my way. At night alas I am wracked by deeper worry, for nigh two weeks it has bene (or more) since last I read your sweete words on some page. I am sick at heart for your news, and of the baby; and though your dayes be not so ful as mine I swear I would no less gladden to heare of them. Here at Fingrun-town it has been all madness and storms. As you no dowt have read in my letter sent two days yester, I have lost the company of my garrisonn. The enemy has stollen many secrets about the mines at Orrath and our forces are sent to head off his attack. Imagine the surprise of Jordacs men when he arrives to find nigh three hundred of our finest troops awaiting him.

It has left me lonley, as I have but thritty men left in reserve, and many who are my best company have left me. I always did get on best with the soldiers than the oficers. But now it seems ~~for but~~ ~~fout~~ quite lucky that they have gone, as we shal be having guests, and I shal not have to put any man out abed for it.

Yesternight I learnt that the Imperiall Scourge, Lord Ashimar, has been West of us hunting fugitive traytors whose secret crimes have offended the Imperator. Well now he presumes to return to the Capital at all haste, as if ever he did a thing slowly. And *his ship being moored upon the coast not far hence at Seton, and his horses being too spent for the journey at speed, he deemes now to take the fastest Post-horses at Fingrun for his use. So he shal feed his men and change horses here, and thus depryved of my coursers I will be stuck for a means to reach you as the snow deepens. But before he comes to me, I may send away one last rider if my pen rides but faster than he.*

Let us hope it came from a swift goose. But for news of the world below the White Crag and its mines, the struggles of the Empire and all beyond this small prison keep and its quiet chalk hills, I am rested and pass my dayes in peace. I do not welcome visitors, a specially not of his kind, though in the summer when you might travell and the way is warm, I would welcome you and now have to me a sturdy house suited well to a young mother.

If you had told me even a year ago that I would be happy in this place, I would not have believed you, The day I met you, with your hair bound for mourning and a bright bundle of gay blue cerulyns clutched in your dellicate arms. The sweete scent of them will live always in my mem―

A mailed fist, pounded hard on the thick door, sent Rendon's quill across the page, scratching a sharp black line through the flimsy scroll of ash-weed paper. His concentration broken, he set the long quill in its stand dripping and unwiped and moved to the door. He gave his ink-stained hand a cursory brush on his breeches, but it was no use; not that the men of the city could expect the warden of a windswept provincial outpost to have the polished look of a city commander.

Rendon brushed at his close red beard nervously before hauling open the heavy door. The young man at the door, broad-shouldered and smiling, set him immediately at ease.

"Gods have mercy, Tannock," he sighed. "I took you for the Scourge."

"Not yet, Captain," said the younger man. "Though he's not far off. He's sent his fastest riders out with news of the fugitives. I expect he had to gather them all back to him before he could ride in, else he'd leave them behind."

"Small blessings," said Rendon. "What's this about, then?"

"Fresh arrivals, sir. Only Travalaith's finest. Ready for processing."

Rendon nodded. "Bring me the ledger. I'll have a look and see where we need them most."

"Likely the deeps," Tannock volunteered. "We lose most of them at the bottom." But he did as he was told, and brought the book, opening it and holding it down so that Rendon might turn over the pages one-handed.

"I know it," said Rendon, running a finger down the page. "But it grieves my heart, what's left of it, to fill the deeps with bread-thieves, or drunks who take a swing at the wrong Legion man, or… look at this? What is this word?"

Tannock leaned over his shoulder. "Besmirched," he read. "She besmirched the honour of the Imperial Harper."

Rendon tried to catch a laugh in his throat, but it slipped out. "Besmirched the honour."

Tannock grinned. "I didn't know he had any."

"I've met him a few times," said Rendon.

"And?" Tannock pressed him.

Rendon shrugged his shoulder. "If that's evil, then evil is a far sight duller than the Occupation led me to be believe. What, a woman had the guts to call him a feeble, buck-toothed, pasty-faced yantan to his face, and for that I'm to chain her in a fracture tunnel and have her delve herself to death?"

"The deep veins are rich," Tannock offered, but Rendon shook his head.

"Put her to the bloomery," he decided. "It's hard work, but at least she'll see the sun. If she works out until summer, no trouble, we can move her to the farm gangs, house her in Little Town."

"You're starving us for talent in the deeps," said Tannock. "Ever since your last trip to the Capital, you've been soft on the women, and they're some of our best. Thinner arms and smaller hands, can reach places the men can't. No fighting, at least not with their fists. No revolts."

"Man or woman," said Rendon, "we live and die by the deeds of our hands. Killers and thieves, fine. For crimes of the hands, man or woman, I'll do my duty with delight. But this…I've no desire to hand her a death sentence for crimes of the mouth. What's next, shall I condemn the boy who talks back to his father? Shall I fill the tunnels with women who gossip?"

"Word of that might get out," said Tannock, and Rendon laughed.

"And look here," said Rendon, turning over the heavy page awkwardly. "Murder. Murder. Passion slaughter. Rapist. Another murder. Tannock, you'll have no shortage in the deeps from this lot."

"It was a large arrival," said Tannock. "I thought there might be a few."

"This one, four murders," said Rendon. "Fratricide. Poisoned four brothers, his own brothers, to become the estate heir. Bury him a mile deep, for all I care. And look: treason. Treason. Treason and espionage. Treason and sedition. Treason and murder."

Tannock raised his eyebrows at the ledger. "We're becoming unpopular."

"There's your deep delvers," said Rendon. "You want a small-handed woman? There, look at that one. Treason and espionage. Whored herself to an overseer of great esteem, and betrayed his vital secrets to the Selikhan rebels, to the death of dozens."

Tannock let out a low whistle. "I'll take her," he said, "if she's still hale enough to dig after the interrogation she's probably had."

"Pull them all for inspection," said Rendon. "From here to…down to here. All the treasons. I'll give you the best of them for the deep shafts."

Tannock closed the book and bowed politely. "Your will, Captain," he said. "And the rest?"

"This lot today," said Rendon, looking wistfully back to the half-finished letter on his desk. "The rest tomorrow. I've got reports to finish before the transport team returns to the Capital. If we can feed them and roof them for the night, I'll have a letter to send back with them under seal."

"I'll let them know," said Tannock. "Will you be long?"

"Not an hour."

"Come down to the square when you're done. I'll have the treasons ready for you."

Tannock bowed again and left him at speed, with an energy Rendon recalled from his first days in the Fifteenth. Beneath his jovial mood, Tannock could be cruel, but there was a boyish innocence to him, and it pleased Rendon to see him so far from the front. Many survivors of the Danhorn had used their medals and scars to buy their way to the Fingrun mines, far from the fighting, and nearly all had a world-weary affection for men like Tannock, who was not so young in years, but had never walked the fields of fire or smelt the flesh of a brother in arms baking within his own armour. As much as he envied Tannock for being whole of body, it was a comfort to him that the boyish soldier was still whole of spirit. With these wistful thoughts he sank back into his chair, seized his ragged-feathered quill with an ink-stained hand, and found again on the page his own rite of healing.

Deep in its chalky white bones, Fingrun was a very old place. In the age of the True Kings, when the Age of the Moon was yet young, a lonely watchtower had stood atop the white jutting cliff like a pale accusing finger admonishing the restless sea. The present keep, a squat square building of mottled limestone, sat upon the fallen wreck of the ancient watchtower, but the low crumbling wall surrounding it was part of the original construction. By Rendon's count—and his head for numbers and figures was better now than it had once been—the wall had stood stubbornly against the patient ravages of the salty air for more than two thousand years.

In most places the wall had sunk or fallen to waist height, or even crumbled away entirely. The watch at Fingrun had never bothered to shore it up or rebuild it: the keep was bounded on three sides by high cliffs of chalky white stone, and on the fourth by Town, as it was known to the soldiers and locals, and by Little Town, the prison camp that was home to Fingrun's less voluntary residents. The mines were farther down the cliffside, dotting and spotting the white surface like man-sized termite holes in the soft rock. Farther down the coast, the sea retreated from the cliffs, leaving several yards of sandy beaches. But within close proximity to Fingrun's jutting crag, there was nowhere to hide, no place to take the keep by surprise whether by land or by sea.

It made the ancient wall a bit unnecessary, Rendon supposed, though he hoped still to rebuild it if Travalaith had ever sent prisoners enough to do the work. He was of a mind now to leave the place in better condition than when he had arrived, and with his wealth growing and a child on the way, he knew he could not stay forever.

The heaviness of a coming storm weighed on him as he traced the line of the old wall down to the courtyard, where everyone was assembled and ready. Tannock stood by the firepit with one of his men, tending the flames gently as the branding irons heated. The fresh prisoners, hooded by grey linen sacks and shackled together in lines of six, had already been loaded off the wagons and secured to tall posts in the yard. Most swayed and shivered in the cold air, for the walls were not like those of the Iron City or even the border keeps, and did nothing to tame the coastal winds.

"Welcome to Fingrun," said Rendon, approaching them with a

calculated air of very slight pleasure. These first moments of contact, he had learned, had a profound effect on how prisoners fared in their first few months.

"I am the Overseer of the Fingrun mines," he continued. "You will address me as 'my lord,' if it suits you. The young man who took you down and stuck you here will be your Keeper. You'll address him as 'my lord Keeper.' It's by his grace or by his displeasure that criminals to the Imperator live or die in this place. You'd do well to remember it. But neither should you despair. Despair makes for weak work, and weak work will not earn you the privileges that may yet come to you. You will be kept, or not, in kind to the work you do. Lesser criminals work the fields and tend the sheep that keep hard workers warm and fed. The Grand Army does not draw on the supplies that are meant for the mines, so long as there is no unrest in the region. A few seasons, a few years, and if you have put your all into your toil, you may find yourself among the field-workers, with the wind on your face and the sun in your eyes."

As he walked to the head of the line for inspection, Tannock, who was stationed behind them stepped forward and began to pull their hoods off one by one. They were staked facing south, toward the low-hanging winter sun, and as their hoods came off the men and women squinted and recoiled from the harsh light: the traitors, especially, had likely come all the way up in prisoners' hoods.

"That may not sound appealing," said Rendon, matter-of-factly. "But time enough in the deeps, and you'll miss it."

He started, as Tannock had suggested, with the traitors. With every load of prisoners he was surprised by the sheer variety of them. Some of the traitors were forgers—educated and lettered men with soft hands and soft spines who wept at their fate. Others were true soldiers for Jordac—well-conditioned of body and mind, fine miners but prone to revolt if the chance was given. The women he never knew what to make of, or what to do with. Many among them were more tearful and timid than the men, especially those native to Travalaith; but many were more defiant, too, and stared him down at these first meetings with a will that would not be broken.

In the time he had served as Overseer, the work had made him a fine judge of character, and the first traitor to the Empire was an easy read. Towering and square shouldered, the traitor's wide Selikhan moustache was stained red with the blood from his broken nose. He had fought them somewhere along the way, and he was still strong. He would be a hard worker, keeping the peace and a low profile until his moment came to revolt or escape—and that moment would not come before he was too sick at heart to try it.

"This one," said Rendon, and Tannock nodded. He motioned to one of his men at the fire, who shook his head.

"The brands are not quite ready," the soldier called. Rendon nodded and moved on.

The second prisoner was a woman so advanced in age that she reminded him of his white-haired grandmother, when she had been alive. Her face was a mask of weariness, except for her dark brown eyes, which smoldered with hatred.

"Gods and fishes," said Rendon. "This one must be eighty. What did you do, old woman, sit in your chair and spin wool for the Mage?"

The old woman narrowed her eyes and sneered at him. "*Sif Traualat'thi azeler tsehro,*" she spat. "*Itt z'bentse nan'doru sif.*"

Rendon turned to Tannock, who had served in Selik and had picked up some of the local tongue. "Well?"

"She says she poisoned six Travalaithi soldiers," said Tannock. "Though clearly, not the right six soldiers."

"Spirited," he said. "I like this one. Clean her up and keep her for the laundry." He ought to have sent her to the deeps for that, but something in her careworn face moved him to pity. With a dismissive wave he moved to the next prisoner.

"If that old woman's half as quick with—"

Rendon's tongue caught in his throat. His mouth went dry as his gaze fixed on the next woman in line.

Here at the end of their road, there were many who wept or trembled. There were many who shrank from him in fear on that first meeting. But there was something altogether queer in the way she clutched at the post and bowed her head in shame, and would not meet his eyes. He raised her chin hard with his hand, and though she was filthy and bruised from the untold mischief of her captors, there was no mistaking the cinnamon curls that shone gold in winter. There was no mistaking the delicate slope of her nose, or the wintry paleness of her graceful neck. Worst of all, the eyes that had once looked on his so brightly were dulled now by despair and shame and every kind of terror—as, no doubt, were his own.

"Lysandra," he breathed. "No, Sana, no."

"Madge," Tannock corrected helpfully. "This one here is called Madge Dunny. Treason and espionage. Says here she duped a high official into turning over Imperial secrets for more than half a year."

He saw her cracked lips mouth his name, but no sound came at first. Her voice was no more like music, but like the groan of a rusty gate wrenching free from disuse.

"Rendon," she breathed at last. "You look… well. Healthy."

"There must be some mistake," said Rendon. He raised his hand as if to brush her face, but he turned to Tannock. "Tell me, Tannock. Tell me there's been a mistake."

With a look of confusion, Tannock consulted the ledger. "None I can see, Captain," he offered. "They haven't given us the details, but the transport order was signed by Mardon Black. Not his clerk, mind you—the Master of Iron, he himself. Why do you ask?"

But Tannock and the others seemed so very small and distant in that moment. The crumbled walls and sunken battlements of the old watchtower fell away from thought, and even the chill of the sea air seemed to vanish from his skin. In that moment, he and the woman he knew as Lysandra were the only two among the high plateau. She was beaten, bruised, and wind-chapped besides, and her bright curls were matted and tangled. Her slender face had gone to sallow and her eyes and cheeks were sunken some by hunger and neglect. But in her green eyes he still saw the fields of summer, and heard her sweet words upon the meadowgrass far beyond the city wall. She had never really laughed, though: neither of them had.

She looked upon him then with the eyes of a stranger—a hateful stranger—and he knew what she saw as well. Behind his crisp uniform, his strong military gait, his clipped beard and strong jaw, she saw a vagabond, a cast-off and wounded drunkard waiting only for death. Reflected in the shimmering wetness of her teary eyes, his red hair whipping wildly in the wind, that was the miserable man he saw too. However disciplined his step, however stern and handsome his countenance had once more become, that bedraggled and wretched tramp was never far behind him.

He pressed a balled fist to his tightened mouth in anguish. As he fought for his composure, his mind played out the steps of his betrayal and found in them a truth for which he had no answer. Twice he tried to speak, but settled only for shaking his head. There could be no words for this, not in the Merchant's Tongue, nor in any other tongue still spoken by the living.

Stunned into petrified silence, Rendon was saved by the sudden blast of a horn from the top of the Fingrun keep. He turned, paced toward the high wall, as if turning his back on her would push her out of the world, let alone out of his mind.

"Speak, then," he called to the lookout upon the parapet. "What do you see?"

"Riders in red," called the lookout. "Approaching from the south.."

"And the Scourge?"

"Aye, Captain," said the lookout. "Leading them, and he's coming fast. That's no parade-gait."

"I hear you," said Rendon. His eyes darted to the southern tree line, then back to the tower, then to…the woman.

"Lord Ashimar?" Tannock asked him. "If he's nigh, we've got to get the best new miners below ground before… well, before…"

In the end, Tannock trailed off, finally understanding that there were grander and stranger stories at work here than his own. With stoic discipline and a voice of command he had borrowed from his father like a set of boots two sizes too big for him, Tannock began herding the strongest diggers away to safety. As he busied himself unchaining them, Rendon strode back and cupped Madge's jaw tightly in the furious claw of his hand.

"Answer me this," he ordered. "Answer me, this one time, before I send you to your rewards. Was there a child? Was there *ever* a child? Or was that a lie too?"

Madge leaned in toward his furious, pleading eyes. Her countenance, formerly dulled from despair, blossomed suddenly into a supremely vengeful hatred.

"My husband," she seethed, "was Hafard Dunny, son of Fardleif. He was a cooper and a weelwright. He was born upon the banks of the Ban—*never* call it the Vostarban—and raised among the Hidradi of Creslyn Wood. He was felled by an arrow on the seventh—"

Coiling his whole body for strength, Rendon backhanded her across the face.

"The child!" he roared, wild-eyed, his temper finally unleashed.

She straightened with cold pride, and the bleeding corner of her mouth turned up in a defiant grin.

"If there had been a child," she whispered through a bloody mouth, "a child by *you*...I would have dashed it on the rocks and thrown it broken into the sea."

The fight went out of Rendon after that. His proud shoulder slumped and his eyes fell. He motioned for Tannock, who had stood faithfully by, and who uncharacteristically put a gentle hand on his Captain's shoulder.

"Your will?" the young man asked.

Rendon bit his lip. "Brand this one," he said. "Brand her well. Mark her deep. I want the Fingrun sigil to pain her the rest of her days. And sink her down the deepest shaft you can find."

"Captain—"

"That's all."

Rendon staggered away from the post where she was chained. He could not bear to look on her, and dared not let the emotion show in his face when the fastest of the Red Captain's retinue had come into sight.

He did not have to wait long. Without horn or banner, without pomp or fanfare, but with the weariness of men hard at campaign, the bloodguards broke from the treeline at speed, their mounts frothing with exertion. The winter sun was far behind them, but the day was bright enough that the grime and wear of days or weeks in the field had stained their red cloaks brown and pitted their immaculate, bestial armour. Only their leader's cocoon of impenetrable plate seemed none the worse for wear, and as he jerked his horse to a stop, he dismounted so violently that the animal nearly reared and threw him. It jerked aside from him, tossing its head, eager to be rid of its rider.

Rendon clapped his far shoulder in a gesture of salute and bowed low as the Red Captain approached. He found himself, quite unexpectedly, staring into the flawlessly polished face of a wailing child whose tears were enamelled red as blood. Bristling in spite of himself, he knelt low like a common servant to avoid the Scourge's stomach-turning countenance.

"My lord," he said. "We did not expect you till after midday."

"As I intended," said Ashimar dispassionately. "We seek fresh horses, as my rider advised you. But we are also searching for two fugitives."

"He advised us of that, too," said Rendon, steeling himself to look up at the Scourge. "A young girl, wasn't it, white-haired in Havenari attire, and a deserted bloodguard. The name eludes me."

"Kellan Fyldron," said Ashimar. "See that you do not forget it again. He will not be dressed as a bloodguard now. He is uncommonly tall, dark-haired. Hard to miss."

"I have seen no such man," Rendon swore, "and no such girl."

"We shall see," said Ashimar. "I would like to see your prisoners."

Rendon laughed nervously. "Surely you don't think—"

"Forgive me," sad Ashimar. "I misspoke: you will take me to your prisoners immediately."

Rendon stood and started moving, but was stubborn and not easily cowed. "You cannot think I would dare hide them," he protested. "Not from you."

"Someone has betrayed us," said Ashimar. "An Imperial of significant power in the region. My scouts would have found the fugitives by now—unless they were receiving aid from someone. Someone close."

Rendon nodded solemnly. "If it's traitors you want, I've more than a few. Most are in the mines proper."

Ashimar looked back to his men. "Seal the mines first," he ordered. "My men are weary. We will search old Fingrun Town by day, as it's the villagers who can come and go most easily. On the morrow we shall search the mines, and make our way. I expect you will have fresh horses for us by then."

"We can spare enough for all your men," said Rendon. "You'll have food and lodging."

Most of the bloodguard had dismounted, but one or two stayed close to their exhausted mounts in case the fugitives tried a desperate flight from Fingrun Town. But the town, too, was bounded on three sides, and offered little chance of escape once its inhabitants were boxed in.

"Take the others and search the town," Ashimar told one of his men, a tall bloodguard in a mantis-headed helm. As he and his panther-headed companion headed off to do his bidding, Ashimar threw out a gauntleted hand.

"Not you."

The panther-headed bloodguard, a stockier man with shoulders like a bull's, held his position.

"We can't have you warning your friend that we're coming," said Ashimar. "You stay with me."

The bloodguard bowed his helmed head, but said nothing. Rendon had dealt with their kind before; this one did not seem like them. He wondered if the bloodguards, the legendary First Legion of the Shield, had finally opened their ranks to regular soldiers, and had done with the fanatics raised from birth to protect the Imperator.

"If there's nothing else," said Rendon gently, "I would take my leave." Haunted still by the sight of the woman he knew as Lysandra, he was eager to be out of the Scourge's sight and to leave Tannock or one of the other Keepers in charge. The open sky was the same clear blue it had been in the summer months, when they had lain among the flowers together, and he was eager to have it off his head. There was a bottle of strong wine in the pantry beneath his chambers—he knew exactly where—and it was the only place now that was small enough for him to hide in his shame and anger.

"Call a feast for my men," Ashimar ordered. "Meat and fish, if you have them. They have come far on a fruitless errand, and I would keep up their fighting strength for when we return."

"As you wish, my lord."

"Have a private chamber made up for me," said Ashimar. "Any size will do. Bring me strong wine, and balm of Seythe for my wounds."

"We have no wine," Rendon lied, with the unimpeachable sincerity of a drunkard.

"Wineseed and vinegar, then," said Ashimar. "And do not disturb me after nightfall."

Rendon bowed low. "I would sooner disturb the restless dead," he swore, "than the Imperator's scourge at campaign."

"There is no more campaign," said the Scourge. "We are going home."

The crisp snow crunched and squeaked under Roald's boot as he stepped over the drift and down into the clearing. He might have gone farther, but a long arm darted out from the shadows of the treeline, and snagged him by the edge of his cloak.

"Stop," urged Venser's deep voice, as loudly as he dared.

"Stop?" Roald asked.

"Come back," Venser said. "Carefully. Quietly."

Roald knew enough not to second-guess the old veteran. He searched the drift carefully for signs of danger—a bear trap or snare wire, or some other hazard. His eyes darted across the clearing to the little cabin, but the morning was still and quiet. Even so, he waited until he had regained the cover of the trees, then dropped to his knees in the shadows, head below the windblown snowdrift, and looked to the senior soldier.

"You see something?" he asked.

Venser frowned and shook his head.

"I see nothing," he said. "And that's worse. No smoke, no tracks. The weather's clear, too. It's been days, maybe."

"You think it's deserted?"

"It shouldn't be. Not this time of year."

"We should tell Robyn."

"Aye," said Venser.

"I was hoping for a hot meal."

The two men crossed the lightly wooded shadow of the hill and trudged down the slope with the lazy care that comes from experience. The Havenari were circled defensively on the road below, resting the few remaining horses and their tired legs. It had been slow going from the Sunderhouse with the company half-mounted, and would have been even without waiting until Bram could be moved. As it was, they had waited until Ursula's healing had done its work—until Bram had recovered enough that he could disarm any two of them from his knees, and even stand for a few moments if he had to. After that, they had made a crude litter for him, which was hard going until Roald, who was from the far North, had the idea of fashioning it into a little sled that could be drawn across the snow. When Robyn demanded a second for the heavier gear, some of the men could double up on the horses for a while, and that made for easier going. But they were still some days later than anticipated, and given the circumstances, they were all on edge for it.

Robyn's long spear was in her hands as they came down the slope, but she relaxed her grip when she saw that they came easily and at leisure.

"Did you find him?" she called.

"Maybe," said Venser, and her face fell.

"What's maybe?"

"Something between a no and a yes," he said, and she swatted him.

"We went to Halgeir's cottage," said Roald. "As close to it as we are to that rock. But we think it's deserted. We saw no tracks, no smoke. Venser pointed out the weather."

"It's either deserted," said Venser, "or Tsúla's made it to look so. Either way, he doesn't want to be found there. We decided not to barge in, the two of us, to give him away."

"Wise thinking," said Robyn. "We're better off to barge in all together. Havenari! Rest is over. Spears and spurs, now."

They had not planned on stopping for long, and were ready to go in an instant. Despite the tension that wore its lines on their bundled faces, they moved with the concerted grace of a flock of snowbirds at need. None of them forgot why they were on the move, after all.

It was not far up the trail to the narrow ridge that led to the cottage, which backed onto a precipitous drop and was surprisingly defensible. Robyn rode at their head with Venser beside her, intrepid as always, though his weak arm had never healed quite right.

"I see what you mean," she said. "If all had gone well, they'd have a roaring fire going for us."

"We might still get one," said Venser, nodding to the side of the cottage. "Plenty of firewood."

"I don't like the looks of that, either," said Robyn. "Banlanders don't cut what they won't use—do they, Roald?"

"That's a hard day's work," said Roald. "My papa would've bled my ears for leaving a pile that high behind."

"Let's have a look," said Robyn. "Venser, on me."

From his sled at the back of the company, Bram stretched himself up, keeping the weight off his bandaged leg.

"It's close quarters," he advised. "Leave your spears. Go in swords and knives—and be ready to drop your swords or half them if it's too tight."

The door was unbarred, though it had swelled some in the frame and took Robyn and Venser both to budge it. The smell of death hit them as they entered, though the cold had done much to keep it from getting out of hand.

"Gods," Robyn breathed. "That's rank. Can you get this open any further?"

"I'm trying," grunted Venser, grinding the door against the floor of frozen packed earth. "It's come right off its hinges."

"C-captain?"

Robyn looked up toward the timid voice. The place looked derelict, ransacked for anything of value and abandoned with its few contents in a broken heap. But among the scattered and cracked bed-frames, one bed was still propped upright. Behind it, in the shadows, Tsúla stood with his shaking dagger at the ready, hood drawn tight over his face.

"Tsúla?" she asked.

"Captain," he breathed again. "Are—are you alone? Are we safe?"

"We're safe," she said, motioning to him. "Come here; we're safe." She lowered her blade and reached out her arms as he staggered shaking over the furniture, and wrapped him in a tight embrace—but not before she nodded to Venser to keep his weapons at the ready."

"I knew you'd come," said Tsúla, clutching her tightly.

"Sorry we're late," she said.

"I'm not," said Tsúla. "I'm relieved. You have Bram with you?"

"Yes," she said. "He's going to be all right, in time."

"I know it," said Tsúla. "You would have come a lot faster if—if he wasn't."

"Tsúla—what happened here?"

Tsúla let his dagger drop to the floor, which was still stained a ruddy brown.

"I wasn't here," he said. "I went to the village. I warned the Reeve. I told them everything. I didn't think to warn the miners. I didn't think he'd be looking for them too. I didn't think—"

"This isn't your fault," she told him. It was not Tsúla's way to weep, but there was a heavy weight in his shoulders and he would not meet her eyes.

"We left the village. Everyone. We took what we could carry. Left some of the stock, some of the stores. They've gone north and west, into the deep wood. And it's a good thing they did. He came to the village. He came—when he was done with them here."

"Did he find anyone?" Venser asked.

"Only this place," he said. "They're all dead. I found Jory. Red. They took Halgeir's head clean off."

"Eleven wounds," said Robyn.

"I've...moved them. They're around back, I covered them. But there's no digging to be done, now, and I dared not risk a pyre."

"And Aewyn?" Venser asked, eager for news. Tsúla shook his head.

"They burned the moot-hall," he said. "Burned it to the ground, because they could. I took the villagers to green, covered their tracks as best I could. I waited until they were on the move before I came back. I was afraid they'd slaughter her and leave her—a message to the village. You said this was about Celithrand."

"That is what Ashimar told me," said Robyn. "But I do not trust him."

Tsúla nodded coldly. "I'm beginning to see why."

"Focus," she snapped. "They came, they slaughtered the men, they burned the hall. What then?"

"They left," said Tsúla. "Abruptly. There was no one left to interrogate, no one to threaten. There was nothing worth pillaging, if they even had greed for anything but human life. They loaded up their horses—*our* horses—and left by day. I saw them on the Serpent Trail and came back to Widowvale. I was so afraid I'd find her there, but—nothing. No body."

"She's alive," said Venser.

"Did you see her with them?"

"I took care never to get so close," said Tsúla. "I didn't see her, but they *definitely* didn't see me."

"Good man." Venser clapped him on the shoulder as Roald knocked at the splintered door-frame.

"Captain?" he said.

"Bring wood for a fire," said Robyn. "We water the horses, we feed the men, and we ride. Venser, the Serpent Trail? Where are they going?"

Venser knit his thick eyebrows in thought. "In this season? Aslea, maybe, or Seton if they're ambitious and don't mind the wind so much. You can get to the coast that way, too. If they came by sea, they may be trying to get back to their ship."

Tsúla shook his head. "I don't like where this is going."

"She's one of ours," said Robyn. "She's one of *us*. She wears the Leaf, as much as you, or Venser, or Bram. Those boys are a long way from home. The Code of Veritenh gives us jurisdiction over the Protectorate.

Even the Imperator's attack dog has to respect that. And if he doesn't—"

"If he doesn't, what?" asked Roald. "You'll kill the Imperial Scourge?"

"After what he's done to Bram?" Robyn asked. "Aye, why not?"

"We're on the same side," Roald warned. "At least, we're supposed to be. If the Scourge is killed in Protectorate lands—we could be siding with the Uprising in the East."

"Roald—"

"I'm not refusing," the young man was quick to answer. "I'm not saying I won't follow you into Tamnor's open mouth, if that's where you send me. I'm only saying, there's politics to this. There's consequences. And I follow you because you think them through before you give me an order."

"That's more than Toren ever did," Tsúla said, clasping arms tightly with Roald as they reunited.

Robyn turned to Venser. "Tell me," she said. "What sort of trouble am I in for?"

Venser laughed fearlessly. "Every hell if I know," he said. "I know if a scout or a courier gets dead, they send half a quire of troops. If a quire of troops gets dead, they deploy the Legions. If they lose a Legion, they're at war, and the whole vasily falls to the Master Generals to sort out. And, gods help you, if you kill one of the Master Generals, they send the Scourge."

Robyn set her jaw in a way that both pleased and unsettled the younger men in her command.

"Venser," she said again, "whom do they send if you kill the Scourge?"

Venser shook his head, smiling incredulously.

"Every hell if I know."

Robyn eased her sword-point back into its sheath, for now.

"If there's one strand of weird fairy hair out of place when we find her," she said, "I imagine we'll find out."

"He slaughtered these men indiscriminately," said Tsúla. "You know Halgeir. You know Red. This did not have to come to blows."

Roald inhaled sharply. "They killed Red?"

"They did," said Robyn. "Are you still for thinking about this some more?"

"Let's find the bastards," said Roald—only this time, he said it without ego, without bluster or posturing. He said it half to his chest, with his head low, for his sorrow was such a burden that there was no room for bravado beneath it.

"You're quite right, of course," said Venser. "Travalaith is not a lawless Empire. Quite the opposite. There are rules and laws of every sort you can imagine. Perhaps some of them are suspended during wartime; I don't know. And it is of course the prerogative of the Imperial Scourge to work outside them, as the hand of the Imperator who made those laws and can easily strike them. But if the Scourge chooses to forgo the law, he'll forgo its protection, as well."

"He'll have to rely on his sword, then," said Tsúla. "Pity, that. Truly a disadvantage for the man who bested Bram."

Robyn shot him a harsh look. "Get a fire going," she said. "Be quick about it. We'll burn the dead, too. I'll tell the others what's happening and where we're going. How far have they got on us, Tsúla?"

Tsúla raised one of the thatched shutters and peered out of the little cabin. "In this clear weather? With that many men, on these trails, riding our own horses? Not nearly far enough."

"You're sure?"

"I can tell Rascal's shit apart from any other horse's in the company."

Venser laughed and cringed at the same time. "Just what I needed to hear," he said. "We'll water the horses and move on straight away. I've suddenly lost any urge for breakfast."

"That might be best," said Robyn. "If we're on them fast enough, we may just catch up with them on our own ground. Venser, sweep the cabin. I'll have a word with the others." With that, she strode to the door, and seemed to grow a foot taller with each step.

"Quite a woman," Roald said in awe. "I was wrong, I think, not to back her for command from the beginning. She's a fine leader."

Venser nodded as he searched the ransacked hearth for a tinderbox. "You just keep watching," he said. "She's a finer leader still, when she's this frightened."

After the reeking smell of death in Halgeir's cabin, and the stagnant swamps around Wescairn, and the ungelded stallions and unwashed men of the Grand Army, Aewyn was pleased beyond words to come at last to the shores of the Pale Sea, where the salt marshes gave way to the glorious silver-blue waves she had only seen at Seton, and the fresh and crisp scent of the ocean in winter overwhelmed everything else. After a lifetime inland, with only the cool and salty northern air to tell her that a world lay beyond the forest, the sea was a magical place to Aewyn, a place of infinite possibility.

She recalled Robyn's promise that when the weather warmed they would go out along the coastal roads, sweeping the whole north coast of Haveïl and the fishing-towns that dotted its shores, before returning home to Widowvale in the fall. She wondered what it would be like, to come home with the smell of the sea in her hair, and wondered if the youngest children would run alongside her horse as she had done in her childhood each fall when the Havenari came home.

She wondered now, looking out across the terrifying infinity of the Pale Sea, if she would ever be home again, or if she had a home at all.

The dark-skinned woman with the long sabre ushered her gently into the rowboat that would bear them out through the shallows of the marshy coast to a fast, sleek-looking ship farther out in the water. Grimwulf had been taken in another boat with most of the men. Aewyn's boat was filled with cargo: bushel upon bushel, in great heavy sacks, of wild winter cerulyns. The smell of them was rich and musky, altogether different from the mild and fragrant blooms in the height of their summer. Their blossoms were closed tightly against the cold, but they were the hardiest of the Maidens and could weather the winter happily within the shelter of the wood where they had been found.

"You're fighting against Travalaith," said Aewyn.

"Against the Travalaithi Empire," said the woman. "We have no quarrel with the city."

"I don't much like what I've heard of either," said Aewyn. The woman's wide smile gleamed white.

"Rahasta I am from, girl," she said. "Many people from many lands in Rahasta. I can see you are asking."

"I know of it," said Aewyn. "South beyond the Verdant Wastes. Outside the borders of the Empire."

"But…you're not like the others. I mean, Selik…I was told they fight for independence, for sovereign rule."

"They fight for many things," said the woman. "You are right. Rahasta did not come to the North during the Occupation. We did not help the people against your evil god. And the ruling marches, Outlands you call—Selik, and Creslyn, and Haukmere, even far Ulitsa—they call us cowards and traitors to free people. But then, for their aid, the Imperator made to them an alliance, and promised that united all the North would stand. In his youth, in my grandfather's time, it was a strength of good people. But in my father's time the alliance has been bent. The Empire that united warring nations against a common evil turned instead to men making power over others. And if you refuse to come under their chain, you stand with the enemy."

"I imagine it's more complicated than that," said Aewyn.

"For magistrates you are right," said the woman. "For vasils and generals there is more. But for the farmers, the traders, the foot soldiers, there isn't complicated. There's men who disagree, and men who crave dominion on the weak. The fear of Tamnor, fear of a world evil no nation can conquer alone, excuses it conveniently."

"I don't believe in world evils," said Aewyn. "I was the Chosen One, once. I was a young girl, and came from the dryads, and my hair turned these magical colours. There was a prophecy and everything—or a piece of one, at least. Nothing ever came of it, anyway. Nothing but trouble."

The woman laughed, and rowed, and laughed again. "I was a Chosen One too," she said. "I was the oldest daughter in my family. I was destined to marry a rich merchant prince, and restore the fortune of my family."

Aewyn was too earnest to laugh with her. "And did you?"

The woman's smile faded.

"Do you have a name?" Aewyn asked, when the silence became to much.

"Elodia," said the woman.

"It's beautiful," said Aewyn.

"It's my name now," said Elodia. "The Widows took new names, beautiful names, when they came to the Uprising. I wanted one too."

"Grimwulf is not Grimwulf's name," said Aewyn.

"I don't care," said the woman called Elodia. But she glanced across the water at the other boat, could hear them talking. These two had a story; there was no question about it.

"Have you sailed on a ship before?" she asked.

"No," said Aewyn.

"When they ask you this," said Elodia, "when Baran the aeril asks you this, you will say 'yes.' You will tell her you know how to tie all the knots, the hitches, the bends, and know when is the right time for each."

"Why would I do that?"

"No one stays on the ship," Elodia warned. "When we get to Fingrun, there will be fighting. The girls of this country, you can't fight. Only those who can sail us quickly away, only those stay on the boat."

"I can fight," said Aewyn, though the words reminded her of Castor Stannon, and her flushing cheeks betrayed her uncertainty.

"I have chosen this life," said Elodia. "We all have. It is not fair that our war pass to you."

"The Iron City sentenced a friend of mine to death," said Aewyn. "If I can help you free your friends, I will."

Elodia raised an eyebrow. "Ah, will you?" she asked. "You at least have the choice. Your friend there, he is big and has the look of a fighter. I think staying behind to tie knots will be no choice for him."

"He can take care of himself," said Aewyn. "I don't know if he's much good with a sword. But he's mean."

The woman looked across to the other rowboat. Dissatisfied with the speed of his new companions, or his new captors, Grimwulf had taken both oars from them and was rapidly outpacing her, speeding out to the Adâni ship with all the haste he could muster.

"We are all mean, when we must be," Elodia said.

The Adâni ship was deceptively large, and had dropped its anchor deceptively far out to sea. They rode the waves in silence for a time, but the water was watched, and before they had come within a hundred feet of the ship its ladders and fall ropes had been thrown down to secure the smaller vessels and make for a speedy embarkment. The deck of the boat, but for a few auburn-haired Adâni tribesmen, was mostly manned by ragged-looking men and women in rust-spotted gambesons that betrayed their typical use beneath crudely maintained armour. A round-faced Travalaithi with the look of a seasoned mariner hooked his foot handily under the wale of the ship and bent over the side to them.

"Hand me the flowers," he said. "Take care not to get them wet."

Elodia handed up the flowers before prompting Aewyn to climb; by the time she reached the deck, Grimwulf was already clasping arms with some of the men and women. It was positively disturbing to see him smile so broadly.

"Hormer, you didn't tell us you were recruiting," said one.

"Recruiting?" Grimwulf laughed. "As if I needed a good reason to come crack some Imperial heads." All eyes were on Aewyn then as she stumbled to his side; the ship was not so still in the water as she imagined it to be.

Grimwulf leaned in close to her. "Try and show a little enthusiasm," he said.

"I can't be excited about cracking skulls," said Aewyn. "It's not my way."

Elodia snorted as she lifted another bag of cerulyn blossoms up to the round-faced man. "She must not know these skulls like we do, *ne*, Odi?"

The man called Odi frowned. "Hormer's ship or no," he said, "this ship is no shelter for wayward girls. You weren't sent ashore for sightseers and passengers."

"We can pay our way," said Grimwulf.

"I've no need for your silv—"

"With steel," Grimwulf clarified.

Odi sized him up appreciatively. "You, if we could trust you… what about this one? Have you ever swung a sword, young lady?"

Aewyn looked down sheepishly. "I can't hold one without pain," she said. "And I've no desire to."

"Don't look at me, rebel," said Grimwulf. "I brought her this far. Where she goes now's not my concern."

"We're only going one place," said Odi, hauling up another bag of blossoms.

Elodia, hauling up the last sack before climbing aboard herself, tugged at his shoulder when she reached it.

"*Kul pabile serbek*," she whispered to her companion. He looked at Aewyn and shook his head no.

She nodded yes.

Odi sighed deeply. "How do you feel about freeing slaves?" he asked.

"Slaves?" Aewyn scrunched up her face slightly in confusion.

"Slaves," said Odi. "Prisoners. It's all the same, trust me. The Travalaithi criminals are transported to the mines. Sometimes for a fixed time, sometimes forever. Most don't last a year."

"I've known miners," said Aewyn. "It's hard work, and sometimes dangerous."

"Not miners like this, you haven't," said Odi. "Freed miners and prison miners are very different folk."

Aewyn thought at once of the miners she knew. She thought of T'ar Dzenkhalh, the boy called Fletch, whom the Havenari had saved from the mines for a time. She thought of Fen'din, who had served in a prison mine before and lived to tell of it, though it had destroyed his good health. She thought of Halgeir after that, who had bested her at the bow in the last Harvest Fair. There was nothing left of him, now, but the memory of the stink of blood in his cabin—and this time, instead of turning her stomach, the memory tightened her jaw with quiet anger.

"I want something from you," said Aewyn. "I want your word that my actions will not be taken as those of the Havenari."

"We'd swear you the Red Moon itself, if it would get us another friendly sword," said Odi.

"I can't hold a sword," Aewyn said. "But I am small and quiet. I can move without being seen, and I have no love of the Iron City or those who make it their home. If I can free these unfortunate souls for you, I will."

Odi and Elodia looked to each other and exchanged a few more whispered words in Selikhan.

"Let me speak to our commander," said Odi, and moved away toward the ship's sterncastle.

"It is dangerous work," Elodia warned her. "We can put to you a position that you will not have to kill. But we cannot put to you a promise you will not be killed yourself."

Grimwulf raised his eyebrows. "That's the most honest thing I've heard in a long while," he said. "Put me with your raiders, and I'll do what I can to see she gets ashore without getting dead."

Elodia nodded. "If you have the courage and the will also to fight for us, sir, you will have safe passage to the place of your choosing."

"It'd be courage," said Grimwulf, "if I wasn't sure I could handle myself. Alewives and carpenters who take up the sword, that's courage. For me, it's paying work, same as picking up a hammer and saw. There's finally a straight line now between me and freedom. That's what I like best. If the road is straight and the way is clear, I don't much care if it's an easy road or not."

"No complications, you mean," Elodia offered.

He nodded with admiration. "Exactly. No complications."

Odi returned from the sterncastle with two women. In the brightly coloured silks of an eastern trader, a stately, severe woman with the alien features of a pure-blooded aeril led a smaller, more graceful young woman who was armed and attired for battle.

"Providence to you, travelers," she pronounced. "I am Baran val-Veril. I am a principal of the Mage's Uprising and protector of the free provinces. I hear that you know what sort of ship you are seeking passage on, and where we are headed."

"They mean to help us," said Elodia. "And I believe them, though I would not put them in a position to hurt us if they lie."

"Certainly not," said Baran. "They will not join our fighting men."

"Perhaps if they were to free the prisoners," said Odi, "and wreck the tools."

"Yes!" said Baran. "That will do nicely. Have you names?"

"I am Aewyn," said Aewyn. "Of the Havenari of Haveïl, though my actions here are my own."

"Grimwulf, I suppose," said Grimwulf with some reservation.

Baran turned to her side. "Catrine, take these two belowdeck and see that they're prepared for what's to come."

"As you command."

Grimwulf tightened his mouth and narrowed his eyes.

"Catrine?" he asked.

"Yes, that's right," she said, oblivious to his thoughts.

She was small, delicate, and very well-shaped, in all the ways Rasten had been insufferably eager to describe. Her exquisite blonde hair was tied back from the wind, though it was dried and tangled some by the ravages of the winter sea. It was impossible to be sure, he decided, without provoking a line of questions he was in no mood to answer.

"No complications," Grimwulf muttered again as he bowed curtly and followed her into the belly of the ship.

"You had better be right about them," Baran whispered to Odi when they had passed from sight.

"Doesn't matter much," said Odi. "They have no way of warning Fingrun now that we've taken them on. Scouts say they were evading a quire of Grand Army cavalry when they came across our flower-picking party. I don't know much about her, though the Havenari are well-trained. But that man's a fighter. Easily worth two of three of our forgers and Widows in a fight."

"If he's on our side," said Baran.

"Everyone who gets off this boat is on our side," said Odi. "The Fingrun guards will hole up in their keep when they see they're outnumbered—but rest assured they'll loose arrows on whoever they can from the tower. If they're not our ally, they will be once the Grand Army sends a few arrows their way."

"They ought not to see us until we're beneath the cliffs," said Baran. "We hope to take them at the mines and at the keep at the same time."

Odi looked down at the sacks of cerulyns. "That's what the flowers are for."

Baran nodded. "You understand."

"Not at all. I mostly take your word for it. D'you get any of this wonder-weaving, Elodia?"

The taller woman shrugged. "On our side," she said. "Better than on theirs."

Odi nodded. "That's the long and the short of it."

"When the time comes," said Baran, "I'll be quite weak. To weave as I do, you must have a source. The cerulyns, where they grow wild, are still resonant with the energies of this world. These will help immensely with the work to come. But I'll need protection when the boat is moored. I want you to stay with me, Odi. I'll keep Catrine with us as well."

"That's a relief," Odi said with a smile. "You'll send all the others?"

"I lead the fighters to attack the keep," said Elodia. "Thirty soldiers we face, lightly armoured. Maybe not so much soldiers, if they fear enough for Orrath. They are well trained, but nearly two to one we will outnumber them. If we strike fast, and rely on our strength in numbers, they will retreat to the keep and hold it against us while they send for aid."

"You never meant for the weakest of us to fight."

"Oh, you'll fight," said Baran. "But we can't afford to lose you. The mines won't be completely undefended, though a few forgers, smugglers, and spies will be able to handle themselves if we can keep the reinforcements pinned down in the keep. Our second quire—including the new arrivals, I suppose— will come up the cliffside, take the foremen and overseers by surprise, and start putting weapons in the hands of the prisoners who'll fight for us. There's got to be fifty miners there with strength enough to fight. They're not worth a soldier, one-to-one, but they're one more advantage for us, one more hedge against the unexpected."

"Many will be in no condition to fight," warned Odi. "Many will be afraid."

"They will be fighting for their lives," said Baran. "Fear and desperation make for the worst fighters, and also the best."

"We're like to lose a few," Odi said. "We've got the stronger force, but things happen."

"Not you," said Baran. "And not me. Jordac says we are too important."

"You are," said Odi. "I'd believe that. As for me…"

"You make a difference," said Baran. "Jordac knows it. Not a feather stirs on the wing of a bird from his flock that he doesn't."

Odi turned the phrase over in his mind "Feather…flock…I'm too seasick for such things."

"Enjoy it," said Baran. "You'll be no happier when we make landfall."

Odi sighed and leaned over the railing, watching the rippling swell of the ocean as Elodia set about weighing anchor. It had been three years since he had seen her last: they had met by night in a rotted barn, in a hilltop village on the edge of the Verdant Wastes. The rich soil of the old karach graveyards proved surprisingly fertile, and it had been a spring of plenty for the villagers, who rightly feared the return of the Legions and had fed them well. But Elodia had been a frightened young woman then, thin-armed and poorly trained. But she was tall enough to wear the captured armour of the Travalaithi soldiers; and he could read and write, and stumble through the languages of the more exotic traders—and he had the look of a local, not only among the pale natives of the northern coast, but nearly anywhere he went. Their paths had been different ever since, and they had fought according to their own proficiencies.

Three years had made a beast out of her, he noted with admiration. She had filled out to lean muscle, and moved with the swagger of a veteran. Being thrown among the fighting men had made her loud and fierce and foul-mouthed, and a fine study with axe and spear besides. That was the kind of person he felt safe around, and he lamented that she would be fighting up at the keep while he made do with gentler, more delicate women on the cliffs below.

"Come help me," she ordered, and he went. In shallow water, she could easily turn the heavy capstan that raised the anchor on her own, but here at sea the length of chain beneath the water made the load many times heavier, and too much for any one man.

"You're an optimist," Odi grunted, but set his back to the work and began to budge the chain with her.

"You look worried," said Elodia. "Surely you will be the last to die."

Odi laughed so hard he nearly lost his grip. "I'd prefer you said I was least likely."

"We will do what we can," she said. "A few of us are strong fighters. The new fellow was a good find."

"I think so," said Odi. "These men are always desperate. He just wants a way from here. If he lives, perhaps Hormer will take him on when we're done with him."

"Perhaps," she said.

The load grew lighter as it came up and the chain left the water. When the anchor was at weigh, they both fell back, exhausted for the moment, and took their rest among the bags upon bags of cerulyns left on deck. Even with the sea breeze hitting the deck hard, their delicate perfume filled the air with a thick, robust, persistent scent. It was a scent of longing and insistence, and perhaps of hope, and though Odi's stomach was unsettled by the churning waves, they put him at ease.

"Magic flowers, hm?" he said. "That's where we've come to put our trust. Magic flowers."

"That is what she says," Elodia sighed. "I believe her."

"Do you have them down south?"

"No."

"Before they became flowers of mourning," said Odi, "before they became a symbol of peace beyond the grave… I think they were considered quite lucky. The poets used to have some pretty things to say about them."

"Perhaps they are still lucky," said Elodia.

Odi shrugged. "Not to the men laid to rest at Vairhurst. And not to the men who died fighting them."

Elodia sighed restlessly and stretched the tension out of her muscled shoulders. "To the women, then, perhaps."

"Here's hoping," said Odi. It's been a hard year for us all. It'd be nice if our luck held out a while, just this one time."

Elodia smiled. "My scouts reported two hundred men, almost the whole of Fingrun's defenses, headed south to reinforce Orrath four days ago. Is that not luck enough?"

Odi turned his thoughts to the fifty other men and women—fifty-two, counting the new arrivals—who were anxiously waiting for landfall and for the fighting to begin.

"Here's hoping," he said again, as he rapped the ship's deck with his knuckles for luck.

SIXTEEN

OLFERTH'S TRUEBLACKED ROBES were better at keeping out the light than the cold, and he shivered in the late evening chill as he made his way down the drafty cloister to the centre block of the Lornock citadel. Beneath the limestone and imported marble, beneath the palatial opulence of his own offices, beneath even the upper catacombs of the Imperial dungeon known for its restless hanging chains as the Rattle, the Chapel of Slaves still stood in mute unholy reverence to its absentee master. Like the Cîr-Valithar itself, the place was still suffused with Tamnor's essence and was so damp with his resonant malice that even Olferth, one of the most spiritually stunted men in the Iron City, could sense that some eldritch malevolence still burned in its walls of spotless black iron.

There were only two who dared to quarter in such a spiritually foul place, and with the Scourge away on campaign, he had only one reason left to come down to the depths. It was for Moriath alone he had come to the thorny iron gates of the profane inner sanctum, and not eagerly. But he came always at her call when the matter concerned Illyria, for the girl was more than an idle curiosity to him. She was a political tool, that much was to be sure, as all things and all people were political tools at need. But more than that she was a mystery to him, and one he hoped more earnestly to unravel with every passing year. He could not shake the feeling that many wrapped up in the girl's story—Ashimar himself, the old schoolmaster Osgrim, and especially Moriath, the old dowager Veritenh, knew more about the girl than he did. Among the many feelings he despised, the feeling that he was shut out from the truth about her was one he despised the most.

At the rap of his pale knuckles, an armoured figure appeared at the twisted subterranean gate, robed in crimson with a helm in the shape of a fanged adder's head. "Speak," the bloodguard said.

The Imperial Harper cleared his throat. "You know me. In the name of his Illustrious Majesty Valithar, I demand to speak with the Lady Moriath."

"She expected you some time ago," said the bloodguard, turning the tables on his command. Warily, he unbolted the iron gate and bowed curtly as the Imperial Harper crossed into the Chapel.

"Ruling over an empire is a busy affair," he said as his eyes adjusted to the dimness. "If it was so urgent, she ought to have come to me."

"I am certain her reasons are just," said the bloodguard.

He knew the way by heart now. Ashimar's chambers were on the right; Moriath's were on the left. And in the centre, upon the black wall none dared to look upon, an unbreakable image of Tamnor the Incarnate leered down at all who dared to enter. His sneering face was wreathed in shadow, glimmered in the fire, and too utterly sickening to stare upon for long, as was the seat of his throne, whose foundations where the tormented figures of men and women suffering unspeakable acts of vileness to their bodies and souls. Olferth shielded himself from the statuary as he might shield himself from a sun burning black instead of bright, and ducked hastily into Moriath's chambers without lingering too long before it or casting his eyes up in its direction.

"Gods, I hate this place," he spat. "You'd better have a fine reason for bringing me down here."

From the darkness, her voice answered. "Osgrim cannot hear what I have to tell you," she said. "This is the one place he will not listen."

"Osgrim?" he asked. "The schoolmaster?"

"You have quite forgotten him," she said. "You have forgotten who he is, or his spells have made you forget."

"I know that he was once the Purple Captain of the Stormguard," said Olferth. "But his spells must have faded along with theirs. I presume that is how he came to his office. I would appoint no schoolmaster as Magistrate, not even for Records and Lore, if a good soldier was available."

The sharp tapping of Moriath's cane preceded her arrival from the bedchamber.

"I would call you a fool," she said, "but this time you are no fool. Spells or no, he has an agenda of his own, and I cannot pierce his mysteries myself."

"He is a washed-up soldier become a washed-up historian," said Olferth dismissively, with such disregard that Moriath saw no use in pressing the matter.

"Most in the city, even on the Council, pay him no mind," said Moriath in spite of herself. "Even you seem to forget him. Why I do not, why he seems to have no power over my wits, is a mystery to me."

"Women's ways," said Olferth, impatient to be on with business.

"Perhaps," said Moriath. "But we have more pressing matters. Illyria is grown, now. Fifteen years old, and the flower of her youth will be upon her. Within the next white month."

"You believe her visions will return."

Moriath nodded. "Yes."

"Can't you do something?"

"I have done more than I should have dared to command those tides," said Moriath. "But even I cannot stop the passage of time. The spheres move where they will, and a woman's body is not a dog to be chained."

"Perhaps I could find a wiser midwife with a stronger chain," said Olferth; but she ignored his vanity.

"She will become harder to control if we let her," Moriath warned. "And so, in turn, will Ashimar."

"It is the way of girls that age to be unruly," said Olferth. "I have every faith you will keep her in line."

"How old were you," Moriath asked, "when first I brought Illyria's mother to the Travost? Twenty, perhaps? Althea was fourteen and already flowered. It was an unruly time, too. The betrothal did not suit her."

"These are not my concerns," snapped Olferth. "Keep them to yourself, but tell me of the visions."

"It is too soon to say much," said Moriath, "but you should be ready. In her cloistered innocence, far as I can see, she is connected only to Ashimar. But even that is enough. She has seen him fighting at great need in the west."

"The west?" Olferth asked. "But we have held every trace of the Uprising east of Carmac."

"Even so," said Moriath. "He will bide at Fingrun, northwest of his ancestral vasily. It is there he shall meet with the enemy."

"Impossible!" said Olferth. "Her visions told you that much?"

Moriath shook her head. "No. The bloodguards report to me, when they can. One reached a waystation a week ago when Ashimar sent him to report a bounty. They reached their destination, and are returning to us."

Olferth clenched his hands into fists. "Without Celithrand, no doubt."

"There was no trace of him."

Olferth thumped the iron wall in frustration. "Fools!" he roared.

"He cannot be allowed to escape."

"He will never press his claim to the Tower. And you know as well as I he would not run with Jordac's insurgents. He is an ancient, Olferth, born while the Baron-Kings still ruled Travost, within spitting distance of the True Kings themselves. The petty dynastic affairs of our Empire are probably well beneath him."

"Ancient or no, a stout noose would crack his neck as easily as any other," said Olferth. "Anyone who lives and dies as a man, however long he lingers, can have ambitions. Fears. Dangerous thoughts. And if his thoughts ever turned to dividing this Empire—"

"Don't steer into the ice while you're watching the stormclouds," Moriath warned. "We have an immediate problem at Fingrun. That is where Ashimar is headed, by the reckoning of his own men. And if the fog is lifting from Illyria's dreams, he may be in terrible danger."

Olferth's mouth tightened so hard that even his pasty cheeks began to flush with anger. "This is Mardon Black's fault," he said. "He demanded, *demanded* we reinforce the mines at Orrath when the maps and records were stolen."

"It seems he was tricked," said Moriath. "And Magistrate Black is no easy man to trick."

"How fast can we get a command order to the Scourge?"

Moriath shrugged. "I'm just an old woman. You'll have to ask someone in the Grand Army. But I venture they won't be fast enough. The time to strike us is now. Jordac must have known."

"The Legions of the Shield are ready to be emptied," said Olferth. "I can put five thousand men on the Iron Road by sundown."

"You might as well send five hundred," said Moriath. "If Jordac takes the mine, he will not hold it. He knows that as well as you—maybe better. No, he will sack it and move on, and those men will be wasted when he mounts another offensive in the east."

Olferth paced nearly back into the center hall of the Chapel; only his dread of the terrible statuary arrested him. Like a caged animal, he turned, paced, seethed.

"You are saying we've lost the mine already."

"No," said Moriath. "I'm saying its fate has been decided. The men we have at the mine—the overseers, the soldiers, the bloodguards—are all that we have. It's up to the Scourge now, and to the defenders."

She stroked her chin thoughtfully. Olferth's icy eyes darted back and forth as he considered his options.

"I'll send a thousand men," he said. "Two hundred fast riders, light lances, ahead of the others. The rear guard I'll send with tradesmen to do the rebuilding. If Ashimar triumphs or no, I imagine there'll be need of them."

Moriath nodded. "It will go best with us," she said, "if Ashimar knows to expect trouble."

"I thought you said no messenger could make the ride in time."

"None can," said Moriath. "A detailed warning is beyond our capability. But I have ways of putting him on alert."

"See to it," said Olferth.

Moriath was a woman without pretense to beauty or the need for gaudy adornments. The two of them left the Chapel of Slaves at once, with Olferth making the ascent to Lornock to coordinate the reinforcements as Moriath curled her way like a shadow up the long stair toward the Cîr-Valithar. She came first into the Black Forges, where below her the magistrates and their consorts took in the perfumed baths at ease. With a hard rap of her cane, she called the attention of one of the grubby domestic servants, a slow-shuffling craven who gazed deferently down at his feet as she turned him around with the crook end of the cane.

"M'lady," he breathed in a low voice.

"Bring me myrrh and lavender oil," she ordered.

Atop the winding stair, only a level or two below the Imperial throne room, the two karach standing guard shifted uneasily. The lone human stationed with them, a young veteran recently elevated to the Cerulean Guard, looked up from his half-sleep as they stirred.

"Something wrong?" he asked.

They sniffed the air and their lips curled back from their teeth.

"Moriath," one of them hissed. "We wait below. Join us when you unlock."

"Below?" the young Cerulean asked. "Are you sure that's wise?"

"Below," the second karach confirmed, flattening his ears. "This is a dark visit."

In the broad chamber, by the latticed window, Illyria was reading while there was daylight to read by. The cold stung her shoulders, and there was little heat in the winter sun, but the air outside did not smell wholly unpleasant, and the brightness of the light was a welcome companion when all others were gone.

She heard Heward's low, rolling bark from the hallway first, then the tapping of the cane. Glad for the company at first, she draped her gown higher over her shoulders and straightened her silver-blonde hair as best she could.

"Grandmother," she said, bright-eyed. "I'm so glad you've come."

Moriath crossed slowly from the inner gate to the anteroom to the chamber itself. "Guards," she snapped. From the closets and hidden chambers where they lay waiting, the silent bloodguards of the tower slipped into view.

"Leave us," the old woman ordered. "Bar the gates and take the dog out." She set about tending to the little oil lamps around the room as the bloodguard organized and stepped out.

"Grandmother, you—"

"You won't be glad," Moriath interrupted. "How are your dreams of late?"

"Troubled," the girl admitted.

Moriath busied herself with a phial of oil. "Tell me."

Illyria shut her book and carried it back to the shelf, as if to protect it from her words. "It was Rasten," she said. "I know you said I would forget him. But I have seen him again, almost with my waking eye. He was dancing with a child—no, with a man in red. The man, the handsome young man whose face is always red with tears."

"What else?"

"There was a monster," she said. "A great green monster whose gnashing teeth were jagged white rocks. A crocodile, maybe? But…something in the deep. The deep water, a deep beneath the deep."

She shuddered and turned back to the window, basking in what little light she could.

"And then?" Moriath asked, kindling the lamps.

Illyria shook her head, trembling. "It's too much. I only know what I saw…or thought I saw. My friend Rasten. He was hurt. I saw his blood, Grandmother. I saw—oh Gods, I saw him fall—"

"You disappoint me, Illyria," said the old woman. A ferocious scowl had carved itself into her haggard face. The deep lines beneath her eyes were trimmed with darkness.

"I—Grandmother, why?"

Moriath tilted her head sympathetically. "I told you to forget him, child," she said. "I told you what vile designs he had on you, what wicked and terrible things fill men's minds…"

Illyria stood to protest. "But n-never," she stammered, "never in the t-time I knew him… always he took such care… he was the timid one…"

Moriath crossed to the girl's side as the room behind her began to fill with the acrid smoke of burning oil and incense.

"Oh, my sweet duckling," she sighed, clutching Illyria and gently shaking her head. "My poor, poor child. Your weak heart has made you so very kind, and your kindness has made you so very weak. The grown man you thought was your friend—you cannot imagine half his cruelty. Not even with an imagination as powerful as yours. Those places are far too dark for a young girl's mind to go."

Illyria shook her head. "It can't be true," she began. He was a good—"

Her words trailed off as the scent of myrrh and lavender hit her, and stole the fight from her arms and her voice. She curled against her grandmother, who brushed at the wispy silver-blonde hair over her forehead.

"Grandmother, no, I'm sorry, please…"

"A good man, was he?" Moriath said, with a plaintive voice only slightly condescending. "A good man in your dreams, perhaps. But in the waking world? Child, you would not believe the things we unearthed when, praises to the Ten, we took him from you."

"In my dreams—"

"He killed a horse," Moriath spat out, straining to remember the report of the bloodguard sent on from Wescairn. "A beautiful mare."

Illyria shook her head. "No, that's impossible. He loves animals... he wouldn't."

"Beat it to death," said Moriath. "Furious. Roaring. He killed it, Illyria, he did. And left it in the field for others to see. Grandmother's family guards told her all about it. A nobler creature you would not find, child. He just chopped it up with his savage axe."

Illyria's face paled even more. "No," she begged. "He couldn't. He would never..." but even as she spoke, her voice seemed suddenly helpless and far away.

"Couldn't he?" she asked, watching Illyria's eyes as the truth wove itself into her story. "Haven't you seen such things? Haven't you dreamt of that, too?"

Illyria shook her head furiously and ground her fingers into her tangled hair.

"No... no... no..."

"Of course you have, my love. You've known all along. These boys go to war, and they come home... broken. Deranged. Bloodthirsty and unnatural." Illyria's words, wailed through a taut mouth, were unintelligible ouside the prison of her own mind.

"Fancied himself a poet, too, of the worst sort," said Moriath. "But never aspired to the great skalds of the north, did he? No, if only he could trick an innocent girl with his honeyed words, he was happy."

"Please—"

"And if he couldn't trick her, if he couldn't have his way through his lies and sweet words—well, he'd just take what he wanted, wouldn't he? Find a lovely young woman on the road, that was his way... bind her hands, carry her screaming through the snow..."

In her mind's eye, the girl was there, arms lashed behind her, screaming herself hoarse as a man in bloody armor—Rasten—hauled her to her feet. Rasten's gauntlet was bloody where he touched the girl's face with something like tenderness. She wanted to believe it was tenderness. But there was so much blood, and the side of the white-haired girl's face was already swollen shut.

"I'm sorry," Illyria whispered. "I'm sorry, I'm sorry, I'm sorry…"

"I suppose not every young girl cares for poetry, does she? The smart girls, the lovely rich girls with tutors and books in their palaces, maybe. But not the farm girls, the ones who couldn't read. Perhaps when you're older, I'll tell you the tricks he has for them."

"I'm sorry, I'm sorry," said Illyria, though the words had passed into mantra. They were sounds without meaning, now that the storm of denial was out of her.

Moriath sat close and held her tightly. "You are so very lucky, my sweet duckling. You are lucky your old Grandmother was looking out for you, then and always. You are so precious to me and to your father. And my eye is on you, every hour of every day. This could have been the end of you, my dear. Sometimes men want to hurt you because of who your father is, yes? You know this, yes? And always we catch them and keep you safe. Sometimes they do not wish to hurt you. It is simply the politics of their people, or the hurt of the war. But other times, wicked men are not redeemed by their politics or their agendas. Sometimes, they simply have foul designs, cruel appetites. And those men are harder to catch, and harder to stop. This was a very close call, child. The closest we've had."

Illyria shuddered and clutched her grandmother's shawl for comfort.

"I…I'm sorry. Really I am."

"It's all right," said Moriath. "It's all right. He's gone, now. All you're left with now is a harsh lesson to learn. After that, you'll be safe again."

"Help me, Grandmother. Help the nightmares go away."

"Roll up your right sleeve, dear."

Illyria did as she was told.

"And you'll forget all about your handsome young poet friend Rasten."

At the mention of his name, Illyria's stomach turned and she felt suddenly cold. The images in her mind's eye were fleeting, but there was no denying their truth.

"I will keep only the company you say, Grandmother."

"Good. Will you ever speak to the Ceruleans again?"

"No, Grandmother."

"Will you ever open the gate to an intruder again?"

"No, Grandmother."

"Those are the bricks and mortar of a happy life, child."

"Yes, Grandmother."

"Do you love me, Illyria?"

"Of course, Grandmother."

"Good." Moriath paused. "The punishment will not be light this time."

Rasten jolted awake suddenly, and was fully alert by the time his hand reached the haft of the axe leaned against his bed. It was his first real bed in some time, and just half a night in it had refreshed him more than he expected. The barracks at Fingrun Town, where the usual garrison slept, were the kind of quarters he was used to from his time on the frontier. Everything about it reminded him of a common soldier—not a pampered Cerulean elite guardsman, not a bloodthirsty and hardened member of the Scourge's retinue. It was nothing to complain about—and with growing cynicism, Rasten knew that meant it could not last forever.

He did not expect, however, to be awakened by the sound of two of his unlikely companions throwing on their armour in the middle of the night. Already attired for axe-work, the mantis-headed bloodguard was helping Astagar into his armour, securing outer plates over the mail and clutching his antlered helm with measured discipline.

"What's going on?" Rasten asked.

"Hush," said Astagar. "Listen."

It was the first time he had heard the Weeping Man weep. From the hallway, through the banded door of the captain's chambers, a man's voice wracked with sobs seemed so far away from the icy composure of the Imperial Scourge that he could hardly recognize it for Ashimar's. But there could be no mistake: the seemingly heartless Scourge had unlocked his emotions at last—and Rasten was at once nostalgic for the impassive, unfeeling statue he had come to know over the past few weeks.

"That's unsettling," he said.

"It usually means trouble," said the mantis-headed bloodguard. "You should get your armour on."

Reluctantly, Rasten wiped the sleep from his eyes and threw his legs over the side of the bed, forcing himself to rise. His shoulders were broad, his arms were not overlong, and it was a hard struggle wriggling back into the layers of his armour with none of the other bloodguard offering to help him. It was a misshapen mess, half-strapped on, when the door swung open and Ashimar emerged, fully armed and moving with deadly purpose.

"Everything all right, my lord?" asked Astagar.

"Arm yourselves," said Ashimar, with no mind to the fact that his men were already reaching for their helmets and buckling them into place.

"Trouble?" Rasten asked anxiously.

"You tell me," said Ashimar. "You have just spent the better part of your night in an abandoned barrack."

"It's hardly derelict," said Rasten. "The men headed for Orrath have only been gone—ah, and you mean to follow them to the fight?"

"The fight will come to us," warned Ashimar.

The bloodguard buckled their sword-belts as Ashimar made for the door.

"Meet me at the foot of the keep stair as soon as you are ready," he ordered. "You, Rasten, with me."

As he crossed the yard in Ashimar's shadow, hastening from the low-walled town barracks to the towering keep, Rasten wondered whether he was singled out because he was slowly endearing himself to the Scourge, or because he had proven almost fatally untrustworthy. He found himself thinking of the girl who had fled with Kellan, wondering if he had indeed bought her freedom, and whether that could ever repay her for the treatment she had suffered under his scheming. Coming up with a plan was not hard, he realized; it was ensuring the plan had no unforeseen consequences that eluded him entirely. He wondered where Kellan was now, and where Catrine was, and whether his old room in the Storm Quarter still smelled of her perfume. He did not know if she stll lived there, or if she had given him up for dead and found comfort in the arms of a new lover. If word had reached her of the company he kept and his reasons for going, giving him up for dead would certainly have been the safer bet.

Ashimar's knock at the high door of the keep was viciously hard and loud, but the gate-warden was slow in coming. The Scourge's knock carried no extra weight, Rasten realized, when those on the other side could not see him or know him from any of the other night visitors. Upon revealing himself at the door, however, the gate-warden led them in hastily, offered them wine, and warned the Scourge that the Overseer was already retired to his chamber for the night.

"Take us there at once," said Ashimar.

Rasten could tell the gate-warden meant to refuse him, meant to insist that the Overseer was asleep and that the matter could wait till morning. But instead the man's jaw worked itself emptily with no words of protest. Drawing back from the door, he admitted them at once and led the way up the keep's winding stair by the light of a flickering taper.

Rendon's chamber door was of stout Nalsian oak and could have withstood a heavy assault, but it was not barred against entry and resisted them only as far as its natural weight would allow. A candle still burned here, too, and Rasten was surprised to see the one-armed Overseer sitting awake at his desk before a plate of white ash. He had been burning something, Rasten realized—though the last page of it was alive in his hand. He stood quickly enough to stir the flame, and the orange candle-light danced angrily across his severe features from below.

"What is the meaning—ah, my lord, uh, Your Dread, what brings you to my door at this hour of the night?"

"The dawn is nearly upon us," said Ashimar. "Wake your garrison—what is left of it. Send your archers to the parapet, heat some pitch for them. Send me your spearmen and heavy infantry, if you have any. The keep wall is too low, but we will make do."

"My lord?"

"Your keep is under attack," said Ashimar. "They will come with the dawn."

Rendon hastily set the last page of his letter to the candle-flame, then moved to his mail-coat and purple tabard, which were polished on a stand by the foot of his bed, clean and unmarked in its perpetual disuse.

"I'll need help," he said, and at the Scourge's nod, Rasten rushed to ready him.

"Call the men as soon as you are ready," said Ashimar.

"What's happening?" Rendon asked, though he did not wait for an answer before complying.

Ashimar rubbed his right gauntlet thoughtfully with his free hand as Rendon readied himself.

"There is trouble approaching," said Ashimar. "It comes from the northeast, and comes with the dawn. Given the sorry state of your garrison, and your empty barracks, I presume you are about to be raided by an adversary who knows of your weakness."

"Northeast is by water," Rendon said. "There must be some mistake. They can't hurt us from the water, not up here, not with half the fleet."

"I know not the nature of the threat," said Ashimar, "save that it comes with the burning light of day. Against this terrain, I expect they will make landfall and send a ground assault up the cliffs."

"Footmen?" Rendon asked. "No horse can make that climb. Footmen we can handle. We have rations for a year, with a full garrison. With our reduced numbers, even counting Your Dread's men, we'll survive any siege until Travalaith sends one of the Legions.

"Besieging you is not their plan," said Ashimar. "Your keep can protect your people, but it cannot protect the mines. They mean to lay waste to the mines, break your machines, free your prisoners and bring them to the Uprising."

At that, Rendon's face was a mask of conflicting emotions.

"We will make ready as you say."

"Make haste," said Ashimar. "Keep only those men you need to defend your gate. The rest will be useless to you if they are caught by surprise within the walls.

Rasten was not well-loved among the men, but he asserted command more forcefully than usual in a bid to conceal the fear behind his wild eyes. There was no mistaking who had truly given the order to arm, and as the dawn approached and the sea to the northeast changed from moon-glistening black to a broader wine-dark colour under a hastily brightening sky.

Stout spears of linden-wood were raised as the men rushed to the low keep wall, and the heavy shields they carried were locked against one another's iron-banded edges and laid behind the wall to be taken up quickly. Tannock, who was late roused and slow to rise, made great complaint to Rendon that the word of the Scourge could not be trusted, and they had too few men for a proper shield-wall besides; but the Overseer would not listen. He was too shaken by Ashimar's commanding presence, and by the renewal of a grisly war he thought he had left behind him. By the time he came down to oversee the strength of the wall and give his customary speech to the men, as his marshal had done to him on the fields beneath the Danhorn, he had his sword strapped awkwardly behind him to facilitate drawing it with his remaining hand. Tannock did not know if he could still fight one-handed. Perhaps Rendon did not know, either.

Stationed at the foot of the keep stair, well back from the shield-wall, Rasten listened with divided intent to both Rendon's uninspiring battle-speech and Ashimar's instructions to the Bloodguard. Surprisingly, the Scourge was thoroughly distracted, clutching repeatedly at his forearm as if already wounded, and even delegating some of the strategy to the senior bloodguard.

There was briefly some talk of manning the cliffs themselves, and making use of the higher ground to counter-ambush the landing party. But it was decided, in the end, that they knew not whether they stood against a hundred men or a thousand, or more: for that reason, Ashimar ordered them to wait just inside the open mine shafts, both to protect against a prisoner revolt at the first sign of outside struggle, and to emerge once the insurrectionists had advanced on the keep and take them from behind. If the force was small, they could be surrounded and wiped out; if the force was so large that the garrison could not defeat it even with the bloodguard's help, it would be too large to feed easily. Ashimar meant to make for their ships, sail them back to the *Providence*, and scuttle them among the rocks. If they were spoiling for a fight when they landed, they would not make the climb with their provisions: separating them from their ships, he decided, would cut off a large force's supplies and means of transport. The survivors might take the mine, or the town, or both, but with months of winter still ahead they would starve for it.

Rasten understood the principles of the defense, but had no real knack for battlefield tactics. He knew as well as any veteran that Ashimar's plan would be foolproof until the first arrow was loosed. After that, it was all up to the whims of Kedwyn, for better or worse. What pleased him the most, though, is that in his mind's eye he could see them rushing up the hill toward him, axe-wielding Esmen and hordes of savage Selikhan radicals, just as it was in his dreams of Jalen. He loved and missed his brother, and the perfect beauty of standing back to back with him like a single, unstoppable four-armed warrior.

But that four-armed warrior had been wounded, and the wound had turned to rot, and the rot had turned to a cold and unforgiving memory stone on lonely and windswept Vairhurst, forever wreathed with rotting violets and words of love shared only too late. Jalen was above all things forgiving, and in the space between their clashes with the enemy he had been kind beyond the measure of most men. But he was no master-at-arms, and in his mind it was Ashimar at his back now—a tireless, peerless killer in unbreakable armour, as indifferent to pain and fatigue as to mercy. His thoughts turned again, against his will, to Catrine, and to the hope that he might one day see her and touch her again, not among the peaceful clovers of the Evermead that awaited the war-spent after death, but here in the real, visceral, sweet-smelling realm of the living. He missed her now above all things, and though he longed for the companionship of his brother, he was glad for the company of the monster at his back.

The sky in the east was already burning with the light of the Three Maidens: streaks of deep azure, violet, and simmering deep scarlet adorned the far horizon like the makeup of an Eastern bride awaiting her suitor. The shelters housing the prisoners were emptied, and the bloodguards led those suited to mining deep into the shafts. A single guide from among Rendon's men came to unchain them and bind their manacles together to prevent revolt. A few who had seen combat in the east knew immediately what was about to happen, but the fearsome presence of the Red Captain kept them in line. As daybreak approached, Ashimar parted company with his men and ascended to the mouth of the central cave, which opened onto a narrow and treacherous path skirting the cliff's edge. Below him, the thundering sea churned and pounded against the jagged white rocks as the contrary moons, opposed in their first and last halves, fought bitterly over control of the tides. A heavy mist lay upon the water to the northeast; to the true east, the fens of Haukmere that stretched to the red horizon were grey and shadowed beneath the rolling fog. Clutching his sword-arm, willing away the searing pain that lingered in the skin and flesh, he watched the horizon in perfect stillness and silence.

"Show yourself," he said breathlessly. "Come to me."

The sun exploded over the horizon in a burst of golden light, and a searing yellow glow spilled across the red curtain of twilight and into the sky. The fens and wetlands of Haukmere gleamed in answer, shining white-hot beneath the sun as it cut through the mist and poured its rays across the flood plain. Only on the water, upon the cool grey skin of the open sea, did that light fail to penetrate. The fog was thick there, and the coastal birds wheeled away from it warily as it rolled forward over the waves, billowing gently toward the coast against the current of the wind.

Behind and far above him, the high parapet of the Fingrun keep was crowned with keen-eyed archers standing lookout over the land, the sea, the cliffs and trees. They too leaned out between the crenellations and watched as the weather changed—but there was no ship to be seen, no raiding party to espy. As the dawn broke and the sky lightened, the mists finally cleared, and the lookouts at last confirmed to one another that no enemies were coming after all.

Then, in the blinding brightness of the morning sun, as if from out of a dream, they came.

SEVENTEEN

ELODIA'S POWERFUL LEGS PLUNGED into the saltwater as she leapt over the railing. The water was deeper than expected, but she slipped into the water silently, gritting her teeth as the cold of the sea shot to her waist.

"Three feet," she warned. "Hold aboard."

The Adâni ship cut through the churning waves, nearly scraping its keel as it tore close to the bank. But Hormer, its captain, coaxed the hull nimbly through the shallows, and shouted heartily to the men, for his words seemed far away and all but lost in the roiling fog. With the rocking motion of the ship, he leapt to and fro across the deck and guided his crew with a firm hand on their shoulders and gentle words against their ears. He was an unproven warrior, but a seasoned sailor and navigator; he had taken off his boots, perhaps superstitiously, and claimed he could feel the waves and counterwaves against the rocks and sea-bottom through the calloused soles of his bare feet.

He took care not to circle too close to Baran, who stood squarely on the quarterdeck between two smoking braziers of cerulyn blossoms. The coiling blue-grey smoke that poured up and over the rim of the braziers hung thick over the deck, filling the air with a heady and powerful scent that was much transformed from the delicate scent of the unburnt flowers. Jordac's navy, such as they were, rubbed at their eyes and tried not to cough too loudly in the smoke as they waited for Elodia's order. They wore patchwork armour of leather and mail, and stood on deck in a ragged row. There were only a few more men than women; the war had taken its toll on the fighting men in the east, and many of the women were draped in heavy mail-coats that belonged to the men of the family who had gone before them. The Grand Army had disallowed women for as long as they could remember; the scattered forces in Selik had done the same until the first generation of them were dead, and Jordac had come to command the scattered remnants of the Selikhan militia groups with hard eyes and an open mind.

Behind the line of earnest young warrior women, the man called Grimwulf stood impassively a head above them, staring into the smoke. Behind the broad-shouldered men, Aewyn stretched high on her toes a she peered into the mist, hoping to catch at least a glimpse of the majestic white cliffs of Fingrun before the shore was upon them.

The ship scraped hard against a jagged white rock, but its hull held true. Angrily, desperately, Hormer leaned over the side of the boat to Elodia, who had waded in to shore.

"It's as close as she comes," he called. "Now, or not at all."

"Now," Elodia called back. "*Isn'à Yerdach! Isnik huryett!*"

"*Isnik huryett*," the raiders answered, though they were too prudent to shout it. One by one, as quietly as possible, they plunged into the shallows.

"That's 'go,' I suppose," said Grimwulf, squirming uncomfortably in his borrowed, ill-sized armour of boiled leather, wishing now he had kept his bloodguard's armour or at least his helm.

"It means 'for freedom,' sir," said one of the insurgents as he followed his comrades into the water.

"Freedom," said Grimwulf, nodding with raised eyebrows. "That's what they call this." But he drew his sword in spite of himself and looked down to the young woman at his side.

"There they go," he said. "There's time yet to change your mind, if you've the stomach for a doublecross."

"For freedom," she said, and leapt down into the waves.

"To every hell with it," sneered Grimwulf, following.

The water where they landed was cold and silty as the churning tides stirred up the sand that lay along the sea bottom and between the jagged white rocks that erupted here and there in the water. The drop-off was steep, or Hormer would not have been able to bring his ship all the way in, but above the rocks it was a steady march of sixty feet or more to dry land. The raiders moved as quickly as they dared, trying not to stir the surface of the water, unsure if the mist that protected the ship would still guard them. The beach reached inland only a dozen feet or so before the climb, but it was better than the cliff surrounding Fingrun itself, which jutted straight down, or even retrograde, to the water without even a pretence to beach or shoreline.

"Climb here," Elodia ordered as the vanguard reached the white rock and began their ascent. The grade was steep and the way perilous, and many looked longingly at the lazy path that extended down almost to the sand. But it was more likely to be patrolled, and was a longer road to the keep by way of the town. If the surveys held true, there was a second path extending up from a low plateau that would take them up to the mines themselves. But coming that way without alerting the mine guards would take all the silence they could muster, and the first part of the climb was not easy going.

The path appeared behind a line of chalky scrub as if out of thin air. It was well-hidden from the sea and from the beach, and they had come by it only on faith. But Elodia waited until they had mustered on the narrow path before making her final speech.

"Straight up hence, to the high fork," she said. "The fork may be marked, or it may not. Siege team up and to the left, rescue team down to the right. Siege team, keep your shields high. Make straight for the tower and seal that door. Brace it any way you can. If there's any resistance outside the tower, don't stop for it. Proceed to the objective quick as you can. The support team and I will be right behind you as quick as we can. Leave them to us. Concentrate on sealing the main garrison within that tower. Leave the fighting to us until the deed is done."

In near-silence, Elodia led the main raiding party forward and upward. Grimwulf and Aewyn left her company at the fork, and came down toward the mining tunnels with the rescue team. They were about halfway down the gentle slope of the mining path before Grimwulf's nerves began to stand on end.

"There's eyes on us," he warned, looking upward to the cliff top. "Can't say whose."

One of the rescuers taking point beside him, a spindly man in patchwork armour, redirected his eyes to the path ahead with the point of his sword.

"Leave those eyes to the siege team," he said. "Focus on our objective."

The path to the mining tunnels bored into the cliffside widened where another trail joined it, but never to a comfortable width. Two heavy ruts had been riven in the dirt where mine-carts loaded with iron ore hand been hauled out and up from the mines for many years, but the paths could not even accommodate a horse abreast. Here and there, wooden posts were sunk into the earth around which tow ropes might have been routed, but the operation of the mine was a precarious mystery. The iron was sunk deep here, and going in at the cliffside must have been faster and easier, if more dangerous, than excavating from the earth high above. Grimwulf puzzled at how the operation could possibly have been made safe, until he realized it wasn't.

"Get in," he breathed. "Get out. As quickly as possible. No complications."

He rounded a bend in the cliffside trail to find himself staring down the length of Ashimar's greatsword to his terrible, weeping face.

In utter surprise, in abject terror, he laughed. Even his foulest cursewords eluded him.

"Right," he breathed at last, and struck.

It was to his advantage that Ashimar, who was prepared for the advance of nearly any adversary, was just as surprised to see his old recruit again. Unready for Grimwulf's brutality, but aware of it, he gave the first ground, jerking his heavy sword high to block Grimwulf's reckless lunge, then down before he could counterattack to swat aside the vicious kick that followed it. He thrust in with the point of his sword, but the big man's fine blade—a bloodguard's blade, he realized—swung down to parry, then darted in before he could defend.

Rocking on his heels, Ashimar leaned into the blows, taking the sword-edge on his forearms and shoulders, angling its thrusting point to where his plates were strongest. Levering the heavy sword down, gripping the blade in his hands, he pinned Grimwulf's sword beneath the parrying hooks and clubbed him hard in the head with the pommeled hilt.

Grimwulf stumbled, but stumbled forward, and threw his weight against the tangle of swords. His shoulder, which was armoured well enough, he shoved against the sharp edge of Ashimar's blade, and with a desperate surge of his arms he threw the smaller man backward before disengaging.

"Back," he ordered. "Back!"

The raiders coming up behind him had perceived instantly that someone was opposing them, but had not yet guessed at the level of dnager that faced them. One of them rushed past Grimwulf on his back side, skirting the cliff edge to land a hard thrust of his spear, but it clanged ineffectually off the side of Ashimar's great helm. Although the Scourge had little room on the narrow trail to swing a weapon of unusual size, there was nothing but open air on his left, where they stood suspended over the rocks. In an instant, the greatsword flashed out to its full length, cutting a wide and bloody arc in the air as the spearman's face was opened to the wind. He went down clutching his face, and as Grimwulf retreated and Ashimar advanced, a hard kick to the shoulder was all it took to send him over the edge. The rocks below, mercifully, put an end to his screams before they could sap the morale of the others.

"Back!" Grimwulf ordered again, and this time the others complied.

The easy death of a raider on the rocks gave everyone, Ashimar included, a healthy respect for the narrowness of the path and the sheerness of the drop at their side. They fell back to where the mine path joined a second trail, where there was a little room to stand and fight. Ashimar gripped the hilt of his long weapon with both hands, glad for the room to swing it, and the trail behind him filled out with more bloodguards stirred by the sounds of fighting.

"Aw shit," muttered Grimwulf, having found his words again. Above them, at the top of the cliff, Elodia held her team cautiously in place as they made ready with pitch and flame to block the keep's gate and smoke the soldiers within who might try to break their barricade. Then, with shields held high to defend from arrows above, they advanced with speed and purpose. The archers crowning the keep were massed on its east side, looking out to the cliffs and readying their bows. It was the ideal time to strike.

"Move," called Elodia, and they crossed the grass to the foot of the keep stair.

A cry of alarm went up as the first of them crossed the threshold of the ruined wall. A line of troops crouched in the shadow of that low wall rose at their flanks and came forward with spears at the ready. Turning on their heels, the rear guard became the van, and the little unit tightened their formation against the defenders, who rapidly locked shields and began to rout them toward the wall of the keep with menacing thrusts of their spears. Now at their rear instead of their front, Elodia looked back to the keep door in time to see it open as a second string of Travalaithi soldiers began to pour down the steps toward her.

"Defensive formation!" she called, and their attack plan was broken.

The raiders below were never meant for an assault, and lacked the discipline of Elodia's team: they were likewise forced into a defensive circle, but the gaps in their ranks only swelled as Ashimar's whirling greatsword cut in again and again. At his side, a half-dozen bloodguards had fanned out to pin down the rebels, and their superior equipment and technique more than made up for the rebels' strength in numbers. Those who knew Ashimar by description or by rumour knew, too, his value as a prized target, and moved to fight him as Grimwulf, who knew him by skill, wisely disentangled himself and engaged the other bloodguards. His former companions had been well-trained, but travel with Ashimar had in some ways made them soft: weeks on the road had made them weary, and a life of murder was no substitute for a life of battle. Eager for Grimwulf's blood, they came to him, but found him unwilling to shed it, and with a rage to match their own he beat at their blades, circled to where they could barely see him in their heavy helms, and by determination and spite he managed to put his sword clean through one, landing its point at the armpit of his cuirass and shoving in so hard that the blade bent once, twice, then punched through the mail beneath.

A hostile sword like his own lunged in and Grimwulf had to let go his weapon to save his skin. The blade had punched fatally through the mail and the ribcage beneath it, but drawing it free again was another matter entirely. Disarmed and flailing against the others, he reached back desperately.

"I'm unarmed," he shouted. "Give me something!"

Grimwulf slipped a deadly thrust and had to push the bloodguard back to block a swing from his companion. His mailed fist landed an explosive hook to the mantis-headed helmet, but he felt his knuckles split beneath the mail as the helm took the brunt of the assault.

From the centre of their defensive circle, where she had been striking over shoulders and under legs, Aewyn handed up the heavy spear they had given her—the only weapon she could bear to hold.

"Take it!" she cried. She had to shout it twice to be heard over the scream of the man at her shoulder as Ashimar's greatsword took his arm on the first swipe and circled back to open his stomach on the second.

"We can't stay here," one of the raiders shouted as his companion fell. "We need the miners!"

"Tighten up," Grimwulf shouted back. Ashimar's greatsword swung down into the man at his side so fiercely that Grimwulf's cheek was stung by a shattered link of rusted chainmail as he looked back.

"Give me the weapons," said Aewyn. "The weapons and the key."

"We've got one key," one of the raiders shouted back. "*One.*" But the momentary distraction cost him his concentration, and the stag-headed bloodguard claimed an eye with one vicious, twisting headbutt of his antlered helm. The raider reeled, screaming, but kept his footing and pushed back hard to keep their defensive circle from imploding.

"My belt!" he screamed. "It's on my belt!"

Aewyn looked for it, spotted it, circled him. A bloodguard's sword leapt in and cut him deep, and he began to fall.

"Grimwulf!" Aewyn cried as she went down after the body. "I need cover!"

The big man stepped to her side, thrusting his spear into the throat of the stag-headed bloodguard. Its point did not penetrate the armour, but the force of the blow sent him backward, reeling and choking.

"You'll get yourself killed," Grimwulf warned. But she knelt at the body's side as it fell, and her little obsidian knife flashed out, sawing at his belt where a heavy brass key was suspended on a chain.

Grimwulf's eyes darted between the tiny knife in her hands and the greatsword that wheeled and spun on its right. He saw a woman's arm fold unnaturally under Ashimar's greatsword as she parried it, saw her transfer her blade to her other hand as she continued to oppose him. He wondered if he could reach her in time, but knew he could not.

"Can you go over them?" he asked. "If I spring you?"

"I can try," said Aewyn. She stripped the key off the dead man's belt and shouldered a heavy peddlar's sack.

Grimwulf chanced a glance back at her and tapped the butt of his spear. "Get ready," he said.

The wait was interminable as the stag-headed bloodguard, Astagar, came in with renewed fury and a thirst for vengeance. Between the spear and his natural height, Grimwulf's reach advantage was supreme, but it was a defensive advantage and he could not take the time he needed. With impatience and frustration, he steeled himself and let a swing come through, taking it on the ribcage with a grunt of pain. He felt a rib give out under the force, felt the rings of his mail-coat split but not shatter as the blade swung home; and as he locked the blade down with his arm, he turned it so that only its flat lay against his exposed flesh. With his free arm, he shoved the spear-point under Astagar's helm and shoved hard—again, it did not penetrate, but the force of it sent the bloodguard sprawling backwards. In the instant before the circle closed in again, he leaned back and planted the butt of his spear against the blood-soaked earth.

"Here," he said, wrenching the spear shaft upward almost immediately.

Aewyn gripped her sack tightly in both hands as she set both feet on the end of the spear. Like most of the raiders' weapons, it was crudely made, but the awkward thickness of it helped it support her weight without bending as a finer weapon would have. With one smooth, powerful motion, as if launching a shovel full of rocks or coal, Grimwulf heaved the spear upward and outward, and Aewyn leapt from it with all the force she could muster as the weapon neared the top of its travel.

What ought to have been graceful was tremendously clumsy as she kicked and coiled herself to be clear of the flashing weapons below her. But none of the bloodguards had quite expected her to wind up where she was, and in an instant she was past them, first trying to grip the cliff wall above, then rolling helplessly down its edge, then scrabbling to save herself from going over the side of the path altogether. But she found herself tumbling to a halt on bruised knees on the far side of the bloodguards, and as the first of them turned in surprise she was off and running.

At the edge of her vision, she saw Ashimar turn to track her, saw him signal to one of his men. It was not much, but it was all she needed to see. Heedless of her impressive vault, heedless of the ache in her joints and especially her weak leg, she sprang for the cave mouth with all the speed she could summon. Over the fading sounds of battle, she could hear the footsteps of pursuit that did not diminish with distance, and sprinted until her breath was ragged and painful, then kept on until the mine was upon her. Whether she truly leapt or lost her footing was a question for the gods, but she slid into the cave mouth on one leg with a cloud of dust behind her and raced downward into the darkness.

Catrine frowned in anger and dismay as the din of battle erupted from the cliffs above them.

"They're in trouble," she said. "Something's gone wrong."

Odi looked down to the dazed aeril lying weakly on the deck. At the moment of Baran's collapse, he had caught her and dragged her away from the noxious smoke of the burning cerulyns, piled the burlap sacks behind her head, and made her comfortable as he awaited word of the easy victory they had anticipated. But his orders began and ended with keeping her safe—and Hormer's began and ended with piloting them near enough to the the cliffs to make landfall. Odi did not know what price could persuade him to wait out the battle and flee with the survivors, if any—but it was more than he had in his purse.

"We can't stay," he said. "Not with her in this state."

Catrine glanced back at him angrily. "This is hostile country, and reinforcements are never far. If we pull out now, those people are all dead."

Odi nodded. "I know they are." He cast his eyes to the cliffside. "From the sounds of it, our waiting here isn't going to change that."

At his feet, Baran groaned softly. "What's happening?"

Catrine knelt beside her. "We don't know. It sounds like there's hard fighting."

Baran tried to sit up. The mist still curled around the boat, shrouding it from view.

"That's outside," she breathed, listening to the screams and clashes of steel. "We failed to keep them in the tower."

"Sounds that way," said Odi. "They're having a hard time of it. We fear they may be lost."

"Get me up," said Baran. "I'm weak. I don't know that I can make the climb on my own."

"Out of the question," said Odi. "We've lost too many. I'm not about to explain to Jordac that we lost you."

Baran's eyes, even in her weakness, were daggers of ice. "Then you can explain to him how you disobeyed me," she said.

Odi sighed and lifted her to a sitting position.

"Obeyed with protest," he corrected. "Obeyed very faithfully, but only after protest much and loud, and against my better judgment and my every instinct as a spy."

"That'll do," said Baran softly. "Catrine, help him."

Odi half-expected moving a living body to be as hard as moving a dead one, and was pleasantly surprised. Baran still had her wits and some measure of strength; she was lighter than expected, and Catrine was in fine shape for her small size and carried her share of the load admirably. It was easy going with her, even on the difficult slope, which pleased Odi immensely until he remembered with disdain where they were headed.

"We're going to die," he sighed. "We're no fighters. Our place is not in the fray."

"Speak for yourself," said Catrine. "I've trained for this a long time."

"Thought you'd fallen in love with the enemy," Odi said with a grunt of exertion, heaving Baran roughly over a rocky outcropping onto the main trail.

"One man," Catrine retorted. "Just one, in the whole Travalaithi Empire. The rest, I've been waiting for years to put a sword through."

"My aim was to be such a good spy that I didn't *need* a sword," said Odi.

"Ease off, both of you," ordered Baran. "I need to concentrate." She was helping them now where she could, though her legs would not yet take her full weight.

Odi tilted the aeril's head up so she could see the fight as they crested the cliff's edge. The raiders, caught unaware and pinned between the keep and its surrounding wall, were losing ground where they could, and losing lives where there was no more ground to give. Surrounded on all sides, they had adopted a makeshift, clumsy tortoise formation: the few shields they had were angled upward against that rained down from the roof of the keep. At first the Travalaithi archers were reluctant to loose on them, fearful of hitting their own men, but as the lines solidified and the raiders were penned in, a central mass of the enemy became more clearly defined and they began to empty their quivers on the men and women below. At Baran's direction, Odi and Catrine mounted a white, stony hill that would give them the high ground against footmen, though it put her in the open against the archers.

"Stand me up," Baran said.

Catrine and Odi hoisted her to her feet.

"What are you going to do?" asked Catrine.

Baran sighed with effort. "Something very vulgar," she said.

With her arms outstretched and palms splayed, the magic came. The jewelled pendant that rested against her breastbone flared brightly; one by one, the falling arrows shot down from the tower sparked and caught fire, blazing with an eerie blue flame—then swerved outward to the edge of the battle, taking the Grand Army soldiers in the heads and arms. Their cries of agony were shot through with anger as they cursed their own men for loosing so recklessly—then, as the hail of blazing arrows continued to harry them, cries of betrayal arose along with the shouts of pain.

A few quick-thinking archers realized what was happening as soon as it happened, and held their bowshots. One or two even began looking for the offending mage. But the rest were slow to react and slow to cease their assault, and a second volley, then a third, plunged down into the Travalaithi soldiers. Baran was not hard to spot on a high hill, and one of the archers squinted away the sun as he nocked and loosed on her. But his arrow too, burst into flame at a downward wave of her hand and arced straight downward into the shield-wall of confused Travalaithi soldiers, punching through a soldier's mail-coat with enough force to leave a shallow wound in his shoulder.

The raiders, hard pressed and in sore need of a sudden advantage, did not waste the opportunity of the Grand Army's momentary distraction. Held at bay until now by the coordinated thrusts of Travalaithi spears, Elodia slipped at last past the deadly spear-points in the moment of confusion and came upon the first row of spearmen with her wickedly curved Selikhan sabre, darting over their guard and striping their necks and shoulders with precise cuts that bled hard, but not hard enough. Even in their momentary disorder, the Travalaithi armour held true and would not be cloven by her one-handed strikes. With some reluctance she let go the sabre and went for the mace at her belt, and armour or no, the front lines troubled her no more. Some were still reaching for their daggers when they fell to the earth with crushed arms and legs, only to be finished by the arrows that descended from above. Where Elodia pushed, the wall was made weak, and where it was made weak the men and women rallied and began, with toil and a great deal of blood, to fight their way free of the deadly pincer.

Cries of "Mage! Mage!" had begun to erupt from the soldiers, which had the effect of nothing but the ruination of their tactics. More than a few still recalled the massacre at the Danhorn in a field of fire, and had come to the far frontier precisely to avoid it. Frustrated at last by the failure of their only weapon, the archers on the keep's roof put up their bows and squatted down behind the crenellations, eager not to be burned alive themselves. As their rain of arrows abated, Baran swooned and collapsed into the waiting arms of her companions. Through the sweat and the sheen of her pale skin, her veins could be seen burning brightly as she fell.

"Hold me up," she breathed. "Let them think I maintain the—"

She passed into shocked silence and said no more.

Rendon strained to hear the screams of the soldiers as he struggled mightily with his sword-belt. At first he had thought himself claver, but it had betrayed him on the first draw, and he figured he might as well go without it.

"What are they saying?" he demanded.

Tannock leaned out at the keep window, listening hard. Then, in spite of the Overseer's pride, he came to unbuckle Rendon's scabbard with some haste.

"I think they're crying 'Mage,'" said Tannock. "You should not go, my lord."

Rendon's stomach, at least, agreed with him. But he tested the weight of his naked sword: it was ungainly, but quick enough.

"You would have me hide in my tower while my men burn?"

"That is the way of lords," said Tannock, with neither doubt nor resentment. "I am your commander. The place on the field should be mine."

"There is no *place* on the field," said Rendon. "And in the fighting I'm not your better, or the better of any whole man. Ranks and badges and pretty cloaks are for parades, and maybe for meetings in the command tent the day before. When the time comes, commanders may shout their commands, but in red mud of war you're never more alone. You've served; I thought you'd know that."

"I kept the peace in Selik," said Tannock. "Border crossings, goods inspections. I never drew steel on a Mage before."

"Come on," said Rendon, leaving his chambers as well-armed as he was going to get.

Outside, his bodyguards bristled at seeing him arrayed for battle.

"You can't go out there, my lord; they have a Mage with them."

"Then someone's got to kill him," said Rendon. "I'm a soldier. It's what soldiers do. Follow, or don't."

Even the winding central staircase was a hard descent for a one-armed man. Constructed "southwind," as the engineers called it, the stair was meant to restrict the sword-arms of attackers and to free up the sword-arms of defenders. Rendon was therefore left with no railing to grip as he stumbled down the darkened stair with his commander at his back.

"There's a mage to be taken out," said Rendon. "Anything else I need to know? Other hidden perils?"

"Not that I can think of," said Tannock. "Normally I'd fear for the mines. When the Selikhan rebels had weapons to spare, they'd liberate the prisoners and arm them. Instant reinforcements. As it is, with Ashimar down there, I'm not worried."

Rendon stumbled on the stair and nearly went down. "What do you mean?"

"He'll kill the prisoners, of course," said Tannock. "If we're attacked, the soundest tactic is to execute the miners. We've got veterans down there, remember. Real warriors. Some men, myself included, still fancy themselves men of honour, and don't have the stomach for exterminating those wretches—but I doubt the bloodguard lose any sleep over it."

"Stop," Rendon ordered, motioning back up the stairs. "You'll move faster than I will. There's a key on my desk. The master key for the manacles. You have to get it."

"My lord?"

"Bring it to me," said Rendon. "We'll slip out the postern and you lot will find that Mage and take him down once and for all. There's something I have to do."

On the mine-trail below the keep, Ashimar had heard the cries of "Mage" just as clearly. Having routed the raiders to a wide parcel of land, he was nearly done with them. His personal retinue had suffered more casualties than he would have cared for, but sixteen men and women lay dead on the chalky plateau, and the four that remained—veterans, all—would not be long in following them.

Towering above the other three, even on a sorely wounded leg, Grimwulf had tirelessly kept the bloodguards at bay, and was canny enough to avoid the wild swings of Ashimar's greatsword while doing so. But he was feeling, now, the powerful effect of their superior armour against the ill-made, hastily scrounged weapons of the rebels. His own sword was a fine enough tool for butchery, but was not so finely honed that it could thrust through plate or even sturdy chain. He had managed to retrieve it from the body where it had been lodged, but its edge was a mass of cracks and pits. The cries of "Mage" and the screams from the summit of the cliff told him how little time he had for such personal matters.

"Put down your sword, Kellan," Ashimar ordered. "The battle is lost, and your new friends will be destroyed. Your courage is utterly pointless."

Grimwulf had the nerve to laugh at him. He banged lazily at one of the bloodguard's helmets, and the man charged in angrily. With a few beats of his weapon, Grimwulf sent the bloodguard back to his master's side, bloodied at the wrist and barely able to keep his sword aloft.

"Courage?" said Grimwulf. "You don't understand a damned thing. I just hate you people; that's not courage." He defended another lunge, though as he was doing so, Astagar slipped to his side and hurled his dagger into one of the other raiders. Only three left standing, now.

Ashimar advanced. "Lay down arms," he said. "Things will go better for you."

"Aye," said Grimwulf. "I'll become Lord of Egestor, will I? Can I collect my own reward? Is there a landgild if I'd sooner have the coin?" Ashimar came on himself, then; Grimwulf parried the first swing, but lost the tip of his sword in the process as the Scourge's greatsword hacked cleanly through it and nearly through the bracer supporting it.

"Jordac's up there," said Grimwulf, jerking his head to the cliffside. "You heard it yourself. He's burning up everybody and everything while you're down here parleying with me. You think I have the power to stop him? You think anything you have to say to me, by tongue or by steel, will make this a victory for you?" He scoffed. "You're wasting time with the wrong man."

Ashimar looked to the cliffside, then back to the three bloodied raiders who remained.

"I never took you for a needless talker," said Ashimar.

"You thought you'd surprise us?" shouted Grimwulf. "We knew you were here! You think we care a whit about a few starving prisoners? Our job is to keep you pinned down while Jordac takes the town and the Keep. You gilded dunce! You were the only threat to this plan from the beginning. And now you're all mine."

Ashimar came on in a fury, then, heedless of his own defense and trusting in his immaculate armour to repel his opponent's hardest swings.

But Grimwulf was no longer interested in striking home. Again and again, he held up his defenses and passed up the opportunity to try for a futile riposte. At his side, with an embarrassing amount of difficulty, Astagar had finally dispatched one of the other two raiders, though it cost him a wound to the stomach that would hurt him on the climb, and might turn foul enough to kill him in a few hours or days.

"You cannot win," said Ashimar. "You are tiring. Your leg is wounded. Your tale ends here."

"I've already won," said Grimwulf with a desperate smile. "My men are seizing the objective for Jordac as we speak. You've been played, Your Dread, from the very beginning. The Imperator's going to be very, very disappointed to lose this particular jewel from his crown."

While Grimwulf could not have known it, and while it was not the Imperator Ashimar feared most, the message had a chilling effect. Ashimar came in on Grimwulf's weak side, swung hard enough to cleave sword and armour alike if the blow had landed, and when Grimwulf desperately threw himself out of harm's way, the Scourge slipped past him and took four great strides up the trail to the summit.

"Leave him," Ashimar ordered. "Let him rot. He won't get far on that leg. We'll come back for him when the Mage is dead."

The bloodguards followed, though their burning hatred of Grimwulf could not be concealed. Bewildered by an exchange that could not possibly have been based in truth, the last raider at Grimwulf's side took the desperate opportunity to lunge at Ashimar while his back was turned. As the bloodguards rushed to his defense, the Scourge wheeled one last time on his heels, clapped the raider's head hard with the flat of his greatsword, and sent him tumbling half-conscious into the sea. Here where the cliff was sheer and the beach nowhere to be found, there were no rocks to speak of, but from a hundred feet or more, it did not matter: too dazed even to scream, he fell flat as a corpse and was broken upon the waves.

Grimwulf made to follow them, cursed them for cowards, boasted as bravely as he dared, and held his sword high and threatening, until it was clear they had made their decision. When they had cleared the crest of the hill and passed from view, his sword fell from his hands and he pitched forward into the dirt, beaten at last to exhaustion and helpless to maintain the ruse any longer. Weakly, trailing blood from his wounded leg, he crawled away from the circle of death, away from the keep and the caves, back toward the ship and the sea.

Atop the cliff, the raiders' momentary advantage had allowed them to sunder the Travalaithi shield-wall and break free of their deadly ground between the keep and the wall. With the Grand Army's formation broken and no commander to rally it, the fighting descended into a clamorous melee beneath the keep. What few proper reinforcements had lain in wait now emptied into the snow-dappled courtyard, but the fray was too mixed now for the archers to do much good. They were evenly matched, more or less, until Ashimar crested the ridge with the remainder of his bloodguard and set them immediately to wolf's work. Arriving at the raiders' backs, shrouded by the awful noise of battle, their first few swings were little more than butchery, and quickly the numbers were very much in their favour again.

On a nearby hill somewhat removed from the fighting, Odi and Catrine crouched in the snow with Baran's inert form and watched the new arrivals with muted horror.

"They're not on our side," said Catrine.

"They're bloodguards," said Odi. "Ashimar's personal legion. Gods be loud, Catrine, what are they doing here?"

With a pale, unsure face and a trembling hand, Catrine pointed back down to the hill to where a solitary figure in immaculate armour had broken off from the others.

"They're here with him," she said.

"What do we do with her?" Odi asked, jerking his gaze back to Baran.

"Don't know," said Catrine. "Back to the ship with her?"

Odi looked down the hill to the grisly battle. "Seems wisest," he said.

But the Weeping Man was watching them—moving toward them.

"Come on!" Catrine cried, leaning hard to drag Baran's inert body.

For lack of a better plan, Odi pitched in, steering them back southward toward the ship.

"He's following," said Odi. "Gods protect me, he's following."

"Of course he's following," said Catrine. "*Pull.*"

They dragged the aeril roughly down the back of the hill, and for a moment, the Red Captain was out of sight. But Odi remembered suddenly Madge's panicked flight to the pier, and the trouble they had endured to protect their base of operations in the city.

"We can't go back to the ship."

Catrine's eyes were wild. "What?"

"We can't lead him to the ship. Hormer needs a crew of ten men—eight, at least—or that hulk doesn't sail. If we lead him to the ship, to that crew, and he cuts down even a few...none of us leaves."

Catrine cast her eyes to what she could see of the fighting.

"There won't be many coming home," she said.

The tip of Ashimar's greatsword, held high, crested the hill before he did. He was closer than he should have been—striding quickly, tirelessly, with the measured pace of a man who knew he would not be outrun.

"Fly," said Odi. "We scatter."

"She knows more of Jordac's plans than anyone," said Catrine. "We can't let him take her alive."

Odi had a knife—not even a dagger, really—and his hand went to it, but he did not draw.

"I'll kill a man in a fight if I have to," he said. "But this? A defenceless woman? My own friend?"

"I'll do it," said Catrine. But the aeril moaned softly, and Catrine's hand trembled on her own weapon.

"You won't," said Odi. "You can't do it either—and that's not a weakness."

"What do we do?"

"This way. Back to the fighting. Perhaps a few can disentangle themselves and help us."

At the summit of the rocky hill, where the snow was shallow, Ashimar broke into a run.

"We're not going to make it," said Catrine.

Odi glanced down to her hip. "Is there a sharp point on that sword?"

Catrine sighed and set her jaw. "Yes, there is," she said gravely.

"Best take it out, then," he urged. "My little knife's not going to be much use on its own."

"Or any use at all," she said. "Get her back to the ship. Over the rocks, not through the snow. Don't leave a trail. I don't think I'll hold him for long."

"Catrine…"

She let go of Baran's body and snapped out her sword.

"Go," she said. "If you value your own skin, go."

"Jordac of Travalaith," called the Red Captain. "Your uprising ends here."

"What?" Odi mouthed.

"You," whispered Catrine. "He has no interest in her. He thinks you're the Mage."

"He's about to be very disappointed."

"Run," said Catrine. "Take her and run."

"You cannot escape," said Ashimar, moving closer.

"I can bluff him once," said Odi. "Make it count." He raised his arms as if to do…he wasn't sure what. Something wondrous, maybe. A desperate miracle.

Catrine advanced, sword at the ready.

"Now!" shouted Odi. "Get down!"

She dove out of the way—and so too did Ashimar.

Nothing happened, of course, as was Odi's way with the arcane. Ashimar had taken a knee in the snow, well clear of the phony mage, though he had caught himself on his hands before tumbling right to the earth. As he reached for his greatsword where it had fallen, Catrine gripped its distant edge with her gloved hands and hauled it up with all her strength. It was heavier than she expected, and she had to wrench it hard to pull it free of his grasp in time. But by a sliver of a second, she was the faster, and with a half-turn and all her strength she made to hurl it clear into the sea. Odi threw himself low as the massive weapon spun through the air, arced, and fell slightly short: it clanged across the exposed white rocks, skipped and skidded, teetered on the cliff's edge—and finally tipped over the side.

"No!" Ashimar cried in frustration.

With at least a moment's courage, Catrine turned to face him, sword-point at the ready.

"I'd tell you to drop your weapon," she said wryly.

Without missing a beat, Ashimar's left hand reached for the barbed scourge coiled at his hip, and her smile faded.

"Keep going," Catrine said to Odi.

"Don't be long," he said optimistically. He resumed dragging Baran's body, though slower than before on his own.

"That was a rare blade," said Ashimar. "It will cost you deeply."

Catrine took the first swing. Ashimar did not move, but let her arming sword skip lightly off the plates of his shoulder. He waited until the shock of the hard strike had numbed her hands before flashing out with the scourge. It uncoiled in flight, and she jerked her head back. She saved her eye, in the end, but a half-dozen ragged cuts opened up along the side of her face and hot blood began to stream down her cheek and neck.

"I do not envy your interrogators," said Ashimar, advancing. "They will have to devise new methods to question you, when I have exhausted all of the old ones at my pleasure." He swung again, and though she made to parry, the bands of the scourge snaked around the blade of her weapon: she shrieked as a few barbs and sharpened keys streaked her face and hands again.

Warily, she backed away, feeling the pounding pulse of her heart in hot waves down the side of her face. Panicked but determined, terrified yet resolute, there was no more time for taunting or posturing.

"Come on, then," she said simply. "Come on."

At strategic junctions of the upper mine, polished mirrors of silver glass directed and diffused natural sunlight into the tunnel as deep as their ingenious engineering would allow. The effect was most pronounced in summer, though, and in the depth of winter the north-facing cliff caves offered nothing more than a faded grey dimness. Even so, Aewyn smashed or bent the mirrors where she could, and turned away those polished metal discs she could not break. She could see well enough in the dimness, or at least make her way by touch, and perceived that the man at her heels would be at the greater disadvantage: the deeper darkness of the low tunnels hindered his pursuit more than it did her escape.

Heart pounding, she bounded lightly down the tunnels, staying clear where she could of the little alcoves lit by trembling oil lamps. The work would have gone easier by torchlight, to be sure, but the air was stale and sick enough as it was, and the smoky flame of a full-sized torch would have done them no good in the deeps.

The prisoners were chained and crowded far below, and in the time it took Aewyn to reach the first signs of them she became coldly aware that she was being followed—then hunted.

In the deepening shadows, when she was sure she had enough cover of darkness, she chanced a shout.

"Men of the Uprising!" Aewyn called. As soon as the words were out, she threw herself low and crossed to the far side of the uneven tunnel, listening for answer.

A voice in the dark came back to her: "Who calls?"

"A friend," she said. "I've come to free you."

"Gods be praised!" the man shouted. "Follow my voice. Follow my voice!"

With caution and care she wound her way through the tunnels in search of the voice, which kept up its shouts with surprising vigor. She found herself doubling back on herself, searching the shallower tunnels, until of a sudden, the voice fell silent.

"Don't give up," she called. "I'm nearly there."

Perhaps she felt the movement of air on her face, or perhaps behind a mask of innocence there was some canny understanding of men's cruelty at last beginning to grow in her. But on a sudden impulse of fear, she threw herself to the side of the tunnel and ducked low as a blade flashed out in the darkness. Catching the scattered light of the little oil lamps for only a minute, it clanged off the stone where her head had been, and the resounding noise of metal on stone stunned her in the silent deep. She came up on her feet moving backwards as a second swing, then a third, came after her; but the ground was uneven and she stumbled. The bloodguard who had followed her into the darkness had drawn her back to him, and with expert strokes of his weapon he herded her backwards to a jagged crevice in the lower cave. She had nothing to parry with, nothing with which to return the fight, and the little obsidian knife that found its way into her hand extended barely more than an inch beyond her fist.

"You won't live to see a slaver's chain," he hissed as he forced her to the ground with a few wild swings. Then, raising his sword to thrust home, he grunted in pain and alarm, turned his blade, and fell aside. A second heavy stroke to the back of his neck split the seam of his greathelm and sent him moaning and twitching to the ground. She recoiled in fear as a figure emerged from the darkness with the face of a terrifying greatcat—but recognized him for who he was when he knelt beside the twitching bloodguard and gently leveraged his axe in both hands to deliver the mercy stroke.

"You," she breathed.

"Me," the figure confirmed. He unbuckled his helmet and removed it—a difficult process—to show his face.

"What is your name, bloodguard?"

"I told you," he said. "I am no bloodguard. Name's Rasten. And this...this is not what I do."

"I remember you. You came here with Ashimar."

"I did," he said. "But...I'm not leaving with him. Those are civilians fighting with you out there. Not soldiers. Jordac's got everyone fighting for him. Women. Boys. Old men. Old women. Tailors and coopers. Whole innocent villages corrupted to his cause. That's not who I trained to kill."

"I mean to free the prisoners," she said. "Will you kill me?"

"No," said Rasten, thoroughly shaken, voice trembling. "I've seen enough of killing. Enough for a lifetime. There's more of them down below... so many more."

"They're fighting above," said Aewyn. "If you're really through with him, don't go outside."

"Outside?" he breathed. "Not on your life. I gave up on him the moment I had cover of darkness. Slipped away when he started executing the prisoners. If he finds me now, I'm a deserter. I'm as good as dead—and if ever I had a natural friendship with him, I've long since squandered it. If the Grand Army finds me, I'm a deserter. As good as dead. If the men of the Uprising find me—I'm a bloodguard."

"As good as dead," Aewyn said with him, and had little reason to think otherwise.

"How did you get back here?" said Rasten. "I thought Kellan would have to put as many miles as possible between you and us."

"Who?" she asked. But Rasten hushed her and pushed her back down with a strong arm, back into the shadowy crevice where her life had nearly ended.

"Quiet," he whispered. "Someone's coming." He crowded closer to her in the little space and sat perfectly still.

She did not recognize the silhouette that passed her. This far into the tunnels, the oil lamps were not enough to make out his features beneath a mass of unkempt hair. In the diffuse light from the upper tunnels, though, his silhouette was strangely lopsided, and it soon became clear he was missing his entire right arm, almost to the shoulder. He moved past them so closely that Aewyn could feel the wind of his passing in the still air. Then he was gone into one of the smaller deep tunnels with intent and purpose.

"Who is that?" she asked.

"I've no care to find out," said Rasten.

Aewyn's fingers traced the brass key she had lifted from one of the raiders. "He has a key," she said. "Like mine. Perhaps he's here to free them, as I am."

A pained look came over Rasten's face, and he shook his head slowly.

"I already told you," he said. "There's none to free. Ashimar thought you might come. Didn't know how many you were, but he didn't want another fighting force at his back. He's seen the mines revolt before. He took care to set them free himself—his own way."

"No," Aewyn breathed.

"I swore an oath," said Rasten. "I swore to follow the orders I've been given. I followed him through a lot. But not through that."

"Lysandra!" a voice called out in the darkness. "Lysandra!"

"Come on," said Rasten. "You need to get out of here." But she slipped past him, and past the dead bloodguard at his feet, and made her way silently toward the deeper caves. Rasten made to follow her, but lingered a moment over the first man he had ever killed from behind, unaware. The sight of it haunted him already, but in a moment of what he felt was dignity, he bent down to unbuckle the man's sundered helmet and remove the beast's head—to let him go to his gods, or to the worms if he preferred, as a man rather than a bloodguard of Ashimar.

"I'm sorry," he said, and followed the young woman.

The lower chamber, the lowest of the mine's top level, was littered with the bodies of the dead. Still chained together in grisly rows, the two dozen assigned to this chamber were relatively new arrivals. Pressing haste must have stifled Ashimar's creativity, for all of them, one after another, had been executed by a swift stroke to the throat. At the far end of the chamber, in stunned silence, the one-armed man knelt in the blood, clutching the lifeless body of a young woman to his breast. Her manacles were the only bindings he unlocked, and the pale flesh of her dangling wrists was unmarred: she had not been a prisoner for long. He was silent as death himself, barely breathing, but on his face was an anguish so complete that Aewyn had seen it captured only once before, by the mad artisans who wrought Ashimar's war-mask. The man's jaw worked vainly, but his mind was far away and no words came to him. Until he spoke, Aewyn was not even sure he had seen her.

"Who are you," he mumbled. It wasn't even a question, really. He wasn't even there.

Aewyn held up her key. It was of cheap brass where his was iron; hers was a crude counterfeit copy where his was a Lornock-forged original. But it was the same key.

"I came to set them free," she said. "I'd hoped to do it while they lived."

It seemed so foolish, now. Maybe it had been a fool's errand all along.

"Me too," said the man. "Me too. Me too, me too."

Rasten, moved by a sudden pity, stepped into the light. The one-armed man, in Grand Army colours with the rank badge of an overseer, set down the body as Rasten approached, made to stand, made to draw and make his stand. But Rasten's helm was off; his brown eyes were such clear pools of stunned sadness that it did not matter what he wore: this was no bloodguard.

Rasten looked down at the body. She was a young woman, to be sure, no wispy young girl; but she was slender and finely boned, and beautiful in all the ways he imagined a Selikhan beauty could be. Her hair shone more to red than to sunlit yellow, but she reminded him so much of Catrine—as all beautiful women might, he supposed. Frozen by tender sorrow, he asked the only thing he could think to ask:

"Was she kin to you?"

The overseer looked up at him with the tearless eyes of a thoroughly broken man. He cleared his throat and seemed to speak from far away.

"No," he said. "Not to me. I suppose, really…truly…I don't know who she was at all."

Looking over the rest of the bodies—there were two dozen in this chamber alone--Rasten bit his lip to keep from grinding his teeth. His hands tightened to fists.

"This is not the way," he said. "This is not the way to make war." But no one seemed to be listening to him, now. He made to leave, but looked back to the girl and the overseer.

"Will you come?" he asked finally. "There's something I have to do. But I swear to you, there's nothing more down here for you. I'll see you back to your ship safely first, if you're going."

"Go," said Aewyn, dismissively. "I've a job to do as well." Gently, unsure if the one-armed man would let her touch the body nearest him, she cradled the next corpse over and unlocked its manacles at the wrists and neck.

"Don't take too long," Rasten warned. "It's not going well for your friends." With that he was gone, and Aewyn was left in the near-darkness of a lamplit cave with a Travalaithi soldier as broken and spiritually dead as any of the bodies in their shared company.

For a moment, they both stood in silence. Then, crouching down over the next body, and then the next, she struggled to unlock each set of chains as her counterfeit key fit each lock almost precisely, but never perfectly.

"Why?" the overseer asked.

Aewyn did not look up from her work. "Why what?" she asked.

"Why—these people," said the overseer. "They're dead. They're all dead, already. All, all dead." He gestured to the heavy bag of weapons she had been carrying.

"You'll find no reinforcements among the dead," he warned.

Aewyn looked back to the dead woman cradled in his lap.

"Do you have a name?" she asked him.

The overseer shook himself from a thoughtful daze. "Rendon," he said.

"And did she have a name?"

Rendon struggled to remember her truename, shaking his head in frustration. "Lysandra," he said at last. "Her name was Lysandra, and I loved her."

Aewyn paused to jiggle a sticky lock. The old man's hand shackled beneath it had already grown cold and white. When she looked back at Rendon, where Rasten's eyes had shown tenderness, there was an anger in hers that burned deep beneath her gentle voice.

"I imagine every one of these people was somebody's Lysandra," she said. "Every single one."

She had nothing more to say to him after that, and he had no words in response. She left him to cradle the only body he had selfishly unlocked as she carefully, methodically went about releasing the others. When it was done, when all the dead were freed, she cast a final look at the master of Fingrun. She imagined it would have been easy enough to end him—perhaps even with his own sword. But it all felt so empty now, so pointless. It was by fortune alone that she had never taken a life, and she could not bring herself to start now. With her work done, she stood to rejoin the others.

Around her, as her eyes adjusted to the dimness, she could see the skeletal shadows of great wooden wheels and pulleys, picks and mauls, buckets and ropes and chalk-dusted wheelbarrows filled to heaping with iron ore. There was no shortage of equipment to smash, if that was what the rebels intended to do. There was every abundance of hurt still to be done to the Travalaithi mining operation. But that was not what she had come to do. Turning away from it all, she lingered on the edge of the lower cavern until, half-lost in his own grief, the overseer looked up at her again.

"You… why do you stand there?" he asked. "What do you want from me?"

"I've never been in a war," she said. "Tell me, soldier. Is all this… is this what it's really like?"

Rendon cleared his throat, idly brushed at the woman's hair in his lap.

"Yes," he said at last. "Yes, it's all very much like this."

She lingered just on the edge of the lamplight, as if to say something more. But when the earth above them growled with the low sound of distant hoofbeats, she abandoned him too, springing back down the passage toward the grey light of a cold and unforgiving morning.

EIGHTEEN

BY THE TIME AEWYN HAD REACHED the top of the cliff, the battlefield had descended into total chaos. To see a true battle, it was longer and harder work than she expected, though the numbers of the raiders had begun, steadily, to dwindle. Helpless to fire into the fracas once the opposing forces had swarmed into each other, the archers from the keep had come down with freshly-forged swords and spears, and the rebels were close to being routed. Wholly unarmed, unprepared for the cruelty of battle, Aewyn meant to return to the ship, but could not tear herself away from the horrid spectacle. Crouching low in the scrubby, snow-covered brush that lined the crest of the hill, she watched and waited.

Fighting in full for their lives now, none of the combatants had the chance to notice her where she hid. The Weeping Man himself was covered head to toe in ghoulish streaks of blood, and warily circled a young woman who steadfastly refused to die, though she too was a grisly sight to behold. The sight of him filled Aewyn with sorrow and anger, but raising a weapon to him felt like folly, even if she had not left her heavy sack of short blades and clubs down in the mines. She puzzled a long time, or what felt like a long time, over what to do before remembering that the bloodguard must have been mounted to cover the ground from Widowvale to Fingrun. With whatever hope remained after the sights of despair she had seen, Aewyn rushed for the stables nearest the keep, hoping that the rest of the Havenari's horses had survived the trek to the coast.

Behind her, on a low plateau between the bulk of the fighting and the open cliffside, Ashimar kept up his relentless assault against Catrine, who could do little now but roll away from his strikes and swing with fading strength to keep him at bay. Much of the blood streaking his armour was hers, and the coldness of the winter air was settling into many of her seeping wounds with an unforgiving bite. Her breath was coming in ragged gasps, and it was all she could do to maintain her defenses as Ashimar's assault rained tirelessly on.

Catrine looked back over her shoulder for Odi and Baran, only to see the exhausted spy struggling along the cliff's edge with the dead weight of her body, searching for the narrow path that led back to the ship. Whether the remnants of Ashimar's bloodguard or even more Travalaithi regulars awaited them, she could not know; but there was nothing to be done for it now. Again and again she glanced up in the hopes that they were gone, and kept up her dwindling defenses as well as she could. When at last she could no longer see them, she fell to her knees, but even on her knees she thrust and parried with her battered old sword until the Weeping Man snared it with his scourge and jerked it away from her. In the end, with her blistered hand laid on the frozen earth, she felt the low rumble of hoofbeats, and knew that the Grand Army had sent on its next wave and the day was lost. She cried out the alarm, or perhaps only thought she did, before slumping over and waiting for the end. It would be slower to come by the scourge than the sword, she knew, and many times more painful. But it would come just the same.

"Rasten," breathed Ashimar. At the name, she tried to look up.

"Your Dread," said a voice that was clearly Rasten's. "I hope I'm not interrupting."

She had never heard such an edge to his voice before. She had never heard him speak unkindly—and she knew, long before anyone else could have known, that he had not returned to Ashimar's side to serve.

"I had not expected to see you again," said the Weeping Man. "I thought you had deserted me. But even at that, it seems you have failed."

"You killed them. You killed them all."

"Some of them were skilled veterans. You would not have wanted them at your back."

"And the women? The old? Are you afraid to have them at your back as well?"

"Be careful," Ashimar warned him. "The women of the Uprising are strong—not like the cravens now bred in the Capital. This one here has given me more than my share of trouble."

Rasten looked down at the bloody woman. There was something oddly familiar about her.

"Ras," she breathed, as if from far away. The effort set her to coughing, but her voice was not lost on him.

"Cat?" Rasten asked. "Catrine, my Catrine?"

When she fell, with her eyes shut and her arms curled, he saw her as she had lain beside him in the Storm Quarter, saw her ivory skin as it looked in the red light of an early dusk. It was something out of a fever-dream to see her here, in this godless place, cringing beneath the merciless barbed chains of Ashimar's weapon of office. Questions flooded his mind, and he did not care at all for the possible answers—but they did not matter, he supposed. When Ashimar raised his bloody scourge to strike her again, Rasten thrust his gauntleted arm into its path.

"What?" Ashimar spat. The movement, impossibly, had caught him off-guard.

The tails of the scourge snared tightly around the vicious spikes of Rasten's red gauntlet, locking the two men together. With only his left hand free from the grapple, Rasten could not reach his sword, but his brother's axe was within easy reach: with every frustration of the past month alive in his lungs, screaming into the enamelled metal face of the weeping child, Rasten twisted with all his strength and came down on Ashimar's neck with it.

The broad beard of the axe did not go through cleanly, but skipped against his immaculate gorget and deflected down into his upper chest. But so true was the strike, and so great its power, that the Weeping Man's breastplate was stove in hard. A second swing and then a third forced a deep canyon of anger into the surface of Ashimar's armour. Ashimar threw his free arm against the haft of Rasten's axe, but it was weakened by some hidden wound and could not slow its descent. On the fourth bite, the axe drew blood, which seeped out as black and thick as molasses where the blade clove through the beaten crack in the plates.

Ashimar's shriek of pain was profound, but his wits did not leave him. Tightly snared to Rasten at the forearm, wrestling hard to keep his footing, Ashimar hauled his opponent toward Catrine's bloody form and kicked her onto her back. In the weak morning sunlight Rasten saw, nearly a moment too late, the glint of the vicious little spurs mounted onto Ashimar's steel boots for hard riding. Half lunging, half falling, he made to put the point of the spur through the delicate flesh of her neck, and only by jerking him backward at full force did Rasten keep the little point from striking home.

The momentary distraction was all Ashimar needed to seize the slender dirk from his tangled gauntled and thrust it home into Rasten's side.

With the strength of ferocity, desperation, and hate, Ashimar punched straight through the battered links of Rasten's mail. He above all people knew where to strike best. Rasten gasped, got his elbow down in time to wedge it in front of Ashimar's arm and keep the blade from going too deep. It might have reached his heart if he had not twisted and stopped it short. As it was, the agony of the thrust was unbearable, and he felt his strength fading fast where the Red Captain's fury seemed only to grow. He knew then that he could not win this fight, nor keep it up for long. But as long as he kept up his momentum, lifting and dragging, Ashimar could not find his footing. And so Rasten lifted and hauled with frantic desperation as the dirk came free of his ribs and plunged back in thirstily. This time, the fine armour of the bloodguard did not suffer its point to pass, and while the sharp agonizing force of the blade bruised his side again and again, it found no purchase like the first wound. Rasten likewise clubbed at Ashimar's gleaming face with the flat of his axe: the blows did little more than distract him, but for a few final moments, distraction was all he needed.

With or without the desperate, bloody battle at his back, Rasten's mind was haunted by the sights and smells of the dead. He saw as clear as day the big, round eye of the horse Ashimar had frighted and maimed nigh unto death; he saw members of the bloodguard dead in the snow at the Sunderhouse, the little cabin littered with the bodies of peaceful miners, the burned village. He saw the dozens upon dozens of dead in the mines—not just the ones in the upper chamber, but those in the deeps he had not had the heart to tell Aewyn about. Most clearly of all, he saw Catrine at his own feet, shuddering in the grip of panic. And locked in his arms, struggling to find his footing, was the man responsible for all that death.

He chanced, selfishly, one last look at Catrine. Her face was red with her own blood, which streamed down her cheeks as she called out painfully to him. But the sea called to him too, and vengeance called to him, and justice called loudest of all—and though he feared its calling to account after all he had done, its song was sweet just the same.

Grappling madly with Ashimar as the two men struggled and stumbled, Rasten let go of his brother's axe and reached for the buckles of his armour. The heavy plates over his fine mail-coat were more of a hindrance than a help, now. Where he had to, he turned Ashimar's dirk aside, heedless of the injuries he sustained controlling its point.

He knew where they were headed. He knew how long he needed the blood in his veins for. It was not long. Tending to his leather straps as much as to Ashimar's murderous weapon, Rasten tugged the last strap free and let his cuirass fall away into the dusting of snow, like two halves of a shelled nut.

As soon as Ashimar sensed and felt the high winds at the cliff's edge, he let go of his scourge and tried to disentangle himself from his opponent; but Rasten held him tightly, with heavy hands that seemed not to tire with the rest of him. Far away from the insistent sting of Ashimar's last blade, Rasten cast his mind back to the Black Bridge Inn. Before the Grand Army, before Selik, before the madness of his adult life set in, he had frequented the old Travalaithi inn and sometimes served as its enforcer. Stout and well-muscled even in his youth, he had more than once seized a drunken Travalaithi soldier by his jutting pauldrons and thrown him out into the gutters to sleep off his anger. *That's all this is*, he told himself. *Seeing to the gutter trash, as I've always done.*

Madly, desperately, Ashimar struck his spurs against the white stone of the cliff's edge, hoping to find some purchase while he sank his dagger to Rasten's heart. But he was not so tall or long-legged as his fearsome presence caused men to describe him: in the end he was only a man—as one Havenar had said at the Sunderhouse, a man pushing sixty, and slowed by sixty pounds of steel plate.

Rasten hoped it would be enough.

If the young soldier had been anything less than totally committed, Ashimar might have wrenched free of him in the last moment, might have twisted from his grasp and fallen away to the safe earth. But so sure were Rasten's hands, and so fierce his resolve, that there was no escaping them. He held the Weeping Man aloft, and hurled him hard, and when at last Ashimar let go of his dirk and locked his grip onto his opponent, Rasten did not give him the resistance he needed, but fell with him, plunging off the cliff into the open sky. A swift kick at the cliff's edge, a silent leap as both men arced over the side in a twisted, fell embrace, and they were gone.

On the snowy earth, not far from the precipice, Catrine awaited the cold relief of unconsciousness, but it would not come. The sight of Rasten—it must have been—flooded her veins with a last desperate surge of fighting vigour, and though she wanted nothing more than to slip away, satisfied that she had served her country, her chosen lord, and her husband's memory to the limit of her endurance, the gentle darkness did not come for her, but left her alone to her searing pains, her confused thoughts of woe, and the churning waves of nausea in her stomach. Sensing and feeling little else, and resentful of feeling even that, she lay still in snow made red with courage, too spent to move or speak.

With her ear against the ground, she could clearly hear the hoofbeats before the men and women tangled in the desperate fighting heard them. She did not know whether to cry out in terror or to spend her last breath in warning the raiders of the reinforcements at her back. But as she slipped away from the waking world, she spied the rich forest green of their battered cloaks, the rough patchwork that heard them together, heard in their charge the whistling of Travalaithi arrows and the shout of a woman's voice above the clamour of battle.

There were no women in the Grand Army, she knew; and with that to give her solace, she did not much care who had come to her aid. With her own battle over, for better or worse, she lay her heavy head down in the red snow and at last took her rest.

While their cloaks were patched and ragged, while they rode seldom in formation and lacked the pomp and pageantry of the Travalaithi Legions, the Havenari could be disciplined and focused when they had to be. But they had arrived to find the battle already underway. After the kidnapping of Aewyn and the wounding of Bram, even Robyn could not well control them—nor, if truth be told, was she much inclined to.

When they had come close enough to spy the red glint of the bloodguard's armour, when they were close enough to cross the whole crucible of battle at full gallop, there was no stopping them. The first few charged without her command, then the next few, and finally Robyn had no choice but to charge herself unless she wished to break formation.

All told, between the raiders, the Grand Army, the bloodguard, and the wandering souls who were never really a part of any of them, perhaps a hundred people had shed blood at the foot of Fingrun keep. Many were dead or dying already, and when the horses burst from the tree line, all of them looked up fearfully, unsure which direction the riders' spears would be pointing when they landed. But these were no ordinary spears. They were the *kolgari*, the iconic spears of Janus Veritenh's Dragons, and it had been long years since the Havenari, long the keepers of the peace in the Outlands, had lowered them in a charge.

"Hold!" Robyn cried from the back ranks. "Hold!" But there was no holding them. It was a reckless, thundering charge kicked to a full gallop: Roald and Tsúla, among the youngest and most inexperienced, were at the head of their driving wedge, coming on full tilt, not because they were seasoned veterans, but because they charged all-out as the lightest riders with the fastest horses.

"Hold!" she cried again vainly. But they had come for one reason alone, and until that debt was paid she would have no diplomacy from any of them.

"Hold formation!" she ordered at last, as if it were the command she had been giving all along. Lowering her own spear into the charge, she led her spirited mare almost to the front of the line before they clashed.

Caught unaware, stuttering and stumbling in their steps, none of the combatants knew what would befall them until the horses were upon them. It became clear, in a wave of brutal force, that of all the forces assembled that day, the bloodguard had done the most to earn the riders' ire, for it was here they drove their spears with deadly precision and thundering force. A few arrows whistled down at them as they came, but their horses were fresh and moving too fast. Like a red wave the bloodguard were driven out of the melee, knocked down to the earth and trampled or pushed back toward the cliff.

The men of the Grand Army, surprised by the full righteous fury of a local force they had long known as peacekeepers, turned at last on those that remained. But they were hard winded from the earlier fighting, and the speed and ferocity of the newcomers was too much for them. One of the riders, a lean man with a bandaged leg swaying uneasily in the charge, they managed to pull down from his horse and surround, thinking him easy prey. But he wrapped his arm around one guardsman's neck as he fell, and blinded him with a flash of his sword as it leapt free of his scabbard. Though he was too weak in the legs to stand on his own feet, he kept his arm locked around the neck of the taller, stronger soldier who stumbled blindly through the battlefield. Clutching at his face and swinging wildly with his own weapon, the guardsman twisted to and fro, trying to reach his unwelcome passenger; but wherever he angled his back, the stranger's sword flicked out again and more soldiers fell.

"Surrender!" the woman shouted. "Weapons down, all of you! Surrender and see the morrow!"

"Ashimar!" bellowed a man's voice, deeper. The name alone gave men pause who had fought on through orders of surrender.

"Where is he?" bellowed the man. "Drop your weapons and give us the Scourge, or die with him!"

The woman in command rode to his side as the soldiers finally began to lay down arms.

"Enough, Venser," she said. "That's enough!"

"I want him, Robyn," the big man snarled. "His men are here, all over the field. I want him."

"Easy. We'll calm them down, and they'll talk to us."

"The Iron City never has to know. We throw him in the bloomer with the slag from the mine, melt him down, send them back some horseshoes."

"Easy, Venser. We'll find him."

With a healthy fear, the Grand Army and the raiders separated from one another. The last of Ashimar's bloodguard, to a man, lay slain or trampled by the charge, and the sight of their elite guardsmen wiped out in a single stroke compelled some of the Travalaithi soldiers to lay down arms and stand as prisoners. A few of the raiders, seizing their moment, broke off and fled for the cliffside. One of the Havenari wheeled his horse around, but their commander shook her head.

"Just as well to let them go," she said. "Go and help Bram."

The one called Venser threw a leg over his big horse and dismounted, trudging across the battlefield. The blinded soldier had fallen at last, stunned and in shock, and without another man's legs to support him at a man's height, Bram had tumbled with him to the snowy earth.

"We are the Havenari of Haveïl," said the woman. "My name is Robyn. I carry First Spear of the Havenari, by the Code of Veritenh. Janus Veritenh was Companion of the Owl to the Imperator, Valithar. Every man here—every man living—who has sworn an oath to the Imperator is by that Company our comrade-in-arms. The rest of you wear no colours. You have no rank and carry no banners. This is a Travalaithi outpost, and I can see that you have no lawful business here. You have thirty minutes to collect your dead, or pay them your respects, and return whence you came."

A vicious murmur went up from the men who had been fighting. With a gesture, Robyn sent two mounted men to ensure the raiders and the soldiers were segregated.

"You're turning them loose?" one asked incredulously.

"There has been enough bloodshed here today," Robyn called to him. "We have business to be done, and we can't do it in the midst of a civil war."

"You're a long way from Haveïl, Outlander," said one, and she ignored it.

"You can't!" another shouted. This one Robyn rode up to directly.

"You can tell us what we can and cannot do," she said, "on the day we no longer have to ride fifty miles out from our Protectorate to make sure your heads stay on, and to defend your keep for you." He opened his mouth to protest, and she thumbed her own sword out of its scabbard. He understood then—perhaps for the first time, since he was young—what it meant to have had enough of battle for one day.

With measured patience, as if separating bickering children, the Havenari drove the Travalaithi soldiers nearly to the wall of the keep and the rebels nearly to the far hill across the field. The dead were sorted and the living tended to, and the day's first joy for many was to learn who, among their comrades, had gone down to wounds that might not claim their lives after all. The tension was fierce, but none tested Robyn's resolve to shut down any further fighting that broke out. With great care some of the Havenari laid out the corpses of the bloodguard who had made it to the top of the hill. Roald was filthy with their blood when he rode back to her side.

"How am I doing?" she asked him quietly.

"You've kept the peace," said Roald. "I'd say brilliantly. Though your hands are shaking something fierce."

She looked down to her iron grip on the reins, relaxed it slightly.

"You found something?" she asked.

"I've found nothing," said Roald. "That's what troubles me. No Aewyn. No Ashimar."

Robyn steeled herself for more bad news. "Think they're together?"

"Unlikely," said Venser, riding up behind his companion. "The way the Purples tell it, he was pitched over the side by one of his own men."

Robyn looked to the red-armoured bodies laid out on the snowy earth.

"Really…any of them up to talking?" she asked, though she already suspected the answer.

Venser lowered his head and sighed, not quite meeting her eyes.

"The Purples, maybe," he said. "But it grieves me to report that not one of the men who took Aewyn from us still draws breath."

Robyn nodded. "Hm. Not one? The boys must have led a strong charge."

"Must have," agreed Venser, looking away. "Did you talk to the Fingrun men?"

"A little," said Robyn. "Still, I'd like to be gone before the Grand Army sends more troops."

"You said it yourself," said Venser. "Who do they send if you kill the Scourge?"

Robyn smiled slightly, in spite of herself. "I've no desire to find out. It's a big loss for Travalaith—the Scourge and a half quire of his personal bloodguard."

"If you want to know the truth," said Venser, "a full quire, and then some. We found the rest of them, slain on the mine-paths below."

"Captain!" shouted Tsúla. "You'd better come. We have one alive."

Robyn rushed to the side of the young man, who was cradling the head of a blonde woman as a child cradles a broken doll. She stirred softly but made no move to speak or open her eyes as the young Havenar gently washed the blood from her face with handfuls of snow.

"Don't do that," said Robyn. "If the frost burns her cheek before we get her indoors, it will go bad for her."

"Sorry," said Tsúla, who had never seen winters quite like the winters in Haveïl.

"Ras—" she breathed suddenly, struggling to open her eyes. "Rast… Rasten. No."

"You're safe now," said Robyn. "Do you understand? You're safe. No one can hurt you anymore."

"Gods," said the woman, weeping silently.

"Easy," said Tsúla. "You don't need to sit up. Just rest. Robyn, these are deep."

"We need bandages," said Robyn. "Go. Find me the Overseer of this place, if he still lives."

"I'll get on it," said Tsúla. She turned to Venser next.

"Have you got a little of the anger out of your blood?" she asked him.

"Not even slightly," he answered. "But if you mean to give orders, I mean to follow them."

"Water the horses," said Robyn. "The Scourge was here—maybe minutes ago, maybe an hour or two. If Aewyn's alive, she'll be with him. I mean to set out at once, soon as we put these men to peace."

"It's a peace that won't last," said Venser. "Soon as we leave, they'll be right back at each other. You haven't seen a real war yet."

"Haven't I?" said Robyn, with such ice in her voice that Venser bowed his head in apology. "Never mind the horses. I'll do it myself. Go get my brother."

Fully cowed, with his heart in his throat, Venser crossed the field of blood to where Bram lay, waiting as ordered to be moved before he tried to stand.

"How's the leg?" Venser asked, reaching down with his strong hand to help Bram up.

"No worse than your arm," said Bram, gesturing to Venser's weak side. "And still on the mend. I'll be dancing the halling again in a red month."

"We'll all be glad for it," said Venser. "I do believe I've insulted your poor sister's honour."

Bram laughed. "You're not the first man, nor the last," he said. "And you're sure as every hell not the worst, either. She angry with you?"

Venser grunted as he hauled Bram shakily to his feet and helped him stumble to his horse. "Afraid so."

"Oh, then it's *my* honour you've insulted somehow," said Bram, not really caring.

"I'm sorry," said Venser. "Truly. I suppose we've all seen our share of hard times."

"Venser?" asked Bram.

"Hm?"

"Don't send me into the mines where the dead are."

It was Venser's turn to laugh. "The dead?" he asked. "The dead are all up here, Bram. This one—watch your step—I put there on the way in."

Bram shook his head. "If Ashimar knew we were coming—knew *I* was coming—they'll be dead all the way down."

Venser shifted the strength in his arms not to carry, but to comfort. Bram was still underfed, still frail. He seemed so young in Venser's old arms.

"I don't believe the dead are any of our business," he said, "if indeed they're ever the business of the living. But we're not going down. Soon as the raiders are back on their ships, and the poor frightened folk in Fingrun Town are told the stupidity of war is over and they can come out from under their beds, she means to press on after Aewyn."

"She won't have to," said Bram. "Look."

Venser squinted his eyes. "Pots and tossers," he swore, breaking into a wide smile. "That absolute bastard girl!"

Hair-draggled and blood-spattered, but no more the worse for wear, Aewyn had come up the hill from Fingrun Town and was leading a team of spirited horses strung together behind her. The black horse at their head jerked and pulled at his reins fiercely as the smell of battle hit him, but there was a lightness to his step and his freely swinging tail as soon as he heard the Havenari's voices on the wind.

"Rascal?" called Tsúla. "Rascal!"

The black horse took off toward him and the others, tethered, had no choice but to follow suit. Even Aewyn had to follow or risk being trampled herself.

"Aewyn!" Venser cried, waving a big arm over his head. Fixated on the horses, it dawned on her slowly who was calling out to her, and why; then she was bounding across the field to him, and to Bram, and to all the rest of the Havenari as they gave up a thunderous cheer and moved to put their hands on her, as if doubting whether she were real.

"It's really you," said one.

"Thank the Ten!" cried another. "We thought you were dead."

Aewyn's smile took on a tinge of sadness. "The folk in the mines weren't so lucky."

"I'm sorry you had to see that," said Bram. He put his arms around her tightly: of all the men whose tears had burst the threshold of their eyes at her return, only his were tinged with sadness.

"Ashimar killed them," said Aewyn, her young voice edged with troubles. "He killed them all."

"Gods," said Venser. "How many?"

"Almost two dozen," she said. "All killed, in cold blood, every one of them."

"That's not right," Venser started. "What about the lower—"

Bram held her tight to his breast, cradled her little head in his hands, and shot Venser a look of cold warning the big man had never seen from any but Bram's sister. Venser clapped his jaw shut.

"How terrible," said Venser, knowing full well how many were truly down there.

"We're glad you're not among them," said Bram softly. "Glad as hounds at homecoming. And you found the horses!"

"All but Hendec's horse," said Aewyn. "My horse, I mean. Melia…

they killed her."

"I'm so sorry, lass," said Venser.

"She was lamed on the ride. She knew better than to suffer Ashimar to ride her. She died unbroken, I suppose." But there was a limit to even Aewyn's good cheer, and she fell weeping to the men, who as tender with her as they might have been with the daughters they never had.

From atop the hill where the blonde woman lay close to death, Robyn watched the men surround a white-haired girl, cheering and laughing, as those who had lost horses pulled them from the confused pack and stroked their manes with voices gentle as loving suitors'. She touched Acorn's mane gently, but could not yet go down to Aewyn, for Tsúla had come to her with a wounded Travalaithi soldier—and enough bandages from the keep, she hoped, to save the young woman's life.

"Are you the Overseer?" she asked him. The young man, hiding his fear as poorly as she had done only a year before, straightened to his full height and shrugged.

"I...I might be," he said. "Name's Tannock. Tannock Keldron. Companion of the Eighth Legion of the Shield, or at least I was."

"You were?" she asked.

Tannock cast his eyes over a green rocky field littered with the bodies of his fellows-at-arms, taking stock of those he knew, and those he was beginning to like.

"I was," he said. "I came up here to get away from the fighting. If you haven't found a living man named Rendon—tall man, red beard, one arm lost at the shoulder, sour fellow—then I suppose I'm your Overseer. At least until the bigger wolves get back from Orrath."

"Can you dress a wound, Tannock?"

He nodded. "I dressed my own."

"You're going to do what you can for this woman."

"Of course," he said. "Is she the only prisoner we took?"

Robyn's confusion lasted only a moment. "The only one," she said. "The rest have gone."

Tsúla brushed at her shoulder. "You hear all that noise below?" he asked. "Sounds like they stayed to clean out the mines after all. Smash the machines, burn the timbers, throw the iron stockpiles into the sea."

"Impossible," said Tannock. "Everything we worked for…we don't have the men to make a second go of it?"

Robyn forced a smile. "It wouldn't be wise, sir," she said. "See to this prisoner. Soon as we can ride, the Havenari will head down the coast, see what we can find."

"If you can find Rendon the Reckless," said Tannock, "he's the real Overseer. He had some mad design to go down into the mines. I hope to the Gods he's still alive. I don't want to be in charge when the Imperator hears we lost the mines, the prisoners, the equipment, a whole year's supply of iron."

"See to her," ordered Robyn, though she made it sound like she was entreating a superior officer. "The Havenari will take care of the rest."

The day wore on as they tended the wounded, and the winter sun was warm and bright in a sky of cloudless blue. The raiders worked diligently on the cliffside as the Havenari kept what was left of the little garrison away from the mine-trails, and the only work-song that rang up from the cliff below was the crack of timbers and sharp ring of refined iron raining down the white rock and into the sea. The young woman was delirious from the loss of blood, but Tannock cleaned her wounds and bound them as best he could, and swore to the Havenari she would live to be questioned. The men of the Havenari were overjoyed to see Aewyn alive and well, but their joy was no less at being reunited with the horses who were almost family to them: to the Travalaithi soldiers, especially the couriers and cavalry on campaign, horses were as much a commodity as hardtack and salt pork for rations, or war-karach bred for digging ditches and hauling wagons. But to the outriders of Haveïl, most of whom had named their mounts and known them since they were foaled, there was a lingering joy in their safe return that did much to take the sting out of carrion-work.

Even under the warmth of the afternoon sun, the ground was too frozen to bury the casualties, but the Havenari took the time to carry them far out from the Keep and especially from Fingrun Town, that the villagers there might be spared the heartache of seeing the bodies as they met their end. Aewyn, untroubled by their cold bodies, dragged them with great and painstaking effort to the top of the little hill, and there she laid them out and removed their helmets so that their dead faces might look upward to the sky. Even the bloodguards' helms she removed and laid aside, curious as to their faces, and wondering what sort of men they might have been—and who they would have become if they had not been raised from the cradle to serve the Red Captain.

"You fought well," she told them, in spite of her distaste; she imagined it was all they would have cared about. "You did your duty. Crows take your eyes, soldier. And crows take your eyes, sir. And eagles, sir, Great Royal eagles take yours." By the time she left them to their end, after secret rites that only the karach still observed, the great carrion-birds circling above the high cliff were only to keen to oblige.

In her mind, Baran was among the aerils in a place of great and ancient magic. The cobblestones where she lay seemed to move and shift beneath her, and though she felt the Floating City at her back, she was too dizzy to rise and could not bring herself to look upon it. It felt familiar to her, yet the cloudless skies were streaked with darkness: strange shadows had come to Varphann, and if they had come even hither, there was no place to which they had not.

The world, if not in ruin, was beginning to rupture. The tapestry of existence all around her seemed to bleed at its seams with some far horror she could not name. The cold terror of its presence shocked her out of her reverie, out of a half-conscious stupor and back to the word of the waking.

Beneath her, the ground rocked softly. Voices shouting her name called up from far away, and a mile or more beneath her she could hear the rush and roar of the distant sea.

"Come back to us," a voice said softly. "Come back to us."

Baran opened her eyes so suddenly that the shadows of her episode still lingered at the edge of her vision. She was lying on her back, on the deck of Hormer's ship. Beside her, Odi likewise lay out in exhaustion but clutched a knife tightly in his hand. She brushed her own thigh, felt for the Harrod knife, and was relieved to find its slim comforting weight there.

"What's happened?" she asked.

"Accounts differ," said Odi.

"Did we lose the mine?" Baran asked.

"It was never ours to lose," said Odi. "But it was Valithar's mine to lose—and lose it he did, at least for a while."

She tried to sit up, but settled for an uneasy shifting of her weight.

"Tell me," she said. "Tell me how it ended."

Odi cleared his throat. "The cost was high. A lot of good folk died today. We never took the tower, in the end—not that we could have kept it for long. But the Havenari rode onto the field as we fell."

Baran could hardly turn any paler. "Rode for whom?"

Odi shrugged. "Themselves, I suppose. The ordinary folk of the land. They put an end to the fighting, but not by more force than needed. There were few enough of us left to fight them, and they were fresh fighters, armoured and mounted. We were easy enough to separate from the Purples, and they just…let us go."

"What? Why?"

"Seems to me they were here to keep the peace, and that's all."

"They're on our side?" asked Baran incredulously.

"I never said that," said Odi. "But they did let us return to our ships. You can bet Elodia was furious. Sent home from battle like a stern schoolmaster excused her. So she took some of the survivors and smashed up the mines before we left."

Baran leaned in hopefully.

"And the iron?"

"It's in the sea," said Odi, frowning. "Just as we planned it. It's gone, except for what we can carry for ourselves."

"Every pound of iron counts," said Baran. "How many are left?"

Odi rubbed at his chest, as if massaging the stubborn words out of his throat. "Not many," he said, grief filling his voice. "Twelve, I think. That's counting yourself, me."

"Catrine?"

Odi's eyes betrayed him so honestly that he needed say nothing. "She took on Ashimar alone," he said at last.

"Gods," Baran sighed. "Why? Why would she do such a thing?"

"To save you," said Odi. "She saved me, too. It's disgraceful, isn't it—a woman giving her life on the field for a man."

"A soldier," said Baran, "protecting another soldier. That is the way of war, Odi. You'll have to learn that if you're to keep spying. You cannot carry that guilt."

Odi looked her in the eyes for the first time in a long while.

"It's not guilt," he said. "I know what needs doing. But I'm going to miss her."

Baran, somewhat uncharacteristically, put a slender arm around him where they lay on the deck.

"That iron was destined for the Black Foundries beneath Cîr-Valithar," said Baran. "Not all of that profane place has been turned into baths for the pleasure of the gentry. It would have been forged into better armour and weapons than we can hope to find for ourselves. It would have gone to Thurmod's legions, or Harrod's. It would have gone into the guts and necks and eyes of our own men—and their widows after them. It's a pity we can't carry it all back to Jordac ourselves."

"It's not the iron I came for," said Odi.

"The iron is why we were sent," Baran reminded him. He shook his head ruefully.

"The men and women of the mine—I'd hoped we could save them," said Odi. "That's what I meant to do. It's why I started in on playing this game to begin with. It's why I took care to get good at it. Don't mistake me: I have the ear of half the honest moneylenders in Travalaith, and near all the crooked ones. I know what will come of this. I know the price of iron will leap high as the moon when word of what we've done reaches the Capital. But mark me on this, Baran, for I'm a man of few pronouncements: whatever the price of iron, the worth of blood will always be higher. My web dwindles by the day. Two hundred men and women of all shapes would've gone far to rebuilding it for you."

"Nearly three hundred," Baran corrected him. "At least, by Madge's last report."

Odi's face grew ashen. "I spoke with the men who were up smashing the equipment," he said. "They found Madge, too. She didn't make it."

Baran shut her eyes tight. "She did very well by us," she said. "This raid was as much her handiwork as anyone's. It's a shame she never lived to see it."

"There are a few who did," said Odi. "In the deepest tunnels. When the slaughter began up above, they broke from their captors and drove as deep down into shadow as they could. Most of them didn't survive. The few survivors we found—Elodia's been rounding them up."

Baran breathed a sigh of relief. "When we're a safe distance out from the coast, I'd very much like to hear what they have to say about the enemy operations."

"So would we all," said Odi. "I think the panic of being hunted in the dark got the better of them. We've hauled in perhaps a dozen, and they've all gone to babble. Raving mad. I'd give them a day or two to rest, sleep off their misadventure before we start to go at them with hard questions."

"So it shall be," said Baran. "For my part, I'm quickly growing tired of being able to see the beach from here. "How are we doing on the mines?"

"Their facilities are totally destroyed," said Odi. "A few stragglers are up there throwing wheelbarrows full of ingots into the sea."

"I don't want them there after dark," said Baran. "The Havenari may keep the peace for now, but the minute a few grieving soldiers get the idea they can sneak out under cover of darkness and have the last word, we're in trouble."

"Good. And the Havenari won't turn on us?"

"Near as I can figure," said Odi, "they came for that girl. She was telling the truth. She's dear to them. She got mixed up with the Scourge over something. If it came down to it, I think they were ready to cross swords for her."

"Did they kill him?" Baran asked.

"If they hadn't," said Odi, "we wouldn't be having this conversation...but nobody seems to know the particulars. The men are asking around. The rumour that's making the rounds says he fought too close to the edge, and somebody pitched him over into the drink."

Baran peered up at the wave-battered wall of dappled white rock, gauged the distance, looked to where the drop would take a man onto the rocks, and where it might take him, if he were lucky, directly into the sea.

"A good diver could survive it," she said. "I think."

"The fall, aye," said Odi. "If he had Kedwyn's favour and didn't break his back on the waves. But if the fall didn't end him, you can bet that silver skin of his would drown him. If he fell in the shallows, he's dead. If he fell where it's deepest, he's dead."

Baran stood, though her head throbbed and she stumbled uneasily, and staggered to the rail. The feuding moons had passed as the morning turned into afternoon, and the churning seas had calmed into an almost glassy stillness. With keen eyes she scanned the surface of the water.

"He's dead," she repeated.

"Aye." Grunting with the effort, Odi rose and joined her at the railing. Distantly, to the south, a small landing-boat was putting out from the narrow strip of beach, carrying the last of the surviving raiders with a heavy chest sealed in wax. They had found one last survivor in the deeps too, and had taken care to bundle him in blankets as a mother swaddles a child before moving him.

"Jordac will be pleased to know," said Baran.

Lost in thought, watching the last of the raiders rowing hard toward them, Odi was slow to reply.

"To know what?"

"That Ashimar's dead," said Baran.

"Right," said Odi. "Dead." His gaze lingered on the coastline to the south a little longer—then drifted back to the calm and silent sea to the north.

"That's a hard blow struck," said Baran, though there was a low anxiety in her voice. Odi had been a spy for many years; he knew the thinnest edge of doubt when he heard it.

"Aye," he said. They stood together in cold silence and lingering dread for a long moment.

"Weigh the anchor," she ordered, suddenly. "Soon as they're aboard, tell Hormer to get us out of here."

Odi acknowledged the order and hustled away. "No objections here," he mumbled over his shoulder. "I've had about enough of this place."

Baran did not take her eyes off the waves. "Hurry," she said.

Odi set himself to the capstan and motioned for a few of Hormer's hands to give aid. The ship was already starting to move under sail when the last of the raiders reached it, and handed up with great difficulty the heavy wooden chest.

"It's the best of what they had," said one. "Top-grade. Each bar is wax-sealed. I know it's not what we came for, but it's a prize, trust me."

Elodia and some of the surviving raiders came to help hoist it over the side as Hormer's corsairs secured the little boat.

"It's a good find," Elodia conceded. "What about that one?"

She pointed to the lean twisted figure swaddled in blankets along the length of the boat. He was bound so tightly that they handed him up as if moving a log or a carpet. Clutching him through the blankets, she felt that one his shoulders hung weirdly, and she could grip no arm beneath it.

"Was he wounded?" she asked. "Is this new?"

"We don't know," said one of the raiders. "We found him in the deepest tunnels with the body of a young woman."

"Madge's body," another confirmed. "I think it was. I only met her a few times."

"What's wrong with him?" asked Elodia.

"Tried to stick us with his sword," said the first. "That's why he's tied, under there. But he was just protecting the woman's body. I think the fight's all out of him now."

Elodia looked down into the man's face. His eyes were bloodshot, locked wide but unseeing, and his breath came in panicked gasps.

"Thank the gods," he breathed suddenly.

Elodia cradled his head, but took care not to angle her body too close to him.

"Can you speak?" she asked him. "Do you understand Tradespeak?"

"Killed her," he whispered through ragged breaths. "Ashimar... killed her."

Elodia stroked his hollow, haunted face with a callused but gentle hand.

"It's all right," she said. "He's gone. He's gone now."

"Thank the gods, the gods, thank the gods," he breathed.

Elodia smiled in spite of herself. "We too are most glad to be rid of him," she said.

At that, the swaddling came undone and the one-armed man's gaunt hand, stained black and red with ink and dried blood, closed around the collar of her mail-coat near her neck. She tried to back away, but she had been fighting all morning and his grip had the strength of madness in it. Seizing his fingers, trying desperately to pry them away from her throat, Elodia was fumbling for her dagger when he caught her eyes with his own. Fixing her with a stare of horrid panic, his blue gaze bored into hers with a terror she would never forget.

"Thank the gods," he croaked hoarsely, as if with great effort from far away, "that Ashimar found her first."

The others were on him after that, gripping at Elodia's shoulders to tear her away from his grasp, but his hand released suddenly and he fell back to the deck, shaking and gasping, eyes rolling wildly.

"Bind him!" one shouted. "He's loose, bind him!" But none of the twisting, jerking movements of his body would pass for resistance for very long. Stout rope was never in short supply on the deck of an Adâni corsair's ship, and he was soon cocooned like a moth in the strongest cord they had. He was mostly silent now, though occasionally he fell to weeping and spluttering. More than once he let out a sudden scream and was silent.

"That's every kind of troubling," said Odi, transfixed by the commotion.

Elodia nodded. "Make him comfortable. We'll question them tomorrow when they've found their senses."

As the sun began to fall away, Hormer pushed for the open sea—or as open as he dared past Fingrun, in the biting cold northeast of Haveïl's rocky coastline. The seas were calm and there was little wind to be had, and though he beat rapidly into the headwind, his crew were a flurry of motion aboard a ship that barely seemed to move. The sky darkened, and still Baran watched the waves, occasionally darting her eyes up to the high coast. As they came round the horn of Fingrun, the square-topped keep passed from view entirely, though the ancient watchtower would have been high enough to spot them. In the lowering light, Baran listened for greater upset from the coast, but heard little. North of the cliff, where again the land had come down to a shallow rocky beach, a solitary campfire burned and winked from the shore.

"Take us farther out," she ordered Hormer, once he had seen it. "I don't know who that is, but I don't want to be seen from shore."

Like a restless child who can find no comfort in bed, there was no comfort to be had for her. At first, the light had seemed menacing, watching the Adâni ship like a gleaming yellow eye. But as they passed away from it and into the blackness of the northern sea, they passed from the gentle glow of dusk into an immense and impenetrable darkness.

There was soon nothing to be seen in the blackness, but Baran watched it anyway, fearful to turn her back on the lightless sea. She watched it heedless of the cold in her hands and her slender neck, with no regard to the anxious chatter and conversation of the raiders or the periodic wails and screams that came from belowdeck. It was only when one of the rescued prisoners did suddenly, choking and frothing around his own tongue, that the men came to her and insisted she come to tend them.

"It's some sorcery, I swear," said Elodia. "Only you can help them."

Baran was older and wiser than mortal men in the ways of many things. She had studied with the monks of Kazan-Yeng and read the priceless works of medicine and engineering that had come across the Great Sea from Edlana. She had assisted Jordac time and time again in his studies of cadavers—learning through observing, as she lent her graceful hands to his fascinated disassembly of living things, every art of healing that was known to him. Alone among the sailors, soldiers, and spies, only Baran knew upon sight and contact the signs of the Aldwode. In her wisdom she knew the ways that the greater spawn of the Second Craftsman afflicted all those who beheld them in the fullness of their dread majesty. In her wisdom, too, she knew that there was no cure left in the world for that sickness—knew that the knowledge to draw men back from such darkness had been gone now for centuries, passed forever beyond the ken of even her own ancient kind.

"They will die tonight," she said. And she waved away the sailors, soldiers, and spies; and when those were gone, she held the frightened prisoners' hands gently in her own, and she sang to them all through the night, until her crystalline voice was hoarse from use and shaking from sadness as much from the savage coldness of the sea air:

> *Silval fograivect iara silbethaldeom,*
> *Un oluamai nualie, ei nuilad,*
> *Undunda ve li lathtarin*
> *Iaralmaira, miumildarim,*
> *Ver valailu urandi ap verad,*
> *şidril hallom valailu şidrilad,*
> *Lai val silverad ve Silvaldeom,*
> *Ic eşton hallom hil lai hil,*
> *Ic eşton ossil lai ossil.*

Around midnight, after a period of merciful calm, the screams began. The terror came on in waves after that, from one to the next. So pure and so distinctive were the prisoners' cries of horror that the sound of one hellish scream alone was enough to set the next to screaming, like a pack of hounds hard on a scent. The first of them died in the first hour, screaming and writhing so forcefully that he smashed the ribs that were already brittle from malnourishment and bled quietly into his lungs. As the hour grew late and the night fell darker, one by one they succumbed. In the end, she sent for Odi, who knew a thing or two about poisons, and those who suffered too much or too long were brought into a fitful and final sleep from which there would be no waiting. For Odi, who had knifed men in back-alleys, who had betrayed counter-spies and sent good friends to their deaths in war, the business was unbearable, and he wept freely as he followed his orders.

"In all my years," he swore, "in all my grisly business…I've never taken a life before, *never*, that didn't save at least two more down the road." But he went about his mercy-work with a hard sense of duty, and as he criss-crossed the cargo hold half-filled with dry goods for Adân, and half-filled with the dead and dying, he touched Baran's hand or shoulder at every pass, to remind her that he had been a living and kind person once, and so had she, and that only the hell of war itself had made demons of them.

The one-armed man was the last to die. He had suffered the longest, and among even the blood-curdling screams of the other afflicted, he faced his terrors in stony silence. Undressing him at the neck as he approached with a small wooden bowl, Odi watched the broken man's eyes dart down to the cup knowingly before passing back into their sightless dream of terror.

"Ah, you're purple scum, I see," whispered Odi. "Here in the end, I don't suppose it matters much, poor fellow. But being the hated purple scum and all, you'll know about the Mother's Drop, the one all Ceruleans wear 'round their big oafish necks, in case they're ever captured. No one knows what's in them—not really. They're made special in the Rattle. Everyone's got a guess, though. Every alchemist and apothecary has got some idea what's in it, more or less. What's it they say? 'Cerulyns for a Cerulean?' I'm sure that blue flower's got to be part of it—and by the grace of Kedwyn, we had more than a few on board. I can't promise you this'll be as gentle—nothing in the world as gentle as a Mother's Drop, all the poisoners and assassins know. But it's my own brew, courtesy of a longer life of espionage than anyone's got a right to. As far as imitations go, you'll find it on the gentler side."

He lifted the bowl to the man's lips. "Up we go. There's a good fellow. You tell that old Rascal, Tamnor, he's got no hold on you no more. Shh. You're in Odi's hands now, friend. No more suffering. No more scared."

From beneath a tossed tangle of blankets, the soldier's stained left hand reached up as he swallowed. Slowly, he touched the edge of the bowl, then traced Odi's finger to his hand, and his hand to his wrist, which he clutched in earnest. Raising himself up gingerly, as if the height of a few inches was nearly more terror than he could bear, he looked Odi in the eyes one last time with the pleading eyes of a madman on the edge of reason.

"Thank you," he said. "But please—please—"

He slipped back onto the crate where his makeshift deathbed was made, and Odi made to pull away. But still the hand gripped him, and still the dull eyes were fixed on his.

Odi leaned in as the soldier's ribs raised high with great effort.

"Take care of my child," he whispered in his delirium, and was gone.

The sleep of unconsciousness, altogether different from the natural rest he had known, was peaceful beyond description. Rasten clutched softly at the rich, luxurious black fur that cocooned him, and for just a moment in the haze of a dreamless stupor he was completely at ease.

The disasters of the world came back all at once. There was, on his face and protruding knuckles, a chill and bitter wind, and the agonizing pain of fingers that had long been numb. There was the searing fire that burned in his hips and his lower back—and, he soon discovered, at the great bruised and bloody welts at his armpits and waist, along his thighs, over his chest. There was the sharp agony of breathing in and the low soothing ache of breathing out through ribs held together mostly by the sheer dumb optimism of their owner. And though the world above him was a luxurious and warm mantle of fine black sable, the world beneath him was a craggy bed of uneven white stones, a desolate rocky beach of chalk and mud, ringed by tidal puddles of frigid salt water and strands of reeking kelp.

His first sound was to be a shout of pain, but his ribs barely admitted it. It came out as a whimper when he tried to roll onto his back. Every muscle and joint screamed in protest. Pushing himself halfway over with the force of his tireless hands, Rasten lay wheezing on his back, too cold to lie still but too pained to shiver. To one side of him, a blazing bonfire warmed him almost pleasantly, until he turned his head to see a grinning black skull in the flames.

"Gods!" Rasted cried. "Gods, what? No!"

It was a pyre of bodies piled high, for the beach was a treeless expanse of stone with nothing else ot burn. The smell of it, as soon as he realized, turned his guts and set him almost to panic. He was surprised it had not done so instantly—but then, he was already in a world of complaints, and one more burden hardly seemed to make the rest of his troubles any heavier.

"Easy," said a deep voice. "Keep it down. At least till we know if there's survivors."

As Rasten blinked his watering eyes and peered through the rancid smoke of the fire, he could see a tall figure on the far side, balanced delicately on a greatsword whose sinister shape he knew all too well.

"Gods," he said again, gauging whether he was too hurt to rise. The numbess made it hard to tell.

As the wind picked up, a familiar face emerged in the smoke.

"Kellan," he groaned. "What—how?"

The big man shrugged. "If you really want to know, 'what' is playing nursemaid. It seems I've a knack for it. As to 'how,' perhaps one of the gods I always forget is especially fond of idiots with a death wish."

Rasten tested his shoulders and elbows to see if anything was broken.

"I assure you," he said, "I've no wish for death. I'm very interested in cheating it, if I can."

The man he knew as Kellan Fyldron limped around to his side of the fire, using Ashimar's polished greatsword as a makeshift cane with one arm. In the other, he clutched a red-enameled helmet with the head of a majestic stag. The big man gripped it by the brutally sharp antlers, and held it out over the fire with something sloshing inside it.

"Then it'll please you to know that cheating death is almost all you've done all day," he said, jerking his head toward the distant cliffs. "I saw you go over the side. First the fall nearly killed you. That was bad enough. Then, I'm in a bad way here, sore wounded by the leg. You nearly drowned before I got out there. You had the sense to doff most of your armour, but you had enough bits on to ruin my day hauling you back. I watched the water rip your pauldrons right off, going in. Then, it was the wet that nearly froze you to death, then the cold air as I dried you."

"You saved me," breathed Rasten. "Kellan, you saved my life."

"Call me Grimwulf," he said. "I've no more use for my old name. There's a price on it, now. A heavy one."

"Th-thank you," Rasten stammered.

"Death's a house with a thousand doors," said Grimwulf. "I feel like I've been slamming them shut for you all day. I expect after your little swim, you'll die of the grip, or the dropsy, or winter fever. At this point, I swear to every hell, if you so much as sneeze, I'll beat you to death myself."

Rasten shivered, suddenly, brushed at some hidden terror in the back of his mind. The weight of dread, for reasons he could not place, was still heavy in his bones. He looked back to the waves, suddenly frightened, recalling at last the reason for his desperate fall.

"Did you see Ashimar fall?"

"He fell with you," said Grimwulf. "Happiest sight I've seen in months. Plunged straight off the cliffside into the deep. You floated back up, and I'm pleased to say he did not. I saw him earlier, too. We had a heated disagreement as to which of us should be dead. If it's you who won me that argument, I owe you my thanks, too."

Rasten smiled absently but still gazed out to sea.

"I had no choice," he said. "I saw Catrine, during the fighting."

Grimwulf rolled his eyes. "That seems improbable."

"She was there," he insisted. "Fighting with the rebels. Fighting against *him*. I saw her."

"No," said Grimwulf, "you didn't. I think you were mad with it, after all you've been through. And you saw your lady-love in the face of whoever he meant to kill. You'd long since had enough of old tin-britches; even I could see that. Only you've got a soldier's loyalty and a poet's weak stomach for killing."

"There's something more to him—or there was," said Rasten stubbornly. "And I saw her, plain as day, close as you to me. Didn't I?"

"You earned the Blue on the battlefield, is that right?"

Rasten looked down at his ruined gambeson, and the scraps of battered armour that remained. His old uniform felt so far away, now.

"I did," he said.

"Then squeamish or not, you're ready enough to kill a man when it needs doing."

"With honour," Rasten corrected him. "In the field. Not in their beds, not with their wives, not the way the Scourge has done."

"There you go," said Grimwulf. "Someone had to put a stop to him. Fifteen years he's been locked in that armour. Fifteen years he's served as the Imperator's avenging hand, now that the old man's too much the coward to do his own fighting. But there's a dread that follows him, and you've felt it as sure as I. Every man with the sense to oppose him has been too afraid to see it done. So maybe I owe that stupid poet heart of yours an apology. When the time came, when other men—maybe even me—would've lost the nerve to see it through…you did the right thing, man. The right thing. And in the madness of battle, you saw whatever you needed to see to give you that courage."

Rasten covered his face with cold-numbed hands. "I could have sworn," he said. "But I miss her so much. I see her eyes in every face. Every face, man or woman, living or dead."

"Don't I know," said Grimwulf. "War's a lonely business, isn't it?"

"Where will you go?" asked Rasten.

"West," said Grimwulf.

"Not east?"

Raising the greatsword awkwardly, testing the strength of his wounded leg, Grimwulf gestured out to sea. "You see that ship?" he asked. "The Adâni corsairs?"

"Barely," said Rasten. "You have keen eyes."

"It's the ship I came on. They've scant supplies on board. Emptied the ship, mostly, to take on fighters for that little nightmare we all just woke up from. They'll have to drop anchor in Aslea for a day or two. If we meet them there, and give their captain a good sock on the jaw for leaving without me, they may take us on to Adân, or put into a major port, get you back where you're going."

Rasten tried to stand. His joints were working, but everything was shot through with pain.

"Everything hurts," he grunted. "I'll just slow you up."

"Don't be noble," said Grimwulf. "I'll move faster with you than without you. That's not poetic courtesy; I'm putting you to work. I've taken a hard wound, and if I'm not careful it'll split open again. I'll need you to carry everything, just about. So if you're looking to be charitable, don't selflessly lie around moping and waiting for death. Pick up what you can carry and start moving, at whatever pace you can carry it."

Grimwulf had dared not show his face at Fingrun itself, regardless of who now held the keep, but he had skulked and scrounged along the cliff's edge, and along the rocky trail that led down to the mine. The raiders had travelled light, expecting only combat, but a few of the dead carried small bows and quivers of arrows that could be burned. The bloodguard, spent from their long ride, had been better equipped for travel, but there was little in the way of rations left, and less still of the comforts and luxuries afforded to ordinary travelers. There was, however, a familiar axe that Grimwulf had retrieved from the field in haste, and Rasten seized it with relish as he gathered their ragged sack of scrounged belongings.

"You saved this?" he asked.

"Why, something wrong with it?"

Rasten tested its precise weight and balance in his hand. "No, no, it's perfect."

Grimwulf shrugged. "Good. One axe is as good as another, but I'm glad you like it. We won't get far on the coast before we need to rest, but I mean at least to skirt the rock till it comes down to those hills—look there—and make the climb up to those trees. You can wax poetic on your perfect axe all the way from here to there, as long as I get a fire made of firewood instead of bodies. Like normal folk."

"Normal folk," Rasten echoed, and shouldered the sack.

Bent low like venerable pilgrims, their march was slow and pitiful. The two men set out for the hills, which were of course many times farther away than they at first appeared. The cliffs of Fingrun were meant to be defensible, and if the one rocky cove and narrow path had been properly garrisoned, as it should have been, it was long miles in both directions before the sheer cliff could be climbed from the sea. Though Rasten boasted the endurance of a bull, and Grimwulf made no fuss of his pain and was as tough as he needed to be, they were above all survivors, and their stops for rest and water were frequent. Grimwulf had scrounged as much fresh water and trail wine from the others as he could, and though their bellies burned with hunger as night overtook them, they were in fair shape and fairer spirits, eager above all not to be counted among the dead.

"Aewyn is alive, too," Rasten said, somewhere far along their march. "I saw her."

"She was alive this morning, then," said Grimwulf. "When you saw her."

"She came to free the prisoners," Rasten said. "She brought weapons for them."

"Aye."

"I presume she came with the rebels…with you."

"Aye."

"See, I thought you were headed somewhere safe. I didn't think you'd be so quick to put yourself back in harm's way."

"Did she see his handiwork?" Grimwulf asked.

Rasten shook his head. "I couldn't bear to tell her," he said. "She saw a few of the dead, the ones being prepared for mine-work. I couldn't tell her how many waited below."

"You kill any of them?"

Rasten shot him an angry glare.

"You served Ashimar longer than I did," he said. "It seems like a fair question."

"He sent us down," said Rasten. "I slipped away in the upper tunnels. Kept moving so they wouldn't find me. It was a nightmare I'll not forget. The dead down there in those tunnels—"

"That's enough of your dead," said Grimwulf tersely. "I've nightmares of the same kind."

"I find that hard to believe," said Rasten, "after all the killing you've seen."

"I've made my peace with mine," he said. "Did I ever tell you how I came to be in Castor Stannon's service?"

Rasten's lips played idly on his teeth as he thought. "I don't think you've rightly told me who Castor Stannon is."

"Imperial Censor of Haukmere," said Grimwulf. "Lord of Wescairn."

"Wescairn?" said Rasten. "That's remote. That's as far West as the Shield reaches. No wonder you're so uncultured."

Grimwulf bared his teeth at him, but went on.

"I was six months shy of my sixteenth birthday when I joined the Grand Army. It was a man's pay. It was a man's life. It was a way out of my father's House, no questions asked—not on the eve of the Forty-Nine Day Siege. Every man was needed. I left home by night, swore the Oath in Carmac, and met up with the Sixth Legion of the Blade. Harrod was Marshal of the Middle Blades then—he wasn't Master General yet."

"I remember," said Rasten. "Not long after, my brother and I served in the Fifth. I should like to have known you before all this…"

"Straight away they sent us east," Grimwulf continued, interrupting. "I thought it'd be months before we got to the front and saw real fighting. I was just a boy. I didn't understand what was happening."

Rasten half-shut his eyes as they walked, trying to picture the map of the Empire in his head. But his lessons were a distant memory now.

"East of Orrath is through Creslyn Wood," he said. "They didn't take you south?"

"The vasils of Creslyn opposed the Siege," said Grimwulf. "Might have joined the rebels, if they'd survived. They had to be stomped out, for their own sake, to demoralize the First Rising, and to send a message to the other nobles. So my first campaign was against my fellow Travalaithis, under Harrod, at the fall of Draden."

"Watchers deny it," said Rasten. "That massacre? At fifteen?"

"It was a gentle enough introduction to killing," said Grimwulf. "The Fanes betrayed their own. Olferth's family'd had some feud with them going back. Draden Castle could have held us out for years. But their own kin slipped us into the castle, and we slaughtered them to a man. It wasn't a siege. It wasn't a battle. It was a massacre."

"In my experience," said Rasten, "massacres are a bit more one-sided. I heard Harrod lost fifteen quires in that assault…a tenth of the whole Legion."

"Listen," said Grimwulf. "I was fifteen. I didn't know the first thing of what we were doing. But of course, they weren't Selikhans. The Easterners, they fight. Every man, every woman. Every child who can lift a knife. Not so among us weak Imperials. The men stood against us, and the men died, every one. The women and children fled into the family catacombs. Not long after we put the castle to the torch, Harrod called Right of Havoc and sent the men down to take their will."

Rasten shuddered. "You know, every day I woke up on the trail, threw on my panther helm, and followed Ashimar another ten leagues… I'd say to myself, 'he's not Harrod, Ras, he's many things but he's not Harrod.'"

"You're comparing roses and cabbages," said Grimwulf. "But no, I wasn't fond of the man, not before, and not after. I suppose you know the rest of how it went."

Rasten sighed, and slowed his step enough to unlock his singing-voice, which was sharp and not altogether pleasant:

The Season Of The Cerulyn

The green-eyed nobles slept unhelmed,
And in their sleep were overwhelmed
'Til every grave was laid in,
Like wasps within the honeyed hive
We left no man nor child alive
Within the walls of Draden.

There Elgar, son of Edgar died,
His sons and daughters at his side,
And thus their line was ended;
But glory none was won that day
And every triumph chased away,
By what we wretched men did.

Where blood in silent trickles fell
From step to step, we crept as well
In search of spoils or pleasure;
The lifeblood pooled at secret doors
Beneath lords' hoards and nobles' stores—
Where fathers hid their treasure.

The wars that ended Elgar's days
Were well-fought, and in righteous ways
Brought honour to who won them.
But no great victory could they plead
Once Harrod's hounds slipped off their lead
And brought their doom upon them.

Had all of us been slaked by gold,
Or lusted for what could be sold,
Then all the gold we gathered
Would deck with pride our living halls—
Not mournful hooks on barrow-walls
To grieve the sons we fathered.

The Legion's fate was turned and tipped
Upon the threshold of that crypt
Where hungry Death lay biding:
The masters who had lain in wait
Upon the rattling of their gate
Rose up at that ill tiding.

Three nights we scoured the catacombs,
Disturbed the ancient masters' homes
But found no living woman;
Each morning we withdrew in woe,
Half by the high road—half the low—
All too dead to be human.

The wedded rogues who courted doom
Like lustful suitors in the tomb
Found Death a willing maiden;
Two hundred wives in deep despair
Now know the woe of those who dare
Disturb the ghosts of Draden.

For once, too tired of body and soul to protest, Grimwulf let Rasten sing himself out without stopping him. He had skipped a verse here and there, and forgot almost the whole beginning, for which Grimwulf was glad. But it was a Travalaithi soldier's job on the march to drink sloppily and sing boorishly; and it had unnerved him, he now realized, that Ashimar's bloodguard had known no songs of war or soldiering but the eerie silence of death.

"That's it," he said at last. "That's the one. So don't tell me I don't know what it's like to fear caves filled with the dead."

"I had no idea," said Rasten. "Is it true? The ghosts of the old Fanes came to life and cut them all down in the dark?"

"I'd call you a superstitious fool," said Grimwulf, "but I've no better answer. They were one of the oldest of the First Families. Their crypts went down a long way. Most of the song's full of poet nonsense, as usual. Elgar Fane was out of bed when he died. He knew something was awry in the night—we'd set the hounds to barking, or something. His sworn squires were arming him when they killed him with his own blade. Killed the rest of his family, too, and the staff who weren't cross-sworn to the Tarbecks. Put them all down before I even went in. The survivors put up a fight as best they could. Like the song says, they sent their women into the catacombs. I suppose it was Harrod's idea of sport to call Havoc and turn us loose."

"But you survived."

"I wasn't interested," said Grimwulf. "I'll kill a man in a fight. Or a woman in a fight, if it comes to that. But I wanted no part of what was to come down there. So when the castle was emptied, my quire and most of the others went into the crypts, and I went to Draden Town, outside the wall. Listened for reports of my brave deeds to come in. They were not flattering—see, I was a fool once, too. That night, the first Night of the Ghosts…that was the first night I ever got drunk, and that was the whole of it. Next morning, I reported for duty. Thought I'd get three lashes for oversleeping. And instead, my Captain set me to work hauling out the bodies of the men who'd been cut down by the ghosts."

"Gods," breathed Rasten. "I can't imagine."

"Serves them right," Grimwulf said, shrugging. "There's no place for what those men had planned. Even in war. I burned them without regret. It's where I learned to burn bodies so well, if you wanted to know."

"I did want to ask," said Rasten. "That's not a skill you just come by. But then, that's not a thing you ask people."

"The next day, my quire was dissolved, me being the only man left of it. But Olferth was just coming to power, see, and his family were the ruling vasils in Creslyn after that, so they took good care of those who survived. I got my medal for valour—valour, hah—and when I had the power to choose, I took a post as far away from Draden and its ghosts as I could get. As you say, Wescairn's as west as west goes."

Rasten, at a loss, gestured to the green hills ahead, coming down to meet them where they would cross from the vasily of Haukmere into the barely-controlled Protectorate of Haveïl.

"Well, you're west of west now," he said.

Grimwulf chanced a sorrowful glance over his shoulder. "I wish we were headed east."

"So do I," said Rasten. "But I think the road ahead has a few turns in it yet." He reached down, caught Grimwulf's hand as the big man stumbled, hauled him up onto the grassy slope.

"You'll find your way home," said Grimwulf, taking the hill one step at a time. "It's the fools who always do."

NINETEEN

THE BLACK WALLS OF THE CÎR-VALITHAR were alive with shouts of alarm. Kind words whispered there never seemed to carry far, but the dread, the fright, the impatient anger of raised voices and harshly spat curse-words—these things echoed resoundingly through halls of seamless, spotless black iron.

At the crest of the morning, a little before noon, Illyria began to cry out, and to thrash upon her bed as if suffering one of her visions. But there were no strange words, no portents or dreams, only the terrible sound of her choking and wheezing as she shook herself almost to pieces. Her attendants, sworn under pain of death not to move or touch her until Moriath had come, made light enough of their oath to turn her on her side, to open her mouth and clear her tongue from her gasping throat. In their muscled arms, thin and fragile as a fawn, they could feel that she had broken her ribs at least, and maybe more, in the sudden fall from her bed.

Moriath had arrived almost instantly, having taken her rest in an adjoining chamber. She was greeted by the haggard face, swollen and suffocated, of her granddaughter turning a deadly cerulyn blue as she writhed on the floor. As her grandmother entered, she lurched over onto her fragile elbows, onto the arm whose invisible burns still made her sick with agony, and emptied her stomach onto the rich marble tile. Moriath approached, but stood some distance away as the attending bloodguards watched the girl with uneasy horror. When it seemed she had vomited up half the sea and her bile was clear, they lifted her to her bed only to find her nightgown stained crimson with blood in a dozen places. Still gasping for breath, still too panicked by pain and terror to form words, she clutched at the air like a spider in its last throes. In that moment, Moriath sent for Osgrim, and said that she was dying; and with the speed of a flickering shadow he came.

The karach at the outer gate did not react to his passing, and he raced into the room heedless of their crossed spears and growls of suspicion. Alarmed by his entrance, the bloodguards moved to stop him, but he fixed them with his stern schoolmaster's stare and they recoiled from him in pale silence.

"You should not have brought me here," he said. His voice rallied Illyria a bit—it was harsher and more full of venom than ever she had heard it.

"I had no choice," said Moriath. "Look at her. She's dying."

"Leave us,"said Osgrim, without looking up from her mangled body. The bloodguards abandoned their post at once and fled the room, and the heavy iron doors swayed shut behind them.

"A few minutes ago she fell," said Moriath. "She bleeds as if by wasting. She thew up half a bathtub, it seems, all clear. Her ribs are broken, crushed, some of them. Her hips, perhaps. She tried to cry out when they lifted her."

"You cannot ask me to save her," Osgrim barked in a fury. "Not here, not at the foot of Tamnor's throne."

"I beg you," she said, with all the gentle guile of an old woman. "She is an innocent child. And if she dies…you know what dies with her."

Osgrim threw down his curator's robes. The black doublet beneath was no trueblacked finery, but a pedestrian dark grey.

"Some of what dies with her should have died long ago," he said.

"And the rest?" she prodded him. "Or shall men like Olferth govern the North-Kingdom forever?"

Osgrim laid a long, bony hand upon Illyria's feverish, sweat-soaked brow.

"Illyria," he whispered.

"Osgrim," she gasped. "I'm hurt again. I'm sorry. Tell Grandmother I've hurt myself again—"

A coughing fit shook her and the agony of it was nearly too much to watch. Even her eyes, wide-open in terror, had filled with blood at the corners.

"Rest now," he said, with a voice of great power, and she passed from him into a fitful slumber. Osgrim tore the neckline of her nightgown with hands too strong for a master of the library. Beneath her collarbone, a deep gash had split her skin from the near armpit almost to the far breast.

"This is bad," he warned. "Taken all together, it's quite fatal."

"Please," said Moriath, without a hint of pride showing.

Osgrim shut his eyes. "*Tûr thum ulur*," he said—though whether it was a blessing, a prayer, a curse, a steadying mantra, Moriath could not be sure. With his bare hand, staining his doublet and breeches, he brushed away the spilling blood from her collar again, again, again, until there was nothing beneath his hand but pale unblemished skin. She shifted and groaned uneasily, and the simple movement brought a shower of pain to her joints. Osgrim took her shoulders next.

"Tell me she will live," said the old woman.

"Your plaintive cries for mercy," said Osgrim, "would carry far more weight if you enjoyed her suffering less transparently."

"Do not turn your Eleventh Sight on me," Moriath snapped. "I could have let her die today. But the coals of pity have not yet burned out in my heart."

Osgrim gently pressed at Illyria's ribs, her arms.

"You still have a use for her," he said accusingly, without looking up. "Or for Ashimar, at least."

"You say such things as if you do not," she replied. "Do not forget, old man, that you abide in this city by my grace. All the world may forget you, but you have no power over me. My husband saw to that even before we were wed."

Osgrim silenced her, pushed at Illyria's flesh and slowy reshaped the girl, bone by bone, into her former self.

"You think I would need to unbind my powers for you?" he said. "Do not flatter yourself. A swift shove down the tower stairs would put an end to you as quickly as an Oubliette."

"Do go on," said Moriath. "Do talk more of killing—if it pleases your appetites."

With a look of disgusted sadness, Osgrim fell silent and continued his work.

"Will they survive?" Moriath asked him.

"In fifteen years," said Osgrim, "this is the worst he's come off in any fight. It's enough to kill a man, no question."

"But not enough to kill two," said Moriath, hopefully.

The schoolmaster looked down at the silent girl with a profound sadness. "He won't last forever, you know. The way you command him, he cannot survive."

"If he loves her," said Moriath, "he will learn." She brushed a stray lock of the girl's dissheveld silver-blonde hair back into place. It was an especially empty gesture after Osgrim had reordered her whole broken body. Illyria groaned softly, still delirious from the pain. Where her flawless skin had split across the chest, an ugly white scar had swiftly begun to rise.

"I thought you had the hands of a healer," she said, half-mockingly.

"Send for a cellwife from the Rattle, if you wish to lighten her scarring," said Osgrim. "What little power I have is for life and death—not for vanity."

"It was nearly to the bone," said Moriath. "He must have taken his armour off, the trusting fool. I cannot wait to hear what provincial thug nearly bested him."

For a time, Osgrim and Moriath sat poised above the girl's fitfully senseless body, lost in their mutual contempt for each other. In time the bloodguards returned, and Moriath sent them for a proper healer.

"Thank you," said Moriath at last. The words did not come easily from her.

"I do nothing for you," said Osgrim, "nor will I ever."

"It is good, then," the old woman answered, "that you want her to live as much as I do."

"In her reside the dreams of many," said Osgrim. "She is more important than you know. But she is more, you know, than important. She is a human person, Lady Veritenh. Above all else, above your schemes and even mine, she is that."

"Spare me," said Moriath. "I do not burden you with my schemes, and I care little enough for yours, whatever they may be."

"We have a common Enemy," Osgrim warned. "He will return, and the people must be ready."

"My only concern is to maintain the Empire," said Moriath, "for as long as it can be held. So long as you serve that end, old man, you are welcome to hide where you like and meddle where you must."

Osgrim's long face tightened with disapproval.

"The old men of this world are forever meddling in the lives of the young," he said. "It is a trap of vanity, and I have no intention of falling into it."

"And yet you stay," said Moriath. "And yet you meddle."

"One cannot be blind to evil," said Osgrim. "That is a privilege left only for the *Imidactui*."

Moriath brushed Illyria's forehead with a hand that managed somehow to be fat and gnarled at the same time. The girl was cold to the touch, but not dangerously so.

"Miraculous," she whispered. "Mage or no, your kind are not known for their powers of healing. Tell me, Osgrim, however did you come by this gift?"

"It was by love," said Osgrim. "I don't imagine you'd understand."

"She loves you a great deal," said Moriath, almost absently. "And I am glad for it. She lives for your lessons, did you know that? She tells me so, every so often."

"I know it," said Osgrim. "But it is the world she loves—not me."

"And who brings her that?" said Moriath, gesturing deferentially.

"You flatter me," said Osgrim, suddenly on guard. "Why would you do that?"

Moriath looked away from the bed, toward the impenetrable latticed ironwork that surrounded the stairs ascending to the balcony.

"Will you take some air with me?"

"A breath will be enough," said Osgrim. "And only then because the library is stuffy."

They rose together and Moriath led him to iron screen surrounding the balcony stair. With the curtains drawn back, the wind from the sea poured unfettered into the room, shaking the flames in the hearth and filling the bedchamber with the unmistakeable heady scent of wildflowers in the height of summer.

"It will be an early spring this year," said Moriath. "A warm wind is not far off, and neither the swallows nor the starlings far behind her."

"Perhaps," said Osgrim, eyeing her suspiciously.

"As long as the Royal Gardens still bloom," she said, "as long as the Three Maidens open their blossoms within the walls of Travalaith…there is hope that one day the ancient city will rise again."

She smiled sweetly at Osgrim's stricken face. "That is what you told her, yes?"

"It is," said Osgrim, seeing little need nor chance for deceit now. She brushed his sleeve with false affection and leaned in close to him.

"One Mage's Uprising is quite enough, I think," she said. "If you ever incite a second rebellion in my granddaughter's mind with your teachings, I shall take her from this tower, and we shall have a pleasant walk through the Gardens. And she will know them for what they are, and know you for a liar and a false friend."

"It would destroy her," said Osgrim, suddenly fearful. "She is your own blood, Lady Veritenh."

"She takes more after her father," the old woman snapped. "Disobedient. Hateful. Lustful. Heedless of her place. Reckless in her passions, with a liar's heart and a thirst for rebellion."

Osgrim laughed once, so sharply it nearly awoke Illyria from her fitful rest.

"You speak as if these qualities displease you," he said.

Moriath's pallid skin flushed red with anger: those who laughed at her in her moments of sincerity seldom did so twice.

"Do as you like with her," Moriath whispered harshly. "But she is under my control, *mine*, and if you would not meddle in our affairs, you will respect that and leave it well enough alone. Do we have an understanding?"

Osgrim leaned close to the latticework, taking in the heady scent of rare flowers and forest blossoms. He lost himself in that complex fragrance for a long moment, drifting in his mind to deep green places far away: even knowing them to be false, in and of themselves, the mingled scents seemed to spirit him away to deeper and more heartfelt truths—rather like a good story, he supposed.

In a moment, he returned to himself and looked down on the old woman with a smile of serenity, if not fondness.

"If she is so unruly," he said, "and if you despise her for it so—why do you give her even this?"

The old woman looked out to see with a narrow smile.

"Have you ever tried," she said, "to punish someone from whom you had already taken everything?"

Osgrim glanced back at Illyria, slowly waking but still too distressed to speak or rise.

"You know I have," he whispered.

Silently, from a place of great suffering, the girl began to weep, though a lifetime of being chastised for her loudness had taught her to weep in silence. Where her suffering might have risen up in her voice, instead it pooled in her lips, twisting her delicate mouth into an anguished knot. Cleansing tears at least poured from her eyes, clearing the blood from their corners as they painted faint red lines down her shining white cheeks.

The sight of her weeping haunted him. And though he felt utterly inadequate, utterly too wrong for work of the heart, Osgrim crossed the floor to her and took her in his arms, and comforted her as a father comforts a child too sick or hurt to reassure with honesty.

"It's all right," he lied, though he knew it wasn't.

"Osgrim," she croaked.

"It will be all right," he echoed, correcting himself. "It will be all right in time."

All that was left, then, was to have faith that it would be.

On very rare occasions, even the oldest and cleverest women are wrong. There was no early spring that year after all, and the snow that had blanketed the black ramparts of the Shadewall for months maintained its siege well past Yearsend, into Idismaunt, and even through the equinox. The weather was mercilessly chaotic, and for long months the winds fought under raging moons. A few false springs came and went, but it was a hard winter, and it made grim and hardy folk out of those who rode out in it.

It was a lean year in Haveïl, too, where the trade roads disappeared entirely under stubborn snows that pounded the forest relentlessly. The season to seed the onion bulbs and to sow the hardy carrots had come and gone; the stews would be blander for it in the year to come. It was the small things that made the people of Widowvale sorrow and despair, in the end, for there was not much to be done about the large things.

Impatiently they weathered the first week in the wilderness, and might have endured a second if the Reeve's wife had not convinced him to send scouts back to the village. "Scouts," of course, meant Alec Mercy, who knew the way by night or by storm and was the closest thing they had left to a soldier, though his days of warring were far behind him.

It grieved him to see the blackened bones of the moot-hall, for he had worked hard to build it with good men in the years of his youth, and the work and sweat had made fast friends of them. He might lead the work again, he knew, but one winter too many had left the first dusting of snow in his beard. The grey had come first to the tip of his chin, when he grew it out, and in only three or four years it had spread to the hair of his neck, his moustache, the gently arched eyebrows that gave him a look of perpetual seriousness, and at last to the crown of windswept brown locks that had made him a handsome fellow in his youth.

A visitor might have found the change quite striking, but there were none in the village to whom he appeared old: they above all had weathered the seasons with him, and understood the circumstances that had peppered his hair with grey. The bees, too, said nothing about the greying of his hair: among the countless thousands of them, only the queens had been alive long enough to see the change in him, and they had not the heart to tell their hive that even Alec, immortal Alec who had overseen their hive for ten generations, had once been born and would one day die.

With some excitement, he found the town more or less untouched, but for a few stock animals put to death for sport and a few that had died more or less naturally. The houses had been violently searched, but little had been destroyed or taken. When he returned to signal that Widowvale was deserted and it was safe to return there, they did so with fearful reluctance. They sorrowed long over the burning of the moot-hall, for in its generous size and the exquisite carvings of its timbers had lain the aspirations of the town in its earliest years. There, too, burned the last works of some of the men Ashimar had killed, and in the years to come, none could hold or point to a thing they had made before departing the world. Of the free miners who worked up on the ridge below Minter's Rock, Halgeir the Tall was the most sociable and easiest to befriend, and for a long time thereafter he lived in the minds and memories of Widowvale. The others, from different lands, were stranger to the townsfolk, and in this they kept their secret but faded from memory when the ground was soft enough to lay them in it.

In the last days of winter, plans were made for a new moot-hall, and a committee appointed to see to it that the silver spent on the job was spent responsibly. But no ground would be broken, and no timber laid, until the summer had come and the memory of the cursed winter had passed.

In Idismaunt, when the days had grown long and the earth had finally softened, the young men and women returned to their fields, and on warmer days the doors were put open to clear the hearth-smoke from the dark houses. Among the vine-covered hills at Grimstead, it was time for the budbreak of the vines as they woke from their curated hibernation and prepared to flower again. To the untrained eye, the fields were filled with children at play among the vines. But those who watched them long enough knew better, for the children had been schooled to various degrees in the manner of viniculture, and sought out with great patience the places where the vines might have been compromised by insects, or mould, or other kinds of rot that might have set in.

When the rain was less than before, and the winds milder, sound traveled a long way down the trail from the Iron Road, and those with keen ears could hear a company moving at speed. On the twentieth of Idismaunt, from beneath the tops of the low wooden trellises, Rinnie jerked his head upright and listened for clearer sounds on the air.

At first, it was not a loud enough sound to be sure. It was a cold grey day, barely spring at all, and the sound could have been thunder. But again and again he strained to hear against the distance, and watched the skies for signs of rain as only a child raised on a farm can do. All at once, it seemed the sound of riders taking their ease seemed to rise up beneath the gently whistling wind, and Rinnie sprang up from his knees to his feet like a startled bear.

"They're here!" he cried. "They're here! Aewyn's returned!" And like an arrow loosed from a taut bow he sprang from his row in the vineyard, to the great protestations of his sister Ali, who had been tasked with keeping an eye on him. She lunged for him, but could not catch him: he had long praised himself as the fastest runner in all of Haveïl, and every season the boast became a little less empty as his shadow grew longer, and his legs with it.

Also like a boy raised in a farmer's field, Rinnie was a poor judge of how clean or dirty things were. The Havenari had ridden hard through light rains to beat the heavy rains to shelter, and their weapons and armour, though well-tended, had seen more use this year than they had in a long while. But they rode in better formation now than before, too, and as Bram's leg healed and the last of his shakes left him, he rode as a part of their flank rather than as some loose decoration. At the head of their formation, Robyn's thundering mare was a horse as big as a house to a small boy, and atop her shoulders Robyn was no smaller. At her right side, clad in green and gold, Aewyn rode double with Roald, who was small and skilled at taking a passenger. In the first rains after the spring thaw began, her shock-white hair had deepened in colour to the tawny gold of a spring sunrise, though Rinnie had seen it many times in his youth and would know her upon sight, he often said, even in the dark.

"Aewyn!" he cried. "Aewyn! You've come home!"

"Hullo, Rinnie," she said, beaming. "Watch yourself underfoot. Careful."

He rushed almost beneath them before turning and racing the riders back to town; Robyn obliged him, and kicked Acorn into a trot. Somewhere ahead, a silver bell rang. Somewhere behind, it was answered by a peal of thunder.

"Well, that was lucky," Venser bellowed over the sound.

"First luck we've had in a while," answered another voice—a woman's voice.

When the riders streamed out of the woods, off the trail and onto the village green just south of Traitor's Oak, the old Reeve was still hard asleep, having struggled with his nightmares again the night before. But alone in the field with a wide brown jug of mead stood Alec Mercy, his expression flat and his clothes muddy.

"Providence to you, Lady," he said. Robyn raised her chin haughtily.

"Providence, "she chided, swinging her leg over Acorn's saddle-horn. "Am I soon a stranger?"

Alec shrugged, smiled suddenly, searching for words. But she bent down to him and took his bearded cheek in her hand and kissed him hard enough to brush away her secret smile, and the men cheered.

"It's been a long road," he said, as if she had never left. "Your men have ridden hard in defense of the land—and women, begging your pardon, Aewyn," he said, saluting her with the mead. But she raised her hand dismissively.

"Talk! Talk!" she told him, though she moved to slip down off Roald's horse, too.

"It's thirsty work," he said, "breathing light back into the dark for us. Will your Dragons drink of my gold? Will you?"

Robyn held his hands, shared a sad and secret glance with him, and uncorked his mead. Another cheer went up from the men as she threw her head back and took a man's draught from the jug, wiping the sweet gold from her lips before handing the jug up to Venser. She kissed Alec again, tenderly, now that her men were mostly fixated on the sweet spiced mead as it made the rounds. With a swift kick, Venser caught Aewyn's attention before he handed it to the other riders.

"Here," he said. "It's ill luck to refuse a host's welcome."

She sipped it delicately, tasting the woody rosemary and delicate sage, letting its lightness and sweetness play on her tongue, feeling the sharpness of its magic in her throat. It was a drink, men warned, for unchaining one's truest words, and though she had tasted it before, and some other liquors besides, she felt at last like one of the men. She passed it up to Roald, who drank as if he had gone the whole winter on only the rumour of water. As the jug made its rounds, only to return empty, only two refused to drink from it: Bram, who did so with the deepest regret, and the mysterious woman, Catrine, who did not lower her black veil to partake. The men would have insisted, had Bram not raised his hand. The glance they shared, Aewyn thought, was one of shared pain.

As Aewyn watched them, curious, an insistent hand tugged at the shoulder of her jerkin.

"You were gone all winter," said Rinnie. "How far did you ride?"

"Miles and miles," she said. "Hundreds of miles."

"Did you go to the Iron City? Did you see the Imperator in his black tower?"

"Not quite," said Aewyn.

"Was there fighting?"

"There was," said Aewyn. "There really was some, this time. Robyn was very brave."

"Did Bram fight?"

"What an odd question," said Aewyn. "He did, in fact. He was very brave too. He fought like a hundred men."

"He was like me," said Rinnie, beaming.

Aewyn scrunched up her face, hoisting Rinnie as she used to. She had stopped growing, though, and he had not.

"How do you mean?" she asked him.

"Every year, you rode out… the Havenaris, I mean. But you were too little to go. And Bram was too little to go, but he wanted to. Like me. He was always sad when they left him behind. Then you got bigger, and I guess Bram got bigger."

Aewyn laughed. "I guess he did," she said. "He's grown a lot."

"I've grown a lot too," said Rinnie.

"You certainly have." She set him down gently as Alec and Robyn, finally, broke off their embrace.

"Maybe soon, I'll be big enough to ride out too."

Aewyn ruffled his hair and looked up to see Venser smiling down at them with something like pride. His withered arm always made him look a little like he was leaning slyly one way or another. It was not an unflattering look.

"And who's this?" said Alec, looking up at the mysteriously veiled woman riding double with Tsúla.

"This is Catrine," said Robyn. "She—she's lost everything in the war. Her home. Her husband."

"I see. Welcome to our town!"

Robyn leaned close to his ear. "Better not to mention her face," she whispered. "She was lovely—really lovely."

Alec nodded with the knowing sorrow of a man who had ridden to war himself, once, with only his father's spear and his grandfather's songs to guide him.

"She'll find a home with us here," he said, "if she's keen for one."

"Be kind to her," said Robyn. "She's been to the Void and back."

One by one, on curious feet, the townsfolk of Widowvale shuffled out to greet their protectors. As if sensing some new fragility to them, they embraced their friends and heroes gently, and spoke in soft sweet words, and where they met, great laughs and many tears were shed, until their faces and beards were so wet that they realized it was raining. Here and there, heedless of the wet and cold, they walked, and spoke, and Bram bent low enough on his healing leg to pet the miller's dog and scratch his old belly, as one limping animal greets another.

"How long will you stay?" Alec answered.

Robyn's green eyes shone with a sorrow unhidden by the rain.

"Not long enough."

There was not yet a moot-hall large enough to call a moot. The rain took the fun out of meeting outdoors, but those townsfolk who cared to say anything soon rallied around Traitor's Oak, where the great druid Celithrand, hanged for treason, had dangled like a jigging puppet only seven months earlier. It was a somber place and a morose gathering for those who had come to escape the ravages of the war, whatever hometown it had found them in; and when Catrine spoke up about her husband's death on the battlefield, they nodded with understanding, and the widow Karis stooped to put another cloak on her, though she was not cold.

When she drew back her veil to tell her story, her face was perfectly shaped with bright round eyes, the gentlest of curves at the nose and jawline, and a tangled mass of gruesome, jagged scars that clawed their way up her face as a creeping vine crawls up a castle wall. At the gleaming windows of her eyes, at the tips of her cheekbones, at the lustrous softness of her high pale forehead, she was an immaculate beauty, and the contrast of Ashimar's handiwork excited pity in the hearts of many. After much discussion, and many questions about where she had come from and what might please her, the townsfolk agreed to send up some men to the abandoned cottage at Halgerstad, the desolate promontory near the summit of Minter's Rock, and to clear out the mice and winter vermin that had no doubt nested there, and to make such a home for her as they could there. In time, not far from the safety and skilled labour of the village, the Widow Catrine could have her peace and her solitude there. The villagers were above all a practical bunch who could not afford to see a single structure go unused. She could grow herself a little garden, and in the summer, if the weather was forgiving, she would just spy the edge of sea and see the red sun glinting gaily off its edge, if she climbed the hill a little way further. She accepted their offer only with the fullest of apologies and thanks—but the townsfolk took her at her word, and asked her no questions, gave freely of themselves, and made her feel as one of them, just as Robyn and Bram had known they would.

The next day was a bright one of real warmth, and a few men of the village (and boys who wanted to be seen as men) mounted the muddy slope of Minter's Rock and spent a hard morning and a harder afternoon digging out the stale bloodstained sod and thresh from the cottage at the place now called Halgerstad. There they swept, and painted, and the most skilled of them cut and lay thin planks for a real timbered floor. In the village, the few women with the luxury of idleness came down to Miller's Riffle to gather river rushes, which they laid out to dry, then stitched and plated them into fresh floor mats, and seeded them with rosemary and lavender that would scent the place when trod upon, and so drive out the scent of wickedness that still lingered there. And when all that was done, they sent for Catrine, and brought her tools and provender, and such wealth as they had they gave to her.

Every day for seven days, and each week after that, more food and drink, more clothing and dry goods, more gifts of goodwill, were brought up to the cottage by a broad-shouldered young man called Ard Oltman, who spoke jovially but kept his distance and asked nothing of her, but delivered tokens of goodwill and welcome from the townsfolk bundled in his heavy arms. His mother, he said, had been widowed many long years past in circumstances she still did not like to speak of. And so Ard treated her like the woman he imagined his mother had once been, and so accustomed she came to his visits that she would not veil herself upon his arrival. When he looked on her scarred face, it was not with disgust nor even with pity, but with an artless acceptance and pleasure that might, in time, become a son's love, or something like it.

The Havenari did not stay long. She came to understand that while they protected the whole of Haveïl they loved and were loved by Widowvale best of all, and great indeed was the sorrow when they left. She came down to the village for the first time to say her farewells, and to thank the extraordinary woman who had led them to her rescue. It was pleasant enough to be among them, but when it was over she returned to Halgerstad in solitude and wept for a whole day.

The bright spring wore on into a hot summer, and the summer turned toward fall. Though her face and arms would never now be whole, they no longer pained her , and in her solitude she made for herself a garden as she had done in Selik—not a noblewoman's flower-garden, but a proper farmer's garden, with food enough for herself, and perhaps to trade with the other villagers, to thank them for their charity. There were days of darkness between the pleasant thoughts, but always she remembered that kind-faced Ard Oltman would be the only one to find her, and then in a sorry state. She had seen too much death, too much altogether, to think long or much on her own. And so she grew her cabbages and turnips, her cold-hardy parsnips and kale, and in the mornings she would climb to the top of Minter's Rock and watch the sun rise, and look away with her memories to the distant and lonely sea.

When he heard she would not come down to the Harvest Fair, and when he tried and failed to explain anything that was so special about it, Ard Oltman pushed the matter for as long as he had the heart to, and then left her alone in his disappointment. With cries and songs of celebration that rose even to Halgerstad in the fall, the Havenari returned to the village, the miners who lived on the far side of the Rock tramped past her house shouting and singing, and Catrine knew that Ard would not return to disturb her languorous peace unbidden until the fair was past.

Meat and mead! Days of plenty!
Pickmen, pikemen, pay your crew!
Pay your ten and take your twenty!
Meat and mead and days of plenty
Lie ahead for those who do!

Tables told and tables laden,
Tell the silver! count the salt!
Tables tallied, tables laden,
Please as much the hungry maiden
As the censor in his vault!

Raise the fire! Raise your holler,
Strike the flint and strike the drums!
Poor ye boys who lie in squalor,
Raise the fire and raise your holler,
Raise a toast ere winter comes!

Behind and below the little cottage, away from the garden, on a scrap of barren soil that gave way to bare rock, Catrine crept down to a flat peak jutting out over the vale. She was surrounded on three sides by trees and on the fourth by an open cliffside, below which a hundred blazing lights would burn when night fell. Inching out on all fours, heedless of a wind that might soon turn cold again after a summer that seemed to pass like a flickering shadow, Catrine listened to the shouts and songs of the miners as they marched down the southern trails to the village. The sky above her was a blazing deep blue; the day was bright and would be for a while yet. Transfixed by their raucous songs, but chained by some hidden fear to the empty little cottage born out of their kindness, she swayed for a long time on the knife-edge of her decision to stay in the house, and to leave the festival to be enjoyed by the festive.

She was jolted from her thoughts by the sound of a heavy footfall scraping the gravel on the trail. Starting up from her lookout, Catrine rushed to meet her young visitor, only to find him struggling mightily under the load of a heavy crate piled high with all the offerings of the village: squashes and gourds of unfamiliar shapes, potatoes, salt pork, and fresh cheese. The crate was filled with a dozen unfamiliar and strange local delicacies Ard had warned her about with great excitement. In spite of herself, she approached with a gracious smile.

"It seems you've brought the whole Harvest Fair to me," she said.

But the man stopped. It was not Ard.

He had a different shape, a different way of walking—a different voice as he leaned in to admire the short bed of hardy sky-blue flowers she had planted along the edge of the cottage.

"Cerulyns," he said. "Cerulyns for a Cerulean."

At the sound of his voice, she meant to leap into his arms. But Catrine merely stood waiting, still as a mountain, to be sure he was real.

"Rasten?" she asked. "Rasten…"

He bent low and shook the stiffnesss out of his hands as he set down her gifts from the villagers.

"I suppose they answer my question," he said softly. "You're still in mourning?"

She rushed to him, eyes wide. He took her gently at the shoulders, but studied her face, as she studied his, in profound disbelief.

"How—" she breathed. "How?"

Rasten brushed the first tear from her cheek the moment it appeared, but he could not catch them all.

"Who was he?" Rasten asked. "This Cerulean? Does it pain you to speak of him?"

She wanted more than anything to kiss him as she once did, to have him sweep her into her arms as it had been in the beginning. But they stood there upon the cliffside for a long moment, loving each other in fearful silence.

"He was a soldier," she whispered at last, leaning her head against his chest but turning her eyes. "A tower guard."

Rasten nodded. "That's a shame," he said. "I don't think the life suited him."

"H-he was brave," she stammered. "He was...he was my Rasten. But... he fell."

"You *were* there," Rasten said, as much to reassure himself.

"I...I was. I saw you go to your death. I saw you... and Ashimar..."

Suddenly self-conscious, she reached for the edge of her veil, but he pushed it away and met her eyes at last. And there he was, looking into her and through her, past all of Ashimar's handiwork as if it had never had been, past even the lines that natural age and woe had wrought in her face, past every mask she had ever worn for love or hate or duty. There he was, looking at her in her utter naked completeness, and she returned his gaze, trembling.

"There's... I have to tell you something," she said.

"You don't," said Rasten. "Not here."

"I was living a lie," she whispered. Her face was covered in tears, her breathing timid.

"So was I," said Rasten. "A nightmare with no end."

"How did you find me?" she asked.

Rasten looked down sheepishly. "Walking, mostly. I returned to the city. I talked to Elmore. He told me of—of Jordac's Widows...who they were, how they worked."

She placed herself gently in his arms, unsure if anything she did, now—any word, any gesture—was the truth. She desperately needed his comfort, and it made her sick that she knew just how to get it from him.

"I am so sorry, my love," she said. It was exactly what a spy would say, and that grieved her too.

"I thought you might have gone back East, if you'd lived," said Rasten. "But then...I thought you might have fallen at Fingrun. If not when it was raided, in the devastation that followed there."

"I was the one who raided it," said Catrine. "I was one of them. I'm a rebel and a traitor."

"You're nothing of the sort," said Rasten. She clutched at his cloak urgently.

"Have you heard nothing?" she asked. "Do you not understand a word I have said?"

"I came west again," he said. "As close as I could get to Fingrun. I... I didn't know what had happened to you, where you'd gone. But I found the Havenari. I...I've met one. The girl. And I spoke to them of you, and they knew to lead me here."

"Ras..."

He paused to clear the lump in his throat. "I don't know what I would've done," he said. "If...if it hadn't been you."

Through the tears, Catrine fought for the composure she felt he deserved. "I'm not," she said. "I'm not who you think I am."

A look of bewilderment crossed Rasten's features. "Who do I think you are?" he asked.

She tightened her mouth. "I don't know," she said. "I... I don't think *I* know who I am anymore."

Rasten smoothed down the front of his tunic, gesturing with his eyes. There was no uniform. She could not recall if ever she had seen him, except in his perfect nakedness, without some garment of purple, or blue, or red. There was no trace of the Three Maidens in his attire now. There was only...him.

"It was the longest year of my life. I asked after you, everywhere I went. I asked the Havenari, and they told me of the woman in Widowvale who took on Ashimar and won," said Rasten. "They told me all about this place. Do you know who *anyone* is here? Do you know what any of them did before they came here?

Catrine smiled reluctantly. "No."

Rasten smiled. "I don't think we're supposed to care about such things. They certainly don't."

"I betrayed you from the first," she said. "I lied and lied from the start." The tears would not stop flowing.

"You met me on the hill, at Vairhurst."

"Yes."

"You were mourning your husband," he said.

"Yes."

"Aden, was it?"

Her eyes went wide. "You remember?"

"We spoke all night," said Rasten. "You took me to your bed, and you told me of his bravery. You told me he had died in the fighting. You said you had no one, that you were lost and angry, and wanted vengeance for his death."

"Yes."

"You told me where to kiss you, and how."

"I did," she said, blushing.

"And six days later, you told me you loved me." She laid her head on his breast, just as she had done then.

"It was a lie," she sobbed. "It was all of it a lie."

Rasten caught her eyes. "What part?" he asked gently. "Your husband? Your loneliness? Your anger? Your love?"

Catrine bit her lip in thought.

"I am not a clever man," said Rasten. "I'm a fool. I've come to realize that. I have every confidence you're more clever than I am. More cunning. I have no idea how many times you lied to me. I have no ear for lies. I wouldn't know a lie when I hear one. But the truth, Cat—the truth I know straight away. I've no memory of what lies you told. But everything you ever said to me that was from the heart…I remember every word of it, even if I forget all the rest."

Catrine's eyes shone like wet jewels. "If that's what it means to be a fool," she said, "we might yet be happy."

"I mean to be," said Rasten. And she kissed him, and he was.

How the night passed, and the morning, is a matter better left to the poets than the chroniclers. But when the sun was high and the cheery clamour of the village rose too high to be ignored, Catrine made herself a pinned gown of the fine blue linens that Jerrold the Mercer had folded into her basket of welcomes, and left her hair freely unbound after the manner of the country women, and on Rasten's obliging arm she came down the trail and into the merriment of the Harvest Fair.

She suffered no veil, but flashed an easy smile at any who cared to look upon her. She came as much to be seen again as to see the sights, and obligingly she introduced Rasten to men and women she barely knew herself, as he stumbled over his tongue trying to do the same.

For Rasten and Catrine, who had never tasted Alec Mercy's mead or Arran Grimsson's tart and unforgiving summer wine, there was plenty of both to be had. Rasten had earned enough as a Cerulean to be comfortable for a long while in the remote provinces, and to his delight when he first returned to Travalaith, the quartermaster paid him, not knowing him for a traitor—for nearly all of the Red Legion, it was heard, had been wiped out at Fingrun, and no survivors had come forward to speak of his treachery.

For the first time since he had seen them, the Havenari had quit their arms and armour and made their way about the village with light hearts. Some crept off into the woods with their own purses, to hide little copper coins for the children among the trees. But Robyn was not among them, for she was hard at work on the archery butts, fighting to win back the archer's laurel that had been denied to her too many years in the row. To no one's surprise, she won her laurel, and the much-envied grand prize—one of the last sealed jugs of Old Grim's Twainroot, a two-grape winter wine harvested and pressed in the Year of the Twins. It was a hard-won prize, for while Halgeir's masterful archery and easy good humour were sorely missed, Aewyn had come at last into her full strength. With a magnificent bow that had once been a hand too long and several pounds too heavy for her, she matched the First Spear shot for shot, and chased her for victory right down to the last of the Tourney Rings, to the admiration of all.

"We traveled together, for a time," said Rasten, with undeserved pride.

"I'd like to meet her," said Catrine, and they went down together.

The Fair was a time of customs that were new to Catrine—who spoke openly for the first time of growing up in Selik near Estelonne—and so familiar now to Rasten that he had to participate fully in the old rituals just to remember them. When the great bonfire was lit, remarks were made—some more tactfully and some more crudely—that the young lovers would not be missed, and would not be rude, if they left the gathering to pay tribute to gods of a fertile harvest in whatever way pleased them best. But Rasten and Catrine sat around the blazing fire with them, listening to their stories and unburdening their singing-voices until the last Oltman family jig was danced and the tallest of the flames had begun to die away. Their hunger to be loved, in the end, had taken many forms, and to be included in the muttering gossip of the townsfolk—the *other* townsfolk—filled a void in them that neither one had seen, and a void that each of them, alone, could not fill in the other.

In their eagerness for the small joys that made even the poorest of the villagers wealthy beyond the measure of a Tower guard, Rasten and Catrine first outlasted the stamina of the middle-aged—and after that, the stamina of the young. Robyn and Alec had gone to green, and Aewyn and Bram had ventured off alone, away from the lovers and drinkers alike, to speak or not speak of the loved ones they had lost. Soon only the true-widow Oltman was left by the fire with the young couple: she was the oldest woman of the village by far, though for a town called "Widowvale" it skewed curiously young. She had once stayed up drinking and talking with Orin, who was a fine companion for her, but he had taken sick again, and it was said he was likely now, at best, to stay that way. Now, the old woman alone held court in Widowvale, and she did so with as much dignity and gravity as was ever afforded to the Reeve in his moot-hall.

"Don't tell me of loved ones," she said suddenly. "Don't tell me of the dead. Don't tell me whom you miss, or whom you're farthest from. Don't talk of old secrets, and if the wolves in your dreams have lost your scent for a while, don't say a word to help them pick it up again. But I ask it of all newcomers, their first year, and I'll match you in kind, if it please you: name me one thing, from the life you've left behind, that you'll miss here."

Rasten looked to Catrine with smoldering admiration. "I can't imagine life before this one," he said. "But I suppose I had a family once. A big one. I followed my brother to war. We grew up inseparable, and I miss him most of all. But back home, there was a whole pack of us—"

"No loved ones," the true-widow snapped, though she was not ill-natured about it.

Rasten puzzled. "Apart from my family...."

"No family," the true-widow insisted.

"...I suppose I'd have to say it was the cooking, then. Cooking like you wouldn't believe."

"Try me," the old woman said, smiling. Rasten beamed like a gleeful child, and Catrine laughed brightly and musically for the first time in what felt like years.

"Oh, roast game birds, roast pork," he said wisfully. "And the bread. Oh, bread! You may laugh—it sounds mad, but there were a hundred kinds of it. All different, every one. Wheats and ryes, spelts, flatbreads. Dessert breads in pear syrup with slivered pecans. Hardtack for the road that softened to buttery fresh in sour wine, when it was made right. You brought enough of that from home, it'd last six months by the red moon, after all the other men's home rations had spoiled—"

"No family," the woman snapped.

"I'm only talking of bread," Rasten protested, but she raised a wise eyebrow.

"Not with your heart, you're not," she said. Rasten bowed and lifted his palms in a gesture of surrender.

"What about you, old woman?" asked Catrine. "I've wintered in a one-room shack, warmed by naught but piled earth. I've summered in the Storm Quarter, lived in a lordly common-house and dined on an officer's silver. But what's really worth missing, if not the ones we love?"

She wrapped her arm around Rasten's bullish neck in a way the old woman had not yet forgotten. "Our loved ones are the only thing worth missing, in the end."

The old woman turned her face toward the fire sadly. Its dimming light shone brightly across her pale skin, but her face was a mask of well-earned wrinkles, too, and there the light did not go.

"I miss the way men used to treat each other," she said. "I miss the days when men were good at heart and glad of spirit."

She didn't seem finished; the old seldom were. And so Catrine stretched out into Rasten's arms before the fire, sighing contentedly, half-drunk, half-exhausted, and waited for the old woman to speak as only an old woman can.

"You've just come here from a far place," said the true-widow. "I've come from Travost, too. You've both seen it; it's nowhere special. But I've come here from a far distant time, as well. A time when we were *all* kin to one another. When everyone was family. Say what you will of the Second Craftsman. But his war made a family of us—it united mankind, which by all rights should be doomed to divide itself."

She looked away from them, into the fire—no, through the fire, over its last licking tails of flame, to the blackened remains of the old moot-hall.

"Clear as day," she said, "I can remember the day I met Lord Ashimar."

Rasten shivered at the name. Catrine's hand brushed the cobwebbed scars of her cheek anxiously.

"He's…not a man easily forgotten," said Rasten, as diplomatically as he could.

"Gods, no," said the true-widow. "He was magnificent. Twenty years old, fair of face, long and lean in the shanks. Commanding presence, with a fierce wit and a ready laugh. The pride of his house, and Valithar's chosen fosterling. The people adored him."

"Ashimar?" said Rasten. "I believe we're thinking of two different men. It's a common enough family name among the Kelmors, isn't it? It can't be the same man—"

"As I said," the true-widow Oltman sighed, "I mourn for the days when we were all of us better people."

Catrine held herself close to Rasten. "What happened?" she asked.

The true-widow shook her head sadly. "Some say the Imperator got sick," she said, "after the Annexation. Some say he went mad. Some say he never came home from the Annexation—that he died on the field, and his wife died of grief in the Tower, and Lord Kelmor went mad when he heard. Swore a blood oath to devote himself to killing his oath-father's enemies—and that's where you lot, the bloodguard, are supposed to come from."

Catrine looked pleadingly to Rasten. He drew in a deep breath upon catching her eye.

"I'd dearly love to know someday," he said, "how he came from that man to this one." He gestured at the moot-hall with more than a little regret.

"As would I," said the true-widow.

"But for now he's an unwelcome guest in the village, and I see no reason to invite him back to it in our conversations."

"It hardly matters now," said the true-widow. "He's well and truly gone, and all his secrets with him. I only mean to say that the Iron City takes the very best of us, and leaves behind only the worst of us. The legacy of the Craftsman, perhaps. Not long after the Annexation, I left Travost forever. I haven't returned. I know now I won't. And whatever you lovelings have left behind there—believe me, you can be far more happy here."

Rasten smiled, relieved above all that she had taken his redirect gently. "I'm glad we got out before it did the same to us," he ventured.

"If it's bread you love," said the old woman, "we have four fine bakers here. The miller, Aeric; his wife, his two daughters. Soon to be one daughter, as my son Ard is fixing to wed young Melia when she's respectable old."

"Your son is Ard?" asked Catrine. "Ard Oltman?"

"He is," said the true-widow.

"He's been so kind to me," she said. "All the long months Rasten was far from home."

"You speak as if it's always been his home here," said the old woman.

Rasten, still troubled by all he had heard, wrapped his brawny arm around Catrine's delicate shoulders.

"Perhaps it has been," said Rasten. "Perhaps this place has been my home for a long time, whether I knew it or not."

"Best to check with the Reeve," said the old woman with a twinkling eye. "You might be a few years behind on your taxes."

Famished for each other's company, overburdened with stories of the road too eager to get out, Rasten and Catrine had outlasted the archery, and the wine, and the fires, and the festivities. But so glad were they to be reunited that they would not suffer even sleep to part them. Instead, they walked aimlessly the whole length of the village, again and again, until the deep blue sky hanging over the distant east had begun to brighten. The old woman had kept at her wine and drifted off at last, as the fire died away to cold embers; and after some difficult discussion on what should be done with her, they laid her gently in a wheelbarrow and brought her, snoring softly, to the house of her sons Corran and Ard. There, with great care, the two of them lifted her and carried her gracefully across the threshold and into her bed, right under the noses of her snoring sons. She was no easy burden, even for two; for the first time, gentle Catrine surprised Rasten with her considerable strength, and mighty Rasten surprised her with his gentleness.

When they emerged from the true-widow's house, the sun was nearly upon them; again the eastern sky was streaked with ribbons of light in the blazing hues of the Three Maidens at play. By the glow of that sky, they could make out the faces of the Havenari bustling hurriedly about the south-houses, grazing their horses idly as as they were making ready to leave. A few of them, Aewyn included, were stringing their bows.

"Providence to you," said Robyn as they approached. "You're awake early."

"Late," said Rasten sheepishly. "We've not slept. You're the ones awake before the gods themselves."

"There was a rider in the night," said Robyn. "Trouble in Aslea."

"What sort of trouble?" Catrine asked. Rasten only frowned.

"The sort of trouble you string your bows before riding to, I gather," said Rasten. "I swear to you, I wasn't followed."

Robyn patted his shoulder gently. "Not everything's about you, sir," she said curtly. "You'll be safe here."

"You folks intending to stay?" the big man, Venser, asked them as he threw his saddle over his horse.

"We'd like to," said Catrine. "That's the hope."

"Good," said Venser. "You're not weak. Either one of you. I heard what you did at Fingrun. Real courage, the both of you… though perhaps not for the same cause."

Catrine blushed slightly, though her scars were young and hid it well. Rasten tightened his jaw nervously.

"I never served the Red Captain," he insisted. "Not even when… your friend there, Aewyn…"

Aewyn turned at the mention of her name. Rasten was still getting used to the sight of her with brown hair; and now it had ripened to the warm red of autumn.

"He wasn't one of them," said Aewyn. "Not really." It was the last thing Rasten expected to her from her; but when their eyes met, there was a deep understanding between them.

"What I mean is, you can fight," said Venser. "Both of you, for once."

Rasten and Catrine nodded.

"I'll sleep easier knowing you've made your home here," said Venser. "You want for anything before we get back, I've a little money with the Reeve. Talk to him. Above all, don't sell your sword."

"My sword?" Rasten asked.

"I've seen too many Ceruleans go to green out here," Venser said. "Too many deserters, too many eager to let go of that ugly thing forever."

"Hang onto it," said Venser. "As long as you've got an arm to swing it, don't you let that valour-stick go. Not for coin."

"You think we'll have need of it?" Rasten asked, fidgeting nervously with the pommel. Even at the Harvest Fair, he had been loath to leave it behind.

"Not today," said Venser. "And I imagine not before we're back. But I'm a poor soothsayer, even for coin, and you've paid me nothing. I wouldn't lean too hard on any promise I give you about the future."

A fleeting shadow seemed to pass briefly across Aewyn's face. "This town is a dangerous place for prophecies and predictions," she said. "You never know what will come true and what won't."

"We mean to make a home here," said Catrine, with a note of firmness in her voice. "We're no outriders. But if making a home in the village means defending it…we'll be ready."

"I don't suppose you can tell us what we need to be ready *for*," Rasten prodded. He checked the edge of his sword out of habit; it was in sore need of a whetstone.

"The world is changing," said Venser. "Faster than any of us had thought. This Uprising of yours, it could spell real trouble for the Empire. I'd underestimated what a heavy blow it would land, taking out that mine. But trouble seems to come all at once. I don't mean to alarm you, but there's a darkness in these woods—in all the lands that once fell under the Occupation. Old stirrings in the deep wood, old forces we'd thought long gone. A land under the Craftsman's shadow, it seems, is not so easily cleansed."

"You mean to say there are Horrors in these woods," said Catrine. Rasten, after long years as a military man, hid his fear so well that only she sensed it.

"We've fought them before," said Venser. "They *can* be fought. And they can be beaten."

"Venser," Robyn urged. "It's time." She put a hand on his shoulder but did not quit her own preparations to pay him much mind.

"Horrors of Tamnor," Rasten moaned. "And still you come to the village to quit your armour, and drink, and shoot in tourney? And your commander wears her dress and hair unbound and dances upon the green while the woods fill with nightmares?"

"So we do," said Venser. "You're a soldier, friend, so you'll know this even if you don't have the words for it: these merry places, these times of plenty? What we do with our blades, our *kolgari*, makes times like these more important, not less. Tell me, soldier…does Mardon Black still teach military history at the Lower Block?"

Rasten's face lit with surprise and recognition. "You know him?"

"We met a lifetime ago. As I say, you're not the first man gone to green here. He still teaches the recruits?"

"He's… a Magistrate now," said Rasten. "Master of Iron."

Venser laughed. "He'll be right sour about that mine then," he said. "But look—if you've had the pleasure of hearing Master Mardon's account of Travalaithi history…it's a history of war. A history marked by swords and sceptres. Sieges and conquests, and a very healthy supply of backstabbings, murders, assassination. Insufferable people in a bloody dance for power. Three thousand years of it. It's no easy task to make a lifelong study of men killing one another, as he's done…but once it's done, it's easy enough to call that history."

"*Venser!*" Robyn snapped. The tall Havenar turned back to her.

"Ready, coming!" he called. "Look, all I'm saying is… history goes a thousand times deeper than the Imperial war record. There's history in the strange way folks speak out here. There's history in the wheat and the wine. There's even history in Robyn's dress, though she'd skin me for saying so. Learn that history, the true history of a place, and you'll learn *why* we fight so hard. There's reasons we waste our best steel putting it into swords, and our best men putting them into fields of blood. Rest here a spell, and be no stranger to these people…you'll learn."

Rasten might have had a ready answer. More often than not, he was the sort to follow listening with talking. But Catrine silenced him with her eyes as little Aewyn came to retrieve Venser, tugging this time on his weak arm so that she was many times stronger than he.

"Safe travels," Rasten said to her with a gentle bow.

She was at a loss for only a moment for what to say.

"Be at peace," she said at last, and hastened to rejoin the others.

Perhaps, as the rumours held, there was still some trick of druid's magic in the hills, for the easy trail Rasten and Catrine had descended in the afternoon had transformed into a steep and unforgiving slope overnight as they drank and walked. The sun burst over the trees to the east in a blaze of gold as they climbed, and in the light of dawn they saw each other as a free man and free woman for perhaps the first time. There were no words between them as they walked—only the steady company of two people whose strides, like dancers' steps, were in perfect rhythm.

Rasten, as was his way, was first to spoil the walk as the little cottage came into view.

"Gods, I'm half-starved," he said. "We ought to eat something before bed."

"There's plenty to be had," said Catrine. "They've been very kind to me, especially at harvest."

"Oh?"

"The shepherd brought us sweetbread…which I think is some kind of meat…and what he calls sweetmeat, which looks like some kind of bread."

Rasten chuckled. "Queer people, these Outlanders."

"They're good folk," said Catrine.

In the warm months, with the windows unsealed, there was light and wind enough to make the little cottage feel bright and full of life. The sun was drifting ever southward as the year wore on, and Catrine feared they would have no sleep at all. But exhaustion overtook her, as in time it must, and she and Rasten fell hard asleep even in the brilliant golden light of a warm autumn day. She must have taken to the cottage, for even in her dreams she did not venture far from it. Just below the cottage, on a grassy plateau ringed and sheltered by high trees, she wandered through the orderly rows of a freshly tilled field. The sun was too bright in her eyes to see far, but she could hear the men's voices, and the ready thud of their heavy shovels.

There, in a fertile bed of loosened earth, her lovers old and new made merry as they toiled in the earth. With endless strength, Rasten plunged his shovel into the clay-rich soil. With endless patience, poor dead Aden directed him.

"You'll want to use the edge," said Aden. "*Att, att, att.* You're not shovelling to shovel. You're breaking up the soil. What you have here, it's not great. The soil's heavy for potatoes. It packs down tight. You want to turn it up, gently, until it's soft. That's it."

The sunlight was so bright that she could barely see them. It was not a deep slumber she had found herself in, and the veil between sleep and waking was wasted thin with exhaustion. She knew, in a moment, that she was dreaming—and then she stood still, watching them motionlessly, afraid to stir lest she wake herself back into an unforgiving world.

It was no use—their voices were too far away now to make out. As she slipped away from them, back toward the waking world, she saw only that they worked the field as friends; instead of graves, they had dug long raised beds of looser soil where new life had already begun to spring.

Catrine awoke in Rasten's strong arms to find him awake with her.

"Bad dreams again?" he asked.

"No," she said.

"You were restless—but not tossing, as you once did."

"What time is it?"

Rasten looked to the window, which he in his infinite warmth had left brazenly open to the autumn air.

"The hour is late," he said. "If you're keen to head back to the Fair—"

"I like it here," she breathed, still half-asleep. "As if I hadn't truly slept in a thousand years."

"Keep at it, then," said Rasten. "I'll put a kettle on the fire. There'll be tea and honey when you wake."

Distantly, she felt his big hands slide down her body, tucking the coarse blanket tightly around her. And she would have passed back into sleep then, but the old momentary panic stirred her once more, and she shifted uneasily.

"Ras?" she asked him after he had risen.

"Mm?"

"Promise me," she said. "Tell me you'll be here with me when I wake up."

"I will," he said. "I swear it."

For all the miles he had traveled, and all the scars he had collected on his way, Rasten was a man of no small integrity when it came to his oaths. True to his word, not only to her but to himself, Rasten was there waiting in the darkness each time she awoke. It was a promise he would keep all through the first night, and all through the next, and for many long nights thereafter.

**HERE ENDS THE SECOND BOOK
OF THE *TRAVALAITH SAGA*.**

AFTERWORD

Old friends will return to a world transformed by war in

The Season of Rust and Rhyme
being the third book of the *Travalaith Saga*.

Two years after the Battle of Fingrun sparked a devastating series of attacks along the frontier, the Mages' Uprising is in a state of full-blown civil war. As rumours begin to circulate that the Imperator is dead, triggering a powerful succession crisis, a mysterious stranger from the far northern Banlands comes south with tidings that could change the course of the war and cost friends old and new more than they ever could have imagined.

If you enjoyed this book, **please leave a brief review** on Amazon, Goodreads, or the social media platform of your choice. Independent authors & small presses simply do not have the same marketing support as the major publishing houses. Your support is more precious than gold, and I try to read it all: it not only enables me to keep writing new books, but gives me the valuable feedback I need to help make each new book better than the last.

You can find me on the Web at **Lukemaynard.com**, where you can follow my writing and music, and sign up to be notified whenever I have a new release.

Thank you for joining me for *The Season of the Cerulyn*. I look forward to our next meeting.

—*Luke R. J. Maynard*

Acknowledgments

These Acknowledgments are additive. All those kind and supportive souls I thanked by name in the Acknowledgments to *The Season of the Plough* are again thanked and appreciated here. They are not forgotten here; if anything, a second book simply means I have more to thank you for.

Aside from those already named and acknowledged, the village of support behind this series has seen a few new arrivals in the last year.

In the writing community, I owe many thanks (in alphabetical-ish order) to Kurestin Armada, to Charles de Lint, to Ed Greenwood, to Kay Hawkins, to Kevin Hearne, to A. A. Jankiewicz, to Arlene F. Marks, to Sylvain Neuvel, to Brandon Sanderson, to S.M. Stirling, to Amanda Sun, to J. M. Tibbott, and to Sienna Tristen. Some of you are certainly too busy to recall the generosity of spirit with which you welcomed, advised, and engaged with an unsung first-time novelist as if he genuinely belonged at the grown-ups' table. Whether through sharing your tools, your vast insights on language and worldbuilding, or your kind words of support, you have made great contributions to the writing community around you, and to this work in particular, maybe even without knowing it. When you spoke, I listened (let's hope I learned something!), and I will always be grateful for the extent to which you have made the "imagination business" a familiar and welcoming place for new arrivals, and for me especially.

I'd like to acknowledge Corinne Davies, Stephen Adams, and David J. Peterson (all of whom I should have thanked last time) for helping me to think about poetry, prosody, and the music of language in ways that are more important to prose fiction than I ever realized. People without languages, without poems, without songs, never quite become real; and that goes double for people who exist only on the page.

The teachers who brought me the history of language have also gone unfairly unacknowledged. Thanks also to Richard Firth Green, Brock Eayrs, Russell Poole, and Kathryn Kerby-Fulton. Without you, sailors off the coast of Haukmere would not know to steer clear of the snaring weeds. Without the memory-stone of linguistic history, of onomastics, of etymology, the white-breasted squirrels who once built their watchtower nests in the trees atop Vairhurst would be as forgotten as the soldiers whose names have been lost to the wind.

No writer who lives two lives well in one life without living well in the other, and so especially in the context of this book, I owe a quiet thanks to Marcus, to Pearl, to Sébastien, to Akash, and to Lori-Ann. I've seen many in my profession broken down and consumed by the stress of their daily work. Your generous guidance, unrelenting fairness, and commitment to a healthy and supportive practice has made even my hardest-working days a pleasure during the last stages of this book, and left me with enough of myself to get *Cerulyn* done in the small hours of the night. Working anywhere else, even for excellent people, I might not have been so lucky.

Finally, a heartfelt thanks to my earliest readers, to those who supported *The Season of the Plough* largely on spec. A début novel from an unsung author is a hard sell, and your support has made the continuation of this saga possible. Extra special thanks to those who have left a review: the Internet success-robots care very much about such things, and in the mercenary world of publishing, it's very often your kind words that empower me to keep imagining.

Don't stop reading.

About the Author

Luke R. J. Maynard is a writer, poet, scholar, lapsed medievalist, musician, and wearer of sundry other hats in the arts & letters. Born in London, Ontario, Canada, he received his PhD in English Literature from the University of Victoria in 2013, and his *Juris Doctor* at the University of Toronto's Faculty of Law in 2019.

Luke's first CD, *Desolation Sound*, was released in June of 2018. His first novel, *The Season of the Plough*, was published in 2019. Luke currently lives in Toronto.

Lightning Source UK Ltd.
Milton Keynes UK
UKHW011857160320
360436UK00004B/22/J